More Ms. Murder

More Ms. Murder

MORE OF THE BEST MYSTERIES FEATURING WOMEN DETECTIVES, BY THE TOP WOMEN WRITERS

EDITED BY

MARIE SMITH

A CITADEL PRESS BOOK
Published by Carol Publishing Group

Library of Congress Cataloging-in-Publication data

More Ms Murder/edited by Marie Smith
  p.cm.
  "A Citadel Press book"

  ISBN 0–8065–1267–9 (cloth)
  ISBN 0–8065–1274–1 (paperback)

  1. Detective and mystery stories, American. 2. Detective and mystery stories, English.
3. American fiction—Women authors. 4. English fiction—Women authors. 5. Women
detectives—fiction. I. Smith, Marie.
PS848.D4M655 1991b   91–21759
813′.087208352042—dc20   CIP

A CITADEL PRESS BOOK

Published by Carol Publishing Group
Editorial Offices: 600 Madison Avenue, New York, NY 10022
Distribution Centre: 120 Enterprise Avenue, Secaucus, NJ 07094

First published in Great Britain by Xanadu Publications Limited
This selection copyright © 1991 Marie Smith and Xanadu Publications Limited.
The copyright notice on pages 258–259 constitutes an extension of this page.
Introduction copyright © 1991 Marie Smith
All rights reserved

Manufactured in Great Britain

ISBN # 0–8065–1267–9 (cloth)
ISBN # 0–8065–1274–1 (paperback)

Contents

Introduction

This collection of crime and mystery stories by and about women revisits and extends the territory staked out in my earlier book, *Ms Murder*, where I tried informally to track the progress of the female sleuth from Edwardian times to the present day. The warm reception given to that book prompts this return visit, but this time I have sought out not only women as detectives but also women as killers and occasionally—lest things get predictable—as victims too.

Broadening the scope in this way enables me to include some writers who I was sorry to leave out the first time around, though I was obliged to do so for the very blunt reason that they had not written about any female detectives – not at short-story length, anyway. Not only does this redress the balance, for how could any self-respecting collection of crime fiction omit Margery Allingham and P.D. James?, but it also allows me to include such underrated writers as Craig Rice, Miriam Allen deFord and Florence V. Mayberry, who deserve to be much more widely known. Also included are some of the newer writers who are just emerging: I wish them well.

As I say, *Ms Murder* was generally welcomed but if there was any criticism it was along the line of: if women are the equal of men at mystery-writing why separate them off from the main stream?

Would anyone compile a book of stories by men dealing exclusively with men? In fact, there are plenty of these even if they are not labelled as such, but it is nonetheless a point that deserves an answer, and my reply is two-fold.

Firstly, I believe that the best of women writers possess a special talent that is unique and separate from anything else that the field can offer, and this comprises a wonderful blend of insight, sympathy and *toughness*. There are no writers with more understanding of the criminal's mind than Ruth Rendell and Patricia Highsmith, no more ruthless plotters than Agatha Christie and P. D. James, no-one better able to get inside the skin of her characters than Florence V. Mayberry. It's a talent that has scarcely been analysed (and there isn't the space for me to attempt it here), but by heaven it is worth drawing attention to; worth celebrating!

Second, it is surely time that we finally lay to rest all those stock female characters who have burdened our fiction (from both male and female writers) for so long, so that we can write and read about women as *people*. So here is a bullet for the batty old spinster, cyanide for the comic charlady, a grave for the doting girlfriend and a mortuary for all maidens in distress. May they rest in peace, but we don't want to see them any more. Here are tales of woman as *doers*, whether they are detecting murders, avoiding them or (under great provocation, of course) committing them.

Which is which?

Ah!

—MARIE SMITH

KELLY BLAU

What Have You Been Doing All Day?

With the early morning sun pouring onto the pitted formica table she could almost pretend the prison didn't exist except as a part of her imagination, that the wide ever-lengthening bars pressing across her bare arms and down the floor really were the shadowed panes of a plain kitchen window in a plain tract house. Soon her mother would call to her, "Shirley! Shirley! Do hurry, dear, or you'll be late for school!"

She smiled, remembering the elastic grip of bobbysox around her trim ankles and the scratchy wool of a bright plaid skirt against her young thighs; but instead of shiny brown loafers a pair of misshapen tennis shoes now flopped on her feet beneath the scarred chair and the plaid skirt of memory was a wilted cotton shift that sagged limply between her knees.

The coffee in the heavy mug before her was bitter from having been reheated from the night before. Its taste reminded her that her mother would not be calling her, that another day in this prison sentence was about to begin. Oh, they came to visit, her mother and the others. The girls, their hair fixed differently now; and the boys, too—only now without the football uniforms that had made them so exciting. They smiled and smiled at her and she had to grin back until her mouth ached.

"You look so well, Shirley!" they said. Inanities dropped with the aggravation of a leaky faucet until she finally stopped her gay pretension and convinced them to go drivel elsewhere. But now, at least, there was a moment of peace, a pinpoint of quiet before the harrassment began again.

As always, without enough warning, the alarm rang. Her teeth clenched and she had to remind herself to be careful not to ruin

1

the orthodonture that daddy had paid for. Oh, God! That screeching bell! She could not ignore it. She washed her cup at the sink and filled a pail. The floor must be scrubbed first. It must shine and gleam so that you could eat from it, they said. The Man liked it that way. If it didn't glow he would look at her with a slight twist of his cruel mouth and say, "Well, Shirley, what have you been doing all day?"

Push the mop. Wring it out. The women on television did it. Push it until the floor is spotless. Intermittently the bell rang. It would continue to ring until it was obeyed. Another order, another question. What have you been doing this morning? You are expected to participate! You must! Chain yourself to the oven until your face is raw from the heat and bake cookies and cakes until you retch with the sick sweetness. Jab your fingers with a thousand needles until your blood splotches over the stiff denim of unending piles of tattered dungarees that must be mended. Set up the padded board and iron, Shirley. Wrinkles and creases are forbidden here. It does not matter if your knees have locked in an agony of exhaustion. Everything must be cleaned and pressed. It is your duty, Shirley.

Dear Lord, I am too young to be here!

Far away the wailing began. Low, keening, rising now to the pitch of an air-raid siren. Come! Obey me!

But the floor must shine first! Hurry! Push the filthy mop for one last sweep, then put it away and answer the screaming.

The room now, and the screaming muffled not at all by the closed door. Open it, Shirley. It does not look like a cell. There are bright curtains and a brightly colored rug. On the bed the guard with the baby face that she sees in her dreams. So sweet, that face; her young heart had taken to it from the beginning and loved it. She had thought that here, at last, was the one who would comfort her in this place, perhaps even be her escape. But behind the child features was a meanness that delighted in thinking of ways to debase her. Bathe me, slave! Feed me and never act as though you do not enjoy every second.

Mutely she did the baby's bidding until he was content at last. His fondness for the bottle was a weakness she had quickly learned to use. With the warm liquid soothing his belly, he stared drunkenly from her to the ceiling and back again as he cooed unintelligible nonsense. She felt the bile rise in her throat at his helplessness, knowing he would demand again and again and that she must answer. His gurgling laugh pursued her down the hall.

Back to the safety of the kitchen now that he was satisfied. Perhaps she could steal a cup of tea before they remembered her. Just a tiny minute of respite. She waited for the water to boil and idled quietly to the window. The world was out there. Occasionally she had been able to see the normal people—calm, happy, everyday people who did not know and could not understand the woman held prisoner in this place. Today there was only an old man walking a black dog. The animal strained and pulled against the leash. Poor beast. I know what you are feeling. The horrible choking stoppage of your throat so that you must gag or die as you fight to be free.

Oh, help me! *Help* me! I do not belong here. I am innocent. No one told me!

The silent screaming echoed through her skull and her arm lifted to crash through the glass. Call the man! Free the dog! Free me! But the old man was gone and the whistling demand of the teapot made her cringe as she ran to obey it.

The hot tea burned her throat as she gulped it down and the sudden memory of her first cup of coffee made the prison place disappear. It had been after the junior prom. She and Buck had gone to an all-night diner for coffee and she had felt too grown up to tell him that her parents had never let her drink coffee before. It had seared tears into her eyes that night.

She could still feel the prickle of the tulle bodice of the pink dress on her arms. Oh, it had been lovely to be sixteen! Her hair had curled along her shoulders and brushed against the orchid pinned there. She had been the only girl at the prom with an orchid, but then Buck would do anything for her.

She had been such a popular girl. Every boy there had wanted to dance with her. Even the seniors and Peggy MacCracken's cousin who was already in college had waited on line. The music had played on and on but her legs were strong and firm and tireless beneath the wispy bouffant skirt. Music swirled again across her mind, her eyes closed and her tight-lipped mouth eased into a smile.

Noise again. A banging, crashing, thudding of boots and the raucous laughter of the two jailers broke into her reverie. They burst into the kitchen shouting for food and tracking layers of mud across the floor. "Hey! Don'tcha know it's time to *eat*?" She poured the tea down the sink and quietly began making sandwiches, hiding tears of frustration at the soiled floor.

They took their places at the table, ignoring her as she moved about the kitchen, noticing her only when something more was required. It became a game to see how much they could spill. Milk from the carton poured across the formica, seeping into the cracks and dropping in slow motion onto the floor. She felt her anger rise but bit her tongue. It would never do to speak out. Soon they would be gone, back to whatever they did, and she would be left with the floor to clean again, and the dishes, the windows, the beds—the beds, oh, Lord, the *beds!* It was so late and the beds were not made!

The dirty spaghetti strands of the mop snatching at the remains of the lunch reminded her of a bedraggled pompon. Hers had been purple and orange. It had rustled like maple leaves on her upraised hands as she had jumped; laughing, crying in excitement over the touchdowns, goading the team on with a voice that became hoarse. Her legs had kicked drawing the attention of the bench boys with their giant shoulders, their helmets on their knees as they knelt in homage to the contest on the field.

The door slammed and she jumped guiltily, banging her shin against a cupboard door. The Man merely passed through without looking at her.

He came after dark, the eternal brief case clutched in his hand and his suit still immaculate. Did he ever really work or did he come only to torment? He glanced around the kitchen, his face a mask of supercilious contempt.

Once, when she had first come here, he had not mocked her. He had been kind and gentle, even eager to help her. But she had been pretty then. Now his eyes, when he saw her at all, held only ridicule or boredom and his mind had thoughts only for the outside people—those important people who gave him his power to rule this place and the money to keep it running smoothly. The money was very important. He said so. She knew each time the raises came because then he would smile and be happy and things were almost as they had been in the beginning. For a while. Then he would begin to crave more power or decide his domain should be larger, more modern, and the bars would slam down again.

She held her breath but this time he did not ask the question. Her mind did it for him. "Shirley, what have you been doing all day?" Doing all day? All day? Another day passed, time going, creeping away from her.

"It's raining again," he said, glancing at the patches of wet his feet had left on the floor. Then he was gone.

Bed at last. Lights out and beautiful soft darkness. The blanket chaffed at her chin and it was good to feel the realness of it. But it was not over. There was a sound and the Man was there standing beside her bed in the dark. He came to her often and once more her teeth clenched in agony. Not now, not again. She must not cry out. She must not! She lay and forced her mind back to fall afternoons and spring evenings, to pompoms and corsages.

This is not me! This is *not* me! The words reverberated through her head. I can't stand this! No more! I do not belong here! Oh, sweet heaven, what would my mother say if she could see this, know what they are doing to me here? She didn't know it would be like this when she let him take me. I have to get out! I must go back where I belong, now, before it's too late!

She slipped from the bed and crept to the kitchen. There were no bars now, no locked doors. They trusted her, these omnipotent jailers. She giggled with teen-aged glee as she slipped through the passageway into the dimness of the kitchen.

It was late. The rain was streaming in sheets across the roadway when the Man's mother drove past the house on her way home from a bridge party. She could see the lights blazing from the kitchen through the blur of the windshield and decided to stop. One of the boys must be sick. Certainly there was trouble of some kind. Buck and Shirley were always in bed by ten thirty. Buck insisted on it.

The only sound in the kitchen was the dull splat of rain on the roof, and the rest of the house seemed as dark as the sky outside. The fluorescent glow of the overhead fixture spotlighted the litter of old high-school yearbooks and yellowed dance programs on the kitchen table. Happy dancing couples stared at her from a page dusted with the powder of a pressed orchid. Cheerleaders arched in the contortions of pre-game frenzy and orderly rows of self-conscious faces grinned from beneath the faded, scribbled verses across dog-eared pages.

Whorls of dried mud marched haphazardly across the floor and the cutlery drawer beside the stove hung precariously on its hinges. Some of the knives had fallen to the floor to gleam dully in the silence.

Poor Buck. He deserved better than Shirley. The way she had let herself go! The horrible frumpy clothes she wore, and hiding, yes, *hiding* in the house all the time! You couldn't talk to her. She just sat twisting her red hands and staring at you like an imprisoned animal. It was ridiculous. You could hardly call Buck's lovely house a prison!

She pursed her lips, feeling a little silly. They'd obviously just forgotten to turn off the light in the kitchen. But she would just tiptoe down the hall and make absolutely sure everything was all right—

Buck was lying on his bed, blood oozing into the blanket twisted about his waist and blackening the lavender sheet beneath him. The two older boys were sprawled across the bunk beds, grotesque in the feeble glow of the night light. She didn't stop to look at the baby. She could not bear to go into the nursery room.

Neighbours called the police. They were frightened of the mad woman groveling in the rainsoaked lawn and screaming what sounded like "Shirley! Shirley! Oh, my God, where are you, Shirley?"

It was probably just a bunch of kids. The officers from the patrol car pulled slickers over their shoulders and ran into the shelter of the stadium. Wouldn't you know the high-school janitor would start hearing noises in the middle of this downpour? The officers plodded up the ramp and looked out at the field where the white chalk marking had begun to fade in the wet.

Shirley was marching in front of the home bleachers, her arms raised in a victory sign. The officers moved closer. Her face glistened in the glare of their flashlights. The lights wavered down over a faded flannel nightgown, plastered against her thin body by the rain.

As they watched, the woman suddenly crouched against the ground in a graceless squat, then rose into the air, arms and legs thrown out in spreadeagled abandon. Her voice rose over the drumming of the rain—a young, exuberant, exhilarated voice. "Yea Team! Yea! Yea! Yea!"

MARGERY ALLINGHAM

Bluebeard's Bathtub

At five o'clock on a September afternoon Ronald Fredrick Torbay was making preparations for his third murder. He was being wary because he was well aware of the dangers of carelessness.

He knew, 'way back before his first marriage, that a career of homicide got more chancy as one went on. Also, he realized, success was liable to go to a man's head.

For an instant he paused and regarded himself thoughtfully in the shaving glass of the bathroom in the new cottage he had hired so recently.

The face which looked back at him was thin, middle-aged, and pallid. Sparse dark hair receded from its high narrow forehead and the eyes were blue and prominent. Only the mouth was really unusual. That narrow slit, quite straight, was almost lipless and, unconsciously, he persuaded it to relax into a half smile. Even Ronald Torbay did not like his own mouth.

A sound in the kitchen below disturbed him and he straightened up hastily. It might be Edyth coming up to take her long discussed bubble bath before he had prepared it for her, and that would never do.

He waited, holding his breath, but it was all right; she was going out of the back door. He looked out the window to see her disappearing round the side of the house into the small square yard which was so exactly like all the other square yards in the long suburban street. He knew she was going to hang some linen on the line to air, and although the maneuver gave him the time he needed, still it irritated him.

Of the three homely, middle-aged women whom he had

8

persuaded to marry him and then to will him their modest possessions, Edyth was proving easily the most annoying. In their six weeks of marriage he had told her a dozen times not to spend so much time in the yard. He hated her being out of doors alone. She was shy and reserved, but now that new people had moved in next door there was always the danger of some over-friendly woman starting up an acquaintance with her, and that was the last thing to be tolerated at this juncture.

Each of his former wives had been shy. He had been very careful to choose the right type and felt he owed much of his success to it. Mary, the first of them, had met her fatal "accident" almost unnoticed in the bungalow of a housing development very like the present one he had chosen, but in the north instead of the south of England.

At the time it had been a growing place, the Coroner had been hurried, the police sympathetic but busy, and the neighbors scarcely curious—except that one of them, a junior reporter on a local paper whose story was picked up by the wire services, had written a flowery paragraph about the nearness of tragedy in the midst of joy, published a wedding-day snapshot, and had titled the article with typical northern understatement, *Honeymoon Mishap*.

Dorothy's brief excursion into his life and abrupt exit from it had given him a little more bother. She had deceived him when she told him she was quite alone in the world. An interfering brother had turned up after the funeral to ask awkward questions about her small fortune. He might have been a nuisance if Ronald had not been very firm with him. There had been a brief court case duly recorded in a small item in newsprint. However, Ronald had won his case handsomely, and the insurance company had paid up without a murmur.

All that was four years ago. Now, with a new name and a newly invented background, he felt remarkably safe.

From the moment he had first seen Edyth, sitting alone at a little table under the window in a seaside hotel dining room, he had known that she was to be his next subject. He always thought of his wives as "subjects."

Edyth had sat there looking stiff and neat and a trifle severe, but there had been a secret timidity in her face, an unsatisfied, half-frightened expression in her nearsighted eyes. She was also wearing a genuine diamond brooch.

He had spoken to her that evening, had weathered the initial snub, and finally got her to talk. After that the acquaintance had progressed just as he had expected. His methods were old-fashioned and heavily romantic, and within a week she was hopelessly infatuated.

From Ronald's point of view her history was ideal. She had taught in a girls' boarding school during her twenties before being summoned home to look after a demanding father, whose long illness had monopolized her life; now at forty-three she was alone, comparatively well off, and as much at sea as a ship without a rudder.

Ronald was careful not to let her toes touch the ground. He devoted his entire attention to her, and in exactly five weeks he married her at the registry office of the town where they were both strangers. The same afternoon they each made a will in the other's favor and moved into the villa which he had been able to hire cheaply because the holiday season was at an end.

Two things signed her death warrant earlier than had been Ronald's original intention. One was her obstinate reticence over her monetary affairs and the other was her embarrassing interest in his job.

Ronald had told her that he was a junior partner in a firm of cosmetic manufacturers who were giving him a very generous leave of absence. Edyth accepted the statement without question, but almost at once she had begun to plan a visit to the office and the factory and said she must buy some new clothes so as not to "disgrace" him. At the same time she kept all her business papers locked in an old writing case and steadfastly refused to discuss them, however cautiously he raised the subject. Ronald had given up feeling angry with her and had decided to act.

He turned from the window and began to run the bath.

The bathroom was the one room they had repainted. Ronald had done it himself and had put up the little shelf over the bath to hold a small electric heater of the old-fashioned type. He switched it on now and stood looking at it until the two bars of glowing warmth appeared. Then he went out onto the landing, leaving the heater alight.

The fuse box which controlled all the electricity in the house was concealed in the bottom of the linen cupboard at the head of the stairs. Ronald opened the door carefully and, using his handkerchief so that his fingerprints should leave no trace, pulled the main switch.

Back in the bathroom the heater's glow died away; the bars were almost black again by the time he returned. He eyed the heater approvingly and then, still using the handkerchief, he lowered it carefully into the water. It lay close to the foot of the tub where it took up practically no room at all. The white cord of the heater ran up over the porcelain side of the bath, along the baseboard, under the door, and into a wall socket just outside on the landing.

When he had first installed the heater, Edyth had demurred at this somewhat slipshod arrangement. But he had explained that the local Council was stupid and fussy about fitting wall sockets in bathrooms since water was said to be a conductor, and she had agreed to let him run the cord under the linoleum.

At the moment the heater was perfectly visible in the bath. It certainly looked as if it had fallen into its odd position accidentally, but no one in his senses could have stepped into the water without seeing it. Ronald paused, his ugly mouth narrower than ever. The beautiful simplicity of the main plan, so swiftly fatal and, above all, so safe as far as he was concerned, gave him a thrill of pleasure—as it always did.

He turned off the faucet and waited listening. Edyth was coming back. He could hear her moving something on the concrete outside the back door below and he took a paper sachet from his jacket pocket.

He was reading the directions on the back of it when a slight sound made him turn his head, and he saw, to his horror, the woman herself not five feet away. Her neat head had appeared suddenly just above the flat roof of the scullery, outside the bathroom window. She was clearing the dead leaves from the gutters and must, he guessed, be standing on a stepladder.

It was typical of the man that he did not panic. Still holding the sachet lightly, he stepped between her and the bath and spoke mildly.

"What on earth are you doing there, darling?"

Edyth started so violently that she almost fell off the ladder. "Oh, how you startled me! I thought I'd just do this little job before I came up to change. If it rains, the gutter floods all over the back step."

"Very thoughtful of you, my dear." He spoke with that slightly acid amusement with which he had found he could best destroy her slender vein of self-assurance. "But not terribly clever when you knew I'd come up to prepare your beauty bath for you. Or was it?"

The slight intonation on the word "beauty" was not lost on her. He saw her swallow.

"Perhaps it wasn't," she said without looking at him. "It's very good of you to take all this trouble, Ronald."

"Not at all," he said with just the right amount of masculine, offhand insensitivity. "I'm taking you out tonight and I want you to look as nice as possible. Hurry up, there's a good girl. The foam doesn't last indefinitely, and like all very high-class beauty treatments, it's expensive. Undress in the bedroom, put on your gown, and come along."

"Very well, dear." She began to descend while he turned and shook the contents of the sachet into the water. The crystals, smelling strongly of roses, floated on the tide and then when he turned the water on hard, they began to dissolve into thousands of iridescent bubbles. The bubbles grew into a fragrant feathery mass which obscured the bottom of the bath and overflowed the porcelain sides of the tub.

It was perfect.

He opened the door to call to her and just then she appeared. She came shrinking in, her blue dressing gown stained round her thin body her hair thrust into an unbecoming bathing cap.

"Oh, Ronald!" she said staring at the display. "Won't it make an awful mess? Goodness! All over the floor!"

Her hesitation infuriated him.

"That won't matter," he said savagely. "You get in while the foam is still there. Hurry. Meanwhile I'll go and change, myself.

Get in, and lie down. It'll take the sallowness out of your skin."

He went out and paused, listening. She locked the door as he had known she would. The habits of a lifetime do not change with marriage. He heard the bolt slide home and forced himself to walk slowly.

He gave her sixty seconds—thirty to take off her things and thirty to hesitate on the brink of the rosy mass.

"How is it?" he shouted from the linen cupboard.

She did not answer at once and the sweat broke out on his forehead. Then he heard her.

"I don't know yet. I'm only just in. It smells lovely."

He did not wait for the final word; his hand wrapped in his handkerchief had found the main switch.

"One, two . . . *three*," he said with horrible prosaicness—and pulled.

From the wall socket behind him there was a single spluttering flare as the fuse went, and then silence.

All round Ronald it was so quiet that he could hear the pulses in his own body, and he could hear no sound at all from the bathroom.

After a while he crept back along the passage and tapped at the door.

"Edyth? Are you there? Edyth?"

There was no response, no sound.

"Edyth?" he said again.

The silence was complete, and after a long minute he straightened his back and let out a deep sighing breath of relief.

Almost at once he was keyed up again in preparation for the second phase. As he well knew, this next was the tricky period. The discovery of the body must be made, but not too soon. He had made that mistake after Dorothy's "accident" and had actually been asked by the local police Inspector why he had become alarmed so soon; but he had kept his head that time, and the dangerous moment had passed.

This time he had decided to wait half an hour before he began to hammer loudly on the door, then to shout for a neighbor, and finally to force the lock. He had planned to stroll out to buy an evening paper, shouting his intention to do so to Edyth from the front door step for any passer-by to hear; but as he walked back along the landing he knew there was something else he must do first.

Edyth's leather writing case in which she kept all her private papers was in the bottom of her hatbox. She had really believed he had not known of its existence, he reflected bitterly.

He went softly into the bedroom and opened the wardrobe door. The case was exactly where he had last seen it, plump and promising, and his hands closed over it gratefully. There were bundles of savings certificates, one or two thick envelopes whose red seals suggested the offices of lawyers, and, on top, ready for the taking, one of those familiar gray books which the Post Office issues to its savings-bank clients.

He opened it with shaking fingers and fluttered through the pages. The sum made him whistle. £7250! Then a drop as she had drawn out £50 for her trousseau.

£7200. He thought that was the final entry but on turning the page saw that there was one more recorded transaction. It was less than a week old. He remembered the book coming back through the mail and how clever she had thought she had been smuggling it in.

He glanced at the written words and figures idly at first, but then, as his heart jolted in sudden panic, stared at them, his eyes prominent and glazed.

She had taken almost all of it out. There it was in black and white: *September 4th: Withdrawal seven thousand one hundred and ninety-eight pounds.*

His first thought was that the money must still be there, in hundred-pound notes perhaps, in one of the envelopes. He tore through them hastily, forgetting all caution in his anxiety. Papers, letters, certificates fell on the floor in confusion.

The envelope, addressed to himself, pulled him up short. It was new and freshly blotted, the name inscribed in Edyth's own unexpectedly firm hand—*Ronald Torbay, Esquire.*

He wrenched it open and stared at the single sheet of bond paper within. The date, he noted in horrified amazement, was only two days old.

Dear Ronald:

If you ever get this I am afraid it will prove a dreadful shock to you. For a long time I have been hoping that it might not be necessary to write it, but now your behavior has forced me to face some very unpleasant possibilities.

I am afraid, Ronald, that in some ways you are very old-fashioned. Has it not occurred to you that any homely, middle-aged woman who has been swept into a hasty marriage to a stranger must, unless she is a perfect idiot, be just a little sus-on the subjects of *baths*?

You must know that I am a dedicated newspaper reader, and after reading about two women who had met with fatal accidents in bubble baths soon after their marriages, I rather began to wonder.

Frankly, I did not want to suspect you because for a long time I thought I was in love with you; but when you persuaded me to make my will on our wedding day, I could not help wondering. And then as soon as you started fussing about the bathroom in this house, I thought I had better do something about it rather quickly. I am old-fashioned, too, Ronald, so I went to the police.

Have you noticed that the people who have moved into the house next door have never tried to speak to you? We thought it best that I should merely talk to the woman over the garden wall, and it is she who looked up the newspaper items I told her about. She even went a little further and found some cuttings from local provincial newspapers, each of which contained a press snapshot of the husband taken at the funeral.

They are not very clear, but even so, as soon as I saw them I realized it was my duty to agree to the course suggested to me by the Inspector. He told me that he had been looking for a man answering that description for over three years, ever since the two photographs were brought to his notice by your poor second wife's brother.

What I am trying to say is this: if you should ever lose me, Ronald—out of the bathroom, I mean—you will find that I have gone out over the roof and am sitting in my dressing gown in the kitchen next door. I was a fool to marry you, but not quite such a fool as you assumed. Women may be silly but they are not so stupid as they used to be. We are picking up the idea, Ronald.

Yours,

Edyth

P.S. On reading this I see that in my nervousness I have forgotten to say that the new people next door are not a married couple but Inspector Barsford of the C.I.D. and his assistant, Policewoman Richards. They assure me that there cannot be sufficient evidence to convict if you are not permitted to attempt the crime again. That is why I am forcing myself to be brave and play my part, for I am very sorry for those other poor wives of yours, Ronald. They must have found you as fascinating as I did.

With his slit mouth twisted into an abominable O, Ronald Torbay raised haggard eyes from the letter.

The house was quiet, and even the whine of the mower next door had ceased. In the hush he heard a sudden clatter as the back door burst open and heavy footsteps raced through the hall, up the stairs toward him.

CRAIG RICE

Quiet Day in the County Jail

"Cut that singing out, Artie." the girl's voice called. Artie, the head trusty, put down his guitar and walked into the cell that was half of what had been named the Presidential Suite. It was unlocked, because its tenant was only being held in protective custody as a material witness.

"What's the matter, Red?" he asked gently. "You nervous?"

She was beautiful, and she was pale, and she did seem too young and too fair to die. She was sitting on the edge of her bunk, wrapped in a green chenille bathrobe. The hair that had given her her nickname was loose over her shoulders. A cigarette blazed between her trembling fingers.

"Shadow fell over my tombstone, I guess," she said. "Forget it."

He patted her awkwardly on the shoulder and said, "You'd better get some sleep while you can." Right away he knew that had been the wrong thing to say, but it was too late to do anything about it now.

She looked at him with eyes that for a moment were bright with fear. "You don't need to remind me. They can't let me get back to Detroit alive."

"Shut up, Red," he said, even more gently. "That isn't what I meant." His voice managed to get back to normal. "I mean they're bringing in Aggie."

"Hot damn!" A smile and a little color came back to her face. "Well," she said thoughtfully, "the jail does need a good cleaning." She crushed out her cigarette in the fruit-jar top that served as an ash tray. "Artie, is there a drink anywhere in the house?"

17

"Need one?" He looked at her,a mixture of admiration, brotherly affection, sympathy, and a touch of fear. "We confiscated a pint of gin off a guy. Most of it's left. I'll get it."

Her lower lip was trembling almost as much as her pale fingers.

"Red, kid," he said softly, "you're in the safest place in the world. Jail, that is. Everything is going to be all right."

He grinned at her reassuringly, paused at the door, and burst into song again.

"The sheriff spoke in a quiet tone,
She seemed so beautiful and so young,
As he said, 'Tonight you're all alone,
And tomorrow you must be hung—'"

He ducked the folded magazine she threw at him and said,"Take it easy. Red. Even the President doesn't have a better bodyguard. I'll be right back."

The Santa Maria County Jail was as informal as a Sunday-school picnic, and on week-ends and holidays, twice as noisy. Small and fitted with only the essentials, it filled the second floor of the police station. The Presidential Suite consisted of two cells in a far corner reserved for women, juveniles, and special prisoners. Right now Red had it to herself.

Because she wasn't, strictly speaking, a prisoner and because she had her bankroll with her, the cell had sheets, a pillow, and pillow case. Her expensive clothes were carefully placed on hangers. And because Red was a friendly person, a bunch of blue flowers smiled from a jelly glass on an improvised table that had been made of two suitcases and a length of board.

Artie came back, his hand under his tan jacket. The cell was in semi-darkness; Red was still sitting on the edge of the bunk. He picked up the white enameled cup from the washstand, poured in a generous drink, added a little water, and handed it to her.

"Dirty trick," Red said. "Toss a guy in the can and then take his gin away."

"He won't miss it," Artie assured her. "He's the mayor's second cousin, and he's got eighteen dollars on deposit downstairs." He added, "You'd better keep the bottle."

"I may need it," she said. She looked up at him, six foot if he was half an inch, crew-cut blond hair, a deeply lined face. She slid the bottle between the mattresses of the bunk across from her, downed the contents of the cup fast, choked, and gasped, "*Water!*"

Artie rushed it to her. "Next time, hold your breath." He paused. "Red, you aren't really scared, are you?"

"Who, me?" she said, turning her eyes away. Her hands shook as she gulped the water, and half of it spilled on the floor.

"Red, kid," he said, taking the cup from her hands. "All you got to do is wait till they take you back to Detroit, just for you to testify. Then you're in the clear."

"They'll never let me get to that courtroom," she said, very quietly.

"Don't talk silly," Artie said. "You'll be protected. You'll be safe."

Their eyes met. They were both lying, and they both knew it.

She turned away first, punched up her pillow, lit a cigarette, and said, "Let's talk about you. What happens? I saw your lawyer come up here yesterday."

"The case comes up week after next," Artie said. "If the judge gets well, that is. The county's only got two judges, and one of em's sick. Two thousand cases were ahead of me, but they got it down to one thousand nine hundred and forty-four. When this other judge gets over his tonsillitis, or ulcers, or beri beri, or whatever it is, I'm first on the calendar. It'll be a short trial. They reduced the charge to manslaughter, and my lawyer's charging self-defense."

He blew his nose, lit a cigarette. "Red," he said, "I love my wife. She wrote me every day I was in the South Pacific. I love my kids. She brings them to see me every Sunday. I have a nice little ranch, I'm building up a trucking business. I met this guy, he came over to my house, the wife and kids were up visiting her mother, we had a few beers. He went wild and pulled a gun on me. I tried to take it away from him, and it went off."

Red reached between the mattresses for the bottle, poured a generous two inches into the cup, and handed it to Artie. She had a hunch it was he who needed moral support now.

"You'll get off," she told him. "They may even give you a bounty."

That got a laugh out of him, which was what she wanted. He flicked the ash from his cigarette and said, "Hell, it hasn't been too bad here, these eleven months. Since I been a trusty, I got the run of the place. I go out and do marketing, run errands, eat good and sleep good. Could be worse."

She said with a tired quietness, "I'd rather be here than dead in the streets."

"Red, you quit that kind of talk."

"They got to get me before I can testify," she said.

"I told you before, you're in the safest place in the world."

Suddenly the jail seemed to shake. There were sounds from downstairs just a little louder than the Bronx Zoo at feeding time, and about the same pitch.

"That would be Aggie," Red said.

"Couldn't be anyone else." Artie grinned. He rose, locked her cell door, and said, "Sorry I have to do this, but it's only for a few minutes." He called, "Hey, Pablo!"

Red settled down on her bunk and listened to the rumpus. Aggie was resisting arrest in two languages, and from the sounds, it was taking both trusties and Fred, the night jailer, to hold her.

Aggie was probably the best cleaning woman in Santa Maria. She was also probably the loudest drunk. She was happy with a bottle, she was just as happy with a pail of soap and water and a mop. Periodically when the jail needed a thorough scrubbing, the word went down the line, "Tour the bars and pick up Aggie."

Aggie always was brought into the jail sounding like a combination of a major riot and a bomb landing in the next block. Next morning the judge invariably sentenced her to six days, which could be worked out in three, and Aggie, cheerful if slightly hung over, filled a pail with soap and hot water and reached for the nearest mop.

Red put her fingers in her ears as Aggie was shoved into the next-door cell and locked in. Aggie went right on shouting.

Artie unlocked the metal grill door to Red's room and said, "You asleep?"

"Slept right through it," Red said cheerfully.

The other trusty, the small, sad-eyed Pablo, came in with Artie. "This we take from Aggie," he said gravely.

The bottle was passed around solemnly. Red shuddered. "Can't these cops ever arrest anybody with champagne?"

"Me, I like Scotch," Artie said.

She passed the bottle to him. "Shut your eyes and pretend that it's Scotch."

There was more noise from the cell next door.

"That Aggie, she makes with the yell," Pablo said.

"I make with the yell myself," Red said grimly. She raised her voice. "Shut up!"

There was a moment's silence, and then an answering yell. "You're who, and what'cha here for?"

"I'm the ax killer you been reading about in the papers," Red called. "And I've got the ax right here, the one I chopped up seven people with. The police let me keep it because I know the mayor. And my cell door is unlocked, and I've got a key to yours, and I like it quiet when I sleep."

There was a long and what promised to be a nightlong silence.

Artie and Pablo waved good night and went away. That was at four a.m.

By eight o'clock in the morning, the sun had been turning the heat on for an hour and a half. Red stirred restlessly, felt a hand pat her shoulder gently, turned over and opened her eyes.

It was Fred, the night jailer. "Going off duty now, Red. Just came to say good-by and wish you luck."

Suddenly wide awake, she sat up, pulling the blankets around her shoulders. "What do you mean, good-by?"

Fred looked embarrassed. "I thought they were moving you out today."

"Nobody's told me yet," she said. She didn't need to look in a mirror; she could feel her face turning pale.

"Well," he said, "well, in case they do. Good luck. Don't worry, Red. Come back and visit us when it's all over."

"Sure will," she said heartily. "I'll do just that little thing."

He knew she'd never be back in Santa Maria, and so did she.

They shook hands. She said. "Fred, please thank your wife for sending me the flowers." Flowers for a corpse that was still walking around and talking. "Wait a minute, will you?"

She reached for her robe, wrapping it around her, slid off the bunk, and rummaged through the suitcase that was under the bed, until she pulled out what looked like a handful of tissue paper. She sat on the edge of the bunk, untangled the tissue paper, and pulled out a brooch. It blazed green, yellow, and white fire in the early-morning sunlight.

"Please give this to her. It's a phony, just a hunk of costume jewelry, but I think it's pretty. The one thing that isn't phony is the thanks to her that go with it."

"Gosh, Red," Fred said. He choked for a minute, rewrapped the brooch in the tissue paper, and stuck it in his pocket. "Gosh." He paused again. "She wanted to send you some more flowers."

"Tell her to save them for my wake," Red said, managing to keep her voice light. She walked over to the window and stood looking out.

Fred stood for a moment, uncertainty drawn on his broad red face. Finally he walked over and put a hand on her arm. "Red." he said, feeling for words, "if—I mean, if something happens to you—I mean, well, I got friends, we'll find out who did it—"

She turned around, smiling. "Thanks. Now beat it, bum. I've got to get some sleep."

There was something she vaguely remembered from high school. She fished for it in her mind, and all that came to her was "There is a time to sleep, and a time to stay awake." She knew that wasn't right, but it didn't matter now.

She paced up and down the cell. She scrubbed her face and put on fresh make-up. She combed her lovely red hair until it was smooth and shining. She brushed on lipstick and tended to her eyebrows. She put on a pair of dove-gray slacks, a pale-green sweater, and darker-green sandals.

Eight thirty. She remembered Aggie with a sudden sense of guilt. She raced into the main room and yelled for Artie.

"Honey, open up Aggie's door. She's got to be in court by nine, and I've got to wash her face."

"Will do," he said, reaching for the keys. He looked appreciatively. "You're going to be missed, Red."

Again she could feel the color drain out of her face. "Who says?"

Artie avoided her eyes as he unlocked the door to Aggie's cell. After a moment of inspection and thought, Red went next door and collected a comb, make-up, powder, a lipstick, a big fluffy towel, mouthwash, and the remains of the gin. Five vigorous shakes woke Aggie.

"Come on, kid," Red said. "You've got to be in court in half an hour."

Aggie began moaning. An inch of gin in the enameled cup took care of that. She got her eyes open enough to stay that way on the fourth blink, and said, "Red! You still here?"

"Haven't thrown me out yet," Red said, with false cheerfulness. "Babe, do yourself proud in court. Wash your face, and I'll put your make-up on for you and fix your hair." She looked at Aggie's dress and shook her head sadly.

Well, there was one of her own that just might fit. She was as tall as Aggie, and the dress would stretch sideways.

At two minutes to nine, Aggie was on her way downstairs, hair combed, face made up, smelling slightly of mouthwash and Daphne cologne, and wearing a blue jersey dress that would never shrink back into shape again.

At ten minutes after nine Aggie came back up the stairs, beaming. "Six or three," she shouted. "Artie, where's the mop?"

Red called from her cell, "Artie! Pablo! Somebody!"

It was Artie who came to the door. "A mouse?" he asked.

"I want breakfast," Red said.

"Breakfast is served in this jail at six thirty," Artie said. "But since you slipped Frank a buck yesterday to buy eggs, I think we can oblige you." He winked at her. "He got a dozen eggs stashed away in the refrigerator. And the coffee's good this morning."

It was Pablo who brought in the tin tray. The eggs were cooked just right, the toast was the right color of tan, and the coffee was as good as advertised.

She smiled at Pablo. She always smiled at Pablo. Today she had an extra one.

Pablo was short and slender and black-haired, and he was almost a permanent prisoner. Frank, the day jailer, had confided in Red that Pablo had been serving a thirty-day drunk charge for almost two years. It had become a regular routine. Sentenced to thirty days. Made a trusty the next day. Released. Arrested the next day, or even sooner.

Artie swore, and Red believed him, that Pablo had once made the round trip from the jail and back in exactly three hours.

And it was Artie who'd told her how Pablo's wife had run away with another man, how he'd lost his job and seen the bank take away his home, all in one month.

"Señorita Red," Pablo said, "would you like I should go and buy you cigarettes?"

She looked at him with pretended sternness. "The last time I gave you a quarter to buy me cigarettes you were gone for two days, and the judge tacked an extra thirty days on you when they did find you."

"It was a mistake," Pablo said with great dignity. "Perhaps you could lend me twenty-five cents. Believe me, it is for a good purpose."

She looked at him, and her eyes softened. After all, Pablo had only two homes. The jail, and the Frisco Bar and Grill. She pulled her change purse from under her pillow, took out a fifty-cent piece, and said, "I hope you have a lot of fun with the good purpose."

That was at ten o'clock in the morning.

The routine daily cleaning was going on, plus Aggie throwing a mop around in the kitchen. Red stood looking out the window at the roof of the bowling alley next door. She lifted her eyes to the mountains that ringed the little city and saw a tiny speck of silver racing cross the blue. Would they take her out by plane or train, she wondered.

She could hear Artie going through the big cabinet in the main room, sorting out files. She could hear a prisoner rattling tin trays in the kitchen sink. This will be going on long after I'm gone, she thought. Artie will go on sorting files, then his case will come up in court and chances are he'll be freed; the guy in the kitchen will go on washing dishes and serve his sentence and be on his way. But she would be gone before that, far away from here.

A voice said, "Hey, Red."

She turned around. It was Frank, the day jailer. He was a deceptively gentle-looking man with a friendly face, white hair, and a deadly right when he had to use it. He was one more person in the world she would have trusted with her life.

"Chief's on his way up to see you. Thought I'd tell you, case you want to powder your face."

"Bless you, Frank." At that moment she heard the buzzer that announced someone was coming up the stairs.

She was sitting on the edge of her bunk, face powdered, when Chief of Police Sankey came in, Frank close behind him.

"Red," he said. "I mean, Miss—"

"That's all right," she said.

He sat down on the bunk across from her, a worried, fretful little man with reddish hair and rimless glasses.

"Well," he said, "we finally got the word. They're taking you on a plane this afternoon. Papers all signed, everything set."

She opened her mouth to speak, shut it again, and finally managed to say, "I'll be ready."

He looked embarrassed. He said, "You'll be well protected, naturally. So there's nothing for you to worry about." He paused and added, "Well, good luck."

After he'd gone, Frank patted her shoulder and said, "Everything's going to be all right, Red."

"Oh, sure." She forced a smile to her face. "It's just that I like your jail so well that I hate to leave it. Besides, I feel safe here."

He cleared his throat, started to speak, and changed his mind. He patted her shoulder a second time.

"Frank, I saw the whole thing. I was standing right in the doorway of the Blue Casino. Louie did the job himself, and I was right there. All I could think of was to beat it, fast. Threw some stuff in a couple of suitcases, got the first plane to Kansas City. That's where I bought the car and headed south. I could have made it across the border into Mexico easy but you guys picked me up."

"Maybe it's just as well." Frank told her reassuringly. "This guy would have had you followed. This way he'll get convicted, and then you won't have a thing to worry about."

"Oh, sure," she said again. She sighed. "It's just luck that some goon was coming down the sidewalk and saw what was going on. He didn't get close enough to recognize Louie, but I was standing there with a light smack on my face, and he spotted me. The Detroit cops picked up Louie on general principles and started looking for me."

She ran a hand through her shining red hair. "I'm their only witness. Course, I could get on the stand and swear I didn't see a thing, or I could swear it wasn't Louie."

"You could." Frank said. "But—"

"But I wouldn't," she finished for him. "That is, assuming I ever get to the witness stand."

Artie came in, lit a cigarette, and lounged against the wall.

"This Louie." Frank asked, "was he your boyfriend?"

That brought a laugh from her, the first one that day. "I didn't have a boyfriend. I ran the Blue Casino. A gambling joint. I ran that end of it, and my partner ran the nightclub end." She grinned at them. "I came by these diamonds honestly, pals."

"So that's why you've been able to take us at blackjack," Artie said lazily.

"Well," Frank said, getting up, "you'll be protected on the way to the plane, and you'll be protected on the plane, and you'll probably be taken off it in an armored car."

Artie pinched out his cigarette, dropped it on the floor. "Pablo'll clean up in here when he gets back. He's got the car out now, getting potatoes."

At that moment all hell broke loose in the yard outside. Red and Artie were tied getting to the window. Artie gave a loud whoop and raced for the stairs, yelling for Frank to work the buzzer.

Outside, Pablo was having troubles. The car used by the jail for general errands was parked directly under Red's window, and the trunk compartment was open. What appeared to be about a hundred white chickens, but were actually only six, were creating the disturbance. Pablo was trying to move them from the trunk compartment to a burlap bag, and the chickens were resisting arrest. The scene was beginning to draw a fair-sized audience when reinforcements, in the person of Artie, arrived.

Between them, the chickens were shoved unceremoniously

into the bag and tossed, still protesting loudly, into the car. Artie and Pablo got in and drove off.

Frank, who had watched the last act from Red's window, sighed deeply and said, "Sometimes I think they give these trusties too many liberties."

"None of them give you any trouble, though," Red reminded him.

"That's right," he said, "except sometimes Pablo." He looked at her searchingly. "Did you give him any money?"

"I gave him fifty cents." Red confessed. She added, as though in defense, "After all, Frank, it's my last day here."

Frank shook his head sadly. "Another thirty days. Well, he's got to sleep somewhere."

That was at eleven o'clock.

It was some time later when Artie and Pablo came in triumphantly, Pablo carrying a large paper-wrapped bundle. The chickens were not only silent now, but in addition to losing their voices they had lost their feathers and a few other odds and ends, and were candidates for the frying pan.

"Farewell party!" Artie called happily, heading for the kitchen.

Red looked at her suitcases, at the clothes hanging against the walls, at the make-up carefully arranged on the improvised table, and started a half-hearted effort toward packing. But there was plenty of time for that later. She flopped down on the bunk, picked up a magazine, and tried to read. The words seemed to run together and made no sense at all.

Pablo came in the door. He was completely sober, and walking with great dignity. He carried a package, which he presented to Red with even greater dignity.

"For you," he said. "For a going-far-away present."

She unwrapped it. It was a bottle of what was probably the worst wine in the world. This was the important purpose for which Pablo had needed money. She felt tears hot in her eyes.

"Pablo, I thank you," she said with dignity that matched his. She put the package under the bunk, reached between the mattresses for the last of the gin. "For farewell, will you have a drink with me?"

Pablo's dark eyes brightened. "Since you insist upon it."

She rinsed out the enameled cups and divided the gin equally into them. They saluted each other solemnly and silently.

"We will miss you," Pablo said simply.

That was at twelve o'clock.

It was Artie who brought in her lunch, some time later.

"No stew?" she said, looking up and sniffing. "No pinto beans?"

Artie grinned at her as he set the tray down. "Fried chicken." He shook his head thoughtfully. "That Pablo. It isn't enough that he goes out and steals chickens. But he has to steal the chickens from the chief of police."

He went on. "He was going to bring them up here and clean them, but I had an idea. We took them to a restaurant where I know the kitchen help. Result, no evidence."

It was one o'clock when he came to take the tray away and lock Aggie's door. She was, after all, a prisoner, and even in the Santa Maria County Jail, rules were rules. He paused in Red's cell.

"I'll help you pack, after siesta."

She turned her face away. "I can manage, thanks, Artie."

He sat down on the other bunk. "Red, listen. You'll be protected. There's nothing to it. When you get to Detroit they'll put you up in some expensive hotel, with a bodyguard. You testify, and it's all over. There's nothing for you to be scared of."

"Who's scared?" she scoffed, managing to keep her voice steady.

"Red," he said slowly, "Red. Will you let me kiss you, once?"

She stared at him.

"I been here eleven months, Red. I'd just like to kiss a girl again."

She smiled, and lifted her face to him. He kissed her very gently, almost a little-boy kiss.

"It won't seem like the same place without you, Red."

The county jail became silent. Frank had gone out to lunch, and everyone else was asleep. Everybody except Red. She lay on her bunk, her eyes closed, wondering if she would ever sleep again. Finally she gave up. Might as well pack and get it over with.

Midafternoon sunlight was streaming in the windows of the

trusties' room when the sound of the big door clanging shut and footsteps on the stairs woke Artie. He swung his long legs off the bed, and walked into the main room.

That was at three o'clock.

Frank and a stranger had just reached the top of the stairs.

"Detective Connelly, Detroit police," Frank said, puffing, and nodding toward the stranger. "Red all packed and set to leave?"

"I'll see," Artie said.

Red was sitting on the bunk, her suitcase beside her. She had on a light-beige suit and a small green hat. Her face was very pale. Artie picked up the suitcase. She rose and followed him into the main room.

Pablo had come out of the trusties' room. Aggie, mop in hand, was watching. Everyone was silent.

Red managed a wan smile at the Detroit detective.

"All set?" He tried to smile but didn't look as though he relished this job. She nodded.

Frank said heartily, "Now remember, Red, don't you worry about a thing. He'll take you back, you testify, this Louie will go to jail or the chair, and that's that."

"Sure," Connelly said, with false confidence. "That's the way."

"And you will come back to visit us," Pablo said. "I will still be here."

That eased the tension a little.

There was nothing left to say but good-by. Then Red went down the stairs without looking back, Connelly and Frank on either side. The two trusties stood looking after her.

At last they walked to her cell and looked in. There was a faint odor of cigarette smoke, gin, and expensive perfume. Artie straightened a wrinkle in the blankets.

"It seems so quiet," he said.

Pablo looked under the bed, pulled out the package. "She forgets and leaves it behind," he said sadly, unwrapping it. "I buy it for her, a going-away present." There were tears in his eyes.

"You're a bad boy, Pablo," Aggie said from the doorway.

Pablo looked wistful.

"I think she'd have wanted you to open it," Artie said very gently.

Pablo ripped off the cap. The bottle of the worst wine in the world was passed around in silence.

RUTH RENDELL

Front Seat

Along the sea front, between the pier and the old town, was a row of wooden seats. There were six of them, regularly spaced on the grass, and they faced the dunes, the sea wall, and the sea. To some people, including Mrs. Jones, they were known by name as Fisher, Jackson, Teague, Prendergast, Lubbock, and Rupert Moore. It was on this last seat, the one that was curiously known by the Christian as well as the family name of the man it commemorated, that Mrs. Jones invariably chose to sit.

She sat there every day, enjoying the peace and quiet, looking at the sea and thinking about the past. It was most pleasant on mild winter days or on those days of summer when the sky was overcast, for then the holiday visitors stayed in their cars or went off to buy prawns and crabs and expensive knick-knacks.

Mrs. Jones thought how glad she was that last year, when Mr. Jones had been taken from her, that she had bought the house in the old town, even though this had meant separating herself from her daughter. She thought about her son in London and her daughter in Ipswich, good loving children that they were, and about her grandchildren, and sometimes about her good fortune in having a comfortable annuity as well as her pension.

But mostly, sitting on Rupert Moore, between Fisher and Teague, she thought about that first man in her life to whom even now, after so long, she referred always as her darling. She had so accustomed herself to calling him this that to her the endearment had become his name. My darling, thought Mrs. Jones, as some other old woman might have thought of John or Charlie or Tom.

She felt closer to him here than anywhere, which was why she chose to rest on this seat and not on one of the others.

31

On July 15th, St. Swithin's Day, Hugh and Cecily Branksome sat in their car, which was parked on the promenade, and looked at the gray choppy sea. Or, rather, Hugh looked at the sea while Cecily looked at Mrs. Jones. The temperature was around ten degrees, according to Cecily who moved with the times, or 50, according to Hugh who did not. It was not yet raining, though the indications were that it soon would be.

Hugh was wishing they had gone to the Costa Brava where there would have been high-rise buildings and fish and chips and bullfights, but at least the sun would have shone. Cecily had got it into her head that it was bourgeois and unpatriotic to go abroad for one's holiday.

"I wonder why she always sits there," said Cecily.

"Who sits where?"

"That old woman. She always sits on that particular seat. She was there yesterday and the day before."

"Didn't notice," said Hugh.

"You never notice anything. While you were in the pub yesterday," said Cecily with emphasis, "I waited till she'd gone and then I read the inscription on that seat. On the metal plate on the back. D'you know what it says?"

"Of course I don't," said Hugh, opening the window to let out cigarette smoke. An icy breeze hit him in the face.

"Do close the window. It says, 'Rupert Moore gave this seat to Northwold in thanks for his deliverance. I was in prison and ye came unto me, Matthew, chapter twenty-five, verse thirty-five.' How about that?"

"Remarkable." Hugh thought he knew all about being in prison. He looked at his watch. "Opening time," he said. "We can go and get a drink, thank God."

On the following morning he went out fishing without her. They met in their room before dinner, Hugh bracing himself to face certain sarcastic questions, not without precedent, as to whether he had had a nice day. He forestalled them by telling her they had caught only one small mackerel, for her censure would be greater if he had enjoyed himself. But he was soon interrupted.

"I've got the whole story about the seat out of that nice man with the beard."

Hugh's memory was poor and for a moment he didn't know which seat she was talking about, but he recognized the nice man from her description. A busybody know-it-all who lived in Northwold and hung about the hotel bar.

"He insisted on buying me a drink. Well, two, as a matter of fact." She smiled archly and patted her hair as if the bearded know-it-all had, at the very least, invited her to Aldeburgh for the weekend. "His name is Arnold Cottle and he said this Rupert Moore put that seat there because he'd murdered his wife. He was put on trial and acquitted and that's what it means about 'deliverance' and being in prison."

"You can't say he murdered his wife if he was acquitted."

"You know what I mean," said Cecily. "It was ages ago, in 1930. I mean, I was only a baby." Hugh thought it wiser not to point out that at ten one is hardly a baby. "They acquitted him, or he got off on Appeal, something like that, and he came back here to live and had that seat put there. Only the local people didn't want a murderer and they broke his windows and called after him in the street and he had to go."

"Poor devil," said Hugh.

"Well, I don't know about that, Hugh. From what Arnold said, the case was very unsavory. Moore was quite young and very good-looking and he was a painter, though he had a private income. His poor wife was much older and an invalid. He gave her cyanide they'd got for killing wasps. He gave it to her in a cup of coffee."

"I thought you said he didn't do it."

"Everyone *knew* he'd done it. He only got off because the judge misdirected the jury. You can't imagine how anyone would have the nerve to put up a sort of monument, can you, after a thing like that?"

Hugh started to run his bath. Resignedly he accepted the fact, from past experience, that part of the evening would be spent in the company of Arnold Cottle. Cecily was not, and never had been, particularly flirtatious except in her own imagination. It was not that. Rather it was that she liked to get hold of causes or what she called examples of injustice or outrage and worry at them, roping in to assist her any helper who might be on hand.

There had been the banning of the proposed motorway, the petition against the children's playground, the eviction of the squatters down the road. She was not always reactionary, for she worshipped free speech and racial equality and health foods and clean air. She was a woman of principle who threw herself whole-heartedly into upheaval and change and battles that right might be done, and sometimes into cults for the improvement of her soul.

The unfortunate part of all this, or one of the unfortunate parts, was that it brought her so often into the company of bores or rogues. Hugh wondered what she was up to now, and why, and hoped it might be, though it seldom was, a flash in the pan.

Two hours later he found himself with his wife and Arnold Cottle, standing on the wet grass and examining the inscription on the Rupert Moore seat. It wasn't yet dark and wouldn't be for an hour. The sky was heavily overcast and the sea the color of a recently scoured aluminium pot. No one would have supposed, thought Hugh, that somewhere up there in the west was the sun which, contrary to all present evidence, science told him was throwing off light at the rate of 250,000,000 tons a minute.

The others were too rapt to be distracted. He had a look at Fisher (In memory of Colonel Marius Fisher, V.C., D.S.O., 1874-1951) and at Teague (William James Teague, of this Town, lost at the Battle of Jutland) and then he prodded Rupert Moore and announced, for something to say, "That's oak."

"It is indeed, my dear old chap." Arnold Cottle spoke to Hugh very warmly and kindly, as if he had decided *a priori* that he was a harmless lunatic. "You could get oak in those days. This seat was made by a chap called Sarafin, Arthur Sarafin. Curious name, eh? Corruption of seraphim, I daresay. Fine craftsman, lived up the coast at Lowestoft, but he died quite young, more's the pity. My father knew him, had some of the furniture he made. You can see his initials up there where the crossbar at the top joins the post. A.S. in a little circle, see?"

Hugh thought this quite interesting. He had done a bit of carpentry himself until Cecily had stopped it on the ground that she needed his workshop for her groups. That had been in the days when she was into Gestalt. Hugh preferred not to think about them. He had a look at Prendergast (This seat was placed here by the Hon. Mrs. Clara Prendergast that the weary might find rest) and was about to ask Cottle if this one was oak or teak, when Cecily said, "Where did he get the cyanide?"

"Moore?" said Cottle. It was never actually proved that he did get it. He said they kept some in their garden shed for killing wasps and that his wife had taken it herself. In point of fact, Mrs. Moore had written to her sister, saying her life wasn't worth living and she wanted to put an end to it. But this gardener chappie said he'd thrown the wasp-killing stuff away a year before."

"It must have come from somewhere," said Cecily in such a hectoring tone and looking so belligerent that Hugh felt even more sympathy for Rupert Moore.

Cottle didn't seem to mind the tone or the look. "Moore had been to several chemist's shops in the area, though not actually in Northwold, and tried to buy cyanide, ostensibly for killing wasps. No chemist admitted to having let him have it. There was one in Tarrington, up the coast here, who sold him another kind of vespicide that contained no cyanide, and got him to sign the Poison Book. Dear Cecily, since you're so interested, why don't you read up the case in the library? Perhaps I might have the pleasure of taking you there tomorrow?"

The offer was accepted with enthusiasm. They all went into the Cross Keys where Hugh bought three rounds of drinks and Arnold Cottle bought none, having failed to bring his wallet with him. Cecily fastened on to the barman and elicited from him that the old woman who always sat on the Rupert Moore seat was named Mrs. Jones, that she had come to Northwold the year before from Ipswich, and was of Suffolk, though not Northwold, origin.

"Why does she always sit there?"

"Ask me another," said the barman, presumably meaning this rejoinder rhetorically, which was not the way Cecily took it.

"What's so fascinating about that seat?"

"It seems to fascinate you," said Hugh. "Can't you give it a rest? The whole thing's been over and done with for going on fifty years."

Cecily said, "There's nothing else to do in this damned place," which displeased the barman so much that he moved off in a huff.

"I've got a very active brain, Hugh. You ought to know that by now. I'm afraid I'm not content to fuddle it with drink or spend ten hours pulling one poor little fish out of the sea."

The library visit, from which Hugh was excused, took place. But books having been secured, a journey had to be made to the house in which Rupert Moore had lived with his wife and painted his pictures and where the crime had been committed. Arnold Cottle seemed delighted at the prospect, especially as the excursion, at Cecily's suggestion, was to include lunch. Hugh had to go because Cecily couldn't drive and he wasn't going to lend his car to Cottle.

The house was a dull and ugly mansion, now used as a children's home. The superintendent (quite reasonably, Hugh thought) refused to let them tour the interior, but he had no objection to their walking about the grounds. It was bitterly cold for the time of year, but not cold enough to keep the children indoors. They tagged around behind Arnold Cottle and the Branksomes, making unfriendly or impertinent remarks. One of them, a boy with red curly hair and a cast in his eye, threw an apple core at Cecily, and when he was reproved he used a word which, though familiar, is still unexpected on the lips of a five-year-old.

They had lunch, and throughout the meal Cecily read aloud extracts from the trial of Rupert Moore. The medical evidence was so unpleasant that Hugh was unable to finish his steak *au poivre*. Cottle drank nearly a whole bottle of Nuits St. Georges and had a double brandy with his coffee. Hugh thought about men who had murdered their wives, and how much easier it must have been when you could get wasp killer made of cyanide and weed killer made of arsenic. But even if he could have got those things, or have pushed Cecily downstairs, or fixed it for the electric wall heater to fall into the bath while she also was in it, he knew he never would. Even if he got away with it, as poor Rupert Moore had, he would have the shame and the fear and the guilt for the rest of his life, again as had been the case with Rupert Moore.

Not that Moore had lived for long. "He died of some kidney disease just twelve months after they let him out," said Cecily, "and by then he'd been hounded out of this place. He had Sarafin make that seat and that was about the last thing Moore ever did in Northwold." She scanned the last chapter of her book. "There doesn't seem to have been any real motive for the murder, Arnold."

"I suppose he wanted to marry someone else," said Cottle, swigging brandy. "I remember my father saying there were rumors he'd had a girl friend, but nobody seemed to know her name and she wasn't mentioned at the trial."

"She certainly wasn't," said Cecily, flicking back in her book so rapidly that she nearly knocked Hugh's coffee cup over. "You mean, there was no clue as to who she was? How did the rumors start, then?"

"Dear Cecily, how do rumors ever start? In point of fact, Moore was known often to have been absent from home in the evenings. There was gossip he'd been seen in Clacton with a girl."

"Fascinating," said Cecily. "I shall spend the rest of the day thoroughly studying all this literature. You and Hugh must amuse yourselves on your own."

After a dreadful afternoon listening to Cottle's troubles, how enemies had prevented his making a success at any career, how his two attempts at getting married had been scotched by his mother, and how his neighbors had a vendetta against him,. Hugh finally escaped. Though not before he had lent Cottle ten pounds, this being the lowest of the sums his guest had suggested as tenable. Cecily had had a wonderful time, making herself conversant with the Moore case, and now she was in the bath. Hugh wondered if a mighty thump on the bedroom side of the bathroom wall would dislodge the heater and make it fall into the water, but this was merely academic speculation.

After dinner he went for a walk on his own in the rain while Cecily made notes—for what purpose Hugh neither knew nor cared. He poked about in the ruins of the castle; he bought two tickets for the repertory theater on the following night, hoping that the play, though it was called "Murder-on-Sea," might distract Cecily; he wandered about the streets of the old town and he had a drink in the Oyster Catcher's Arms. On the whole he didn't have a bad time.

The morning being better—a pale sickly sun was shining and making quite attractive tints on the undersides of black clouds—he thought they might go on the beach. But Cecily had other plans. She got him to take her to Tarrington, and in the little shopping center she left him to his own devices which included buying two pairs of thicker socks. After that, because it was raining again, there was nothing to do but sit in the car park. She kept him waiting two hours.

"What d'you think?" she said. "I found that chemist, the one that sold Rupert Moore the wasp killer that hadn't got cyanide in it. And, would you believe it, it's still the same firm. The original pharmacist's grandson is now the manager.

"I suppose," said Hugh, "that he told you his grandfather had made a deathbed confession that he did give Moore the cyanide after all."

"Do try not to be silly. I already knew they had cyanide wasp killer in the shop. It said so in the library book. This young man, the grandson, couldn't tell me much, but he did say his grandfather had had a very pretty young girl assistant. How about that?"

"I've noticed that very pretty young girls often do work in chemist's shops."

"I'm glad you notice something, at any rate. However, she is not the one. The grandson knows her present whereabouts, and she is a Mrs. Lewis. So I shall have to look elsewhere."

"What d'you mean, the one?" said Hugh dismally.

"My next task," said Cecily, taking no notice, "will be to hunt for persons in this case of the name of Jones. Young women, that is. I know where to begin now. Sooner or later I shall root out a girl who was an assistant in a chemist's shop at the time and who married a Jones."

"What for?"

"That right may be done," said Cecily solemnly. "That the truth may at last come out. I see it as my mission. You know I always have a mission, Hugh. It was the merest chance we happened to come to Northwold because Diana Richards recommended it. You wanted to go to Lloret de Mar. I feel it was meant we should come here because there was work for me to do.

I am convinced Moore was guilty of this crime, but not alone in his guilt. He had a helper who, I believe, is alive at this moment. I'd like you to drive me to Clacton now. I shall begin by interviewing some of the oldest inhabitants."

So Hugh drove to Clacton where he lost a pound on the slot machines. Indefatigably Cecily pursued her investigations.

Mrs. Jones came back from morning service at St. Mary's, and although she was a good walker and not at all tired, for she had slept well ever since she came to Northwold, she sat down for half an hour on her favorite seat. Two other elderly people who had also been in church were sitting on Jackson (In memory of Bertrand Jackson, 1859-1924, Philanthropist and Lover of the Arts). Mrs. Jones nodded pleasantly to them, but she didn't speak. It wasn't her way to waste in chat time that was more satisfactorily spent in reminiscence.

A pale gray mackerel sky, a fitful sun. Perhaps it would brighten up later. She thought about her daughter who was coming to lunch. Brenda would be tired after the drive, for the children, dears though they were, would no doubt be troublesome in the car. They would all enjoy that nice piece of sirloin and the Yorkshire pudding and the fresh peas and the chocolate ice cream. She had got in a bottle of sherry so that she and Brenda and Brenda's husband could each have a glass before the meal.

Her son and daughter had been very good to her. They knew she had been a devoted wife to their father, and they didn't resent the place in her love she kept for her darling. Not that she had ever spoken of him in front of their father or of them when they were small. That would have been unkind and in bad taste. But later she had told them about him and told Brenda, in expansive moments, about that long-past happiness and the tragedy of her darling's death, he so young and handsome and gifted.

Perhaps, this afternoon when the rest of them were on the beach, she might allow herself the luxury of mentioning him again. Discreetly, of course, because she had always respected Mr. Jones and loved him after a fashion, even though he had taken her away to Ipswich and never attained those heights of talent and success her darling would have enjoyed had he lived.

Tranquilly, not unhappily, she recalled to her mind his face, his voice, and some of their conversations.

Mrs. Jones was disturbed in her reverie by the presence of that tiresome woman. She had seen her before, hanging about on the promenade and once examining the seat that Mrs. Jones thought of as her own. An ugly thin neurotic-looking woman who was sometimes in the company of a sensible elderly man and sometimes with that shameless scrounger, old Cottle's boy, whom Mrs. Jones, in her old-fashioned way, called a barfly. Today, however, she was alone, and to Mrs. Jones's dismay, was approaching her with intent to speak.

"Do excuse me for speaking to you, but I've seen you here so often."

"Oh, yes?" said Mrs. Jones. "I've seen you too. I'm afraid I have to go now. I've guests for lunch."

"Please don't go. I won't keep you more than a moment. But I must tell you I'm terribly interested in the Moore case. I can't help wondering if you knew him, you're here so much."

"I knew him," said Mrs. Jones distantly.

"That's terribly exciting." And the woman did look very excited. "I suppose you first met him when he came into the shop?"

"That's right," said Mrs. Jones, and she got up. "But I don't care to talk about it. It's a very long time ago and it's best forgotten. Good morning."

"Oh, but please . . . !"

Mrs. Jones ignored her. She walked far more rapidly than usual, breathing heavily, along the path toward the old town. She was flustered and upset and very put out. To take up all that now just when she was thinking of the lovely events of that time! For that day, though not, she hoped, for the future, the encounter had spoiled the seat for her.

"Had a good day with Cottle?" said Hugh.

"Don't speak to me about that man. Can you imagine it, I phoned him and a woman answered! She turned out to be some creature on holiday like us who was taking him to Lowestoft in her car. I could come too if I liked. No, thank you very much, I said. What about my finding the girl called Jones? I said. And he was pleased to tell me I was getting *obsessional*. So I gave him a piece of my mind, and that's the last of Arnold Cottle."

And the last of his ten pounds, thought Hugh. "So you went on the beach instead?"

"I did not. While you were out in that boat I researched on my own. And most successfully, I may add. You remember that old man in Clacton, the one in the old folks' home? Well, he was quite fit enough to see me today, and I questioned him exhaustively."

Hugh said nothing. He guessed who had been exhausted.

"Ultimately," said Cecily, "I was able to prod him into remembering. I asked him to try and recall everyone he had ever known called Jones. And at last he remembered a local policeman, a Constable Jones, who got married in or around 1930. And the girl he married worked in *a local chemist's shop*. How about that?"

"You mean she was Moore's girl friend?"

"Isn't it obvious? Her name was Gladys Palmer. She is now Mrs. Jones. Moore was seen about with a girl in Clacton. This girl lived in Clacton and worked in a Clacton chemist's shop. Now it's quite evident that Moore was having a love affair with Gladys Palmer and that he persuaded her to give him the cyanide from the shop where she worked. The *real* evidence is that, according to all the books, that was one of the few chemist's shops from which Moore *never tried to obtain cyanide*!"

"That's real evidence?" said Hugh.

"Of course it is, to anyone with any deductive powers. Gladys Palmer took fright when Moore was found guilty, so she married a policeman for protection, and the policeman's name was Jones. Isn't that proof?"

"Proof of what?"

"Don't you ever remember anything? The barman in that Cross Keys place told us the old woman who sits on the Rupert Moore seat was a Mrs. Jones." Cecily smiled triumphantly. "They are one and the same."

"But it's a very common name."

"Maybe. But Mrs. Jones has admitted it. I spoke to her this morning before I went to Clacton. She has admitted knowing

Moore and that she first met him when he came into the shop. How about that? And she was very nervous and upset, I can tell you, as well she might be."

Hugh stared at his wife. He didn't at all like the turn things were taking. "Cecily, it may be so. It looks like it, but it's no business of ours. I wish you'd leave it."

"Leave it! For nearly fifty years this woman has got off scot-free when she was as much guilty of the murder of Mrs. Moore as Moore was, and you say leave it! It's her guilt brings her to that seat day after day, isn't it? Any psychologist would tell you that."

"She must be at least seventy. Surely she can be left in peace now?"

"I'm afraid it's much too late for that, Hugh. There must be an inquiry, all the facts must come out. I have written three letters, one to the Home Secretary, one to the Chief Commissioner at Scotland Yard, and a third to the author of this very incomplete book. There they are on the dressing table. Perhaps you'd like to look at them while I have my bath."

Hugh looked at them. If he were to tear them up she would only write them again. If he walked into that bathroom now and dislodged the heater from the wall and it fell into the water, and she died and it was called an accident . . . The letters would never be sent, he could have his workshop back, he could chat with pretty girls who worked in chemist's shops, and go on holiday to the Costa Brava and be free. He sighed heavily and went down to the bar to get a drink.

Thank goodness, thought Mrs. Jones, that woman wasn't anywhere to be seen this morning. The intrusion of yesterday had upset her for hours, even after Brenda arrived, but she was getting over it now. Unfortunately, in a way, the weather had taken a turn for the better, and several of the seats were occupied. But not Rupert Moore. Mrs. Jones sat down on it and put her shopping bag on the ground at her feet.

She was aware of the proximity of the barfly who was sitting on Lubbock (Elizabeth Anne Lubbock, for many years Headmistress of Northwold Girls High School) and with him was a different woman, much younger than the other and very well-dressed.

With an effort Mrs. Jones expelled them from her mind. She looked at the calm blue sea and felt the warm and firm pressure of the oak against her back and thought about her darling.

How sweet their love and companionship had been! It had endured for such a short time, and then separation and the unbearable loneliness. But she had been right to marry Mr. Jones, for he had been a good husband and she the wife he wanted, and without him there would have been no Brian and no Brenda and no money to buy the house and come here every day to remember. If her darling had lived, though, and the children had been his, and if she had had him to sit beside her on his seat and be the joy of her old age . . .

"Do forgive me," said a voice, "but I'm a local man myself, and I happened to be in Lowestoft yesterday and someone told me they'd heard you'd come back to this part of the world to live."

Mrs. Jones looked at the barfly. Was there to be no end to it?

"I've seen you on this seat and I did wonder, and when this friend in Lowestoft told me your present name, all was clear."

"I see," said Mrs. Jones, gathering up her shopping bag.

"I want you to know how greatly I admire his work. My father had some charming examples of it—all sold now, alas—and anyone can see this seat was made by a craftsman compared with the others." Her stony face, her hostility, made him hesitate. "You are," he said, "who I think you are, aren't you?"

"Of course I am," said Mrs. Jones crossly, another morning spoiled. "Arthur Sarafin was my first husband. And now I really must be on my way."

CHARLOTTE ARMSTRONG

From Out of the Garden

Maude Seton, aged twenty-eight, was a girl who trotted around the city of New York in the most bizarre high-fashion clothing she could find, with a very thin attaché case hanging by a strap from one shoulder as the badge of the newspaperwoman she was hell-bent to be. Nobody loved her; nobody even liked her; but Maude Seton had settled, long ago, for just being envied. She was already an aggressive and accomplished pest.

She was swinging down a side street one summer afternoon, plotting how to "angle" the assignment she had nagged out of Ben Crawley a few days before.

"Okay, toots,' Ben had said wearily. "How about twelve hundred words, for January, on the fifteenth anniversary of the mysterious disappearance of the famous and beloved Elizabeth Rose?"

"Aw, come on, Ben. You know I purely hate sugar."

"Take it or leave it," he had said. "But kindly and firmly leave my midst. I got work."

"Okay, toots," she had said. "Maybe I'll solve the mystery. When Seton digs, she digs."

Maude had already ferreted out the daughter and had talked to her. Today she had an appointment with the husband and the mother. The old house, for which she was now bound, was the only residence that still stood on the south side of the street, where it seemed stuffed in at the bottom of a tall crack between towering new office buildings.

Maude skipped up the steps, noting that this brownstone had once been remodeled; its face had been covered with white brick,

44

although the white had turned dingy, and the green paint on the door was no longer bright.

A small gray-haired woman, with plump and matronly contours, opened the door. She was, she said, Mrs. Allen, the housekeeper, and would Miss Seton please come in? Mr. Mortmain would be down in a moment. Sniffing and peering, Maude followed her in.

The entire house was only about twenty-five feet wide. At Maude's left, as she entered, a gray-carpeted stairway went up, almost immediately. At her right a white door was ajar, and she caught a glimpse of a fairly modern kitchen. The passage seemed very long and narrow, between the stairway and the wall, and it ended with three steps leading down into a large sitting room which overlooked, through a wide glass door—of all things!—a garden.

Maude, frankly staring all around and storing up things to describe, caught a glimpse of the dining area adjoining the kitchen—up three steps as if it were a stage. She could see in her mind's eye the famous beauty sweeping her guests to a little late supper.

"Are these her things?" she asked with the expected awe.

"Very little has changed," said the woman. Cold light from the garden beyond the glass door was falling on the pale and delicate texture of her skin. "That is her piano. That is her portrait, of course."

"Oh, yes," said Maude, who had seen it as a print. Over the mantel (where else?) hung Elizabeth Rose. Oh, Gawd, thought Maude, observing the pink and white of the face, the flat-topped hairdo that now looked so antique, the gold of the curls, the baby-blue of the eyes, the pink and simpering mouth, the white lace dress with the rosebuds on it. How utterly *icky!*

Maude turned to look out at the garden. Beyond a pavement of cemented brick, some grass was trying unsuccessfully to be a lawn around a central bird bath. There was one discouraged-looking tree. But at the far end, massed in an arc, there was a bank of tall marguerites.

"How unusual to see a garden in the city," said Maude. She spotted the wrought-iron supports. "Oh, I see the balcony. That's where the child fell, isn't it?"

"Won't you please be comfortable," said Mrs. Allen primly.

"I've met Mrs. Sidney, you know—Miss Rose's daughter," said
Maude chattily, not sitting down yet. "She and her husband
sailed for Europe this morning, I believe."

"Is that so?"

"A nice girl," said Maude, who thought Barbara Sidney
deserved this flabby adjective. "The deformed arm isn't conspicuous at all, is it?"

"I am glad to hear that," said Mrs. Allen quietly.

"She couldn't tell me a thing about the night her mother
vanished, having been in the hospital at the time, and only six
years old, besides. She has never lived here since?—Barbara, I
mean."

"No," said the housekeeper. "There is only her stepfather here
and her invalid grandmother. A little too depressing for a young
person."

"I see." Maude tended to agree. This place had charm, but it
was an embalmed charm. "Were you here?"

"Not at that time," the woman said coldly.

Maude thought the garden was really weird. On three sides
were the blank twenty-odd-story walls of three office buildings.
What bird would be caught dead in that ridiculous bird bath? The
patch of garden must be like the bottom of a well.

"May I just step out?" she asked.

The housekeeper said, "Oh, no. Please sit down. I'm sure Mr.
Philip—"

"Miss Seton?" a man said.

Maude Seton knew that her latest costume must be silhouetted
against that gray light, in all its saucy outlines, but that her face
was in shadow. She was glad of it. Maude had had, of course, the
usual casual adventures, but she hadn't been exactly enchanted by
any of her temporary partners. Her first sight of this man was
sending a ripple along her nerves that was quite a shock to her.

He was tall, a little stooped, elegantly thin, with dark hair and a
face that seemed surprisingly unlined. It was pale; he had no
outdoor look. But he seemed very, very male just the same. Even
his clothing had some quality of elegance she couldn't define,

although it was verging on shabbiness. And there was something—her heart had actually jumped.

Maude resented this fiercely. She went into her pitch. Her Editor felt so-and-so. People were still so-o-o interested. She sat down. So did he. "I am hoping," said Maude, "that I can give the story a little touch of something new."

"I don't know what that could be," he said sadly.

"Fifteen years ago, next January? Tell me—"

So they went through the well-known biography—the familiar list of great, and now classic, musicals in which Elizabeth Rose had starred, and all the worn-out anecdotes of Elizabeth Rose's heyday in the theatre. Philip Mortmain had a pleasant voice and he spoke willingly, yet he gave the impression of being a very quiet man.

Maude was dying to ask how old he was, but she refrained. (She could find that out easily enough in the files.) He was the famous star's third husband, and sometimes these women, ageless themselves, kept marrying younger and younger men.

"Everybody knows," she said, "that your wife disappeared on the night that little Barbara fell. Do you think that might have been, in some way, pertinent?"

"Elizabeth was certainly very much upset," he said gravely.

"She wasn't in the house when it happened?"

"No. Barby was already in the hospital when Elizabeth came home. By that time the child had been in surgery and was all right, you know. Elizabeth saw her in the hospital, of course. But then she followed the venerable tradition. The show must go on, mustn't it?" He smiled at her.

"I understand she gave a brilliant performance,' said Maude, a little cattily. "You were in the theatre that night, Mr. Mortmain?"

"Oh, yes, But after the curtain I was detained by some friends who had heard about Barby and were concerned. By the time I reached backstage, Elizabeth wasn't there."

"And no one has ever seen her since." Maude sighed. "It *is* a famous mystery."

"I suppose so," he said wearily.

"But I wonder." Maude leaned forward in her taut and forceful way. "I couldn't help noticing that this neighbourhood has deteriorated. Why do you stay on here, Mr. Mortmain?"

"Why, because," he said gently, "one of these days Elizabeth may return."

Oh, now, come on! thought Maude. You can't really believe that! "Elizabeth has never been declared legally—?"

"Dead?" he supplied. "Oh, no."

"But she must have had a considerable estate." Maude was thinking, All those hits! And this piece of land alone must be worth a fortune.

"Elizabeth's estate is in the hands of trustees," he told her patiently. "A bank allows funds for the maintenance of her home, the care of her mother, the education of her daughter, and the board and keep of her husband." His voice was very calm.

"I see. But surely some day—"

"Some day it will all belong to Barbara."

Ah, so? thought Maude. It will, will it?

"What do you do, Mr. Mortmain?" she asked him boldly.

"Oh, I dabble. Read. Study."

"You used to be in the theatre, yourself?"

"A long time ago." He smiled.

"I see," said Maude. To keep on feeling attracted toward this man was perfectly ridiculous, so she took care to think, cynically: Turning on the old charm, aren't you, my friend? She rose energetically. "Now, may I see the garden?"

He rose. "You can see it all from here, Miss Seton."

"I'd like to go out there."

"I'd rather you didn't," he said gently.

Maude gazed rebelliously through the glass door and said, with a bit of an edge, "How does your garden grow? There can't be any sun."

"No, not any more."

"Those are potted plants?"

"Yes. Elizabeth was always very proud of her garden. That means, you know, a walled or guarded place. I'm afraid the city is overdoing the walls just now. No, nothing really grows. When those fade I'll bring in chrysanthemums."

"Because," she snapped, so outraged that she let it show, "she may yet return?"

She was thinking, what *is* this? An obsession? Is he really languishing around here, still romantically in love with darling Elizabeth, who is going to show up any minute, after fifteen years? What a waste! I don't think I believe it.

"Mr. Philip?" The housekeeper spoke behind them. "Mrs. Rose is ready to see the young lady now."

"Oh, yes, Mrs. Allen. Thank you. Miss Seton, I know that you wish to speak to Elizabeth's mother, but may I ask you not to talk too long? Mrs. Rose has not been well. Will you watch me, please, for a signal?"

"I promise," said Maude.

At the foot of the stairs he let her go first, with old-fashioned good manners—the man behind in case of a fall. Upstairs he led her along another narrow hall, this one neatly wallpapered, and then into a large bedroom that also looked out on the garden. Across its bank of windows and another glass door ran the white wrought-iron tracery of the balcony's low rail.

But Maude only glanced that way. She bent her attention to the woman who was propped high in the huge bed, against white satin pillows.

"I have been admiring your garden," said Maude, when the introductions were over. She didn't know what else to say. This woman was ill, all right. Her wrists were thin to mere bone. Her face was fallen in—the gray flesh sagged. Her white hair was disagreeably streaked with yellow. And her eyes! Ah, so, thought Maude, is the poor old crone loopy?

Philip Mortmain began to prompt the conversation. Maude noticed that the housekeeper remained standing silently in the room, as the woman in the bed started to speak of her daughter with such idolatrous praise that Maude felt sickened. It seemed that Elizabeth Rose had been the most beautiful, the most charming, the most talented, and the kindest, the sweetest . . . Was there a cult? Was this house a shrine?

But Maude, as she listened, began to watch more closely those slippery eyes and the old lips which said, "Philip adored her, of course."

"Of course," he agreed softly.

So Maude said, in polite malice, "Your daughter was married

three times, I believe, Mrs. Rose?"

"Yes, my daughter—" The eyes fled; the old lips began to tremble.

Philip Mortmain rose and said, "We mustn't tire you. Mrs. Allen, we'll go down for tea now."

"Yes, Mr. Philip." The housekeeper went away.

But Maude Seton ignored the signal. She did not rise from the low chair. "I would so like to have known your daughter," she gushed. "Tell me—"

Whatever the old woman was mumbling, she couldn't hear, because Mortmain's hand took hold of Maude's arm and pulled her up."Please excuse Miss Seton now?"

"Yes," said the old woman with a sigh. She gazed out at the shadowy space,–toward the garden where no sun shone and nothing grew.

He took Maude forcefully along the upper hall, saying nothing. Oh, he was angry. But at the stairs he let go of her, and as a gentleman should, he started down first. So Maude, behind his back—because he couldn't order her around, no man could!—turned and scooted back as fast as she could to pop her head into that room. The old woman lifted on one bony elbow.

"Where is your daughter?" Maude spoke low, but in her own forceful and insistent manner.

"My daughter is buried in the garden," the old woman whispered, with terror in her eyes, and sank back.

Philip Mortmain came behind Maude and put cruel hands on her shoulders. "I thought I had dropped my pen," she cooed, but he said nothing. He wasn't going to let her loose again. Mrs. Allen, going up swiftly, passed them on the stairs, heading toward the sound of weeping in the bedroom. Her look was severe. There would be no tea.

At the bottom of the stairs the man said coldly, "I don't believe you will have any trouble finding a photograph—*somewhere else*," (He was going to put her out, was he? Well, Maude had been put out of better places.) "You will mail me a copy of what you write," he said sternly. "If I do not approve, you will not submit it to the magazine. That was agreed."

"Of course. I promised. And thank you very—"

But she was now back on the stoop and the door was shut. Maude ran down the steps savouring her bruises. Yah, yah! All that guff about she-may-return. Romantic devotion—in a pig's eye! He'd boss Seton around, would he? Well, we'll see.

Two days later she had Ben Crawley cornered in a cocktail lounge. "I'm not going along with the gag, Ben. There's something phony about the whole bit. For one thing, this dame was married three times, and that doesn't make her the sweet dewy little rose she was cracked up to be. Not in Maudie's book, it doesn't. Thirty-one when she so-called vanished. She'd be forty-six today. He's only thirty-eight—I looked it up."

"Who is only thirty-eight?"

"Mortmain. Mr. Dead Hand."

"I'm supposed to be shuddering?"

"You are supposed to be listening. I dug up her first husband. Sol Divine. That's his name, believe it or not. He didn't want to talk. Says it was all a long time ago. He forgets. You bet! I get the feeling that Elizabeth Rose may not have been *all* sweetness and light. This Sol is bald as an eagle, which he slightly resembles—a real solid type. Fat jolly wife and a pack of kids around. Elizabeth divorced him. The second husband, Barby's father, she divorced, too. He's dead."

"This is news?" said Ben sourly.

"So listen. The day the kid lands on those bricks and greensticks her bones so they never do grow even, guess who was in the house? Servants' day off. Elizabeth wasn't there. So who? None other than Mr. Philip Mortmain, the kid's stepfather. Now, don't tell Maudie that a young sprout of twenty-three, madly in love with gorgeous, adorable, fabulous Elizabeth Rose, is going to be all that nuts about a six-year-old brat of hers from a former marriage.

"Say our Phil happens to get peeved at the brat and happens to kind of push her off that balcony? Oh, well, he didn't mean it, and besides, nobody's there to see. So he calls Doc. Ambulance. Hospital. Surgery. When Elizabeth shows up in a cab, he takes her tenderly in his arms, says the kid had an accident. Elizabeth goes to bedside and emotes. Then to the theatre for her brilliant performance. Yah!"

"But whaddaya say, afterwards the great lady gets home like usual? Late, and the cook asleep in the basement. *Now* she finds out what really happened to the kid. So, she *not* being all sweetness and light, they get into a knockdown drag-out fight, and pretty soon, by gosh, there she is. Dead.

"Maybe he didn't mean that either, but what's Philip going to do? The kid can't remember a thing—she told me so herself. So she's no problem. But a dead rich wife, whose name means front-page headlines, that's inconvenient."

"Just come on out of the gaslight, willya, kiddo?" Crawley gulped liquor.

"How come dear Philip—who looks as if he crawled right out of Edgar Allan Poe, believe me, Ben—how come he hangs on to that house? How come he doesn't sell it for one hell of a lot of money and go enjoy life, aged thirty-eight? How come he's got his sick old semi-loopy mother-in-law *imprisoned* there?"

"Naaaah!"

"You just listen," said Maude. "Because I'm telling you that old woman was looking mighty sly. You should have seen her little old eyes peeking at me, by the corners. But *they* were in the room, you know. Not only Philip but the housekeeper, too. Taking no chances. So I'll tell you why Philip doesn't have Elizabeth declared legally dead, which he could do, and sell that house. He *can't* sell it. Somebody would build, dig up the garden. Elizabeth Rose is buried in that garden and the old lady knows it."

Crawley was shaking his head sadly from side to side.

"She told me so," said Maude.

"Who did?"

"The old lady."

"She told you *what*?"

"She said these very exact words. 'My daughter is buried in the garden.' Verbatim, my friend."

Maude explained and Ben said, "Take it to the cops, toots. You're not selling it to me."

"The old woman is half nuts, I will admit. But I'll tell you what I'm *going* to do. Little Maudie's going to find out."

"Pinch yourself first, kiddo."

"Oh, I don't know. He's living easy, meanwhile. After the old lady conks out, she can't talk. Maybe he figures to leave the house vacant—"

"And this housekeeper keeps quiet?"

"Oh, in the meanwhile," said Maude nastily, "this housekeeper is pretty well-preserved."

Ben Crawley looked at her with distaste. "Get away from me," he said. "For your own sake, Seton, I'm warning you, get off this kick."

"Don't you worry about me being murdered," said Maude, "I don't walk around unarmed, you know. I've got a little idea dreamed up."

"Say, what's all this?" said Ben with sudden intuitive suspicion. "How come you took such a prejudice against this Philip Mortmain?

He was gratified to see the blood rise in Seton's cheeks.

"Oh, he's *charming*," she said viciously, "but nobody can charm the brain out of my head, you know."

"Go, soak your head, why don't you, Seton?" said Ben gloomily.

"And while you're at it, run a little soap around the inside. I want no part of this."

"You'll be on your knees, friend," said Maude confidently.

Maude got nowhere with the Police Department. Their backs were up; they didn't like her. So she researched old news accounts and the police reports in them. She discovered that by the day after the significant day Philip Montain's mother-in-law had been in the house. Ah, so? thought Maude. And never got out again?

The only servant mentioned was a Mrs. Pelham, the cook, and Maude was disappointed to find that this woman had died four years ago. Oh, well, there was still the little idea that she'd dreamed up.

She banged out a sugary story, working in her messy little apartment where she never entertained because she didn't know how. On the top copy she typed one extra final paragraph. That should do it. And when it did, she would know she wasn't wasting time, no matter how long the digging might take.

Digging? Yah! Under the bird bath? She wondered . . .

Whenever she was in the streets, Maude carried a gadget with her, manufactured by a firm that had scented profit from the plight of women-alone-on-a-city-street in this year-of-our-Lord. It was a small gun that fired tear gas and was supposed to enable a woman to blind and thus escape an attacker.

So Maude Seton, with her attaché case holding the top copy of her story, and with the little gas gun in her pocket, convenient to her right hand, went swinging down that street one afternoon, uninvited, unexpected, and hell bent.

He opened the door himself. She felt the same shock. He *was* like something out of Poe. Yet what else was it about him? Maybe I go for murderers, thought Maude—they're usually strong characters. An extension of this flickered through her mind. *Stronger than I am?*

She dismissed the thought quickly and said, as girlishly as possible, "I've written the story, Mr. Mortmain. Will you please read it, now? It's very short, and I do need your approval, right away."

So he let her in, led her to the room overlooking the garden, and took the typescript. She sat down as near as she could to the passage leading to the street door; she kept her right hand in her pocket.

Ordinarily Maude Seton would rather be whipped than watch anybody read her stuff. But this time she kept count of the pages as they slipped behind each other in his lean hands. She wasn't afraid, she told herself. She had a weapon. She could escape. She would see what he would do when he realised he hadn't fooled Maude Seton.

He came to the last page and Maude braced herself. She had written, in the final paragraph. "The whole story has never been told. Only Mr. Philip Mortmain knows how angry his wife became that night when she discovered what he had done to her child. Only Mr. Philip Mortmain knows where he buried the beautiful body of Elizabeth Rose—in her own garden."

His eyes raced. He froze. His hands crushed the sheets of paper into a twisted roll. He sprang from the chair, holding the paper as if it were a club.

Maude pulled the weapon out of her pocket. "Hold it, mister," she commanded. But he didn't recognize the threat—he was too close to her. She shut her eyes and pulled the trigger.

She heard him roar. She squinted and saw him stagger. He had dropped the typescript and was pawing his face. Maude nipped out of her chair and down the passage. He roared again and it gave her a deep satisfaction. She reached the street door and yanked it open. She heard a woman's voice call down the stairs, "Philip?"

Maude Seton's brain knew that although she had infuriated him, she had not found out anything conclusively. She slammed the street door. But she had not gone through it. She slipped, instead, through the white door to the kitchen, and stood, hidden and trembling, against the kitchen wall. One of her own eyes was streaming. She made her hands check her little gadget and cause another cartridge to take position for another shot. She could always get out. But first, she must find out.

She could hear his shuffling progress. He must be blind, but she looked behind her for a hiding place. She was startled when her cheek came into contact with a telephone on the kitchen wall. So much the better. Where was he now?

"Philip, what's happened?" The woman must be on the stairs.

"Where is that Seton?" he raged.

"I heard the front door slam. Somebody went out?"

"She's gone? You don't see her?"

"I don't see anyone. Philip, are you *crying*? What—"

Now another woman's voice shrilled, "Philip? Darling? Oh, what is it? What's the matter?"

"I'm all right," he called. He must be just the other side of the kitchen wall. "Nothing to worry you, dearest." Then he lowered his voice. "Don't come down. The place is full of some sort of gas."

"But why?" Now Maude recognized the first voice—the housekeeper's.

"That little monster wrote that I buried Elizabeth in the garden," he said bitterly.

The other voice above was screaming. "Darling, if anything's happened to you, I can't bear it! You know I can't! Darling, come up. Please!"

"Oh, hush, Elizabeth," said the housekeeper wearily.

"I'm coming, Elizabeth," he called up.

"Hadn't we better phone?" said the housekeeper.

"I can't see to phone. Can't come up yet. You go to her."

"Yes, and I'll phone."

Maude heard the stairs creak. Then shuffling. The street door must have opened because fresh air crept around the partition to where she was. Phone? she thought, feeling stunned. Phone for what? What do they mean, *Elizabeth*?

Holding the gas gun firmly in her right hand, she shifted position and with her left hand lifted the kitchen telephone from its moorings.

". . . can't you get in touch with Dr. Carlson quickly?" the housekeeper was saying on another instrument. "Mrs. Rose has been badly upset and we need him—as soon as he can possibly get here."

"Right away, Mrs. Allen," said a girl's voice.

Maude hung up. She had better get out and go somewhere and *think*. But what if he were standing at the door to the street? She listened to the old house, which had its mysterious noises. Finally she began to slide softly sideways toward the crack of the door.

He caught her forearms from behind and dragged her backward. He had come from the dining room. "Drop it," he commanded. Mrs. Allen pushed through to the kitchen. "Take that thing away from her," he ordered. The woman's small hands fought at Maude's fingers. Then her weapon was gone.

"So there *was* someone on the extension," said the woman indignantly. "You rotten little sneak! What shall we do with her? We'll have to—"

"No time," he said. "Go up. Say I'll be right there."

Maude Seton, with her arms pinned behind her, thought she might be murdered in another instant. She had one glimpse of his red-rimmed eyes, as he wrestled her across the sitting room to the wide opening where the glass door had been slid aside, to air the room. But he simply put her out into the garden, closed the glass door, locked it, and went away.

Maude stood still, all her feathers ruffled, frightened, of course, and yet in a curious way, delighted. She called on her wits. Get out. (He couldn't do this to her!) But how *could* she get out? She didn't dare throw her body against the glass door to break it. She would find a heavy stone.

She ran across the bricks toward the bird bath. There were no stones. She searched with her eyes for some opening, some gap, some way out of here besides the way back through the house; but all around her rose those tall, blank, eyeless, earless walls.

Then she was among the flowers at the far end. Here were the pots—rather, the black metal cans. She could drag one of them and heave it at the glass. Too heavy. Pull out the plant? Dump out the soil? She grubbed at roots. Wait! He would hear the breaking of the glass.

But what other way out? She was locked in at the bottom of a twenty-odd-story well? Maude began to feel the adrenaline of panic in her blood. She would choke, faint. No. She held her cheeks and told herself to think. Think, Seton, think! It wasn't so much that she refused to be murdered. She *wouldn't* be licked. Then she literally saw a light.

She hurried back toward the house. There was only one thing to do. She could climb one of the wrought-iron supports of the balcony. Perhaps, if the old woman was alone, she could get in, through the door or a window, scoot through that lamplit bedroom, down the stairs, and out. Or hide.

So she cast off her attaché case and put her foot in among the curving designs. It was better to be climbing. The exertion relieved her panic. She drew slowly upward. She could hear nothing from the house. There was only the constant roaring of the city, outside this horribly deep well that she was in. As her head drew to the level of the balcony floor, Maude made herself moved very, very slowly.

She could see into the bedroom easily, through the glass door. A yellowish lamplight spilled out. The old woman was visible in the bed, high against the fat and shining pillows. She was in tension. Her hands were hooked into each other by curved fingers and the fingers pulled against each other. Her neck cords were tight. She was staring across the room—but not staring Maude's way.

Maude could see no one else in the room. This seemed strange. Then she heard the glass door below rumble. Then she heard his voice. "Come down from there," it commanded softly.

Not me, friend! Maude's foot hunted for a higher notch. Her hands on the railing pulled and, slowly she went higher, higher, over the low railing, onto the balcony—

In the room the old woman's hands let go of each other. The thin arms flashed; she threw off the covering and leaped out of bed. She was wearing a long nightgown of some filmy pink stuff. Her emaciated body fled, like something wild, with a knifing action of those old sharp knees, and the woman was screaming, screaming, as she vanished into the upper hall.

Maude saw the other woman, that Mrs. Allen, rise up out of a wing chair, look once Maude's way, and then hurry after the old woman. There was one long echoing cry. The man below shouted, and she knew he was running.

Scrambling and clinging, Maude went back over the railing, down the wrought-iron support, and dropped to the ground. Yes, the glass door below was open. Maude picked up her attaché case and crept inside. Where were they? Could she escape now?

She looked down the passage and saw that she could not. He was kneeling over a heap of the pink stuff lying at the bottom of the stairway. As Maude watched, the housekeeper came out of the kitchen, carrying a long cloth. Maude seemed to know that it was a tablecloth. The woman began to spread it over that fallen heap. The man slid back to let her do this, but he did not rise.

Then the housekeeper saw Maude. She touched the man's shoulder gently and began to walk in Maude's direction. Maude shrank backward in the heavy, heavy silence of this house.

She made herself remember that this woman now had the weapon. But the woman did not brandish it. She said, "Sit down. We knew we'd have to tell you. She's dead now, so I'll tell you. Sit down."

Maude sat, scheming how to elude the woman and the weapon and the man who was still so near the only exit. It seemed necessary for Maude to keep on believing in her own peril. She wondered if there really was a doctor coming.

"My daughter Elizabeth," the woman said, and Maude's whirling thoughts came to attention, "used to do her breathing exercises and calisthenics on the balcony. Little Barby forgot to take them serious that day, and when Elizabeth's arms flung out with her usual impatience, they hit the child and Barby fell over the low railing."

She wavered for an instant, but a look of strength came over her face and she stiffened. "It was Philip who rushed the child to the hospital where what could be done for her was done," she said unemotionally. "Meanwhile, my beautiful and famous daughter, Elizabeth, put into her veins whatever drug she was on at the time and crept up to the top floor—to dream it had never happened. Are you listening, Miss Seton?"

"But Elizabeth wasn't here," gasped Maude, as her wits began to rally.

"Oh, yes, she was. *I* was the one who came in that cab. Philip phoned me from the hospital and told me what to do. Wear Elizabeth's mink that she had once given me. Wear one of her hats that she had given me. Go to Times Square. Hail a cab with Elizabeth's famous gestures. When I arrived here, he met me and put his arms around me, and whatever neighbors—oh, there were neighbors then—who had seen the ambulance and were curious—they took me for Elizabeth. So my daughter had her alibi."

Maude Seton gave up pretending for the moment that she was going to be murdered this afternoon. "Really?" she said feebly.

"Elizabeth was told that Barby didn't remember anything, and being what they call "high," she insisted on visiting the hospital. Philip had hoped to force her into a doctor's care, but she got away and went to the theatre. He was detained, as he has said, although he was doing the best he could to watch her. So— Elizabeth disappeared."

Maude's brain was now buzzing. "Are you trying to say that— *that* is Elizabeth?"

The woman lifted one hand to demand silence as if, now that she had begun to tell, she could not bear an interruption. "Barby really didn't remember anything. We thought that if Elizabeth had gone running blindly to her death, then at least Barby would never need to know how she had come to be so cruelly hurt. And maybe her mother's legend wouldn't have to be destroyed. So we found the strength to wait."

The voice had steadied. "Thirteen days later Philip found her, doped, debauched, dirty, in some filthy room. He wanted me to dismiss all the servants except our Mrs. Pelham, who kept our secret until she died, God rest her loyal soul. And Philip brought Elizabeth home. With Dr. Carlson's help, with more agony for us all than you can ever imagine, we took Elizabeth off narcotics. When Barby was ready to leave the hospital, we sent her with Mrs. Pelham to Florida—for convalescence in the sun, we said. Then we put Barby in the very best schools we could find."

"I still don't—"

"You see, Elizabeth wasn't—well, right.She was very confused. Some days she wouldn't believe that she had ever had a child."

"Why didn't you show her the child?" said Maude, who was feeling almost her normally bold self.

"Because we would have had to show the child her mother," the woman said quietly. "Of course, we had to account for Elizabeth somehow, so she became Mrs. Rose, and I became 'Mrs. Allen.' That meant I couldn't visit Barby or have Barby come here, since she would have recognized me. So it was Philip who watched over Barby. He went to her little celebrations. Advised and comforted her. She has grown into a fine young woman. She has married well. She is happy." The woman's head was proud. "As for the two of us," she continued, "we kept on, sometimes hoping that one day Elizabeth would come back—come back to herself.

"Now it's over," the woman continued. "Will you help us, Miss Seton? Let us bury her quickly as Mrs. Rose. No one will pay much attention any more. Will you please not force us to tell Barby, now what her mother had become and what her mother had done to her? Will you let the legend rest? It does no harm to anyone. Elizabeth really was, *once*, very beautiful and talented."

"You were a little foolish to let me see her, weren't you?" said Maude saucily.

"She liked to read about her own legend. She didn't really understand how much time had passed. She always supposed that next month, next fall, next spring, she would be beautiful again and go back to her former eminence. She could take pleasure in the skill she thought she had—to act the part of a sick old woman."

"I see," said Maude. "You just thought you'd fool *me*—just for the fun of it."

"Yes," the woman said calmly. "And *I* see. You still intend to tell the story."

"If I promise not to," said Maude, with belated caution, "then may I go?"

"Your promises are worthless," the woman said with quiet resignation. "I shouldn't have bothered. Just go, if you like." She was fumbling in the pocket of her dress. "I believe this is your property."

Made got up and took the small weapon from that steady hand. She was settling her clothing, not to be seen on the street in such a disarray, when Philip Mortmain appeared at the end of the passage. His eyes seemed dusty. He stepped aside politely.

"May I leave now?" Maude said.

"I don't know," he answered vaguely, not seeming to give his full attention to her, not really seeing her. "When the doctor comes . . ."

"I've told her and begged her," said the woman, "But it's no good, Philip."

"No," He didn't even glance at Maude, but moved into the big room and sank into a chair. Maude flitted to the open passage. Up the three steps, and she would be safe. She had her weapon. She had her story. She must only pass between that—that heap on the floor—and the wall, then open the door. But *who* was dead? Maude hesitated.

The housekeeper had gone to the man. He said to her drearily, "We needn't worry about Barby, I suppose. She can understand it, now."

The woman said softly. "Yes, if she must. You have raised her well. And to Elizabeth, my dear, you have kept all your promises. 'In sickness or in health,' you said, "until death do us part'."

Maude Seton, listening from the passage, thought, Oh Gawd! She was infuriated. How icky can you get? Did they still think she was going to fall for this junk? As if anybody took the mouthings in the marriage service for anything *but* mouthings! And a third husband, at that! How simple-minded did they think she was? If they were putting on this sickening act for *her* benefit—but *why*?

"I see," she said loudly. "You *want* me to tell the world that the old woman was Elizabeth Rose."

And that's pretty cute, she was raging to herself. Just fool Seton and you've got it made. Oh, wouldn't you like to bury Elizabeth Rose again, and publicly, *and somewhere else*! Oh, wouldn't you just!

"You know she is," the woman said coldly. "You heard."

"Philip, *darling*, eh?" Maude had begun to snarl. She hated Philip Mortmain with her whole being. She must hurt him! "Did the poor silly old thing sometimes have the delusion that she *was* her own adorable daughter? Being mad—about her daughter's charming husband, for instance?"

He stood up and came toward her. She held her gas gun ready. But she was not displeased to notice that he was seeing her now.

"What's wrong with you?" he asked quietly.

"What's bugging me?" she said flippantly. "You don't know, then, that she told me? 'My daughter is buried in the garden,' she said."

Then Maude's heart lurched as the woman moaned dismay.

Philip Mortmain said, with sudden force, "And you intend to tell *that* to the world?"

"Oh, when I am given an assignment," she said, "I do like to tell the whole story." She was being perfectly reckless and her heart was banging, but there was a savage joy in it, and suddenly the dusty look was gone from his eyes.

The doorbell rang and made her jump. But he just stood there, looking at her. "Her daughter was buried in the garden," he repeated slowly. Then he bowed slightly. "Why, yes, that is true. Excuse me."

He wasn't going to kill her. It seemed he wouldn't bother. He was merely going to answer the door. Maude put her back to the passage wall. She just stood there. Her brain seemed to have stopped.

It was a doctor who had come. She saw him crouch to throw back the tablecloth, and she saw Mortmain kneel. Yah! *Still* playing pious devotion to that—that scarecrow! What if the doctor's in the plot too?

The two men began at last to walk toward her. "Why the devil everything has to come out now," the doctor was saying crossly, "I can't see. Listen, Philip, Missing Persons have known exactly where Elizabeth was, and in what condition, for fifteen years now. And so has her manager. And her bank. Everything's been in order. Now, *why* does every lip-licking twerp in the city have to have this private tragedy dished up at breakfast? Keep on thinking about Barby, I say."

He stopped to stare at Maude. He was a rosy-fleshed, somewhat rotund, middle-aged man, and seemed almost ludicrously respectable. "Who is this?"

"This is Maude Seton," said Philip Mortmain coldly, "a journalist of some sort. She came here, uninvited, to accuse me of murder, to blind me with tear gas, to upset Elizabeth, to hear us call her name—"

"What the devil is it her business?"

"She says it's her business to tell the whole story."

"Is that so?" the doctor said angrily.

"I'm very sorry, Doctor," said Maude brightly, now that she had managed to slip along the wall and was between them and the way out. Whether the doctor was a dupe or not, let him look after himself.

"Just a minute," said Philip Mortmain, "Are you going to tell the *whole* story?"

"Philip?" The doctor sounded worried.

"Then you'll tell," Mortmain went on, "that when Elizabeth accidentally knocked her small daughter over the railing, she thought she had killed her. You must also tell how Elizabeth had nearly finished burying the living child when I came on the scene and pulled the unconscious little girl out of the earth just in time."

The doctor said angrily, "Damn it, Philip, why did you have to bring up that gruesome bit? Elizabeth was mad as a hatter, half her brain eaten away, but you could have spared Barby that part of it."

"No," said Philip, "the world must have the *whole* story. You do understand? I put Miss Seton in the garden because I couldn't talk to her until I'd soothed Elizabeth. She climbed up to the balcony. Don't you see what happened?"

He turned. "Tell it all," he said, "or, I promise you, *I will*."

He went into the sitting room and pulled the draperies closed. He sat down in the gloom, far away.

The doctor was looking at Maude in a curious way. "Well, well," he murmured. "Seton is the name? Miss Maude Seton? I must phone the authorities."

"Wait," she said. "Listen."

"You *will* be a bit of a freak, won't you?" This doctor wasn't ludicrous any more, but a shrewd citizen of Maude's own country. "Climbing up the back of a man's house? Why? Carried away by melodramatic fancies? Or in a fit of paranoia?

Maude was a moth against the wall and the pins were going in. "Please, if you think its all better—"

"Too late," the doctor said cheerfully. "What Philip Mortmain promises to do, he will do. Don't think he won't. An unusual man, eh?

She whimpered; he was too shrewd for her.

Then the doctor touched her, benignly enough, just pushing her a little. "Could be, you don't yet realize what happened? What part *you* played?" Then he left her and went off to the kitchen phone.

So Maude Seton looked into the mirror on the wall and realised there was also a mirror in that bedroom upstairs. Then she saw what had sent Elizabeth Rose at last to her death. A white female face, rising so slowly and so silently from out of the garden, all streaked and smudged with the black earth—just come from her grave.

No! But no use crying "no." Seton knew that she was destroyed. A temporary titbit at the bars and after that a fool forever. Who in the world would pity the *whole* story? Pity these hands that had grubbed in a flower pot, frantic to escape—

On guard! On guard! Lest anything as uncomfortable as sun or rain or love or faithfulness or sacrifice should fall upon Maude Seton and she should grow!

P. D. JAMES

The Girl Who Loved Graveyards

She couldn't remember anything about the day in the hot
August of 1956 when they first brought her to live with her
Aunt Gladys and Uncle Victor in the small east London house at
49 Alma Terrace. She knew that it was three days after her tenth
birthday and that she was to be cared for by her only living
relations now that her father and grandmother were dead, killed
by influenza within a week of each other. But those were just facts
which someone, at some time, had briefly told her. She could
remember nothing of her previous life. Those first ten years were
a void, insubstantial as a dream which had faded but which had
left on her mind a scar of unarticulated childish anxiety and fear.
For her, memory and childhood both began with that moment
when, waking in the small unfamiliar bedroom with the kitten,
Sambo, still curled asleep on a towel at the foot of her bed, she
had walked bare-footed to the window and drawn back the
curtain.

And there, stretched beneath her, lay the cemetery, luminous
and mysterious in the early morning light, bounded by iron
railings and separated from the rear of Alma Terrace only by a
narrow path. It was to be another warm day, and over the serried
rows of headstones there lay a thin haze pierced by the occasional
obelisk and by the wing tips of marble angels whose disembodied
heads seemed to be floating on particles of shimmering light. And
as she watched, motionless in an absorbed enchantment, the mist
began to rise and the whole cemetery was revealed to her, a
miracle of stone and marble, bright grass and summer-laden trees,
flower-bedecked graves and intersecting paths stretching as far as
her eyes could see. In the far distance she could just make out the

65

top of the Victorian chapel gleaming like the spire of some magical castle in a long-forgotten fairy tale. In those moments of growing wonder she found herself shivering with delight, an emotion so rare that it stole through her thin body like a pain. And it was then, on that first morning of her new life with the past a void and the future unknown and frightening, that she made the cemetery her own. Throughout her childhood and youth it was to remain a place of delight and mystery, her habitation and her solace.

It was a childhood without love, almost without affection. Her uncle Victor was her father's elder half-brother; that, too, she had been told. He and her aunt weren't really her relations. Their small capacity for love was expended on each other, and even here it was less a positive emotion than a pact of mutual support and comfort against the threatening world which lay outside the trim curtains of their small claustrophobic sitting room.

But they cared for her as dutifully as she cared for the cat Sambo. It was a fiction in the household that she adored Sambo, her own cat, brought with her when she arrived, her one link with the past, almost her only possession. Only she knew that she disliked and feared him. But she brushed and fed him with conscientious care as she did everything and, in return, he gave her a slavish allegiance, hardly ever leaving her side, slinking through the cemetery at her heels and only turning back when they reached the main gate. But he wasn't her friend. He didn't love her and he knew that she didn't love him. He was a fellow conspirator, gazing at her through slits of azure light, relishing some secret knowledge which was her knowledge too. He ate voraciously yet he never grew fat. Instead his sleek black body lengthened until, stretched in the sunlight along her window sill, his sharp nose turned always to the cemetery, he looked as sinister and unnatural as a furred reptile.

It was lucky for her that there was a side gate to the cemetery from Alma Terrace and that she could take a short cut to and from school across the graveyard avoiding the dangers of the main road. On her first morning her uncle had said doubtfully "I suppose it's all right. But it seems wrong somehow, a child walking every day through rows of the dead."

Her aunt had replied: "The dead can't rise from their graves. They lay quiet. She's safe enough from the dead."

Her voice had been unnaturally gruff and loud. The words had sounded like an assertion, almost a defiance. But the child knew that she was right. She did feel safe with the dead, safe and at home.

The years in Alma Terrace slipped by, bland and dull as her aunt's blancmange, a sensation rather than a taste. Had she been happy? It wasn't a question which it had ever occurred to her to ask. She wasn't unpopular at school, being neither pretty nor intelligent enough to provoke much interest either from the children or the staff; an ordinary child, unusual only because she was an orphan but unable to capitalize even on that sentimental advantage. Perhaps she might have found friends, quiet unenterprising children like herself who might have responded to her unthreatening mediocrity. But something about her repelled their timid advances, her self-sufficiency, the bland uncaring gaze, the refusal to give anything of herself even in casual friendship. She didn't need friends. She had the graveyard and its occupants.

She had her favourites. She knew them all, When they had died, how old they had been, sometimes how they had died. She knew their names and learned their memorials by heart. They were more to her than the living, those rows of dearly loved wives and mothers, respected tradesmen, lamented fathers, deeply mourned children. The new graves hardly ever interested her although she would watch the funerals from a distance then creep up later to read the mourning cards. But what she liked best were the old neglected oblongs of mounded earth or chipped stones, the tilted crosses, the carved words almost erased by time. It was round the names of long dead that she wove her childish fantasies.

Even the seasons of the year she experienced in and through the cemetery. The gold and purple spears of the first crocuses thrusting through the hard earth. April with its tossing daffodils. The whole graveyard *en fête* in yellow and white as mourners dressed the graves for Easter. The smell of the mown grass and the earthy tang of high summer as if the dead were breathing the flower-scented air and exuding their own mysterious miasma. The glare of sunlight on the stone and marble as the old women in their stained cotton dresses shuffled with their vases to fill them at the tap behind the chapel. Seeing the cemetery transformed by the first winter, the marble angels grotesque in their high bonnets of glistening snow. Watching at her window for the thaw, hoping to catch that moment when the edifice would slip and the shrouded shapes become themselves again.

Only once had she asked about her father and then she had known as children do that this was a subject which, for some mysterious adult reason, it was better not to talk about. She had been sitting at the kitchen table with her homework while her aunt busied herself cooking supper. Looking up from her history book she had asked: "Where is Daddy buried?"

The frying pan had clattered against the stove. The cooking fork dropped from her aunt's hand. It had taken her a long time to pick it up, wash it, clean the grease from the floor. The child had asked again: "Where is Daddy buried?"

"Up north. At Creedon outside Nottingham with your mum and gran. Where else?"

"Can I go there? Can I visit him?"

"When you're older, maybe. No sense is there, hanging about graves. The dead aren't there."

"Who looks after them?"

"The graves? The cemetery people. Now get on with your homework, do child. I'll be wanting the table for supper."

She hadn't asked about her mother, the mother who had died when she was born. That desertion had always seemed to her wilful, a source of secret guilt. "You killed your mother." Someone, some time had spoken those words to her, had laid on her that burden. She wouldn't let herself think about her mother. But she knew that her father had stayed with her, had loved her, hadn't wanted to die and leave her. Some day, secretly, she would find his grave. She would visit it, not once but every week. She would tend it and plant flowers on it and clip the grass as the old ladies did in the cemetery. And if there wasn't a stone she would pay for one, not a cross but a gleaming obelisk, the tallest in the graveyard, bearing his name and an epitaph which she would choose. She would have to wait until she was older, until she could leave school and work and save enough money. But one day she would find her father. She would have a grave of her own to visit and tend. There was a debt of love to be paid.

Four years after her arrival in Alma Terrace her aunt's only brother came to visit from Australia. Physically he and his sister were alike, the same stolid short-legged bodies, the same small eyes set in square pudgy faces. But Uncle Ned had a brash assurance, a cheerful geniality which was so alien to his sister's unconfident reserve that it was hard to believe that they were siblings. For the two weeks of his visit he dominated the little house with his strident alien voice and assertive masculinity. There were unfamiliar treats, dinners in the West End, a visit to a greyhound stadium, a show at Earl's Court. He was kind to the child, tipping her lavishly, even walking through the cemetery with her one morning on his way to buy his racing paper. And it was that evening, coming silently down the stairs to supper, that she overheard disjointed scraps of conversation, adult talk, incomprehensible at the time but taken into her mind and stored there.

First the harsh boom of her uncle's voice: "We were looking at this grave stone together, see. Beloved husband and father. Taken from us suddenly on 14 March 1892. Something like that. Marble chips, cracked urn, bloody great angel pointing upwards. You know the kind of thing. Then the kid turned to me. 'Daddy's death was sudden, too.' That's what she said. Came out with it cool as you please. Now what in God's name made her say that? I mean, why then? Christ, it gave me a turn I can tell you. I didn't know where to put my face. And what a place to choose, the bloody cemetery. I'll say one thing for coming out to Sydney. You'll get a better view. I can promise you that."

Creeping closer, she strained her ears vainly to catch the indistinct mutter of her aunt's reply.

Then came her uncle's voice again; "That bitch never forgave him for getting Helen pregnant. No one was good enough for her precious only daughter. And when Helen died having the kid she blamed him for that too. Poor sod, he bought a packet of trouble when he set eyes on that girl. Too soft, too romantic. That was always Martin's trouble."

Again the murmur of indistinguishable voices, the sound of her aunt's footsteps moving from table to stove, the scrape of a chair. Then her Uncle Ned's voice again.

'Funny kid, isn't she? Old-fashioned. Morbid you might say. Seems to live in that bone yard, she and that damned cat. And the split image of her dad. Christ it turned me up I can tell you. Looking at me with his eyes and then coming out with it. "Daddy's death was sudden too." I'll say it was! Influenza? Well, it's as good a name for it as any if you can get away with it. Helps having such an ordinary name, I suppose. People don't catch on. How long ago is it now? Four years? It seems longer."

Only one part of this half-heard, incomprehensible conversation had disturbed her. Uncle Ned was trying to persuade them to join him in Australia. She might be taken away from Alma Terrace, might never see the cemetery again, might have to wait for years before she could save enough money to return to England and find her father's grave. And how could she visit it regularly, how could she tend and care for it from the other side of the world? After Uncle Ned's visit ended it was months before she could see one of his rare letters with the Australian stamp drop through the letter box without the cold clutch of fear at the heart.

But she needn't have worried. It was October 1966 before they left England and they went alone. When they broke the news to her one Sunday morning at breakfast it was apparent that they had never even considered taking her with them. Dutiful as ever, they had waited to make their decision until she had left school and was earning her living as a shorthand typist with a local firm of estate agents. Her future was assured. They had done all that conscience required of them. Hesitant and a little shame-faced they justified their decision as if they believed that it was important to her, that she cared whether they left or stayed. Her aunt's arthritis was increasingly troublesome; they longed for the sun; Uncle Ned was their only close relation and none of them was getting any younger. Their plan, over which they had agonized for months in whispers behind closed doors, was to visit Sydney for six months and then, if they liked Australia, to apply to emigrate. The house in Alma Terrace was to be sold to pay the air fare. It was already on the market. But they had made provision for her. When they told her what had been arranged, she had to bend her face low over her plate in case the flood of joy should be too apparent. Mrs Morgan, three doors down, would be glad to take her as a lodger if she didn't mind having the small bedroom at the back overlooking the cemetery. In the surging tumult of relief she hardly heard her aunt's next words. There was one small problem. Everyone knew how Mrs Morgan was about cats. Sambo would have to be put down.

She was to move into 43 Alma Terrace on the afternoon of the day on which her aunt and uncle flew from Heathrow. Her two cases, holding all that she possessed in the world, were already packed. In her handbag she carefully stowed the meagre official confirmations of her existence; her birth certificate, her medical card, her Post Office savings book showing the £103 painstakingly saved towards the cost of her father's memorial. And, the next day, she would begin her search. But first she took Sambo to the vet to be destroyed. She made a cat box from two cartons fitted together, pierced it with holes, then sat patiently in the waiting room with the box at her feet. The cat made no sound and this patient resignation touched her, evoking for the first time a spasm of pity and affection. But there was nothing she could do to save him. They both knew it. But then, he had always known what she was thinking, what was past and what was to come. There was something they shared, some knowledge, some common experience which she couldn't remember and he couldn't express. Now with his destruction even that tenuous link with her first ten years would go for ever.

When it was her turn to go into the surgery she said: "I want him put down."

The vet passed his strong experienced hands over the sleek fur. "Are you sure? He seems quite healthy still. He's old, of course, but he's in remarkably good condition.'

I'm sure. I want him put down."

And she left him there without a glance or another word.

She had thought that she would be glad to be free of the pretence of loving him, free of those slitted accusing eyes. But as she walked back to Alma Terrace she found herself crying; tears, unbidden and unstoppable ran like rain down her face.

There was no difficulty in getting a week's leave from her job. She had been husbanding her holiday entitlement. Her work, as always, was up to date. She had calculated how much money she would need for her train and bus fares and for a week's stay in modest hotels. Her plans had been made. They had been made for years. She would begin her search with the address on her birth certificate, Cranstoun House, Creedon, Nottingham, the house where she had been born. The present owners might remember her and her father. If not, there would be neighbours or older inhabitants of the village who would be able to recall her father's death, where he was buried. If that failed she would try the local undertakers. It was, after all, only ten years ago. Someone locally would remember. Somewhere in Nottingham there would be a record of burials. She told Mrs Morgan that she was taking a week's holiday to visit her father's old home, packed a hold-all with overnight necessities and, next morning, caught the earliest possible fast train from St Pancras to Nottingham.

It was during the bus ride from Nottingham to Creedon that she felt the first stirrings of anxiety and mistrust. Until then she had travelled in calm confidence, but strangely without excitement, as if this long-planned journey was as natural and inevitable as her daily walk to work, an inescapable pilgrimage ordained from that moment when a bare-footed child in her white nightdress had drawn back her bedroom curtains and seen her kingdom spread beneath her. But now her mood changed. As the bus lurched through the suburbs she found herself shifting in her seat as if mental unease were provoking physical discomfort. She had expected green countryside, small churches guarding neat domestic graveyards patterned with yew trees. These were graveyards she had visited on holidays, had loved almost as much as she loved the one she had made her own. Surely it was in such bird-loud sanctified peace that her father lay. But Nottingham had spread during the past ten years and Creedon was now little more than an urban village separated from the city by a ribbon development of brash new houses, petrol stations and parades of shops. Nothing in the journey was familiar, and yet she knew that she had travelled this road before and travelled it in anxiety and pain.

But when, thirty minutes later, the bus stopped at its terminus at Creedon she knew at once where she was. The Dog and Whistle still stood at one corner of the dusty litter-strewn village green with the same bus shelter outside it. And with the sight of its graffiti-scrawled walls memory returned as easily as if nothing had ever been forgotten. Here her father used to leave her when he brought her to pay her regular Sunday visits to her grandmother. Here her grandmother's elderly cook would be waiting for her. Here she would look back for a final wave and see her father patiently waiting for the bus to begin its return journey. Here she would be brought at six-thirty when he arrived to collect her. Cranstoun House was where her grandmother lived. She herself had been born there but it had never been her home.

She had no need to ask her way to the house. And when, five minutes later, she stood gazing up at it in appalled fascination, no need to read the name painted on the shabby padlocked gate. It was a square built house of dark brick standing in incongruous and spurious grandeur at the end of a country lane. It was smaller than she now remembered, but it was still a dreadful house. How could she ever have forgotten those ornate overhanging gables, the high pitched roof, the secretive oriel windows, the single forbidding turret at the east end? There was an estate agent's board wired to the gate and it was apparent that the house was empty. The paint on the front door was peeling, the lawns were overgrown, the boughs of the rhododendron bushes were broken and the gravel path was studded with clumps of weed. There was no one here who could help her to find her father's grave. But she knew that she had to visit, had to make herself pass again through that intimidating front door. There was something the house knew and had to tell her, something that Sambo had known. She couldn't escape her next step. She must find the estate agent's office and get a permit to view.

She had missed the returning bus and by the time the next one had reached Nottingham it was after three o'clock. She had eaten nothing since her early breakfast but she was too driven now to be aware of hunger. But she knew that it would be a long day and that she ought to eat. She turned into a coffee bar and bought a toasted cheese sandwich and a mug of coffee, grudging the few minutes which it took to gulp them down. The coffee was hot but almost tasteless. Flavour would have been wasted on her, but she realized as the hot liquid stung her throat how much she had needed it.

The girl at the cash desk was able to direct her to the house agent's office. It seemed to her a happy augury that it was within ten minutes walk. She was received by a sharp featured young man in an over-tailored pin-stripe suit who, in one practised glance at her old blue tweed coat, the cheap hold-all and bag of synthetic leather, placed her precisely in his private category of client from whom little can be expected and to whom less need be given. But he found the particulars for her and his curiosity sharpened as she merely glanced at them, then folded the paper away in her bag. Her request to view that afternoon was received, as she expected, with politeness but without enthusiasm. But this was familiar territory and she knew why. The house was unoccupied. She would have to be escorted. There was nothing in her respectable drabness to suggest that she was a likely purchaser. And when he briefly excused himself to consult a colleague and returned to say that he could drive her to Creedon at once she knew the reason for that too. The office wasn't particularly busy and it was time that someone from the firm checked up on the property.

Neither of them spoke during the drive. But when they reached Creedon and he turned down the lane to the house the apprehension she had felt on her first visit returned, but deeper and stronger. Yet now it was more than the memory of an old wretchedness. This was childish misery and fear re-lived, but intensified by a dreadful adult foreboding. As the house agent parked his Morris on the grass verge she looked up at the blind windows and was seized by a spasm of terror so acute that, momentarily, she was unable to speak or move. She was aware of the man holding open the car door for her, of the smell of beer on his breath, of his face, uncomfortably close, bending on her look of exasperated patience. She wanted to say that she had changed her mind, that the house was totally wrong for her, that there would be no point in viewing it, that she would wait for him in the car. But she willed herself to rise from the warm seat and scrambled out under his supercilious eyes, despising herself for her gracelessness. She waited in silence as he unlocked the padlock and swung open the gate.

They passed together between the neglected lawns and the spreading rhododendron bushes towards the front door. And suddenly the feet shuffling the gravel beside her were different feet and she knew that she was walking with her father as she had walked in childhood. She had only to stretch out her hand to feel the grasp of his fingers. Her companion was saying something about the house but she didn't hear. The meaningless chatter faded and she heard a different voice, her father's voice, heard for the first time in over ten years.

"It won't be for always, darling. Just until I've found a job. And I'll visit you every Sunday for lunch. Then, afterwards, we'll be able to go for a walk together, just the two of us. Granny has promised that. And I'll buy you a kitten. I'll bring it next weekend. I'm sure Granny won't mind when she sees him. A black kitten. You've always wanted a black kitten. What shall we call him? Little black Sambo? He'll remind you of me. And then, when I've found a job, I'll be able to rent a little house and we'll be together again. I'll look after you, my darling. We'll look after each other."

She dared not look up in case she should see again those desperately pleading eyes, begging her to understand, to make things easy for him, not to despise him. She knew now that she ought to have helped him, to have told him that she understood, that she didn't mind living with Granny for a month or so, that everything would be all right. But she hadn't managed so adult a response. She remembered tears, desperate clinging to his coat, her grandmother's old cook, tight-lipped, pulling her away from him and bearing her up to bed. And the last memory was of watching him from her room above the porch, of his drooping defeated figure making its way down the lane to the bus stop.

As they reached the front door she looked up. The window was still there. But, of course, it was. She knew every room in this dark house.

The garden was bathed in a mellow October sunlight, but the hall struck cold and dim. The heavy mahogany staircase led up from gloom to a darkness which hung above them like a pall. The estate agent felt along the wall for the light switch. But she didn't wait. She felt again the huge brass door knob which her childish fingers had hardly encompassed and moved unerringly into the drawing room.

The smell of the room was different. Then there had been a scent of violets overlaid with furniture polish. Now the air smelt cold and musty. She stood in the darkness shivering but perfectly calm. It seemed to her that she had passed through a barrier of fear as a tortured victim might pass through a pain barrier into a kind of peace. She felt a shoulder brush against her as the man went across to the window and swung open the heavy curtains.

He said: "The last owners have left it partly furnished. Looks better that way. Easier to get offers if the place looks lived in."

"Has there been an offer?"

"Not yet. It's not everyone's cup of tea. Bit on the large size for a modern family. And then, there's the murder. Ten years ago, but people still talk in the neighbourhood. There's been four owners since then and none of them stayed long. It's bound to affect the price. No good thinking you can hush up murder."

His voice was carefully nonchalant, but his gaze never left her face. Walking to the empty fire grate, he stretched one arm along the mantelpiece and followed her with his eyes as she moved as if in a trance about the room.

She heard herself asking: "What murder?"

"A sixty-four-year-old woman. Battered to death by her son-in-law. The old cook came in from the back kitchen and found him with the poker in his hand. Come to think of it, it could have been one like that."

He nodded down to a collection of brass firearms resting against the fender. He said: "It happened right where you're standing now. She was sitting in that very chair."

She said in a voice so gruff and harsh that she hardly recognized it: "It wasn't this chair. It was bigger. Her chair had an embroidered seat and back and there were arm rest edged with crochet and the feet were like lions' claws."

His gaze sharpened. Then he laughed warily. The watchful eyes grew puzzled, then the look changed into something else.

Could it have been contempt?

"So you know about it. You're one of those."

"One of those?"

"They aren't really in the market for a place. Couldn't afford one this size anyway. They just want a thrill, want to see where it happened. You get all sorts in this game and I can usually tell. I can give you all the gory details if you're interested. Not that there was much gore. The skull was smashed but most of the bleeding was internal. They say there was just a trickle falling down her forehead and dripping on to her hands."

It came out so pat that she knew that he had told it all before, that he enjoyed telling it, this small recital of horror to titillate his clients and relieve the boredom of his day. She wished that she wasn't so cold. If only she could get warm again her voice wouldn't sound so strange. She said through her dry and swollen lips:

"And the kitten. Tell me about the kitten."

"Now that was something! That was a touch of horror if you like. The kitten was on her lap, licking up the blood. But then you know, don't you? You've heard all about it."

"Yes," she lied. "I've heard all about it."

But she had done more than that. She knew. She had seen it. She had been there.

And then the outline of the chair altered. An amorphous black shape swam before her eyes, then took form and substance. Her grandmother was sitting there, squat as a toad, dressed in her Sunday black for morning service, gloved and hatted, prayer book in her lap. She saw again the glob of phlegm at the corner of the mouth, the thread of broken veins at the side of the sharp nose. She was waiting to inspect her grandchild before church, turning on her again that look of querulous discontent. The witch was sitting there. The witch who hated her and her daddy, who had told her that he was useless and feckless and no better than her mother's murderer. The witch who was threatening to have Sambo put down because he had torn her chair, because daddy had given him to her. The witch who was planning to keep her from daddy for ever.

And then she saw something else. The poker was there, too,

just as she remembered it, the long rod of polished brass with its heavy knob.

She seized it as she had seized it then and, with a high scream of hatred and terror, brought it down on her grandmother's head. Again and again she struck, hearing the brass thudding against the leather, blow on splitting blow. And still she screamed. The room rang with the terror of it. But it was only when the frenzy passed and the dreadful noise stopped that she knew from the pain of her torn throat that the screaming had been hers.

She stood shaking, gasping for breath. Beads of sweat stood out on her forehead and she felt the stinging drops seeping into her eyes. Looking up she was aware of the man's eyes, wide with terror, staring into hers, of a muttered curse, of footsteps running to the door. And then the poker slid from her moist hands and she heard it thud softly on the rug.

He had been right, there was no blood. Only the grotesque hat knocked forward over the dead face. But as she watched a sluggish line of deep red rolled from under the brim, zig-zagged down the forehead, trickled along the creases of the cheeks and began to drop steadily on to the gloved hands. And then she heard a soft mew. A ball of black fur crept from behind the chair and the ghost of Sambo, azure eyes frantic, leapt as he had leapt ten years earlier delicately up to that unmoving lap.

She looked at her hands. Where were the gloves, the white cotton gloves which the witch had always insisted must be worn to Church? But these hands, no longer the hands of a nine-year-old child, were naked. And the chair was empty. There was nothing but the split leather, the burst of horsehair stuffing, a faint smell of violets fading on the quiet air.

She walked out of the front door without closing it behind her as she had left it then. She walked as she had walked then, gloved and unsullied, down the gravel path between the rhododendrons, out of the ironwork gate and up the lane towards the church. The bell had only just started ringing; she would be in good time. In the distance she had glimpsed her father climbing a stile from the water meadow into the lane. So he must have set out early after breakfast and had walked to Creedon. And why so early? Had he needed that long walk to settle in his mind? Had it been a pathetic attempt to propitiate the witch by coming with them to church? Or, blessed thought, had he come to take her away, to see that her few belongings were packed and ready by the time the service was over? Yes, that was what she had thought at the time. She remembered it now, that fountain of hope soaring and dancing into glorious certainty. When she got home all would be ready. They would stand there together and defy the witch, would tell her that they were leaving together,the two of then and Sambo, that she would never see them again. At the end of the road she looked back and saw for the last time the beloved ghost crossing the lane to the house towards that fatally open door.

And after that? The vision was fading now. She could remember nothing of the service except a blaze of red and blue shifting like a kaleidoscope then fusing into a stained glass window, the Good Shepherd gathering a lamb to his bosom. And afterwards? Surely there had been strangers waiting in the porch, grave concerned faces, whispers and sidelong glances, a woman in some kind of uniform, an official car. And after that, nothing. Memory was blank.

But now, at last, she knew where her father was buried. And she knew why she would never be able to visit him, never make that pious pilgrimage to the place where he lay because of her, the shameful place where she had put him. There could be no flowers, no obelisk, no loving message carved in marble for those who lay in quicklime behind a prison wall. And then, unbidden, came the final memory. She saw again the open church door, the trickle of the congregation filing in, enquiring faces turning towards her as she arrived alone in the porch. She heard again that high childish voice speaking the words which more then any others had slipped that rope of hemp over his shrouded head.

"Granny? She isn't very well. She told me to come on my own. No, there's nothing to worry about. She's quite all right. Daddy's with her."

RUTH McKENNEY

Dapper Johnny Brown

I never cared for *The Taming of the Shrew*—it makes my hackles rise—but my sister Eileen and I early took for our motto the lines:

> *Such wind as scatters young men through the world,*
> *To seek their fortunes further than at home,*
> *Where small experience grows. . . .*

Father, on the other hand, disapproved of Dick Whittington, Shakespeare, Boswell, Rabelais, Cardinal Wolsey, James Thurber and other adventurers (seedy, excitable, gross, passionate, high-principled, or otherwise) who abandoned the quiet dust of home for the noisier lures of London, Paris, New York City and similar dens of large experience. Father has lived in Cleveland, Ohio, all his life, and he is glad of it. Eileen and I had our glittering, beady gaze fixed on New York City even during the years we whiled away in a grammar school. We regarded Ohio as a mere anteroom, a training ground, the minor leagues. We made up our minds to seek our fortunes in New York so young that now I cannot remember why. Nobody else in the family ever heard of such a thing. The Flannigans and the McKenneys are still cosily established in Ohio. Eileen and I were the only ones of the whole tribe whom the wind scattered.

"What's wrong with Ohio?" father argued. Father was never a fierce man, but it irked him to hear his own daughters talk about going to New York. Father thought there was something unwholesome, something dubious and un-American about a one-way ticket from Cleveland to New York City. He considered it going backward; it was anti-pioneer, anti-Daniel Boone, anti-

80

covered wagon. California, now, he might understand. But New York!

"Rackety place," Father said. "What are you going to do in New York? Smoke cigarettes, drink liquor, and do the Charleston?"

Eileen and I sniffed. We were not sure what people actually did on that towered island of Manhattan, but we were confident that New York was a wider, grander, sweeter world than Cleveland.

"Talk, talk, talk," Father remarked. "You mark my words. You girls will settle down right here in good old Cleveland."

We laughed. Father voted against Al Smith, to show where he stood.

But one year after another passed. Eileen and I grew up. We were eighteen, nineteen, twenty; and nothing happened, nothing important. After dabbling in culture at Ohio State University, I went to work as a newspaper reporter.

Eileen acquired an immense diamond ring, her picture in the society section of the *Plain Dealer*, and a young man named Robert (Bidgie) Thomaston III, Princeton '31, steel scion, and man about Cleveland.

"I'm just marking time," Eileen told me bravely.

I marked time, too. I puttered about with murders, riots, strikes, breadlines, campaigns, marathon dances, spelling bees, and the like. All very banal. Finally I was elected "Ohio's Best Newspaperwoman." My employer celebrated this event by a front-page headline: *GIRL REPORTER, ONLY 21, COPS COVETED PRIZE.* There was also a picture of me, heavily retouched, shyly pointing to my pewter plaque.

Father bustled down from Cleveland. His eyes danced. "I always knew you'd make good!" he said. "This'll show Mrs. Griffin!"

Mrs. Griffin was the Cassandra of East Cleveland; she lived across the street, and had long predicted something dire in the way of a future for Eileen and me.

Eileen and Bidgie were getting married in October, too, father reported smugly. Mr. Thomaston, the steel king (or, anyway, duke), was giving the happy young couple a completely furnished house. "Four bathrooms, built-in tile showers," Father said with satisfaction. "Mrs. Griffin can hardly believe it."

One week later, Eileen and I took the Greyhound bus for New York. We hated to spoil Father's innocent triumph, but we could not cut off our noses to spite Mrs. Griffin. Four bathrooms! Built-in tile showers! Pewter plaques! Ohio's Best Newspaperwoman! Another six months—another six weeks—and Eileen and I would be permanently trapped. Buckeyes for ever. It was now or never; do or die. I was twenty-one, Eileen twenty; we were aging fast. "To horse!" Eileen said, with an attempt at insouciance.

To tell the truth, we were scared to death. We arrived in New York City with no jobs, no diamond rings, no prospects, no place to sleep, not a friend in the world, and fifty-one dollars and seventy-eight cents between us. It was the middle of the depression, and Father said not to bother wiring him for money, just hitchhike home to Cleveland—or walk.

The first four days in New York were nervous. I called on the city editors of New York newspapers, but one and all, they seemed to be very busy. On the fourth day, I went back to the *New York Post*. The office boy presided over a small, stuffy anteroom. "You again," he said. He also pointed out that the city editor, Mr. Bixbee, did not like women reporters, and never, under any circumstances, hired them, especially if they came from out of town.

"Is that so?" I was beginning to dislike office boys. Hoity toity!

"I suppose you don't mind," I said icily, "if I wait—until Mr. Bixbee has a moment to look at my string?" A "string" was a pasted-up file of newspaper clippings; I had my prize-winning Ohio masterpieces conveniently tucked away in my purse.

"Go right ahead," the office boy replied. "Wait, wait. What's the matter? It's raining outside?"

I disdained a reply to this impertinence. There was a long bench across one wall of the anteroom. I took a seat. On my right was a gentleman, not quite clean, but eager. He showed me his blueprints for a global highway to end wars and depressions—four lanes, poured concrete, floating pylons on the Pacific and the Atlantic.

"Instead of wasting money on battleships and guns, the nations will all get together and build a parkway. People will drive around the world and have good will towards one another. The project will make so many jobs that . . ."

On my left was a Prophet of Old. He had a long, mangy beard and wore a burlap robe and tennis shoes. "The Lord cometh," he confided. "I'm giving it to Mr. Bixbee exclusive. He's a friend of mine. It's either the 17th of October or the 5th of next February. We'll have to wait and see."

I looked at the clock: nine thirty-four. At nine forty, the anteroom struck me as much, much stuffier. At ten eleven, I definitely made up my mind: It was the prophet. No doubt he was waiting for doomsday to be washed as white as snow. Why trifle with inessentials, now that the sands were running out?

I changed places. At the far end of the bench, a tall, dark, hawk-nosed gentleman in a Broadway suit and shiny tan shoes grudgingly gave me room. At eleven five, he addressed the office boy in a rough, rude voice. He sounded raspy. "Hey! you wit' the ears! Ya tell this cluck Bixbee I'm waiting'?"

"Sure did, pal." The office boy hummed a tune.

"Ya told him John Brown's here?"

"That's it!" the office boy carolled.

Mr. Brown subsided.

At eleven fifty-five, the office boy went to lunch.

At exactly noon, Mr. Brown stood up. His face was mottled—rage, I feared. He reminded me of some Ohio gangsters I'd met once at a marathon dance. New York was a regular melting pot, all right.

"Listen," Mr. Brown said, suddenly fixing me with his black eyes. "Ya goin' to see this Bixbee?"

I blushed. "Well, if Mr. Bixbee happens to have time, I hope I—"

Mr. Brown took a piece of paper from a natty tan wallet, and carefully wrote: *106-A Greene Street, ring twice, Jersey City.*

"Here. Tell this Bixbee joker I give him until tonight. See? After that, I hit the Telly. Wha's Bixbee think? I got all my life?"

"Yes, but what if I don't—"

Mr. Brown, a dynamic personality, turned on a polished heel and stalked out the door.

I shrugged. Probably Mr. Brown thought he was Napoleon and

wanted Mr. Bixbee to have the news first—for a price. Or maybe Mr. Brown had invented something although he did not look much like an inventor.

Time dragged. The office boy came back from lunch. The prophet unwrapped a vegetarian snack and fell to; but the end-wars man and I did not bother with refreshments. Eileen and I were on a diet, for lunch. The way things looked, we were going to be on a diet for dinner, too, starting about next Monday.

At two forty-one, the telephone on the office boy's desk rang. The prophet, the end-wars man and I came to electric attention. The office boy listened, and then replied in a whine: "I already did tell her, Mr. Bixbee . . . Yes, Mr. Bixbee . . . I know it, Mr. Bixbee . . .Well, I tried to get rid of her, Mr. Bixbee, but she—"

The office boy banged down the phone and pointed at me. "Five minutes. No jobs. Got it?"

Five minutes! My heart leaped up. I did not care what the office boy said; when Mr. Bixbee saw my prize-winning feature, he would be overwhelmed, I hoped. *Orphan, Nine, Starves, As Granny, 82, Is Jailed for Stealing Coal.* Or perhaps Mr. Bixbee would be more interested in my front-page scoop: *Gang Massacre Horrifies Crossroads Hamlet.* It was a nice point. Maybe Mr. Bixbee read fast and I could show him both.

I walked down the aisle of the *Post* city room, weighing orphans against gangsters. But the city room seemed very large (about ten times bigger than Ohio city rooms), and men looked at me curiously as I tramped down what began to feel like the Last Mile. I was stuttering mentally long before Mr. Bixbee asked me my name and how old I was.

Mr. Bixbee, a sophisticated, handsome man, reclined in a swivel chair. He was not like city editors back home. He had clean fingernails. He looked suave. His attitude was languid, relaxed, negligent, even airy.

A considerable audience had assembled for Mr. Bixbee's interview with the girl reporter from the provinces. Amused, weary men in pressed pants, and no green eye shades, leaned against desks, or draped themselves gracefully over typewriters. Newspapermen were more rumpled and alert in Ohio.

Mr. Bixbee waved aside my clippings. He did not care to read about *Orphan, Nine, Starves, As Granny Jailed*; he smiled a wintry smile when I proposed *Gang Massacre*.

"Just give me one good reason why I should hire a twenty-one-year-old girl who came to New York Monday. Be brief. Keep to the point."

I swallowed. "Well, I—"

"Speak up!"

"Yes, sir."

Somebody chuckled, to the right of Mr. Bixbee's elbow.

I took a deep breath. "I was elected Ohio's Best Newspaperwoman for '34."

It appeared that a creamier jest had never been heard in the *Post* city room. People laughed and laughed. Mr. Bixbee had to wipe the tears from his eyes. Men rushed over from the copy desk to get in on the fun.

I regretted I had not brought along a knife, like Charlotte Corday. "Thank you very much," I said bitterly, and started back up the aisle. I thought of running, but decided against it.

Mr. Bixbee called me back. He apologised. He said he was sorry he had laughed. It had been rude. He couldn't hire me, because I didn't know anything about New York City. I wouldn't be of any use to him. Probably I didn't even know how to get to Brooklyn.

"I could look it up on a map."

Mr. Bixbee said well, yes, but it wasn't the same as knowing Brooklyn in your bones. Then Mr. Bixbee became fatherly. It was not just a matter of geography. I was too young. "I tell you what. I'll give you an assignment. If you carry out the assignment, I'll put you on the staff. If you fall down on it, you make me a promise you'll take the next train back to Ohio."

"Okay," I said eagerly, "I'll bet I can do any—"

I heard the mirth, right and left.

"Freddie!" Mr. Bixbee called, trying to keep a straight face himself, "give her the dope on Molliati."

I saw people shake their heads. Some gentlemen were openly sorry for me; they thought Mr. Bixbee was carrying the joke too far.

"Left-handed monkey wrenches!" I snarled. By this time I had given up hope, and did not care what Mr. Bixbee thought of me.

Mr. Bixbee seemed piqued. "No. It's a thousand-to-one shot. But then, it's a thousand to one I'd ever hire Ohio's Best Newspaperwoman. It evens out."

I marched over to Freddie's desk, my nose in the air and my face a rich shade of purple.

Freddie, the assistant city editor, was laconic. On Monday, the day Eileen and I had arrived in New York—what a coincidence— a man, or anyway a voice, name of Molliati, had called up Mr. Bixbee and offered to sell him some kind of a story about a Brooklyn murder ring.

"It must be quite sensational," Freddie said. "Mr. Bixbee's been burning up the staff ever since. I had four men out on the story yesterday. We were supposed to meet this Molliati character in some Jersey City dive—a lot of hocus-pocus about gardenias in buttonholes, signals, and Molliati following our man to the rendezvous. Either we missed connections or the whole thing is a phony. Personally, I think it's Benny Stevens at the West Forty-seventh Street station. Benny's a wit, he imagines. On the other hand, maybe there really is a Brooklyn murder mob, and they decided to use our friend Molliati for target practice. Who can tell?"

Freddie seemed indifferent to Molliati, dead or alive. He tossed over a memo from the *Post's* Centre Street reporter. It appeared that there actually was a Molliati in the police files. He was wanted for various trivial items: throwing acid on pressers during a dry-cleaners' strike, squashing tomatoes and tomato vendors in an effort to "organise" the tomato pushcart industry—that sort of thing.

The reporter's description of Mr. Molliati wasn't much of a surprise to me. The words "Jersey City" were already singing in my soul. Hark, Hark, Molliati the lark, of Jersey City.

Mr. Molliati, the Centre Street man reported, was tall, thin, dark-skinned, dark-haired, and had a Roman nose. He sometimes used the alias John Brown; the police reporter could not think why. He wore sharp clothes (when off duty from squashing things and throwing acid), and was partial to highly polished tan shoes, which he flicked from time to time with a clean white handkerchief. The memo went on: *Started life as bootblack, educated reform schools and one term Sing Sing. Character: bad. Despised by fellow-toilers in Brooklyn vineyards. Possible Bixbee's phone call planted by annoyed acquaintance of Molliati to get M. in bad with Brooklyn employers. Such phone call would get Molliati in something terrible. In fact, might as well start checking morgue for Molliati. Brooklyn organisation puts high premium on loyalty, school spirit, team play, co-operation, etc. Would resent Molliati selling story of organisation's activities to newspaper.*

Freddie took the memo back.

"Quite a joker," he said sourly.

"Well— when would Mr. Bixbee like to see Molliati?"

Freddie looked at me. "Oh, any time," he said gently.

"Should I phone in first?"

Freddie yelled—loudly—across the rewrite bank. "Jeff! Lady wants to know should she give you a ring? Before she brings in Molliati?"

Mr. Bixbee and eight or ten rewrite men tried, without success, to choke back their mirth. "No," Mr. Bixbee said, when he'd stopped laughing, "don't waste time with telephone calls. Take no chances. Don't let him out of your sight. Moment you catch up with him, push him in a taxi and bring him right to this desk. Got it?"

"Thank you, sir."

I hardly heard the merriment. I did not walk out of the *Post* city room; I floated out, on wings of purest joy.

I had a little trouble getting to Jersey City. As Mr. Bixbee had feared, I did not know my way around New York. Somebody mentioned a ferry in connection with Jersey City, so I went to Staten Island; then opinion veered, in favour of taking a tube, and I arrived in Newark. All in all, Mr. Molliati was irritated, when at last I rang his bell in Jersey City. Mr. Molliati said (from a shadowed, dank staircase) that it was about time Mr. Bixbee got on the ball.

When I trotted into Mr. Molliati's crummy headquarters, however, he took a good look at me under the naked bulb. He recognised me right away; I'd been sitting next to him in the *Post* anteroom all morning. Mr. Molliati took alarm. He wondered if I were not a spy, either from the cops or from the Brooklyn mob.

"I am not a spy!" I said indignantly.

Mr. Molliati peered earnestly at my freckled face and stout form. He had to admit I did not look like the ordinary type of spy. Then the wind shifted to another quarter. Mr. Molliati took offence at Mr. Bixbee sending what he ungallantly called a "punk dame reporter" to "contact" him. He considered it *lèse-majesté*.

"When did they let ya outta pantywaists?" he snarled. "Wha'z Bixbee think this is? A lousy society-page story?"

I drew myself up. "Mr. Molliati, I hardly think it's any of your business what Mr. Bixbee—"

Mr. Molliati made it clear that he had expected somebody older, wilier, in pants, no doubt with a hat pulled down over his eyes and a toothpick jammed between his teeth, as in *The Front Page*.

"This is not the movies, Mr. Molliati," I said coldly.

"Well—" Mr. Molliati was dubious. For two cents he'd call up the Telly.

"Mr. Bixbee said to bring you in a taxi. Right away."

It was a cunning stroke, if I said so myself. Mr. Molliati was fired by the idea of riding across on the ferry, all the way to Manhattan, in a taxi. However, I was appalled when we got to the *Post* office and discovered that Mr. Molliati expected me to pay the driver.

"It's practically all the money I've got in the whole world, Mr. Molliati," I argued.

"You mean Bixbee says for me to pay my own taxi fare? He must be some cheap crumb, awright. I never heard of no city editor like him. I should a contacted Winchell."

I paid the fare plus a quarter tip. I could see why Mr. Molliati's friends did not like him. I hoped Mr. Bixbee paid expense accounts from current petty cash. I glanced at the clock in the lobby. It was after six. I hoped Mr. Bixbee had not gone home. What on earth would I do with Mr. Molliati until tomorrow morning? I didn't think Eileen would like Mr. Molliati, he wasn't exactly a lovable personality.

The office boy had left for the day. The anteroom was dark.

Mr. Molliati and I walked right into the city room. It was also empty. Our footsteps echoed. Some cleaning ladies came in a back door and started to sweep up the litter. My heart sank. Then I spotted Mr. Bixbee playing bridge with three cronies in the managing editor's glass-partitioned cubby-hole.

"Come on."

Mr. Molliati hung back a little. His eyes darted around. "Where's all the reporters?"

"This is an afternoon paper," I said patiently. "Now, Mr. Molliati, you don't want to get scared at the last minute."

"Who, *me*?" Mr. Molliati snarled.

The cleaning ladies looked at us. They seemed surprised. I trotted down the long city-room aisle. Mr. Molliati followed, diffidently. Once he stopped to straighten his tie (red roses on bright blue), and flick imaginary dust from his tan shoes.

The door to the managing editor's office was open. I leaned in and began. "Oh, Mr. Bixbee! I'm certainly glad to see you! I was afraid maybe you'd be gone."

Mr. Bixbee was studying his cards. He looked up. He did not seem at all friendly. "I thought I told you to go back to Ohio."

"Huh?" Mr. Molliati said. He narrowed his eyes at me.

"Mr. Bixbee!" I cried hastily. "This is Mr. Molliati! After all!"

Mr. Bixbee had returned to his bridge hand. "I'll bet it is," he replied rudely. "Four spades."

Mr. Molliati was startled, I think, by his cool reception. He peered over my shoulder; he looked at the back of Mr. Bixbee's balding head. He muttered. He stood first on one foot, then on the other.

"Pass," Mr. Bixbee's partner said.

Freddie's partner reflected. "Pass."

"Say, Mr. Bixbee," I ventured. I hoped Mr. Bixbee had not lost interest in the Brooklyn murder mob. In that event, what about my job? And my taxi fare?

Mr. Bixbee drummed his clean fingernails on the desk. "Four no trump," he said.

Freddie laughed. "Double four no trump. Ha, ha, Bixbee's folly."

"Five no trump," Mr. Bixbee's partner cooed, in the voice of a dove.

Mr. Bixbee played the hand at five no trump, doubled and redoubled. Mr. Molliati and I watched. We were a little impatient, but then again, we hated to interrupt. At least I did. Mr. Molliati kept muttering, I believe he was baffled.

Mr. Bixbee made five no trump— by the skin of his teeth, however.

"What dumb, dumb luck," Freddie said. "That last finesse was strictly seven-come-eleven."

"Oh, sure, sure." Mr. Bixbee cut the fresh pack with an expansive gesture.

Freddie noticed me, still standing in the doorway. He got up. He said, "Now, look, Miss-what's-your-name, don't you think you're pressing this act a bit too far?"

Mr. Bixbee wheeled around sharply in his chair. "For the love of God!" he shouted.

Mr. Molliati and I backed up nervously, "Mr. M-m-m-molliat-t-ti," I managed to get out; and I stood aside, to point at my prize.

Mr. Bixbee blinked. He put down the cards. He stood up. He frowned. He pushed back his chair and walked up to Mr. Molliati, very deliberately. Mr. Molliati looked at Mr. Bixbee with a dumb anguish.

"What's your name?"

"M-m-m-mollia-t-t-i." I don't know whether Mr Molliati always stuttered in moments of stress, or whether I had hypnotised him.

Mr. Bixbee breathed deeply.

"I called ya up," Mr. Molliati said piteously. "About some fellows in Canarsie."

"You mean you're Molliati!"

Mr. Molliati and I giggled wildly.

"He certainly is," I put in. "Aren't you, Mr. Molliati?"

"Bet yer life," Mr. Molliati said.

Mr. Bixbee could not get over it. He said, "No!" and "I don't believe it!" several times. He seemed angry. "How'd she find you?" Mr. Bixbee stroked the "she" in a tone of utter contempt.

"I gave 'er my address." Mr. Molliati was bewildered. I

suppose the whole thing did not seem very well organised to him.

"*You* gave *her* your address!"

Mr. Bixbee was shaken. "I see. Old friends, no doubt?" Mr. Bixbee laughed, like Pagliacci. "Now I believe in Tinker Bell. She even looks like Ohio's Best Newspaperwoman. I have not been played for such a sucker since jolly college days."

"Yes, but Mr. Bixbee," I kept tying to say.

"Well, what's your angle, sister?" Mr. Bixbee inquired, after he had calmed down somewhat. "You cut in on this deal of Molliati's? Or do you just deliver the body?"

"B-b-body?" Mr. Molliati quavered. His conscience smote him, I think.

At last I had an opportunity to converse with Mr. Bixbee. I explained that Mr. Molliati and I had sat next to each other in the anteroom all morning. Happenstance, of course.

Mr. Bixbee was deeply grieved by this intelligence. He planned reprisals against the office boy, until I hastily told him about "John Brown."

"I wasn't going' tuh give name a Molliati to no punk kid," Mr. Molliati said loftily. "Anyways, everybody calls me Dapper Johnny Brown. It's my alias, see?"

"Dapper Johnny Brown!" Mr. Bixbee gave a hoarse chuckle. "Ironic, isn't it?"

After these exciting preliminaries, Mr. Bixbee decided it was about time to get down to business. He said if Mr. Molliati would please take a seat at the desk, he would call a stenographer.

Mr. Molliati mentioned money. Mr. Bixbee said yes, yes, he would come to that but first . . .

Freddie added up the score. The other players collected the cards.

I cleared my throat. Everybody seemed to have forgotten me. Mr. Bixbee almost barked. "*Now* what?"

"Well—uh—Mr. Bixbee—"

"Oh!" Mr. Bixbee was enraged. He said he absolutely detested women reporters. They made him nervous. Women should be gun molls or mothers or something. They should not sit around in city rooms, smoking cigarettes. He had no opening on the staff of the *Post*. He was sorry, but he had not expected me to find

Mr. Molliati. After all, it was just a fluke, was it not?

I couldn't think of anything to say.

"I'm sorry," Mr. Bixbee repeated.

"It's all right."

This time nobody laughed. I remembered about the cab fare before I got to the door, but I could not bear to go back and talk to Mr. Bixbee again. I took the subway—to Brooklyn, as it turned out—and then, after some difficulty, to Christopher Street, where Eileen and I had just rented a dismal apartment in the basement. I was depressed. So was Eileen, when I told her about the taxi fare.

"That Bixbee ought to be ashamed of himself!" Eileen said hotly.

"Oh, well, I guess it was just a fluke."

"Don't cry," Eileen exhorted me. "We can always pawn your typewriter."

After a meagre meal, we tried on each other's clothes for a while to cheer ourselves up. A little after ten, the telephone rang for the first time—we had just had it installed, after pawning my winter coat.

"Hello?" I said eagerly, but it was a wrong number.

"Don't look like that," Eileen said crossly. "It's harrowing. Did you give Bixbee your telephone number?"

"I didn't know it."

"Does he have your name?"

I remembered Freddie's "Miss-what's-your-name."

"Then quit looking eager when the phone rings."

At eleven thirty, the telephone rang.

I looked eager. "Hello?" I cried anxiously.

"Honestly!" Eileen was disgusted.

However, it was Mr. Bixbee, after all. I recognised his voice right away. He sounded furious, as usual. "Is this Ohio's Best Newspaperwoman?" he shouted.

"Yes, sir." I hoped Mr. Bixbee had not called up just to be funny.

"Well, why don't you leave your name and address when you ask for a job!" Mr. Bixbee said indignantly. "I had to call the A.P. in Cleveland. Imagine! People think I'm out of my mind. New

York calling! Who's Ohio's Best Newspaperwoman? They gave me the Four-H Champion, too, just in case."

"I'm sorry," I muttered.

"Anyway," Mr. Bixbee went on crossly. "I've finally tracked you down. What's the idea of walking out of the office that way? I turn my back, and you're gone."

"Well, but, Mr. Bixbee—"

"I owe you taxi fare."

"Taxi fare?"

"And a job, I suppose," Mr. Bixbee said biterly. "It's against my principles. When do you want to start?"

"Mr. *Bixbee*! Oh, thank you! Thank you!"

"When do you want to start?" Mr. Bixbee inquired, pronouncing each word loudly and distinctly.

"Tomorrow, Mr. Bixbee. First thing."

"I knew it," Mr. Bixbee said, and, after a groan, he hung up.

I was always very grateful to Mr. Molliati, and sincerely sorry when, a year or so after I went to work on the *Post*, he was found, charred, but only partly cemented, in a Canarsie dump. He would have been pleased by his obituary: *Dapper Johnny Brown Identified By Snappy Tan Shoe, Shreds of Silk Necktie.*

If You See This Woman

Junie's mouse-gray rump stuck out from under the marble-topped coffee table. She had spilled an ashtray, hitting it with the duster, and now there was a mess of ashes and cigarette butts to clean up. She was fumbling with the last of the butts when Mr. Arnold came into the room behind her. She knew that he must be looking at her; she heard him say, "What on earth are you doing? Laying an egg?"

She inched hastily backward, freeing her heavy shoulders from the rim of the table. She squatted, looking up at him, pink in the face from the exertion of stooping and crawling. "Oh, no, Mr. Arnold."

He grinned at her in the way she didn't understand. "Chasing a butterfly? Would you actually be chasing a butterfly, Junie?"

"Oh, no, sir." Junie got to her feet, tugged down the cotton uniform, reached for the fallen duster and the ashtray. "No, I wouldn't do that, Mr. Arnold."

"I know—you were dictating a letter to the little man who lives under the rug. A love letter."

She shook her head, speechless now, backing away gingerly. She wanted to swallow; her throat ached with the nervous need to swallow; but under Mr. Arnold's malevolent grin her throat had dried up.

Mrs. Arnold came into the room from the hall to the bedrooms. "Junie, the baby needs changing." Mrs. Arnold had on the pink satin jump suit, gold slippers, and wore her hair piled on top of her head, all silky darkness and pink ribbons. She looked beautiful. She looked like a doll Junie had once seen in a store window.

94

Mr. Arnold had put his brief case on the coffee table and was lighting a cigarette. Mrs. Arnold looked at the brief case. "You're selling the stock today?"

"Dumping it. Dumping every damned share. Willcutt is in with me, he's selling his too. Then we'll both buy it back for next to nothing."

Mrs. Arnold went to the wall and straightened a picture there. She turned around. Junie was almost at the door to the hall. Mrs. Arnold said to her husband, "Well, just be careful what you're getting rid of, just don't throw out the baby along with the bath water."

Junie hurried down the hall. The words rang in her ears. Mr. and Mrs. Arnold were always saying strange things, but this thing that Mrs. Arnold said every once in a while was the strangest and the scariest of all. Who would throw out a baby in its bath? How could you make a mistake like that? Or . . . could it mean that somebody might *want* to throw away a baby, might want to make it go down, down, down into the deep pipes, the lost places, the rushing water, the dark?

Junie shivered as she turned into the baby's room. Pete, almost a year old, was just beginning to stand well and try to walk. He was a heavy, placid infant. Now he clung to the bars of the crib and gurgled as Junie rushed to him and put protective arms around him.

"Nice Petey."

At Sylvan Slopes Home no one had ever talked about throwing out a baby in its bath. You were taught carefully how to bathe a baby, along with how to dust and clean. But if you'd talked about throwing a baby away—Junie shook her head, trying to imagine the consequences of saying a thing like that at Sylvan Slopes.

They'd have sent you away—the principal, Mr. Willoughby, and the directress of instruction, Miss Gombie. They'd have given you a blue suitcase like the one you got when you were ready to graduate, and maybe some extra underwear, and a Bible, and $10. And may be Miss Gombie might have cried—that a girl of hers had said a thing like throwing a baby away, sneaky-like, in its bath water.

Junie could see it all in her mind, see it quite clearly. She wondered where a girl could go in such a case. Where would you run to? She couldn't imagine.

She tickled Petey gently, got him to lie down, opened his rompers, and changed the didy. Then, since he was obviously all through with his nap, she put him in his playpen. For a while she squatted beside the pen, handing him toys which he threw at her, and once in a while reaching gently to touch the dark curls that covered his head.

"My Petey. My own Petey."

She whispered the words, glancing guiltily at the door to the hall. Miss Gombie had been firm. You must never, never forget that the babies belonged to somebody else. To their parents. Even if their parents had adopted the baby. There had been one whole lesson on just that alone—Miss Gombie had taught it herself. Standing in front of the class in her green suit.

"We must love the children. All of our girls here love children. All of our graduates are famous for loving children," Miss Gombie had said in her forceful way. "We love them but we don't *possess* them."

There had been a short, puzzled silence.

"We don't *own* them," Miss Gombie said, and the word *own* made her mouth round and funny-looking, as if she were getting ready to suck an orange.

Her listeners had nodded their understanding.

For several days Mr. Arnold went around whistling and snapping his fingers, when he was home; and Mrs. Arnold bought a fur jacket and two new hats. At dinner they talked about a new car. They seemed very critical of the car, and yet while she served, and listened, it seemed to Junie that they were going to buy it anyway.

Then for almost a week the house was quiet because Mr. Arnold didn't whistle or snap his fingers any more. Mrs. Arnold took the fur jacket back to the store. The other store wouldn't take back the hats. They no longer talked about the car, but about thousands and thousands of dollars, more than Junie could understand, and about something Mr. Willcutt hadn't done.

When Mr. Arnold noticed Junie, he asked questions like, "You gonna save ol' Massa from de po'house, Junie-bug?" Or "Think they'll take me in at Sylvan Slopes? I'll wear a wig and look retarded."

But Junie had no idea how to answer these strange questions.

Then at the end of the week Junie began to notice how cross Mr. and Mrs. Arnold were getting with each other. One night at dinner Mr. Arnold threw his wine glass at the wall and made a splotch, and Mrs. Arnold screamed. She mad-screamed, not scared-screamed, and in the kitchen Junie choked on her fright.

Then, watching carefully, Junie saw how they both began to get cross with Petey. Not so much at first, but when Petey caught the sniffles and cried at night, Mr. Arnold would get up and walk around and smoke, and say things quiet-like to himself. And Mrs. Arnold would make Junie get up and go to Petey's room and sing to him, and put him on her shoulder while she rocked in the rocking chair.

Then Mr. Arnold put a cot in Petey's room and told Junie she had to sleep in there, though this was against the rules. Junie knew they'd signed a paper before she came, saying she must have a room of her own.

One night when Petey was whimpering and Junie wasn't awake yet to walk around and carry him—she was tired all the time now, and slept heavily—Mr. Arnold came and threw open the door and cursed. He called Petey a damn brat and he called Junie a lazy, feeble-minded slut. His words bounced off the walls like bullets, and Junie cowered in terror.

They didn't love Petey anymore. That was it.

He was sick now, and his face looked rough and red, and he cried a lot. There was no curl in his hair—it looked lank and had no shine to it; and his voice had turned into a hoarse croak.

The doctor came and left some medicine, and told Junie how often to give it to Petey. Mrs. Arnold didn't even come into the room while the doctor was there. She sat in the living room, holding a cigarette, and when the doctor went back in there, Junie heard her saying, "Bill, I don't know when we can pay you," and the doctor answering, "Oh, forget it. And chin up, Betty. Mark's been through worse than this and come out smelling like a rose."

Junie was faithful about giving the medicine, and about

rubbing Petey with alcohol, and rocking him to keep him from crying. At times she would fall asleep in the chair, and only wake when Petey stirred. Mrs. Arnold didn't help at all. She smoked more and more, and stared out of the windows at the skyline, and spent a lot of time talking on the telephone with her mother.

Mr. Arnold came home earlier now. His face seemed thinner and paler. He drank more. And once while Junie was lighting the candles for dinner, bending close with the match, he said, "A vestal virgin. Tell me, how did your high priest—Mr. Willoughby—how did he initiate you virgins? With fire and incense?"

Junie looked at him and wished she might give a proper answer. "We weren't ever allowed to play with matches." For some reason this set Mr. Arnold off into hoots of laughter.

It was going to be winter before too long, but today was mild. The apartment felt overheated and stuffy. Junie served Mr. Arnold his toast and coffee, and took a tray to Mrs. Arnold in bed. Then she bathed Petey and dressed him in the blue rompers with the white collar. His nose was still red, his eyes puffy. She hugged him for a long minute before she set him down in his playpen.

Then she went back into the bathroom, Petey's own private bathroom, and bent to touch the outlet lever for the tub. She was stooped there when she heard the Arnolds in the hall. Mrs. Arnold must have got out of bed and met Mr. Arnold there while he was getting his overcoat at the hall closet.

Mrs. Arnold asked something that Junie didn't catch, and Mr. Arnold answered, "Willcutt made money out of my losses. He was supposed to be with me, but he cut my throat. Now I think I have a chance to get back at him."

Mrs. Arnold said, "So we're going to throw the baby out with the bath water. Is that it?"

Mr. Arnold seemed to get mad all at once. "You're damned right, we're throwing the damn baby out with the damn bath water and we damned well should have done it long before now."

Junie's hand, reaching for the lever, began to shake. She managed to touch the lever, though, and the cold metal sent a

chill all the way up her arm and into her heart. Her heart felt like
a lump of steel ten times bigger than her fist, a hundred times too
big for her chest, pounding coldly there inside her.

"You're determined to go on with this?" Mrs. Arnold said.

"Yes, I am. Damned right I am."

The water began to swirl and growl down into the pipe. Junie
stared at it. Pipes must be dark places. Far, far below the city, she
remembered from somewhere, there were giant pipes like great
dark caves. It would be cold there, cold and slimy, with awful
gurgling echoes, with rats maybe. Junie had seen a woods rat
once.

Who would want to put a baby into a place like that?

The thought scared her so that she ran back to be with Petey.

Mr. Arnold hadn't left yet. They were in the living room now;
she could hear the murmur of voices.

She looked at Petey. He was playing with a rubber elephant,
pulling one of its ears. Junie's heart pounded harder than ever.
What should she do?

She had a telephone number in her suitcase; it was written on a
piece of paper, pinned to the lining. Miss Gombie had told her, if
anything bad ever happened to her, she was to dial Operator and
give her the number and tell her that the call was collect.

Would they help about Petey? Was there anything Miss
Gombie could do? Would Mrs. Arnold catch her using the phone
and stop her?

Crouched beside Petey's pen, Junie began to cry.

An hour went by.

Junie wiped her eyes and tidied up Petey's bed, then went to
the kitchen and washed up the breakfast things. She mopped the
floor, not because it needed it, but because she thought she might
try to use the kitchen phone extension. But then, when she
peeped into the living room, she saw that Mrs. Arnold was
already using the phone. Mrs. Arnold had on a white negligée, all
fluffy, with gold embroidery; and her hair was tied up with a
yellow ribbon. She looked hard and strange.

Junie went to her room and put on her coat. She stole back to
Petey's room, put on his cap and coat and leggings, and took an

extra blanket. Then she remembered her purse. She could never remember exactly how much she still had left of the $10 they'd given her when she was graduated from Sylvan Slopes. Her money was put in the bank for her—the salary she was paid by the Arnolds. There was a little book that showed how much she had and every six months it had to be mailed to Sylvan Slopes, for some reason; but Junie had no idea of how she might get money out of the bank. Now, exploring her little change purse, she found $2.30.

There was money in the kitchen, though, in a funny small jar shaped like a beehive. Mrs. Arnold called it "gin money" and Mr. Arnold called it "the devil's bankroll." Junie picked up the baby and the blanket, stuffed her small change purse into her coat pocket, and stole silently out to the kitchen. She found a ten-dollar bill and three one-dollar bills and two quarters in the beehive. She took it all.

She went out the back way. There was a service elevator here where the janitor took away trash and things, but Junie didn't quite know how to work it. And then too, she didn't want to be seen by the janitor. He might remember. So she carried Petey all the way down the stairs, eight flights, stopping to rest twice.

In the street she paused, bewildered. The day was greyer and cooler than it had seemed from inside the apartment. The trees in the park across the street looked bare and wind-bitten. Aimlessly, Junie walked for a few blocks.

Petey was very heavy. Her arms ached. She knew now that she should have brought the stroller.

Just at that moment she was passing an apartment house and a nice big carriage with a baby blanket in it was standing by the doorway. No one was around, though when Junie touched the cushion inside the carriage, she found it still faintly warm from the baby which had just been taken upstairs. Sometimes Mrs. Arnold had taken Petey out, and had left the stroller for the janitor to bring in; and remembering this, Junie decided that's what had happened here.

She plopped Petey into the carriage and ran for the corner, turned the corner swiftly, then slowed to a walk.

Junie thought, I can be smart like anybody else when I have to be. She felt pleased with herself, alert, vigilant for Petey's welfare, on guard against the world.

After a random stroll of eight or nine blocks she turned back in the direction of the park. She and Petey spent several pleasant hours there. They sat on the grass and Petey patted some dead leaves into dust and then tasted his fingers. He stood up, clinging to Junie's shoulder, and when some fat squirrels ran past he tried to wobble after them.

When she began to feel hungry, Junie put the baby back into the carriage and they went south, toward another part of the city. They ate lunch in a restaurant where you put money in a slot and lifted a small glass door and took out the food. It was an easy way to buy what you wanted. She and Petey had two moist turkey sandwiches and two glasses of milk and four pieces of custard pie. Petey ate well, better than he had for days; the fresh air and the exercise must have been good for him.

Right after lunch Junie realized that she had made a serious omission; she had forgotten to bring diapers. But then she remembered: sometimes in an emergency, when the diaper service had been delayed, Mrs. Arnold had used a kind of disposable diaper that she said came from the drug store.

D-R-U-G.

There one was. Junie went in, pushing the carriage. The person who waited on her let her change Petey in a room at the back of the store. The problem was solved.

She returned to the park. Petey took a nap, snug in the big warm carriage. He awoke later, and again was enchanted with the dusty leaves. But now it began to grow cold and windy. Junie thought over what she should do, and while she was thinking she noticed the buses running on the avenue next to the park.

She pushed the carriage out of sight, deep into some evergreen shrubs, and carrying Petey and his blanket and the package of disposable diapers, she went over to the bus stop. Ever since coming to the city she'd wanted to take a bus ride, but she'd never had the chance.

On the bus she sat in the back. Petey stood on the seat beside her, looking all around, making crowing and squealing noises. Several people noticed him, and smiled.

Junie took three different bus trips that afternoon, to various outlying parts of the city, seeing things she had never seen before. Coming back into downtown on the last trip, she noticed that twilight had drawn in and all the lights were on. It occurred to her that she and Petey had no place to sleep. Impulsively she turned to a middle-aged woman sitting beside her. "I'm going to have to find a room for the night," she said.

The woman looked at Petey and smiled. She coughed gently behind her hand. "Do you—uh—have any money?"

"Oh, yes. Well . . . some."

The woman nodded and in a kind voice she began to tell Junie where to find a room

It wasn't bad. The bed was clean. There was a Bible in the bottom dresser drawer. In the front of the Bible someone had written *God is good*, and underneath that, *God forgives all*. Junie wanted to write *Even me*, but she couldn't find a pencil.

She put Petey to bed in a clean diaper, leaving on his little shirt and his socks. During the night there was laughter and other noises in the hall, and once somebody fell against the door so hard that the panel made a cracking noise. Junie felt comforted by the sounds, the nearness of other people. She wasn't really alone, she thought.

She didn't feel alone until she went out the next morning and heard the news broadcast in the coffee shop where she had breakfast.

At first she didn't realize that the broadcast was about her and Petey. Somebody had kidnapped Peter Bentley Arnold, aged eleven months. The public was asked to be on the watch for June Campbell, aged 22, five foot four, weight 150 pounds, wearing a . . .

June Campbell.

That's me, she thought, almost getting to her feet. She was in a booth, a very small booth back near the kitchen, with Petey squeezed in against the wall. They were eating oatmeal. The little cafe was warm and steamy and pleasantly filled with the odor of fried bacon. The radio speaker was almost directly over Junie's head.

She looked around to see if anyone was watching her.

The waitress noticed and came right over. "More coffee?"

"Thank you." Junie waited, expecting the woman to notice Petey now and to ask, isn't this the baby who was kidnapped, and Junie was going to say, yes, they were going to put him down the sewer, so I had to run away. But the waitress merely went back for the coffee pot and returned to fill up Junie's cup.

It occurred to Junie that she had better leave the city. She must get away from the radio broadcasts. Everyone would be listening, even the Arnolds—they'd hear about it now—and then for the first time Junie realized that the Arnolds must be the ones who had started the broadcasts in the first place. Of course.

. . . *if you see this woman with this child, please notify the police at this emergency number—*

Junie fed Petey a spoonful of oatmeal and kissed the hand that he put against her mouth.

We repeat—this is urgent—please notify the police . . .

Junie formed the words to herself: the police. Notify the police. She suddenly felt cold, empty, and scared. Not scared the way she'd been yesterday, at the Arnolds'. Then, she'd been afraid for Petey, for what might happen to him, and running away with him had been a great relief, almost *fun*, with the feeling that she was finally going to fix things. Now she had to run again, but it wouldn't be any fun at all. Junie didn't understand why this was so, even as she sensed its truth.

Urged by a sudden apprehension, Junie took out her small purse and counted her money. There was very little left. She hadn't realized how much it would cost to eat and to sleep, and to ride buses.

When she had paid for the breakfast there was hardly any money left at all. More scared than ever, she carried Petey out into the street. There were no radio broadcasts out here on the sidewalk but Junie felt conspicuous and exposed. Passers-by glanced at Petey in her arms, and surely pretty soon one of them would run off to notify the police.

There was a friendly-looking man who had a newsstand. He wore an old sweater, pulled up around his ears, and a knitted cap.

His face was red. When Junie paused there, trying to think, he made clucking sounds at Petey, and called him Old Top.

Junie turned to him as she had to the woman on the bus. "I want to get out of town the cheapest way I can," she told him.

"Lady," he said, "the cheapest way to get out of this town is on the Staten Island Ferry. You can go for a nickel and Old Top here can go for nothing."

"Oh, thank you. And how do I get to it?"

"Bus over there. See where the curb's painted yellow? Get the one says South Ferry."

"Would you write it out, please?"

Without curiosity he did laborious lettering on a scrap of newspaper, wetting the pencil stub in his mouth.

Junie wanted to ask, what is a ferry, but explaining it might take time. And something was telling her now that she had better hurry.

At the end of the bus line there weren't a lot of people getting off, but there were enough so that Junie could follow along and find her way and do the right thing without having to ask. The ferry ride was so nice that for a while Junie forgot about being scared, and running, and what might happen to Petey if they gave him back to his father and mother. She took in all the strangeness of being on the water, the sights and sounds of the harbor, the movement of the ferry-boat under her feet, the smells of the sea.

She recognized the Statue of Liberty from a picture in a textbook she had seen at Sylvan Slopes, a feeling of stunned happiness coming over her; she hadn't really connected the picture with anything that actually existed, until now.

She thought, if I had time to take a hundred bus trips, I'll bet I'd see other things out of that book. Maybe they're all real and maybe they're all right around here some place. And then, standing on the deck of the ferryboat in the sunshine, it seemed to Junie that she understood all at once that the world was a beautiful place, that the sky was benign—a sheltering blue umbrella under which everyone could live at peace.

I love everybody in the world, she thought.

Petey most of all, of course.

Not sure what she would find at the end of the ferry ride, Junie bought three egg-salad sandwiches at the lunch counter below, wrapped them in a paper napkin, and put them in her coat pocket. The ferry came into its slip, bumping and sloshing—a scary time—and then Junie saw that the people were hurrying ashore.

She saw the policeman, too.

He was tall, and he looked enormous and frightening in his blue uniform. He was carefully looking at everyone who came off the ferryboat. Junie's first instinct was to duck back out of sight, to hide on the boat somewhere.

She actually turned to run, but then she saw that a man who worked on the boat—he was doing something with a big rope—was watching her. His eyes were dark and moved quickly; they ran all over Junie as if they were memorizing her appearance. She was choking with fear now, and her arms were so leaden it seemed that Petey was going to fall out of them and tumble to the deck.

Suddenly the man finished what he was doing with the rope and came over quickly—Junie was rooted to the deck—and he said, "Can I help you with the baby, ma'am? He's kind of heavy, isn't he?" And he took Petey easily in his big hands and Petey clung to the front of the man's leather jacket.

They walked up the ramp that connected the boat with the dock and went right past the policeman, who gave them an interested glance, as if he'd been told to look over *all* babies—only of course this wasn't the right one. Then by some miracle they were in another big room, almost a duplicate of the one Junie had waited in on the other side of the water.

The man tickled Petey under the chin, then gave him back to Junie. "He's sure a nice big husky kid," the man said.

"Thank you so much."

"It's not far to your bus now."

"Thank you so much," Junie repeated.

The man gave off a sea smell of tar and salt, and the sound of his voice was quiet and kind; the way he handled Petey showed how strong he was, and yet how gentle. Junie thought, I'll never see this man again, and there was a sudden ache around her heart, and a quick stinging of tears in her eyes as he turned away.

She had always wondered how you met a man, how you got acquainted with a man—the way Mrs. Arnold must have gotten acquainted with Mr. Arnold; and now she thought, it must be *this* way. Only for me it doesn't count, because I can't stop, I have to look after Petey.

At the end of the bus line she began to walk. She didn't stop until she found a nice beach. She put Petey down on his blanket and sat beside him. Petey seemed tired now; he looked at the ocean, at the waves rolling in, but he didn't try to find things in the sand and he didn't even want to taste his fingers. After a while he slid over to lie down, and went to sleep.

A woman and three boys of various sizes came to the beach. The boys ran and hollered, and the woman read a book. Junie would have liked to talk to the woman, but the woman wore an air of indifference, of defending herself by this indifference, as if the boys had worn away any ability she had to put up with other people. By and by the biggest boy yelled, "Mom, we're going around to the other beach and look at the old boat."

"Go ahead," the mother yelled back, not looking up from her book.

When the woman and the boys left, Junie went to see what was to be seen on the other beach. She rounded a crumbling small headland and came to a crescent of sand with an old rowboat lying on it. This beach was much more sheltered than theirs, so she picked up the sleeping baby and took him to it.

She investigated the boat. There didn't seem much wrong with it, except that it lay tipped on its side and there was a lot of sand in it, mixed with some orange peels and seaweed. Junie experimented out of curiosity, trying to straighten the boat. She was surprised at how heavy it was, and was unable to move it.

When Petey woke up she fed him one of the sandwiches. She built a sand castle for him, and let Petey knock it down. She took some seaweed out of his mouth.

At first there was just one siren, howling and whining far away, and Junie didn't pay any attention to it. In the city she had seen police cars on the avenue, and fire trucks, and she knew that the howling and whining came from one of these.

After a while, though, there were more sirens. They made Junie think of some sort of queer bird flying back and forth, emitting strange cries, hunting for something.

Hunting for something.

Junie scooped up the baby and the package of diapers, rushed to the rowboat, and crouched there, hiding.

It made a fine place to hide. The bow of the boat was turned a little so that the inside of the boat could not be seen from the bluff behind the beach. Junie listened to the sirens, now close, now far, and Petey chewed on one of the sandy orange peels. Though the air high above seemed to throb, to be filled with the noise of the sirens, right here there was a little island of stillness. She and Petey were shut away from the wind, from the sight of other eyes, from the howls given out by the strange hunting birds—from everything but the sun.

And the sun would not tell anyone where they were . . .

The sea turned gray, cold-looking. A fog began to gather, at first offshore like a misty wall hanging out of the sky, and then creeping slowly shoreward, so slowly that you couldn't see it coming. You smelled it first in the air—a wetness with a flavor of fish and salt.

Junie made a bed for the baby with her coat, snuggling him down so that the dampness and chill would not make his sniffles worse. She kissed each of his eyes to make them close, the way she had always done at the apartment, and Petey's fingers strayed out to tangle in her hair.

"Nice Petey!"

Lying beside him, she kissed the end of his nose.

"My Petey. My own, own, own Petey!" She spoke out loud, dreamily. No one could hear. No one could say, Stop it. And Miss Gombie and the Arnolds were far away.

After a while there were voices, echoing queerly in the fog from the top of the bluff. One man kept calling, "Hey, Joe. Over here," and after a while another man yelled, "Hell, there's nobody. It's a bum steer, that's all."

Junie slept, and when she woke she was shivering. The night

had come and the only paleness in all the dark was Petey's sleeping face. She tried to cuddle under the edge of the coat, to share a little of its warmth, and then suddenly she realized that when she had moved, the boat moved.

She experimented, puzzled, but it was true. When her weight shifted the boat rocked on its bottom.

"Rock, rock, old boat," she said aloud, wanting to laugh at the queerness, and then she stuck a hand over the side into the dark, and found cold water there. She sat up.

The fog must be thick, thick, thick—its wetness pressed against her face and filled her lungs. She stared, but her eyes found no prick of light in the night; it was like looking into a tunnel, or into a well, or like being shut in Miss Gombie's coat closet when you were bad.

"They can't find us now, Petey. We can stay all night in our boat. We'll sail away, even. Tomorrow we'll wake up and we'll be somewhere else."

She kissed Petey's forehead and rubbed his cheek with her cheek. Then she rocked and rocked the boat, but though it moved in a kind of trough, it never did sail away. Junie thought, I'll have to push it.

The voices were back at the top of the bluff now; a man was yelling about bringing the light. "Bring the damned thing over *here*!" And then there was a great moonlike glow, all gold and strongly shining. Junie, in the water beside the boat, was wet to her knees. The coldness, the force of the current, were startling.

A sudden sucking current pulled the boat away, off into the dark, and for a heart-stopping moment Junie thought that it had gone, taking Petey and leaving her stranded on the beach. But then, by a dim reflection from the big light beginning to swing back and forth at the top of the bluff, she saw the stern, dipping against the surf. She caught the rim of the boat and jumped in.

The current took them off quickly. Junie could tell how quickly by the way the big light on the bluff diminished through the fog. She sang softly to Petey and the surf slapped the hull and every once in a while the boat made a quick turnabout, end around end, that almost left her dizzy.

"We're sailing away, away. I'm all wet but I'll be dry," she sang. "By and by, Petey, by and by."

She had gotten dreadfully wet from the ocean—so wet that it took a while for her to understand that all the water was not coming off her clothes. Some of it was bubbling up through tiny broken places in the bottom of the boat.

She tried stuffing the edges of Petey's blanket into the broken places, and finally parts of her coat; but when she realized that these were not going to keep out the sea, she picked up the still-sleeping baby and stood, balancing herself against the boat's movement, holding Petey as high as she could, waiting, loving everybody, and remembering the sky as she had seen it from the deck of the ferryboat that morning.

PATRICIA HIGHSMITH

The Heroine

The girl was so sure she would get the job, she had unabashedly come out to Westchester with her suitcase. She sat in a comfortable chair in the living room of the Christiansens' house, looking in her navy blue coat and beret even younger than 21, and replied earnestly to their question.

"Have you worked as a governess before?" Mr. Christiansen asked. He sat beside his wife on the sofa, his elbows on the knees of his gray flannel slacks and his hands clasped. "Any references, I mean?"

"I was a maid at Mrs. Dwight Howell's home in New York for the last seven months." Lucille looked at him with suddenly wide gray eyes. "I could get a reference from there if you like . . . But when I saw your advertisement this morning I didn't want to wait. I've always wanted a place where there were children."

Mrs. Christiansen smiled, but mainly to herself, at the girl's enthusiasm. She took a silver box from the coffee table before her, stood up, and offered it to the girl. "Will you have one?"

"No, thank you. I don't smoke."

"Well," she said, lighting her own cigarette, "we might call them, of course, but my husband and I set more store by appearances than references . . . What do you say, Ronald? You told me you wanted someone who really liked children."

And fifteen minutes later Lucille Smith was standing in her room in the servants' quarters back of the house, buttoning the belt of a new white uniform. She touched her mouth lightly with lipstick.

"You're starting all over again, Lucille," she told herself in the mirror. "You're going to have a happy, useful life from now on,

110

and forget everything that was before."

But there went her eyes too wide again, as though to deny her words. Her eyes looked much like her mother's when they opened like that, and her mother was part of what she must forget. She must overcome that habit of stretching her eyes. It made her look surprised and uncertain, too, which was not at all the way to look around children. Her hand trembled as she set the lipstick down. She recomposed her face in the mirror, smoothed the starched front of her uniform.

There were only a few things like the eyes to remember, a few silly habits, really, like burning little bits of paper in ashtrays, forgetting time sometimes—little things that many people did, but that she must remember not to do. With practice the remembering would come automatically. Because she was just like other people (had the psychiatrist not told her so?), and other people never thought of them at all.

She crossed the room, sank onto the window seat under the blue curtains, and looked out on the garden and lawn that lay between the servants' house and the big house. The yard was longer than it was wide, with a round fountain in the center and two flagstone walks lying like a crooked cross in the grass. There were benches here and there, against a tree, under an arbor, that seemed to be made of white lace. A beautiful yard!

And the house was the house of her dreams! A white, two-story house with dark-red shutters, with oaken doors and brass knockers and latches that opened with a press of the thumb . . . and broad lawns and poplar trees so dense and high one could not see through, so that one did not have to admit or believe that there was another house somewhere beyond . . . The rain streaked Howell house in New York, granite pillared and heavily ornamented, had looked, Lucille thought, like a stale wedding cake in a row of other stale wedding cakes.

She rose suddenly from her seat. The Christiansen house was blooming, friendly, and alive! There were children in it. Thank God for the children! But she had not even met them yet.

She hurried downstairs, crossed the yard on the path that ran from the door, lingered a few seconds to watch the plump faun blowing water from his reeds into the rock pond . . . What was it the Christiansens had agreed to pay her? She did not remember and she did not care. She would have worked for nothing just to live in such a place.

Mrs. Christiansen took her upstairs to the nursery. She opened the door of a room whose walls were decorated with bright peasant designs, dancing couples and dancing animals, and twisting trees in blossom. There were twin beds of buff-colored oak, and the floor was yellow linoleum, spotlessly clean.

The two children lay on the floor in one corner, amid scattered crayons and picture books.

"Children, this is your new nurse," their mother said. "Her name is Lucille."

The little boy stood up and said, "How do you do," as he solemnly held out a crayon-stained hand.

Lucille took it, and with a slow nod of her head repeated his greeting.

"And Heloise," Mrs. Christiansen said, leading the second child, who was smaller, toward Lucille.

Heloise stared up at the figure in white and said, "How do you do."

"Nicky is nine and Heloise six," Mrs. Christiansen told her.

"Yes," Lucille said. She noticed that both children had a touch of red in their blond hair, like their father. Both wore blue overalls without shirts, and their backs and shoulders were sun-brown beneath the straps.

Lucille could not take her eyes from them. They were the perfect children of her perfect house. They looked up at her frankly, with no mistrust, no hostility. Only love, and some childlike curiosity.

". . . and most people do prefer living where there's more country," Mrs. Christiansen was saying.

"Oh, yes . . . yes, ma'am. It's ever so much nicer here than in the city."

Mrs. Christiansen was smoothing the little girl's hair with a tenderness that fascinated Lucille. "It's just about time for their lunch," she said. "You'll have your meals up here, Lucille. And would you like tea or coffee or milk?"

"I'd like coffee, please."

"All right, Lisabeth will be up with the lunch in a few minutes." She paused at the door. "You aren't nervous about anything, are you, Lucille?" she asked in a low voice.

"Oh, no, ma'am."

"Well, you mustn't be." She seemed about to say something else, but she only smiled and went out.

Lucille stared after her, wondering what that something else might have been.

"You're a lot prettier than Catherine," Nicky told her.

She turned around. "Who's Catherine?" Lucille seated herself on a hassock, and as she gave all her attention to the two children who still gazed at her, she felt her shoulders relax their tension.

"Catherine was our nurse before. She went back to Scotland because of the war. I'm glad you're here. We didn't like Catherine."

Heloise stood with her hands behind her back, swaying from side to side as she regarded Lucille. "No," she said, "we didn't like Catherine."

Nicky stared at his sister. "You shouldn't say that. That's what I said!"

Lucille laughed and hugged her knees. Then Nicky and Heloise laughed too.

A colored maid entered with a steaming tray and set it on the table in the center of the room. She was slender and of indefinite age. "I'm Lisabeth Jenkins, miss," she said shyly as she laid some paper napkins at three places.

"My name's Lucille Smith," the girl said.

"Well, I'll leave you to do the rest, miss. If you need anything else, just holler." She went out, her hips small and hard-looking under the blue uniform.

The three sat down to the table, and Lucille lifted the cover from the large dish, exposing three parsley-garnished omelets, bright yellow in the bar of sunlight that crossed the table. But first there was tomato soup for her to ladle out, and triangles of buttered toast to pass. Her coffee was in a silver pot, and the children had two large glasses of milk.

The table was low for Lucille, but she did not mind. It was so wonderful merely to be sitting here with these children, with the sun warm and cheerful on the yellow linoleum floor, on the table, on Heloise's ruddy face opposite her. How pleasant not to be in the Howell house! She had always been clumsy there. But here it would not matter if she dropped a pewter cover or let a gravy spoon fall in someone's lap. The children would only laugh.

Lucille sipped her coffee.

"Aren't you going to eat?" Heloise asked, her mouth already full.

The cup slipped in Lucille's fingers and she spilled half her coffee on the cloth. No, it was not cloth, thank goodness, but oilcloth. She could get it up with a paper towel, and Lisabeth would never know.

"Piggy!" laughed Heloise.

"Heloise!" Nicky admonished, and went to fetch some paper towels from the bathroom.

They mopped up together.

"Dad always gives us a little of his coffee," Nicky remarked as he took his place again.

Lucille had been wondering whether the children would mention the accident to their mother. She sensed that Nicky was offering her a bribe. "Does he?" she asked.

"He pours a little in our milk," Nicky went on, "just so we can see the color."

"Like this?" And Lucille poured a bit from the graceful silver spout into each glass.

The children gasped with pleasure. "Yes!"

"Mother doesn't like us to have coffee," Nicky explained, "but when she's not looking, Dad lets us have a little like you did. Dad says his day wouldn't be any good without his coffee, and I'm the same way. Gosh, Catherine wouldn't give us any coffee like that, would she, Heloise?"

"Not her!" Heloise took a long delicious draught from her glass which she held with both hands.

Lucille felt a glow rise from deep inside her until it settled in her face and burned there. The children liked her, there was no doubt of that.

She remembered now how often she had gone to the public parks in the city, during the three years she had worked as maid in various houses (to be a maid was all she was fit for, she used to think), merely to sit on a bench and watch the children play. But the children there had usually been dirty or foul-mouthed, and she herself had always been an outsider. Once she had seen a mother slap her own child across the face. She remembered how she had fled in pain and horror.

"Why do you have such big eyes?" Heloise demanded.

Lucille started. "My mother had big eyes too," she said deliberately, like a confession.

"Oh," Heloise replied, satisfied.

Lucille cut slowly into the omelet she did not want. Her mother had been dead three weeks now. Only three weeks and it seemed much, much longer. That was because she was forgetting, she thought, forgetting all the hopeless hope of the last three years, that her mother might recover in the sanatorium. But recover to what? The illness was something separate, something which had killed her.

It had been senseless to hope for a complete sanity which she knew her mother had never had. Even the doctors had told her that. And they had told her other things, too, about herself. Good, encouraging things they were, that she was as normal as her father had been.

Looking at Heloise's friendly little face across from her, Lucille felt the comforting glow return. Yes, in this perfect house, closed from all the world, she could forget and start anew.

"Are we ready for some dessert?" she asked.

Nicky pointed to her plate. "You're not finished eating."

"I wasn't very hungry," Lucille divided her dessert between them.

"We could go out to the sandbox now," Nicky suggested. "We always go just in the mornings, but I want you to see our castle."

The sandbox was in the back of the house in a corner made by a projecting ell. Lucille seated herself on the wooden rim of the box while the children began piling and patting like gnomes.

"I must be the captured princess!" Heloise shouted.

"Yes, and I'll rescue her, Lucille. You'll see!"

The castle of moist sand rose rapidly. There were turrets with tin flags sticking from their tops, a moat, and a drawbridge made of the lid of a cigar box covered with sand. Lucille watched, fascinated. She remembered vividly the story of Brian de Bois-Guilbert and Rebecca. She had read *Ivanhoe* through at one long sitting, oblivious of time and place just as she was now.

When the castle was finished, Nicky put half a dozen marbles inside it just behind the drawbridge. "These are good soldiers imprisoned," he told her. He held another cigar box lid in front of them until he had packed up a barrier of sand. Then he lifted the lid and the sand door stood like a *porte-cochère*.

Meanwhile Heloise gathered ammunition of small pebbles from the ground next to the house. "We break the door down and the good soldiers come down the hill across the bridge. Then I'm saved!"

"Don't tell her! She'll see!"

Seriously Nicky thumped the pebbles from the rim of the sandbox opposite the castle door, while Heloise behind the castle thrust a hand forth to repair the destruction as much as she could between shots, for besides being the captured princess she was the defending army.

Suddenly Nicky stopped and looked at Lucille. "Dad knows how to shoot with a stick. He puts the rock on one end and hits the other. That's balliska."

"Ballista," Lucille said.

"Golly, how did *you* know?"

"I read it in a book—about castles."

"Golly!" Nicky went back to his thumping, embarrassed that he had pronounced the word wrong. "We got to get the good soldiers out fast. They're captured, see? Then when they're released that means we can all fight together and *take the castle!*"

"And save the princess!" Heloise put in.

As she watched, Lucille found herself wishing for some real catastrophe, something dangerous and terrible to befall Heloise, so that she might throw herself between her and the attacker, and prove her great courage and devotion. She would be seriously wounded herself, perhaps with a bullet or a knife, but she would beat off the assailant. Then the Christiansens would love her and keep her with them always. If some madman were to come upon them suddenly now, someone with a slack mouth and bloodshot eyes, she would not be afraid for an instant.

She watched the sand wall crumble and the first good soldier marble struggled free and came wobbling down the hill. Nicky and Heloise whooped with joy. The wall gave way completely, and two, three, four soldiers followed the first, their stripes turning gaily over the sand.

Lucille leaned forward. Now she understood! She was like the good soldiers imprisoned in the castle. The castle was the Howell house in the city, and Nicky and Heloise had set her free. She was free to do good deeds. And now if only something would happen . . .

"O-o-ow!"

It was Heloise. Nicky had mashed one of her fingers against the edge of the box as they struggled to get the same marble.

Lucille seized the child's hand, her heart thumping at the sight of the blood that rose from many little points in the scraped flesh. "Heloise, does it hurt very much?"

"Oh, she wasn't supposed to touch the marbles in the first place!" Disgruntled, Nicky sat in the sand.

Lucille held her handkerchief over the finger and half carried her into the house, frantic lest Lisabeth or Mrs. Christiansen see them. She took Heloise into the bathroom that adjoined the nursery, and in the medicine cabinet found mercurochrome and gauze.

Gently she washed the finger. It was only a small scrape, and Heloise stopped her tears when she saw how slight it was.

"See, it's just a little scratch!" Lucille said, but that was only to calm the child. To her it was not a little scratch. It was a terrible thing to happen the first afternoon she was in charge, a catastrophe she had failed to prevent. She wished over and over that the hurt might be in her own hand, twice as severe.

Heloise smiled as she let the bandage be tied. "Don't punish Nicky," she said. "He didn't mean to do it. He just plays rough."

But Lucille had no idea of punishing Nicky. She wanted only to punish herself, to seize a stick and thrust it into her own palm.

"Why do you make your teeth like that?"

"I—I thought it might be hurting you."

"It doesn't hurt any more." And Heloise went skipping out of the bathroom. She leaped onto her bed and lay on the tan cover that fitted the corners and came all the way to the floor. Her bandaged finger showed startlingly white against the brown of her arm.

"We have to take our afternoon nap now," she told Lucille, and closed her eyes. "Goodbye."

"Goodbye," Lucille answered, and tried to smile.

She went down to get Nicky and when they came up the steps Mrs. Christiansen was at the nursery door.

Lucille blanched. "I don't think it's bad, ma'am. It—it's a scratch from the sandbox."

"Heloise's finger? Oh, no, don't worry, my dear. They're always getting little scratches. It does them good. Makes them more careful."

Mrs. Christiansen went in and sat on the edge of Nicky's bed. "Nicky, dear, you must learn to be more gentle. Just see how you frightened Lucille!" She laughed and ruffled his hair.

Lucille watched from the doorway. Again she felt herself an outsider, but this time because of her incompetence. Yet how different this was from the scenes she had witnessed in the parks!

Mrs. Christiansen patted Lucille's shoulder as she went out. "They'll forget all about it by nightfall."

"Nightfall," Lucille whispered as she went back into the nursery. "What a beautiful word!"

While the children slept, Lucille looked through an illustrated book of *Pinocchio*. She was avid for stories, any kind of stories, but most of all adventure stories and fairy tales. And at her elbow on the children's shelf there were scores of them. It would take her months to read them all. It did not matter that they were for children. In fact, she found that kind more to her liking, because such stories were illustrated with pictures of animals dressed up, and tables and houses and all sorts of things come to life.

Now she turned the pages of *Pinocchio* with a sense of contentment and happiness so strong that it intruded on the story she was reading. The doctor at the sanatorium had encouraged her reading, she remembered, and had told her to go to movies too. "Be with normal people and forget all about your mother's difficulties. . . ." (Difficulties, he had called it then, but all other times he had said "strain." Strain it was, like a thread, running through the generations. She had thought, through her.)

Lucille could still see the psychiatrist's face, his head turned a little to one side, his glasses in his hand as he spoke, just as she had thought a psychiatrist should look. "Just because your mother had a strain, there's no reason why you should not be as normal as your father was. I have every reason to believe you are. You are an intelligent girl, Lucille. Get yourself a job out of the city—relax, enjoy life. I want you to forget even the house your family lived in. After a year in the country—"

That, too, was three weeks ago, just after her mother had died in the ward. And what the doctor said was true. In this house where there were peace and love, beauty and children, she could feel the moils of the city sloughing off her like a snake's outworn skin. Already, in this one half day! In a week she would forget forever her mother's face.

With a little gasp of joy that was almost ecstasy she turned to the bookshelf and chose at random six tall, slender, brightly colored books. One she laid open, face down, in her lap. Another she opened and leaned against her breast. Still holding the rest in one hand, she pressed her face into *Pinocchio's* pages, her eyes half closed.

Slowly she rocked back and forth in the chair, conscious of nothing but her own happiness and gratitude. The chimes downstairs struck three times, but she did not hear them.

"What are you doing?" Nicky asked, his voice politely curious.

Lucille brought the book down from her face. When the meaning of his question struck her, she flushed and smiled like a happy but guilty child. "Reading!" she laughed.

Nicky laughed too. "You read awful close."

"Ya-yuss," said Heloise, who had also sat up.

Nicky came over and examined the books in her lap. "We get up at three o'clock. Would you read to us now? Catherine always read to us till dinner."

"Shall I read to you out of *Pinocchio*?" Lucille suggested, happy that she might possibly share with them the happiness she had gained from the first pages of its story. She sat down on the floor so they could see the pictures as she read.

Nicky and Heloise pushed their eager faces over the pictures, and sometimes Lucille could hardly see to read. She did not realize that she read with a tense interest that communicated itself to the two children, and that this was why they enjoyed it so much. For two hours she read, and the time slipped by almost like so many minutes.

Just after five Lisabeth brought in the tray with their dinner, and when the meal was over Nicky and Heloise demanded more reading until bedtime at seven. Lucille gladly began another book, but when Lisabeth returned to remove the tray, she told Lucille that it was time for the children's bath, and that Mrs. Christiansen would be up to say good night in a little while.

Mrs. Christiansen was up at seven, but the two children by that time were in their robes, freshly bathed, and deep in another story with Lucille on the floor.

"You know," Nicky said to his mother, "we've read all these books before with Catherine, but when Lucille reads them they seem like *new* books!"

Lucille flushed with pleasure. When the children were in bed, she went downstairs with Mrs. Christiansen.

"Is everything fine, Lucille? I thought there might be something you'd like to ask me about the running of things."

"No, ma'am, except . . . might I come up once in the night to see how the children are doing?"

"Oh, I wouldn't want you to break your sleep, Lucille. That's very thoughtful, but it's really unnecessary."

Lucille was silent.

"And I'm afraid the evenings are going to seem long to you. If you'd ever like to go to a picture in town, Alfred, that's the chauffeur, will be glad to take you in the car."

"Thank you, ma'am."

"Then good night, Lucille."

"Good night, ma'am."

Lucille went out the back way, across the garden where the fountain was still playing. And when she put her hand on the knob of her door, she wished that it was the nursery door, that it was eight o'clock in the morning and time to begin another day.

Still she was tired, pleasantly tired. How very pleasant it was, she thought, as she turned out the light, to feel properly tired in the evening (although it was only nine o'clock) instead of bursting with energy, instead of being unable to sleep for thinking of her mother or worrying about herself.

She remembered one day not so long ago when for fifteen minutes she had been unable to think of her name. She had run in panic to the doctor.

That was past! She might even ask Alfred to buy her a pack of cigarettes in town—a luxury she had denied herself for months.

She took a last look at the house from her window. The chintz curtains in the nursery billowed out now and then and were swept back again. The wind spoke in the nodding tops of the poplars like the high-pitched, ever-rippling voices of children.

The second day was like the first, except that there was no mishap, no scraped hand—and the third and the fourth. Regular and identical like the row of Nicky's lead soldiers on the playtable in the nursery. The only thing that changed was Lucille's love for the family and the children—a blind and passionate devotion which seemed to redouble each morning.

She noticed and loved many things: the way Heloise drank her milk in little gulps at the back of her throat, how the blond down on their backs swirled up to meet the hair on the napes of their necks, and when she bathed them the painful vulnerability of their bodies.

Saturday evening she found an envelope addressed to herself in the mailbox at the door of the servants' house. Inside was a blank sheet of paper and inside that a new $20 bill.

Lucille held it by its crisp edges. Its value meant nothing to her. To use it she would have to go to stores where other people were. What use had she for money if she were never to leave the Christiansen home? It would simply pile up, $20 each week. In a year's time she would have $1040, and in two years $2080. Eventually she might have as much as the Christiansens and that would not be right.

Would they think it very strange if she asked to work for nothing? Or for $10 perhaps?

She had to speak to Mrs. Christiansen, and she went to her the next morning. It was an inopportune time. Mrs. Christiansen was making up a menu for a dinner.

"It's about my salary, ma'am," Lucille began.

"Yes?" Mrs. Christiansen said in her pleasant voice.

Lucille watched the yellow pencil in her hand moving swiftly over the paper. "It's too much for me, ma'am."

The pencil stopped. Mrs. Christiansen's lips parted slightly in surprise. "You *are* such a funny girl, Lucille!"

"How do you mean—funny?" Lucille asked curiously.

"Well, first you want to be practically day and night with the children. You never even want your afternoon off. You're always talking about doing something 'important' for us, though what that could be I can't imagine. And now your salary's too much! We've never had a girl like you, Lucille. I can assure you, you're different!"

She laughed, and the laugh was full of ease and relaxation that contrasted with the tension of the girl who stood before her.

Lucille was rapt in the conversation. "How do you mean different, ma'am?"

"Why, I've just told you, my dear. And I refuse to lower your salary because that would be sheer exploitation. In fact, if you ever change your mind and want a raise—"

"Oh, no, ma'am . . . but I just wish there was something more I could do for you—and for the children."

"Lucille! You're working for us, aren't you? Taking care of our children. What could be more important than that?"

"But I mean something bigger—I mean more—"

"Nonsense, Lucille," Mrs. Christiansen interrupted. "Just because the people you were with before were not so—friendly as we are doesn't mean you have to work your fingers to the bone for us."

She waited for the girl to make some move to go, but still she stood by the desk, her face puzzled. "Mr. Christiansen and I are very well pleased with you, Lucille."

"Thank you, ma'am."

She went back to the nursery where the children were playing. She had not made Mrs. Christiansen understand. If she could just go back and explain what she felt, tell about her mother and her fear of herself for so many months, how she had never dared take a drink or even a cigarette . . . and how just being with the family in this beautiful house had made her well again . . . telling her all that might relieve her.

She turned toward the door, but the thought of disturbing her or boring her with her story, a servant girl's story, made her stop. So during the rest of the day she carried her unexpressed gratitude like a great weight in her breast.

That night she sat in her room with the light on until after twelve o'clock. She had her cigarettes now, and she allowed herself three in the evening, but even those three were sufficient to set her blood tingling, to relax her mind, to make her dream heroic dreams. And when the three cigarettes were smoked, and she would have liked another, she rose, very light in the head, and put the cigarette pack in her top drawer to close away temptation.

Just as she slid the drawer she noticed on her handkerchief box the $20 bill the Christiansens had given her. She took it now, and sat down again in her chair.

From the packet of matches she took one, struck it, and leaned it, burning end down, against the side of her ashtray. Slowly she struck matches one after another and laid them strategically to make a tiny, flickering, well controlled fire. When the matches were gone, she tore the pasteboard cover into little bits and dropped them in slowly. Finally she took the $20 bill and with some effort tore bits from it of the same size. These, too, she meted to the fire.

Mrs. Christiansen did not understand, but if she saw *this*, she might. Still *this* was not enough. Mere faithful service was not enough either. Anyone would give that, for money. She was different. Had not Mrs. Christiansen herself told her that?

Then she remembered what else she had said: "Mr. Christiansen and I are very well pleased with you, Lucille."

The memory of these words brought her up from her chair with an enchanted smile on her lips. She felt wonderfully strong and secure in her own strength of mind and her position in the household. *Mr. Christiansen and I are very well pleased with you, Lucille.* There was really only one thing lacking in her happiness. She had to prove herself in crisis.

If only a plague like those she had read of in the Bible . . . "And

it came to pass that there was a great plague over all the land."
That was how the Bible would say it. She imagined waters
lapping higher against the big house, until they swept almost into
the nursery. She would rescue the children and swim with them
to safety, wherever that might be.

She moved restlessly about the room.

Or if there came an earthquake . . . She would rush in among
falling walls and drag the children out. Perhaps she would go back
for some trifle, like Nicky's lead soldiers or Heloise's paint set,
and be crushed to death. Then the Christiansens would know her
devotion.

Or if there might be a fire. Anyone might have a fire. Fires were
common things and needed no wrathful visitations from the
upper world. There might be a terrible fire just with the gasoline
in the garage and a match.

She went downstairs, through the inside door that opened to
the garage. The tank was three feet high and entirely full, so that
unless she had been inspired with the necessity and importance of
her deed, she would not have been able to lift the thing over the
threshold of the garage and of the servants' house too.

She rolled the tank across the yard in the same manner as she
had seen men roll beer barrels and ashcans. It made no noise on
the grass and only a brief bump and rumble over one of the
flagstone paths, lost in the night.

No lights shone at any of the windows, but if they had, Lucille
would not have been deterred. She would not have been deterred
had Mr. Christiansen himself been standing there by the fountain,
for probably she would not have seen him. And if she had, was
she not about to do a noble thing?

She unscrewed the cap and poured some gasoline on a corner
of the house, rolled the tank farther, poured more against the
white shingles, and so on until she reached the far corner. Then
she struck her match and walked back the way she had come,
touching off the wet places. Without a backward glance she went
to stand at the door of the servants' house and watch.

The flames were first pale and eager, then they became yellow
with touches of red. As Lucille watched, all the tension that was
left in her, in body or mind, flowed evenly upward and was lifted

from her forever, leaving her muscles and brain free for the voluntary tension of an athlete before a starting gun. She would let the flames leap tall, even to the nursery window, before she rushed in, so that the danger might be at its highest.

A smile like that of a saint settled on her mouth, and anyone seeing her there in the doorway, her face glowing in the lambent light, would certainly have thought her a beautiful young woman.

She had lit the fire at five places, and these now crept up the house like the fingers of a hand, warm and flickering, gentle and caressing. Lucille smiled and held herself in check. Then suddenly the gasoline tank, having grown too warm, exploded with a sound like a cannon shot and lighted the entire scene for an instant.

As though this had been the signal for which she waited, Lucille went confidently forward.

CAROL CLEMEAU

Curses

"**P**rofessor Nielsen, are you serious?"

"What I want to know is, do these things work? Because I can think of a *couple* of people—"

"Doesn't it make you kind of nervous, giving an assignment like this? I mean, you being a teacher and all?"

Antonia grinned back at the six members of Latin Historical Prose 403.

"Yes, yes, and no, in that order," she said. "I am invariably serious, as you should know by now. Of course they work—would I waste your time and mine composing curses that didn't even work? And what do I have to be nervous about, universally admired, respected, and beloved as I am?" Antonia then glared ferociously at the six, daring them to deny the universality of the respect and affection she commanded. Two of them giggled.

In the back row, her blonde head resting against the green chalkboard, Jessica Hopewell did not giggle. She was looking, as usual, sceptical and a bit tired. She had apparently dedicated her senior year at the university to a pose of blasé world-weariness. This was rather incongruous with what Antonia knew of her in earlier years, but seniors did get into some odd moods as they moved toward the threshold of the Real World.

"The problem with Miss Nielsen," Jessica said, "is to figure out exactly what she's being serious *about* at any given moment. At this particular moment, my guess is she's dead serious about the hortatory subjunctive, or maybe *ut*-clauses with jussive verbs. Whether she's also serious about laying quartan fevers and migraine on people—who knows?"

The class laughed, and Antonia laughed with them. Six years of

126

teaching had convinced her it was not the irreverent students who threatened the effectiveness of a teacher or a class. Those who genuinely feared and distrusted learning typically had a respectful manner and no sense of humour whatever. It was the Jessicas of the academic world, flippant on occasion but fundamentally serious, that made teaching bearable, and occasionally even fun.

"The problem with Miss *Hopewell*," Antonia said, "is trying to put anything over on her, anything at all. And I thought I'd disguised my true purpose so cunningly, too. Yes, Jessica, you're right, it is an exercise in Latin prose composition. We've read enough curse tablets by now that you ought to be aware of some of the constructions most commonly used in them. The infamous Hortatory Subjunctive, the abominable Jussive Noun Clause, the—"

"But what if we also want them to work?" inquired the irrepressible Jessica.

"I have here," Antonia replied, "six small sheets of lead, the metal of earth." She produced them from her briefcase and handed them out, one to each student.

"Lead, as you know, is the most effective material for our purpose. So if yours doesn't work, Miss Hopewell, I'm afraid we'll have to attribute its failure to your Latin grammar, because the tablet itself is absolutely authentic."

The students fingered the lead curiously. The sheer physicality of the exercise, which Antonia had used with previous classes, always intrigued the students—the heavy, slightly greasy feel of the little metal sheet, and later the drag of the surface against stylus or nail-point as they scratched their laboriously assembled Latin words onto it after they had been approved on paper.

"Aside from using the correct writing material and getting your vocatives and imperatives right, there are a number of other things you can do to increase the potency of your curse. Does anyone remember what they are?"

"You can write the whole thing in Greek—Latin words, I mean, but in Greek letters," said a boy in the front row.

"Right," Antonia affirmed. "What else?"

"You can write backwards. Or you can do one of those what-chacallems—boo-something. The thing that means 'like an ox plowing furrows,' backwards and forwards in alternate lines."

"A boustrophedon, right. But have mercy on my failing eyesight, will you? Those things are murder to read."

"How about a few nice potent symbols?" another student suggested. "The Seven Mystic Vowels—or one of those guys wrapped in chains and serpents. I'm going to have lots of those in my curse."

"Fine, but put them on the *back* of the tablet, please. Otherwise you won't have room for all the Latin I know you're eager to write."

The bell rang, signaling the transition from ten- to eleven-o'clock classes. As the others filed out of the classroom clutching bookbags, notebooks, and clipboards, one of the girls stopped at Antonia's desk.

"Professor Nielsen," she said, "I just had this great idea! It's only three weeks till Hallowe'en, and our sorority always has a Haunted House as our annual fund-raiser. I was thinking that instead of a fortune-teller's booth, we could have a booth for getting a curse to lay on your worst enemy, or a love spell on somebody you're not having any luck with. You *said* that's the way they did it in antiquity. You'd go to a professional to get your curse drawn up properly, like a will or a contract. Get it done right, you said."

"And you think I'd be perfect for the role of the professional? Otherwise known as the witch?"

"Oh, no," protested the girl, "it's just that if *you* wrote the curses you wouldn't have to worry about any atrocities we might commit against the Latin language. The kids wouldn't know the difference, of course, but you'd feel better about it, wouldn't you, Professor?"

"Oh, definitely," said Antonia. "I wouldn't be able to sleep at night if I thought there were improper Passives Periphrastic wandering around loose. I'll think about it, Sandra."

After lunch on Wednesday Antonia settled down to read this year's crop of curses. Two students, predictably, had opted for love charms. "Make her do whatsoever I desire, let her touch no food and go without sleep for love of me, let her freeze and burn with desire for me" was the steamy burden of one. The other was more vindictive than amorous: "Let him be as a lump of coal, or a dry stick, or a dead thing, in the eyes of that bitch for whom he left me."

The other four students had composed variations on the cursing formulas they had encountered in the ancient tablets. One boy had enumerated the parts of his victim's body, from eyebrow to toenail, together with a form of mutilation or incapacitation appropriate to each. It made pretty gruesome reading, especially so soon after lunch.

Antonia shifted two nouns from the accusative into the dative case in the last of them, doctored an ailing subjunctive passive, and gave the author a B+.

With a now-for-the-dessert kind of feeling, she turned to Jessica Hopewell's curse.

She had been saving Jessica's paper till last, as she often did. Though not a Classics major—with hard-headed practicality Jessica had opted for Computer Science, in which she was said to be doing brilliantly—she was by far the best Latinist in the class, and reading her papers was a treat.

This one was no exception. Jessica, as usual, had taken a good deal more trouble over the assignment than anyone else in the class.

But aside from its technical correctness, the little exercise was oddly disturbing. Jessica had caught the tone of the ancient tablets almost too well—the mesmeric repetitions and parallelisms, the piling up of verbs of violence, the compulsive reiteration of the victim's name.

The victim. Suddenly Antonia realized what it was about Jessica's curse that had struck her as odd. Other members of the class seemed to have picked the objects of their spells or curses from among their immediate circle of friends and acquaintances— a roommate, a girl friend, in one case a hapless kid brother.

But Jessica—Antonia looked again to be sure, and there it was: *Iasonem Cornelium Giffordum quem peperit Helene.* Jason Cornelius Gifford, son of Helen. More commonly known as Jason C. Gifford, III, son of Gifford Enterprises.

Jake Gifford was currently in his fourth year as what Jessica herself had once called a B.N.O.C., or Bête Noire on Campus.

He was widely regarded as having caused more trouble, of more varieties, to more people, in a shorter time, than any other student in the university's long and otherwise distinguished history. He received poor, though just passing, grades in everything. He was ringleader of the most destructive faction of the most antisocial fraternity on campus, Gamma Alpha, unaffectionately nicknamed Gifford's Animals. His attitude toward women was often compared to that of Attila the Hun, with Attila's invariably adjudged the more enlightened.

He was also very, very rich. Gifford Hall, which now housed Anthropology and Sociology, had been donated by his grandfather to prevent the expulsion of Jake's father, who had recently endowed an Institute of Ecological Studies to prevent the expulsion of Jake. Endowing things was what Jake liked to refer to as one of his clan's "fine old family traditions."

It was axiomatic with the Giffords that real scandal—that is, scandal unfixable by blandishment, threat, or endowment—was to be strictly avoided as detrimental to the family and corporate image. This circumspection had reference primarily to matters academic and sexual. Naturally it did not extend to petty financial affairs such as fines, damages, and personal debts. Jake therefore had considerable leeway in which to exercise his talent for trouble-making before he felt the tug of the parental tether.

Sexual indiscretion was less of a problem than might be supposed, because nowadays there were barely enough unregenerate masochists among the female half of the student body to keep Jake precariously supplied. Or as Jake himself was said to have put it, "It's a good thing I'm graduating in June, because the quality of the womanhood around here sure has gone to hell."

That Jessica Hopewell was, or had ever been, one of those drawn into Jake's orbit—even briefly—was inconceivable. Yet there was his name, all three of his names, in Jessica's firm hand, in the middle of Jessica's curse.

A joke, perhaps. But as a joke Jessica's paper was feeble, a cheap shot at an obvious target, and Jessica simply didn't have that kind of mind. If she had meant to lampoon the already much-lampooned Jake, no reader of her curse would have been in any doubt about it. She would have zeroed in on his all too well known vices—his arrogance, his lasciviousness, his intellectual dimness. She would have been devastatingly specific, probably indecent, and extremely funny.

But Jessica's curse was not funny. It contained the usual array of violent yet vague verbs (crush . . . break utterly . . . overwhelm and utterly slay . . . strangle . . . bind him, break him), verbs that lacked the sting of personal reference that would have raised them to the level of satire.

Telling herself sternly that all this fruitless conjecture was no more than an excuse to put off grading some baby-Greek quizzes, Antonia was about to lay Jessica's paper back on the pile with the others when the last line of the curse caught her eye. *Let my enemy's tongue be mute against me, and powerless. . .*

That too struck Antonia as odd, but she resolutely refused to speculate further and turned to the quizzes.

Twenty minutes later there was a knock on her office door.

Jessica Hopewell was looking even wearier than usual, and this time Antonia thought it was not a pose. She seemed anxious as well as tired. Her left arm, wrapped around an assortment of legal pads and spiralbound notebooks, was stiff with tension. Her right hand was hidden in the pocket of her battered khaki jacket. Antonia would have been willing to bet it was clenched into a tight fist.

"Miss Nielsen?" The girl's voice was wary. "I know this sounds funny, but could I have my paper back? I've written another one." She pulled a sheet hastily out of one of the notebooks and thrust it at Antonia.

As a general rule it was hard enough to elicit *one* paper from a student. To be offered a second as replacement for one that had already ben awarded an A was without precedent.

"I'm afraid I don't understand, Jessica," Antonia said. "There was nothing wrong with your first paper. In fact, I gave you an A on it."

Jessica squirmed uncomfortably. "It's just that I had a better idea after I turned that one in."

Antonia looked at her questioningly.

"I changed the—the victim. I mean, Jake Gifford's such a cheap shot. A cliché, practically. I mean people are always doing take-offs and things about him."

Antonia pulled Jessica's paper out of the pile and held it out to her. The girl seized it nervously and stuffed it into a notebook together with the one intended as its replacement.

"A person's got to have *some* standards, in humour if nothing else." She tried unsuccessfully to make it sound like a joke.

"The assignment was to compose a Latin curse, Jessica, not a joke," Antonia said. "And that is what you did. Your paper was not to tell me whatever it is you're trying so hard not to conceal?"

Antonia's steady gaze was too much for her. Jessica grinned sheepishly and dropped into the chrome-and-vinyl chair which was the only free surface in the cluttered office. For the first time since she had entered, Jessica Hopewell looked her usual self. Some internal dam had apparently given way and let out the deviousness and the nervousness that were so unlike her.

"I should just have taken the stupid paper back and kept my mouth shut, right?"

"I gather it's something to do with Jake Gifford?"

"Partly, yes. But I'd better start with the other part, because Jake only comes into it later. It began last May, during exam week. I had four finals in two days, and by the end of the first day I was afraid I wasn't going to make it through the second."

"But with four exams in two days you could have applied for a deferment on one."

"I know, I know. But I'd never done that and I suppose I was trying to prove something. Juniors can get sort of cocky at times, have you noticed? Anyway, by the time I realized I needed a deferment it was too late to ask for one."

Antonia, who had been searching her memory for anything out of the ordinary concerning last spring's exam period, suddenly thought she saw what the girl was leading up to. "Oh, Jessica, you *didn't.*"

"Yes I did, Miss Nielsen. The fourth exam was your Greek final, and I cheated on it—super-detailed cribsheet and all."

"But you'd been getting A's in that course all along!"

"Oh, I knew the material all right, or I would have if I hadn't been so exhausted. I might have made it—it was just that I couldn't be sure I would. And I just can't afford that kind of uncertainty, Miss Nielsen."

"Now hold on, Jessica. If every student who wasn't certain of getting an A refused to take exams—"

"Yeah, I know, Miss Nielsen. It seems wrong to me too now, but at the time all I could think of was how stupid it would be to risk everything I'd worked for just because for one moment I'd been too conceited to admit I might need a little extra time to rest and study for my last exam."

"Risk everything?"

Once again Jessica looked sheepish. "Oh, I suppose I was being a little melodramatic. But—there was the Woolrich."

Ah, yes, the Woolrich. Antonia had momentarily forgotten the high-paying, high-prestige, high-pressure Woolrich Fellowship. Awarded only once every four years, it relieved the recipient of all financial anxiety for the last two years of his or her undergraduate career and the first two of graduate school, and in this respect was a dream come true for the student and her or his family. But it made correspondingly heavy demands upon the Fellow. Though its provisions were couched in a lot of quasi-legal jargon, what they amounted to was the requirement that the Woolrich Fellow maintain a virtually straight-A average in all courses for all four years.

And Jessica Hopewell was the current Woolrich Fellow. Antonia was beginning to get the picture.

"You cheated on an exam you had a pretty good chance of getting an A on anyway because you were tired and under-prepared and even the possibility of a lower grade was more than you could face."

"The loss of the *fellowship* was more than I could face, Miss Nielson." The girl's voice was much calmer now but deadly serious. "Without that fellowship I wouldn't have been able to study the way I have, without distractions and without squandering my energy on details like staying alive and paying tuition. I wouldn't be the student I am, wouldn't have the graduate-school prospects I have, wouldn't have the same future ahead of me."

Antonia gazed at her for a long moment. Jessica's eyes met hers unflinchingly. "I'm expected to report a thing like this," Antonia said at last.

"Yes, I know," said Jessica."I think that must be why I came. I wanted it to be you."

"I don't understand."

"You're forgetting Jake."

"Yes, what *does* Jake have to do with this? I assumed that you found him a convenient target for your curse. Surely there's nothing more to it than that?"

"I'm afraid there is, Miss Nielsen. Of course there's nothing 'between' us in the romantic sense. I haven't fallen quite *that* low. But there is a bond of sorts between us."

Jessica seemed to brace herself, clutched her notebooks a little closer, and sat a little straighter in the chrome-and-vinyl chair. "By the time that last exam was over, what with exhaustion and guilt feelings and plain fear, I was feeling pretty spacy. I went staggering back to the dorm, thinking about what to do with the damn cribsheet, and I tripped and fell and dropped everything I was carrying. And suddenly there was Jake looming over me, laughing and making gallant remarks about broads not being as graceful as they used to be. He did help me pick up my books and papers and stuff, but while he was doing it he found the cribsheet." She paused and took a deep breath.

"For a long time he just stared at it, with a look like the one I imagine on Mephistopheles' face at the moment he's certain he has Faust in his clutches. Only Jake's face is fatter. Then he folded the paper up and put it in his shirt pocket and walked away without a word."

"But you've heard from him since, I gather."

"Yes, but not for almost four months. It was in early September, a couple of weeks after school started. I was just beginning to hope he'd forgotten about the paper, or never really meant to use it, when he phoned. Most of the rest you can imagine for yourself, I expect."

"He's—blackmailing you." Antonia found it painful even to pronounce the word. The girl nodded miserably. "But what *for*? He's already got more money than he knows what to do with.

Surely he's not making like a Victorian melovillain and forcing you to share his loathsome embraces?"

Jessica smiled without much conviction. "No, though I'm sure he's capable of it. There's a certain mad logic to what he *is* getting out of me, though. Some people might even think it was—funny." Jessica almost choked on the last word.

"He's making me do what I do best—write term papers for him. He's a rotten student, and good grades are the one thing his money won't buy him. Oh, I know you can buy term papers out of catalogues, but this is safer, more *individualized* as Jake puts it—and classier. Jake always goes first class."

Antonia was thinking very hard. Finally she said, "Your idea, I take it, is that I should turn you over to the Discipline Committee, which will try you, find you guilty of cheating, and duck you three times in the village pond. Your conscience will thereupon be shriven, and you will also be in a position to wreak a terrible vengeance upon Jake Gifford. Of course, your career will be destroyed, but no doubt that is a small price to pay for revenge and a clear conscience."

Jessica was looking a little dazed, as if the conversation was taking a turn she hadn't anticipated. "You make it sound as if I had some alternative, Miss Nielsen. My only options now, as far as I can see, are to be reported by you, or by Jake. I won't write his damn papers for him, and that's the only thing that would have kept his mouth shut."

"Have you thought about what you'll do to Jake?"

"As soon as they're through with me, I'll haul *him* in front of the Discipline Committee and tell them what he tried to do. I'll make damn sure they call it by its rightful name too—blackmail."

"But what evidence do you have, Jessica? Have you actually written any of these infamous papers? Do you have a shred of concrete proof of what he's been up to?"

Antonia had never actually seen anyone go pale with anger before. She let it sink in for a long minute before she continued. "That's an interesting color your face is turning, Jessica, but let's not panic just yet. I think I have an idea."

It took nearly twenty minutes of elucidation, expostulation, and exhortation before Antonia could push the girl gently out the door and aim her in a homeward direction. Jessica Hopewell was still shaking her head in disbelief as she left the Humanities Building, but there was a gleam of purpose in her eye which had not been there when she arrived at Antonia's door.

On days when a major paper is due, the atmosphere in a classroom changes subtly.Those students who have completed the assignment look less alert than usual, having had little or no sleep the night before. Those who have not written the paper look more alert than usual, some hoping to convey the impression that they're really terrifically interested in the subject and their failure to do what they were asked to do was attributable to circumstances beyond their control, others aiming for an air of sophisticated nonchalance indicating that such mundane considerations as deadlines, academic requirements, and the teacher's convenience are below them.

Antonia was familiar with both of these attitudes and their permutations, and as a rule paid little attention to the gradual accumulation of multicolored folders and stapled and paperclipped manuscripts before her. Today, however, was different. She found herself waiting with considerable anxiety for the arrival of one student and one paper in particular.

He arrived at last, tossed a kelly-green celluloid folder onto her desk, and betook himself to his customary place in the far back corner of the lecture hall. There he flopped into a seat with the look of bored insouciance that seldom left his rather petulantly good-looking face.

Antonia breathed more easily and launched into the day's lecture, which was one of her favorites. She called it The Great Cheaters of Greek Mythology.

"The ancient Greeks," she began, "loved a good swindle. You have only to recall the gleeful larcenies of the infant god Hermes, the wiles of Odysseus 'renowned among men for his craftiness,' the undetectable thieving of Autolycus, whose name means Lone Wolf—"

The fifty-minute hour passed quickly. When the last student had left, Antonia bundled the term papers into a manageable armload and lugged them to her office. There she rifled hastily through the stack till she came to the green celluloid folder.

She found what she was looking for on page nine. She read it, nodded approvingly, and replaced the paper in the middle of the pile. The faint smile that played about her lips as she leaned back in her chair was by no means one of Christian charity. It partook rather of the pagan notion that an enemy who tries to screw you is a fair target for any retaliation your ingenuity may suggest.

Antonia of the Many Wiles, she thought to herself. That has a nice ring to it.

Four nights later Professor Nielsen appeared on Fraternity Row, walking her big grey Afghan hound, Nike. Although their evening perambulations were a familiar sight around the university, it was unusual to find them on this side of the campus. Their preferred walk centered around the University Museum several blocks to the north where there was more open space for Nike to stretch her legs in.

This evening, however, Nike (who at heart was something of a clown) was at her most businesslike and dignified. She trotted briskly at Antonia's side, looking neither to the right nor to the left, disdaining the enticements of unfamiliar shrubbery and crunchy autumn leaves. She seemed to sense that there was more important business afoot than the mere vulgar investigation of bushes and lamp posts.

Antonia herself, though she was doing a fair job of looking relaxed and casual, was beginning to worry. This was the third night in a row they had toured this sector of the campus, and sooner or later someone was bound to ask what they were doing there.

She saw him just as he turned into Fraternity Row from Higginbotham Drive. Tightening her grip on Nike's leash, Antonia strode purposefully toward him.

Jake Gifford was handsome in a fashion-ad sort of way that Antonia found far less attractive than honest homeliness. His massive neck, rugged jaw, and broad shoulders already hinted—at least to the prejudiced observer—of premature flab not far in the future.

"Mr. Gifford," she said when the distance between them had

narrowed to about five yards.

"Evening, Ms. Nielsen." Jake was the kind of sexist who is religious in his use of anti-sexist jargon. "Nice night for a stroll, isn't it?"

Antonia said, "I'd like a word with you, Mr. Gifford."

Jake looked puzzled, but his prep-school manners never faltered. "Sure thing, Ms. Nielsen. Shall I come see you sometime tomorrow?"

"No, Mr. Gifford, I want to talk to you right now."

Antonia fell into step beside him, heading toward the Gamma Alpha house. Jake looked even more puzzled.

"I've been looking over the paper you wrote. Or perhaps I should say the paper you handed in." She paused for a moment to let that sink in. "I was particularly interested in what you had to say on page nine about Hermes as the embodiment of the business ethic." Another pause, this time to watch the expression on Jake's face. The interesting thing was that there was no expression on his face.

"That entire passage, Mr. Gifford, was lifted direct and unaltered from Norman O. Brown's *Hermes the Thief*. There are," Antonia added with relish, "a couple of people on the Discipline Committee at the moment who are absolutely intransigent on the subject of plagiarism."

They had reached the Gamma Alpha house, but Jake Gifford showed no inclination to turn in at the neat white-picket gate. There was no lack of expression now on his blandly handsome countenace. Anger, fear, and frustration struggled for dominance there, though there was no clear victory when finally, through clenched teeth, he said, "I know nothing about any such passages being in my paper."

"I realize that. Still, it's hardly a line of argument you can pursue very far in front of the Discipline Committee, is it? Sooner or later it seems likely that someone on the committee will ask how it's possible that these plagiarized pages could have crept into a paper which you allegedly wrote without your knowledge. And the answer to *that* question would involve you in even hotter water, wouldn't it, Mr. Gifford?"

"Maybe so, *Professor*." The heir to Gifford Enterprises made it sound like a dirty word. "But someone else'd get scalded along with me."

"That is a dilemma, isn't it?" said Antonia thoughtfully. "Of course," she said, "There is another possibility."

Jake glared at her. "Yeah?" he said sullenly. "Like what?"

"If a certain piece of property were returned to our mutual friend, I believe I could see my way to overlooking the irregularities in the paper you submitted to me."

"She told you about that?"

"I honestly don't think you have much choice, Mr. Gifford. Given the probable reaction of your esteemed father to a scandal of this mag—"

"I could expose *both* of you, you know!" Jake exploded."I could destroy you too, *Professor*!"

Antonia had been wondering how long it would take him to figure out that her career, as well as Jessica's and his own, was at stake. "I realize that, Mr. Gifford," she said, "but I don't think you will. Revenge may be sweet, but it is also extremely expensive just now, from your point of view. I'd like your answer, please."

"All right, damn it! I'll bring you the paper first thing tomorrow morning!"

"Not good enough, Mr. Gifford. There are more photocopiers on this campus than telephones. In all probability there's one in every fraternity house. Why do you think I've been skulking about like this for the past three nights? You'll bring it to me now, and here. I'll give you exactly sixty seconds from the time you enter the front door of the Gamma Alpha house to put that paper into my hands. Sixty seconds out of my sight, Mr. Gifford, no more."

"All right," Jake muttered, "I'll get you the goddamn crib. Probably break my goddamn neck doing it, too."

He didn't, of course, even though he made the sprint in and out of the Gamma Alpha house in just under fifty-three seconds. As he turned to leave, after thrusting a rumpled bit of paper at her, Antonia said, "There's just one more thing, Mr. Gifford."

He turned back, scowling.

"I'll be needing a proper Mythology paper from you. I could let you have, let's see—one week to get it in."

"But you said—" Jake protested indignantly.

"I said I would overlook the improprieties of your first paper. I never said I would evaluate that paper as if it were a legitimate piece of work. One has," she added virtuously, "one's professional ethics to think of." Antonia of the Many Wiles smiled sweetly at Jake's purple face.

Pi Epsilon Tau's Haunted House was a great success that year. Something new had been added to the usual creaking coffin lids, bloodcurdling shrieks and groans, and disgusting cobwebby things that brushed your cheek in the dark. Two of the sisters, technical theater majors, had concocted a sort of grotto, dimly lit and smoky with incense, its entrance adorned with hand-lettered mottoes:

ANCIENT CURSES   ABSOLUTELY
(TABELLAE DEFIXIONUM)   AUTHENTIC

LOVE CHARMS   GUARANTEED 100%
ALSO A SPECIALTY   EFFECTIVE
     OR YOUR DENARII BACK

ZAP YOUR ENEMY
BEFORE
HE/SHE ZAPS YOU!

The interior, as far as one could tell in the prevailing murk, was draped with gauze, spray-can cobwebs, and the lead curse tablets created by Latin 403 and generously loaned (according to another placard) by Professor Antonia Nielsen.

The sorceress who presided over this bizarre little shop was, of course, Jessica Hopewell.

Antonia arrived at the Pi Ep house shortly before midnight, left Nike on the front porch to bask in the attentions of the usual throng of admiring undergraduates, and entered the house. The Cursing Booth was just inside the door and obviously well patronized.

Peering out through the gauze draperies in the mouth of the grotto was the laurel-wreathed head of Jessica Hopewell. Cackling gleefully, the head inquired, "Is their another citizen who desires the services of Domina Canidia? If so, let him step forth and—"Suddenly catching sight of Antonia, the head gave an incongruous giggle and said cheerfully, "Oh, hi, Miss Nielsen! What are you doing here?"

"Could I speak to you for a moment, Domina? I won't keep your clients waiting long."

"*Certe, certe,*" intoned the head, resuming its thaumaturgic character. "*Ini in speluncam meam, obsecro,*" An unseen hand swept the drapes aside and Antonia entered.

"What can I do for you?" asked Jessica when they were alone. "Are you having trouble with a dean or something? I can whip you up a *defixio* that will blow him away in no time." Jessica seemed to have recovered her normal high spirits rather quickly after her flirtation with professional disaster.

"I'm not a customer, Jessica. I've come—" Antonia glanced around in the classic gesture of melodramatic suspiciousness "—to warn you!"

"Warn me?"

"Yes," Antonia went on in a conspiratorial whisper, "about these curses and spells. You must be *very careful* with them. So much power placed in the hands of one so young—" She shook her head dubiously.

"Miss Nielsen, what are you talking about?"

"Well," said Antonia, "considering what that curse of yours has done to Jake Gifford, I think you must have some sort of affinity for these things and I only hope *I* never get on the wrong side of you."

"What's happened to Jake?"

"The University Clinic is calling it mono. Worst case they've seen in years, they say. But to anyone who's read the Hopewell Curse—isn't that it, hanging over their next to the bunch of garlic?—to anyone who's read it, it's perfectly obvious that what ails the poor boy is *not* monoucleosis."

Jessica smiled and took the little sheet of lead from the hook where it hung amidst bunches of garlic, chicken bones, and aerosol cobwebs. In her Canidia voice she chanted, *"Send him fever and chill, sweats and shiverings quartan, tertian and quotidian . . . let his head pain him, his forehead, his chest, his stomach.* By Hecate, you're right, Miss Nielsen, it *does* sound like mono. But it was you who fulfilled the last part." Her forefinger hunted the words scratched into the lead. *"Let my enemy's tongue be mute against me and powerless to defend him, and let his malice be of no avail against me, and empty."*

JESSICA'S CURSE

Kataxin qui es Egipto magnus daemon, tere contere confringe Iasonem Cornelium Giffordum quem peperit Helene; Trabaxian omnipotens daemon, trade Plutoni praeposito mortuorum et si forte te contempserit et rideat de te et exsultetur tibi vince peroccide eum Iasonem Cornelium Giffordum quem peperit Helene; Nokhthiriph cogens daemon, trade illum febri frigori sudoribus obripilationibus quartanis tertians cottidianis, et si forte occansionem invenerit praefocato eum in thermis in viis in quocumque loco; Bibirixi fortissime daemon, compedi frange filium canis, et doleat illi caput frons pectus venter; Rikourith agilissime daemon in Egipto, inimici mei lingua adversus me ommutescat nec illum defendere possit, nec valeat malitia illius contra me sed vana sit.

Translation

Kataxin, who art in Egypt a mighty demon, crush and utterly crush and break utterly Jason Cornelius Gifford whom Helen bore; Trabaxian, demon omnipotent, surrender him to Dis who is set in judgment over the dead, and if perchance he contemn thee and deride thee and make mock of thee, overwhelm and utterly slay Jason Cornelius Gifford whom Helen bore; Nokthiriph, demon compelling, send him fever and chill, sweats and shiverings quartan, tertian and quotidian, and if perchance he find means of recovery strangle him, in the streets, in the public baths, in whatsoever place; Bibirixi, demon most powerful, bind and break the son of a dog, let his head pain him, his forehead, his chest, his stomach; Rikourith, most nimblest of demons in Egypt, let my enemy's tongue be mute against me and powerless to defend him, and let his malice be of no avail against me, and empty.

MIRIAM ALLEN deFORD

Danger—Women at Work

"Eat your egg, Paulie," Edna said. "You'll make daddy late."

"Today I *want* to go to school," remarked little Paul virtuously. "I'm going to be a nomitor."

"Monitor, darling Rick, will you be home early?"

"If I can. It's Friday, you know—the Jenks payroll is getting so large it takes hours to handle it. I can remember when it was only about $10,000, and now it's nearer $100,000—pretty good for a town the size of this one, isn't it?"

"And *my* husband the cashier of the only bank!" said Edna proudly.

"I'd be a smaller frog in a bigger puddle."

The front doorbell rang.

"Good Lord!" Richard exclaimed. "That's not Julia already, is it?"

"Heavens, no—she won't be here for an hour at least."

"What's she want this time?"

"Now, that's not nice, Rick. Paulie, run and open the door, will you, dear? If it's somebody selling something, tell him mother's too busy right now."

Richard smiled apologetically.

"Sure, honey, I know—Julia's your best friend. But she makes me nervous. She always snaps me up so quick."

"Julia's a wonderful friend," said Edna firmly. "And anyway, all she wants today is some advice about clothes. She's—"

Paulie was back.

"It's three men," he announced. "They want daddy."

"Three? What on—at this hour?"

"They said Mr. Fairchild."

143

"Okay. I'll go see. Finish your breakfast, Paulie, if you want to be dropped off at school. I'm leaving in exactly twelve minutes."

There were three men, all right, one tall and thin, the others shorter and stockier. Through the front door Paulie had left open, Richard could see their sedan parked outside, next to his own coupé.

"Mr. Fairchild?" inquired the tall one pleasantly. "Can we talk to you for a minute?"

Richard led the way to the living-room, a bit embarrassed to discover he was still holding a piece of toast. He laid it surreptitiously on the table by the telephone.

"What can I do for you?" he asked. "If it's business, we'd better discuss it at the bank. I'm pretty nearly due there now."

"It's business," the spokesman said quietly.

Richard found himself looking into the muzzle of a revolver levelled at his head.

"What the—" His voice became a whisper.

"Don't get excited. Call your wife and kid in here."

"Edna," Richard croaked. It wasn't necessary—Edna stood in the doorway, Paulie clinging to her. One of the two stocky men had them covered. At a nod from the leader, the other stocky man shut and locked the front door, then went through the dining-room and kitchen to guard the back one.

Richard tried to collect his thoughts. It was all too sudden. All he could think was that they didn't look like robbers; they were neatly dressed, clean and shaved, and the tall, thin man—the others hadn't spoken—talked like an educated man.

"Be quiet and listen, and nobody will get hurt," the spokesman said in the same calm tone. "We've got this all worked out to the last detail—we've been months at it. Do as we tell you, and the whole thing will go through like clockwork. It's no skin off your nose—the money's insured and you're only a salaried employee anyway, no matter what your title is."

"What are you going to do to my husband?" Edna cried.

"Nothing that will harm him—if he plays ball." The leader turned to her politely but his finger remained steady on the trigger. Richard glanced at Paulie. The boy stood with his mouth open, too fascinated to be scared.

"I'm going to give you the entire procedure, so you'll know exactly what's what. Mr. Fairchild, you're going with me to the bank in my car. You'll open up and let me in, with two more of us who are waiting there now. You've got seven employees—I know them all and just when they're due at work. We're going to lock them all up, as they come in—you first—in the Board of Directors' room, and keep you there for an hour."

"Why?" asked Richard hoarsely. Involuntarily his eyes darted to the telephone.

"Because it'll be an hour before the time-clock releases the vault," said the tall man suavely, "and that's where the big money is—the money for the Jenks payroll. When we've got that and are ready for our getaway, the last of us out will unlock the door of the Board of Directors' room. Then you can phone anybody you want. We'll have the licence numbers of our car changed by then—so you needn't look at the ones we have now, when you leave here. We'll have transferred to another car, anyway, long before the police can find this one.

"But if anybody so much as touches the phone in the Board of Directors' room before we let you know we're finished, we'll know it—we'll have an extension open and be listening. It's the only way you could get word outside—the windows are too high. I repeat—if anyone touches that phone, one of our men will phone the two men I'm leaving here . . . Now, I'm sure you're going to be sensible about this, Mr. Fairchild. Because if we *do* have to notify our men, they'll shoot Mrs. Fairchild and your son before they leave."

Richard stared, white-faced.

The tall man glanced again at Edna and half smiled.

"And I know Mrs. Fairchild's going to be sensible too, and not make any foolish moves to try to rescue you. But we won't put temptation in her way; as soon as you and I have left, my friends here will tie her and the boy up. They won't be hurt, but they won't be able to get near the doors or windows, or this phone, either."

There was a sick silence. It was Paulie who broke it.

"But I *gotta* get to school today!" he wailed. "I'm going to be a nomiator!"

Thank heaven, Edna thought wildly, for those blood-and-thunder TV shows, after all! If they did nothing else, they made this into a game in which a threat of murder didn't terrify or even intimidate a seven-year-old.

"Sorry, son." The leader smiled at him affably. "You'll be a hero when you go to school this afternoon, and that will be much more fun."

"And don't *you* try to be any hero, Richard Fairchild!" Edna rapped out suddenly. "I want a live husband. Do as the man says."

"You're a very sensible lady," the tall man approved. "Come on, Mr. Fairchild, let's go."

Richard opened his mouth to speak, then shut it again. He and Edna exchanged a long look. Then, with the gun prodding his back, he reopened the front door.

"Do you have to tie Paulie up too?" Edna appealed to the man still covering her as the last sound of the car was lost in the distance. "He'll be good and just sit here and play, won't you, Paulie?"

"Have to do what the boss says," the man answered. His voice was quiet too, though it lacked the urbanity of the leader's. He whistled, and the other man came from where he had been guarding the back door. He too had his gun out. In his other hand he held a coil of flex. Edna recognised it—it was from the electric iron.

"Be fun, won't it, young 'un?" he said ingratiatingly. "Just like playing Indians." Paulie submitted, wide-eyed, to being trussed firmly into the big green chair. "Here, where's your toys or something? I'll leave your hands free so you can play with them."

"There," said Paulie, pointing. "Are you going to scalp my mother?"

Both men laughed, and Paulie looked offended.

"Nothing like that, kid," said the other man. "Now you, lady. You bring something to tie her with, Bud?"

Bud fished in his hip-pocket with his left hand and drew out the long cord from the vacuum cleaner.

Under the menacing revolver, Edna walked to the chair on the other side of the fireplace.

"Comfortable, M'am? Here, I'll put this little table by you with the cigarettes and the magazines. See, that ain't so bad, is it? Nobody's going to harm you, lady, 's long as your husband shows good sense. And it'll be all over in an hour or so."

"Suppose the phone rings?" Edna asked.

"You just hope it *doesn't* ring, lady. You heard what the boss said. You just hope it isn't the call from him. Any others, I'll say it's the wrong number."

His eye fell on the piece of toast Richard had dropped by the telephone.

"Hey, that reminds me. You folks had your breakfast?"

Paulie nodded. His eyes followed every move the men made; his face shone with excitement.

"Well, *we* ain't. Bud, go out to the kitchen again and see if you can rustle up something for us."

Bud, the handyman, departed obediently.

Edna took a cigarette from the box, and her keeper jumped to light it for her. Once she and Paulie were securely tied, both men had put their guns back in the holsters.

"You won't get away with this, you know," she said, careful to keep her voice from shaking. "The F.B.I. will be after you, not just our local police. You kidnapped my husband."

"You let us worry about that, lady. The boss knows what he's doing. He's got everything figured out. What you got there, Bud?"

They sat down in chairs opposite the bound two, and amiably devoured ham sandwiches and coffee. Paulie watched them, absorbed. Edna chain-smoked. Nobody spoke.

The doorbell rang.

Edna drew a deep breath.

"It's a friend of mine," she said quietly. "She won't go away. We had a date for her this morning."

"You ought to've told us," said Bud's partner reproachfully. He stood a minute in thought. "All right, lady, she can't see into this room from the front door. Untie her, Bud." Bud obeyed quickly.

"Now you—" The revolvers were out again. "You go to the door, and I'll be right behind you, inside these curtains. You tell her—tell her the kid's sick, that the doctor says it's something contagious, and she better not come in. And remember, I'll be right there. If you say a word to give her any funny ideas, I'll let you have it."

"I'll have to talk to her a little, or she *would* think it was funny." Edna was stretching her cramped legs.

"Okay, but watch it."

Nobody, from the doorstep, could see behind the drapes. But Edna could feel the muzzle pressing gently just below her left shoulder blade.

It was Julia. Edna braced herself.

"Julia!" she cried brightly. "How are you dear? . . . Look, honey, this is dreadful, but I can't let you in. Paulie's sick."

"Sick?" Julia looked puzzled. "But then let me—"

"No, it's contagious, the doctor says. I don't want to take a chance on infecting your children with anything."

Julia's eyes widened.

"Rick had already gone to the bank before I called the doctor, so he couldn't let you know," Edna went on hurriedly. "We're going to take Paulie to Farnham Hospital just as soon as the doctor can get a bed in the children's ward."

"Isn't there anything I can do to help?" Julia asked eagerly. The iron below Edna's shoulder blade pressed just a little more deeply.

"Why, yes, there is one thing, if you will," Edna answered quickly. "When you go to the school at noon to pick up your own children, would you mind seeing Paulie's teacher, Miss Schermerhorn, and telling her? I don't want to mention it over the phone—somebody might overhear, and you know how panicky they get about contagion."

"Miss Schermerhorn?"

"Yes, you know—the new teacher who just came this year."

"I'll be glad to do it," said Julia. "Shall I phone Richard at the bank for you and tell him, or have you done that already?"

"No, he's terribly busy at the bank this morning, and besides I don't want to worry him. I'll phone him as soon as we know about the hospital, but that probably won't be till after you've seen Miss Schermerhorn."

"I won't wait till noon, Edna—I'll drive right down and tell the teacher now."

"Oh, that would be even better! I'm very grateful to you. And you do understand, Julia, why I can't ask you in? I'd never forgive myself if I exposed your youngsters."

"Of course I understand, Edna. Don't worry. Just take care of yourself."

"Oh, I'll be all right."

Edna found she was trembling all over as she closed the door.

"You sure gabbed long enough," the man growled. "And what's the point of having her tell the teacher the kid's sick, when he can go back to school again this afternoon? You didn't need to carry it that far."

"I wanted her to feel it was serious, so she wouldn't be offended by my not letting her in," Edna said placatingly. "I had to give her *some* sort of errand to do."

The man marched her into the living-room. She sank with a sigh of relief into the chair and let herself be tied up again.

"Was that Auntie Julia?" Paulie demanded from his chair. "Did you tell her I was sick, like the man said?"

"Yes, dear. And she said she was very sorry."

Paulie wriggled in his chair.

"I'm getting awful tired," he complained. "When are they going to let us go?"

"How about watching television?" said his mother. "Will you turn the set on so he can look?"

"There's nothing on I want to see," Paulie whined. The game was beginning to pall.

"It won't be long now," Bud said soothingly, looking at his wrist watch. "You be a brave scout, and pretty soon the cavalry will come and drive off all the Indians . . . I got kids of my own," he confided to Edna. "I know how they are."

"If we ain't heard from the boss by 10.30 it means everything's clear and we can beat it," the other man added. "Somebody'll be along soon and untie you. We'll be leaving in your car, lady. The cops'll find it for you, so don't worry."

Edna nodded wearily.

"Might as well turn the TV on at that," said Bud, going over to the set. "Give us something to do till it's time to go."

It was a very noisy show, with a military band. Even Edna and Paulie didn't hear the cars driving up. Then suddenly the front door opened and the room was full of policemen with their guns out. It looked like nearly half the police force in town. It was, the other half was down at the bank, taking over the three men there.

"I still don't understand how you did it, darling," Richard said, holding her hand tight. In the reaction Edna had collapsed, and she was lying stretched out on the couch, still weak and shaking. They were all around her—Rick, Julia, the Chief of Police. Paulie, worn out by the excitement, was sound asleep in the chair where he had been tied.

"It was Julia," Edna said faintly, raising her head to smile at her friend. "I could never have put it over with anybody else. Tell them, Julia."

"Well, it was when she mentioned Paulie's being taken to the hospital that I began to realise she was trying to get something else across to me—that something must be dreadfully wrong.

"Of course I didn't know she was speaking with a gun on her, but I guessed there must be some good reason for all that double-talk. Then Edna made that remark about *my* children—and me not married and not having any children! And then her saying that Paulie was going to the children's ward of the Farnham Hospital—which, of course, is just our town's polite name for the County Home for the Aged.

"Well, at last I caught on that Edna was in trouble, I didn't know where the trouble was—here or at the bank, or both—but something else Edna said made me decide to get down to police headquarters right away."

"It just goes to show you," said the Chief of Police. "It was the best planned robbery I ever heard of. Didn't look from their end as if *anything* could go wrong. But they weren't local men, so they weren't on to what every kid in town knows.

"At first I thought the lady was crazy," the Chief added apologetically. "But when she told me Mr. Fairchild's car was still parked outside this house, and yet Mrs. Fairchild said he was at the bank and being 'terribly busy' there—and then not letting her inside the house, and pulling that stuff about the Farnham Hospital to alert her— well, it *could* have been that Mrs. Fairchild was being held as a hostage. And there'd be no reason for that— unless somebody was trying to rob the bank. And it's Friday, the Jenks payday. So I played a hunch—and we were lucky.

"Thanks to you, Mrs. Fairchild, we've got hold of a man the whole state's wanted for a long time, and all his gang too. Won't do me any harm, either—a haul like this, the first month I've been on the job."

"And it won't do *me* any harm at the bank, I might add." Richard squeezed Edna's hand. "We've saved the Jenks payroll, all $98,000 of it, and I'm the fair-haired boy there now, even though it's thanks to my wife's brains."

"There's a reward for that fellow," said the Chief, "and I guess you two ladies will get a good share of it."

"I always knew I had a smart wife!" Richard said proudly. "And she's got a friend who's mighty quick on the uptake too. But I still don't get it, Julia. How did Edna make you realise so fast that it was a police matter?"

"Yes," the Chief put in. "I don't understand that either! You're a brave woman, Mrs. Fairchild. You took an awful chance, with a gun at your back. Just how did you do it?"

Edna and Julia burst into laughter. When Julia could talk, she explained.

"When you've lived longer in a small town like this, Chief, you'll realise that everybody is acquainted with everybody else. Those out-of-town bandits couldn't know it, but Edna and I were fully aware that there is only one person in town named—"

"Oh, I get it!" exclaimed Chief of Police Schermerhorn.

BARBARA CALLAGHAN

Hidden Springs

Last week after I finished bleachin' apples, I sat in the rockin' chair on the porch and watched that storyteller, Frank, straddlin' the steppin' stones in Reuben's Creek. Two college kids was with him, Sally and Keith, real nice young folks. By the time Frank and the kids reached my steps they'd raised up a thirst, so I gave them cups'a water from the well Pappy dug over 45 years ago.

Frank, he introduced himself as the nephew of Silas Coates, a distant kin'a ours who quit these hills years ago to work in the lumber mill down Lawrenceville way. Frank told me he was a bookwriter who was undertakin' a long story about mountain folks who was his kin. "Tracin' my roots," Frank said he was doin'. Then Frank said him and the kids who he called his researchers wanted to ask me questions about old-timey customs that I should answer in my own words and to tell them how me and my family followed the mountain ways. I'd be helpin', Frank said, "to add flavor and authen-ti-ci-ty" to his story. Well, Frank and the kids seemed right friendly and I do get afflicted with loneliness livin' here by myself, so I said I didn't mind talkin' to them.

Sally and Keith, they had big thick copybooks with heaps'a questions written inside and they read off the questions and wrote down whatever I said. The kids asked me about makin' soap and slaughterin' hogs and plantin' by the signs'a the moon and the stars. Lordamercy, how fast their words came trottin' out! I almost swooned from usin' up so much breath to keep up with their chatter.

Finally that Keith, he grinned and said he really wanted to ask

152

about moonshinin'. Well, Sally, she kicked Keith in the shins and Frank, he scowled at the boy. Sally and Frank was steamin' higher than Pappy's old still because they thought Keith had caused me to become wary'a them. "Now don't fret, Sally and Frank," I said. "Moonshinin' weren't nothin' to be ashamed of. My pappy hisself run a still and folks claimed his stillin' was the best in the county."

So Sally and Frank, they stopped tormentin' Keith and we all sat here on the porch. I told them how Pappy named this porch "The Lookout" because my mama and me, we'd sit here, weavin' oak splits into baskets, a chore we could do whilst our eyes wandered down the hill through the hickory trees to catch sight of the law. If we seen any federal people, Mama'd take my basket and shove it behind her chair whilst I run around back'a the cabin to drop pebbles through the evergreen boughs that covered the roof'a the lean-to. When Pappy and my brother Willis heard them pebbles droppin', they'd shut down the still and skeedaddle.

Frank, he wanted to know how we knowed who was federal. That was easy. The federal people was strangers. The sheriff and his deputies was neighbors or kinfolk who knowed the government didn't take kindly to stillin'. Sometimes the sheriff and his men was obliged to break up the stills but they weren't happy about doin' it.

Sheriff Luther Cox, now he was a real gentleman. He'd take his axe to the still, apologizin' to Pappy all the while, tellin' Pappy how he didn't like the excise tax neither and that he knowed Pappy did stillin' to help raise up his family. "I know yer jest doin' yer job, Luther," Pappy'd say. Then Pappy'd go to the springhouse and take out one'a them jars painted on the outside to look like buttermilk was inside'a it. Pappy and the sheriff'd pass that jar back and forth till the sheriff stood up kind of wobbly-like and say, "You make the best buttermilk in the whole county, Jacob."

After I finished tellin' Frank and them kids about moonshinin', I half expected to see Pappy and Willis haulin' sugar bags for the still until I recollected that the still ain't here no more and neither is Pappy nor Willis. I ain't a child no more. Come April I'll be 61 years old. Around these hills 61 ain't old but lately I'm findin' I doze off when my thoughts get heavy and I don't wake up till the chipmunks start promenadin' on the porch roof or the sun starts boring' into my eyes.

That storyteller, Frank, he must'a noticed how my eyes misted up when I talked about Pappy and Willis so he asked me if I'd talk about quiltin' and bottomin' chairs. Sally, she got real excited about them subjects, so she jest shot me questions harder than hail-stones till Frank finally said, "Whoa. Let's give Mrs. Payne time to collect her thoughts."

"Miss Payne," I said. Frank blushed and stammered, "Oh, I'm sorry." I wanted to lift Frank's embarrassment off'a him, so I said, "You ain't got no cause to be sorry, Frank. I ain't your mama."

Directly I wanted to bite off my tongue for funnin' with their boss in front'a them kids but them kids jest hooted and laughed to bust. Sally and Keith weren't bashful at all. Maybe it's better that kids today don't hold no shame about sech things. Frank was mad at them kids, so I recollected Aunt Sarah Payne's old sayin' when members of the family was gettin' ready to whup each other. "Foodin' stops feudin'," she'd say in her soft, little-bitty voice. I asked Frank and the kids into the cabin for some carrot puddin' and cracklin' bread. Law, even that bony Sally asked me for second helpin's.

After they'd done eatin', Sally skipped around the room and squealed over the friendship quilt settin' on the old featherbed. I showed Sally the names of the women who worked on the quilt and stitched their names into the patches. The friendship quilt belonged to my mama. Pappy never held with me goin' to no quiltin' bees. "Yer slow about yer work, girl," he'd say. "Yer always woolgatherin'. I can't letcha off a this farm. The first young buck come along'd have his way with ya."

Pappy didn't have no booklearnin' but he was smart about me. I woolgathered when I shucked corn or stirred the hominy or gathered pears in the old of the moon. Always in my woolgatherin' up till I was 16 years old, I was wearin' Aunt Sarah Payne's lacy white weddin' gown, the gown that she gave to Mama to store at our place on account of the moths that was feastin' on it at her cabin. Yep, Pappy was smart about me.

Sometimes my thoughts trip out'a my mouth and I heard

myself tellin' Sally, "As ye sow, so shall ye reap." Sally put down the quilt and looked at me peculiar because we hadn't been talkin' about plantin'. Then Frank thanked me for the hospitality and asked me if he could leave a little black machine with me, a tape recorder he called it. Frank showed me how to talk to the machine by fillin' up a tape with my thoughts. He said he understood how hard it was for me to answer questions without time to think on them first. He started showin' me the buttons on the recorder and seemed downright surprised to find I could read what the buttons said. Six years'a schoolin' I had before Mama took the fever and died.

Frank wrote a heap'a questions on sheets of yellow paper and told me to take my time answerin' them, that he wouldn't be back till next week. Before they left him and the kids told me they had a right good time.

As soon as they were gone, I studied them questions and the machine. I weren't ascairt of the recorder but I found three'a them questions devilish mean because they roused hurtful memories that crawled partway out'a my mind like wounded creatures beggin' to be unsnared. I tried not to pay no mind to them three troublesome questions but they hankered to get freed'a the traps in my mind. Finally I picked up the little microphone and read off the first of them three questions: "Did you ever know a Dowser?"

"Yep, Frank," I answered. "I knowed a Dowser, jest one." Then I started talkin' about dowsin' like I was in the one-room schoolhouse recitin' a lesson to my teacher. I told Frank how the Dowser found water by puttin' one end'a the stick in his mouth and holdin' the other end with his thumb until the dowsing stick would twitch and act plumb crazy when it was passed over a hidden spring. Then my mind took to dowsin' and swayin' over currents deep inside'a me till them currents bubbled up and swamped that machine.

I told the recorder about me bein' 15 years old and watchin' the Dowser that Pappy had sent for to find a spot to sink a new well. Wore a frockcoat, Dowser did, and looked like a preacher. But Dowser weren't no preacher. He didn't ask the Lord's blessin' on his chore nor did he give thanks when he found the

Lord's own spring. Dowser jest stood on the spot the stick pointed out whilst Pappy marked the place with twigs and brought him four buttermilk jars filled with Pappy's best.

Whilst Dowser was waiting' for the moonshine he fixed his fiery eyes on me and I felt like I was bein' branded by the hot coals of Lucifer hisself. Dowser weren't old and he weren't young. A heap'a lines scored his face. They weren't thinkin' lines nor worryin' lines. They was hatin' lines.

Now Aunt Sarah Payne, she was sittin' beside me, her bein' a new widow and stayin' with us a spell whilst she grappled with her melancholy. A shiver run through her plump body when Dowser's eyes lit on her. For a minute I thought she'd swoon like she done at Uncle Fergus' buryin', her bein' delicate and soft, not like the other women in the family, but Aunt Sarah leaned towards me and whispered, "Dowser's got power, good power and bad power. You stay away from him, hear?"

I promised Aunt Sarah I would and that weren't hard because nobody knowed Dowser's name nor where he lived nor where he came from. My brother Willis, he used to say Dowser were a haint, a ghost from the cemetery on Weepin' Woman Hill, and he wore a frockcoat with the collar turned up to hide his neck where there was a scar, Willis said, from Dowser's bein' lynched by folks years ago for holdin' back his power when drought troubled the land. As God's own punishment to him, Dowser had to leave his grave every time someone needed a well. "That's why he looks so mean," Willis said, "cause he's plumb tired out from never gettin' a good deadman's sleep."

I didn't hold with Willis' opinion about Dowser, so one day after gatherin' berries near Weepin' Woman Hill, I left my pail and tiptoed into the graveyard. All them crows and bluejays was chatterin' mighty loud but I kept myself as quiet as a sinful thought to show them dead folks I held them in respect. Around the graveyard I walked, lookin' at the plots and didn't find one'a them with loose dirt or a slanted marker like they'd have if Dowser came thumpin' out'a the ground.

But I did see a sign in the dirt at the gate to the graveyard, the sign that summoned Dowser. If a farmer wanted to find a spot to sink a well, he'd draw a bit letter V in the dirt, the V standin' for the divinin' rod Dowser used. Oncet the Brownell boyus who was always up to mischief scratched Dowser's sign in the dirt and wrote their Pappy's name under the V when their Pappy didn't need no well. Dowser, he come checkin' the graveyard like he did every day and seen the sign and waited for Mr. Brownell to lead him to his farm. Long about noon Dowser must'a knowed them boys was funnin' him, so he found the Brownell place by hisself.

Dowser, he din't say a word to nobody. He just took his dowsin' stick and walked through the Brownell place to the cornfield behind the barn where the dowsin' stick started twitchin'. Mr. Brownell who was sorely puzzled by Dowser's visit had followed him and he pushed aside some cornstalks and found his son Thaddeus, the sixteen-year-old, huggin' and kissin' the Simpson girl.

Lordamercy, how Mr. Brownell whupp'd that boy! And he gave Dowser jars'a okra and souse in appreciation. After that nobody drawed signs in the dirt for Dowser unless they really wanted a well. I was ascairt of Dowser before Aunt Sarah Payne told me about the Brownell boy but after hearin' that story Dowser became my nightmare man.

"How'd Dowser know Thaddeus and the Simpson girl was there in the cornfield, Aunt Sarah?" I asked.

Well, Aunt Sarah's pretty face turned all red like it done whenever she was obliged to talk about 'indelicate' things. She said, "Dowser finds water, child, and a heap'a kissin' and huggin' raises up a sweat. And sweat is water, very salty water."

Well, I made a vow on the spot not to go kissin' and huggin' and I held true to that vow till the night I wore Aunt Sarah Payne's lacy white dress in the moonlight. Anyways, when word of the Brownell boy got around, Dowser started receivin' signs in the graveyard from folks wantin' him to track down runaways and sech. When the Simpson girl told her little sister she was runnin' off to Lawrenceville, Mr. Simpson summoned Dowser who found her three miles from home crouchin' in a laurel thicket. She was sweatin' and cryin' which is both watery things, so I guessed that's how Dowser found her.

The federal people, they heard about Dowser's trackin' power and they tried to summon him to find a prisoner in the hills but

Dowser never answered their sign. Folks thought that Dowser like theirselves didn't take kindly to the federal people or else that Dowser thought prisoners didn't sweat nor cry.

Lordamercy, I sure wandered off the path of Frank's question about a Dowser and told the machine so much foolishness. But I felt good talkin' about them things and I knowed how the straw must feel when it's pulled out'a the mattresses and aired in the spring. Dowser's still my nightmare man and he hovers over the next two questions. The next question I was drawed to from Frank's batch was "Did you ever know a Granny Woman?"

"Yep, Frank," I said to the microphone, "I knowed a Granny Woman, a midwife you'd call her now. The Granny Woman was God's own creature, wise and comfortin'. Mrs. Florence Trumbill, she'd ride her mule as far away as ten miles right up till she was near seventy to help a woman birth her baby. Out'a her black bag Mrs. Florence Trumbill'd take her clean white apron and white cap and clean white cloths. Then she'd go to work, massagin' and coaxin' and bearin' down right along with the mother, all the time holdin' the woman's hand. Over four hundred babies was helped into the world by Mrs. Florence Trumbill. After the birthings Mrs. Trumbill'd cook dinner for the family and stay on with them for at least a week till the mother and the family got the hang'a the new baby. Nowadays the women go to the clinic down Lawrenceville and have all the mod'rn conveniences but there ain't nothin' invented that'd take the place of the Granny Woman."

Mrs. Florence Trumbill, now she didn't have no special tools, no magic wand like Dowser but she must'a had a third eye that could see deep down into the whirlpools of a person's soul. Somehow she knowed when a body was cryin' inside. I recollect how hard she looked at me durin' the revival meetin' at Carson's Field seven months after I wore Aunt Sarah Payne's lacy white dress and danced by myself in the moonlight till the stranger with the quiet voice and nice smile came out'a the woods and waltzed with me till we both fell down in a heap from spinnin' and spinnin' around.

At the revival, whilst Pappy and Willis was renouncin' Satan at the altar call, I stood off by myself wonderin' if I was sinnin' by prayin' to the Lord that the stranger would come back to me like he said he would and that he'd be powerful happy when I told him about the baby. All of a sudden Mrs. Florence Trumbill touched my arm and beckoned for me to follow her to the apple orchard.

That Granny Woman, her eyes didn't travel over my loose dress like Pappy's did when he said, "Yer eatin' too much, girl, and workin' too little." Mrs. Florence Trumbill jest pushed the hair out'a my eyes and said, "You're lookin' mighty peaked, child. When you need me, I'll come to you."

Well, I jest thanked her and shook my head in wonderment at Mrs. Florence Trumbill's third eye, the one that could read the thoughts that was stuck inside'a you and couldn't get out.

A month later when the pains started, I left the cabin after Pappy and Willis went hayin' in the south pasture. I was standin' next to Reuben's Creek wishin' the Lord'd part the waters for me like He done for His people at the Red Sea when I seen Mrs. Trumbill standin' on the other side, holdin' her black bag and gettin' ready to cross the steppin' stones. "Stay there," she hollered. "I'm comin' over. I dreamed about you last night and I always pay heed to my dreams."

Mrs. Trumbill helped me back into the cabin and into the feather bed. Then she put on her white cap and white apron and was jest takin' a cloth from her bag when the baby birthed herself.

Mrs. Florence Trumbill worked a long time on the baby, even to takin' butter and puttin' some in the infant's mouth to bring up phlegm that might'a been blockin' her breathin'. But nothin' helped. Mrs. Trumbill, she stroked my hair and took care'a me, then she told me to lay quiet whilst she went outside to Pappy's pile of pinewood.

After talkin' about Mrs. Trumbill I had to turn off the recorder for a spell. She's gone now but these hills is filled with folks whose first inklin' of human kindness came from the hands of that Granny Woman. To answer the last and most troublesome question, I had to turn the tape over like Frank showed me. I sat thinkin' for a long time, quarrelin' with myself about whether to keep talkin', but I'd been feelin' a curious kind'a peace since I started, so I pushed the button and said to the microphone, "Can you tell me about burial customs?"

"Yep, Frank," I answered. "I can tell you about the buryin' ways." I told the little tape how the dead person's spirit might'a slipped off by itself but how his kin was surrounded by all the folks who heard the bell tollin' the number'a years the departed one had lived and how they came to the cabin to sit up with the dead and took to singin' quiet church songs together round about midnight. I told the tape how folks brought food to the family and held it a proper honor to be asked to help make the box or dig the grave. Granny Nesbit came to mind when I was tellin' Frank about the buryin' ways. For 35 years Granny Nesbit had her buryin' clothes ready. Made them herself, she did, and aired them in the sun each spring.

After I talked about Granny Nesbit my mind got to dowsin' over them strong currents deep inside'a me and I started tellin' Frank about my little girl's buryin'. Mrs. Florence Trumbill came back into the cabin and started hammerin' a box out'a the pinewood. The box looked so forlorn that I got up and snipped some lace off'a Aunt Sarah Payne's white gown. Before Mrs. Trumbill placed the baby in the box, I had lined the inside with the white lace. Then Mrs. Trumbill made me get back into bed and she set out with the box and a spade towards the hollow.

It jest didn't seem right layin' there without heedin' the buryin' ways more proper, so I got up and went out to the porch. For a spell I stood beside the dinner bell before I started ringin' it and stopped after it sounded eight times, figurin' me and the little girl, we knowed each other for eight months. Directly Pappy and Willis come runnin' in from the pasture, thinkin' that the Dillard boy who was eight years old and always strayin' over to our place had fallen down the well or drowned hisself in Reuben's Creek.

Pappy and Willis and some neighbors kept yammerin' at me to tell them why I rung the bell but I was too ascairt to answer them. When I seen Aunt Sarah Payne come onto the porch, I ran inside the cabin to hide her dress. She ran right after me and spied the dress with the big empty spot gapin' at her hangin' crooked from a nail in the wall. Well, Aunt Sarah started hollerin' and callin' me a demon for shreddin' her dress till I finally told her I needed the cloth for somethin' important.

Aunt Sarah got this canny look in her eye like she was doin' sums in her head. After she totaled the eight rings of the dinner bell along with the extra heaviness I'd been puttin' on, and added to them things the fact that a baby's box is lined with white cloth, she blushed and sighed like she always done when obliged to talk about indelicate things. She turned to Pappy and said, "She had a baby, Jacob, and it died."

Pappy's face went redder than ripe strawberries before he sent the neighbors home after tellin' them we should be alone with our shame. Him and Aunt Sarah jest fired questions at me about who was the father and where was the baby till I jest crawled into bed and covered my ears. Pappy raised his voice and yelled, "Dowser will find the no-account father. Yep, Dowser can find anybody. I'm goin' to summon him now."

When Pappy charged out'a the door, he bumped into Mrs. Florence Trumbill who was standin' on the porch, holdin' the spade, her apron all streaky with dirt.

"The baby's father was a stranger passin' through these hills, Jacob," she said. "Dowser won't find him. And the baby, she never took a breath. I buried her in the hollow in back'a the pine grove."

Pappy, he pulled the spade out'a Mrs. Trumbill's hand and throwed it hard into the woodpile. "Yer a fool, woman," he thundered. "A no-account like that ain't gonna quit these hills. The fox'll tarry as long as there's chickens. He already brung disgrace to our family but I aim to keep him from bringin' sorrow to my neighbors."

After Pappy and Mrs. Trumbill left, Aunt Sarah Payne sat by the bed, rockin' herself and cradlin' the white dress in her arms, croonin' "Dowser will get him. Oh, yes, Dowser will get him. Jest recollect the Brownell boy and the Simpson girl." Aunt Sarah's words worked on me like a witch's lullaby and I fell to dreamin' about Dowser, his frockcoat flappin' in the wind as he swooped down on the Brownell boy, the Simpson girl, my stranger, and me.

Before Dowser came the next morning Aunt Sarah tiptoed out'a the cabin, leavin' me alone to hear him climb on the porch where he sat swillin' down the moonshine as Pappy recited the story of our shame in a voice so pitiful it made me cry.

And my cryin' was a sign to me that Dowser'd find my stranger, the kind stranger who told me how pretty I looked in the moonlight. My stranger'd be cryin' too, lost in the hills like he was and yearnin' to come back to me. Men cry too. Yep, they do. I seen men cryin' at weddin's and buryin's. And my stranger'd be sweatin' from climbin' and hikin'. Cryin' and sweatin' was watery things that'd lead Dowser directly to him. I felt so bad that I come down with a fever that gripped me all the way into the dyin' of the moon.

Pappy made me sassafras tea but mostly he took to sittin' on the porch with his huntin' rifle crosst his lap, waitin' for Dowser to bring him the stranger. Pappy gave up runnin' the still and jest drunk the moonshine hisself that he'd already made. Willis, he got tired'a farmin' by hisself and told Pappy he was leavin' for Lawrenceville to work in the mill. Pappy's spirit was too weary to argue with Willis and he left.

When the fever let go'a me, I started hidin' behind the biggest marker in the cemetery to spy on Dowser when he come checkin' for his summonin' sign. I took to trailin' Dowser real quiet-like through the hills, hopin' he'd lead me to my lost strainger, thinkin' that me and my stranger could hog-tie Dowser and run away together. Tracking' Dowser carried me way into October when the air became powerful cold and the winds clawed at the trees.

Mostly Dowser jest circled farms, stealin' pumpkins and squash when he weren't lookin' for a spot to sink a well. Sometimes he'd set traps for small critters but mostly he'd go back to the lean-to he built hisself up atop'a Lookout Ridge where he'd drink the moonshine till his eyes glowed like they'd been seared from starin' into Hell. Dowser weren't lookin' for my stranger. He was takin' Pappy's payments without workin' for them.

On the last day of October, the eve of the haints, I was wore out from climbin' Lookout Ridge on the other side'a Dowser's hidey place and I vowed not to come no more when I heard voices rumblin' inside the shack. I crept closer and hid myself behind a thick maple tree to listen. What I heard I can't never forget. I can recite them words jest like Dowser and the other man spoke them.

"Drink up, friend," Dowser said. "This stuff's the best in the mountains. I get it once a week from a hillbilly intent on shooting the man who wronged his daughter. The old geezer thinks I'm trailing the varmint."

Dowser's visitor laughed.

"I heard about you in stir," he said. "You were the one that got away, the whole pen's hero. You were my inspiration to bust out."

"I'll drink to that," Dowser said.

Then Dowser's visitor said, "Old-timers like Shorty Grenville and Pump Martin say you're an educated man."

"A certified wreck from Marshall Tech," answered Dowser. "A civil engineer until I turned to banking and a teller and a security guard interfered with my new interest."

Dowser's visitor snorted, then asked, "How come the folks in these hills don't turn you in?"

"They think I've got magic power. They call me Dowser because I find water with this old hickory switch. Hell, these hills are teeming with underground springs. I put on a good show for them by letting this stick go crazy over any likely waterhole. The hillbillies also think I can find lost people and I can. After seven years in prison I like the freedom of roaming these hills. I know every trail and from here I can see everything, all the hiding places for necking couples and runaway kids."

"You got it made," the man said.

Dowser laughed. "The mountaineers got it made too, friend. I'm the guardian angel of every still in these parts. I don't want my sources to run dry, so I protect my clients from the feds. Nine, ten months ago, the feds got tricky and sent an advance scout into these hills, a young fellow dressed like a hiker."

"Yeah," said Dowser's guest, "what did you do?"

Dowser grunted, then must'a filled up with more likker. I stood next to the tree, peelin' bark off, waitin' for his words.

"I let the young fed have his way with a moonstruck farmer's daughter before I threw him down a ravine deeper than Davy Jones', no, Davy Crockett's, locker."

All of a sudden I heard the sound'a hundreds of bees but it were too late in the year for bees. Them bees was swarmin' inside my head, creatin' that woooo noise their wings make when they're coolin' honey in the hives on hot nights. I kept shakin' my head but them bees kept fannin' their wings so I only heard snatches 'a the rest 'a the talkin'—Dowser's tellin' the man he'd guide him to the highway the next mornin' and Dowser's sayin' somethin' about quittin' Lookout Ridge the next day to pass the cold weather in a cabin with the plump windowpane. His talkin' started makin' no sense on account of them bees in my head.

I skittered down the ridge and run through the trails till I reached Reuben's Creek and jumped in to cool my throbbin' head. After I swum acrosst, I hastened to the cabin to dry. A powerful chill overtook me afterwards, so I stayed wrapped in Mama's quilt for two days. Before dawn on the third day 'a November I ate a plate of hominy grits that put strength back into my body. I was cravin' to visit Aunt Sarah to beg her to go to the sheriff with me so's I could tell him what I knowed about Dowser, bein' ascairt to go alone lest Dowser seen me scramblin' off the ridge and was spyin' on me from his new hidey place.

I set out for Aunt Sarah's place in the darkness to be covered from Dowser's devil-eyes, hopin' she wouldn't be too deep into her winter melancholy to go to the sheriff's with me. Every year since Uncle Fergus died Aunt Sarah gathered in supplies all during' October and wouldn't see no family nor friends till March. She said her heart was too froze up with grief to talk to nobody. Uncle Fergus and her never had no young'uns that'd be a comfort to her.

With a full moon guidin' me I reached Aunt Sarah's cabin quick and sat down on the porch to catch my breath when I pierced my hand on an ornery stick. When I picked it up, them bees started carousin' again in my head. The stick were vee-shaped like a dowsin' rod. Fearin' Dowser'd been expectin' me to go to Aunt Sarah's where nobody'd be able to help me, I quick opened the cabin door and went in, gropin' at the place where Uncle Fergus used to keep his huntin' rifle. A heavy coat fell off a hook and jest about smothered me. After grapplin' to get free 'a the coat, I got it off 'a my head and seen the moonlight strokin' the sleepin' faces of Dowser and Aunt Sarah.

Directly Dowser's words on the ridge came back to me, the

words he spoke when them bees was befuddlin' my hearin'. Dowser didn't say he was going' to pass the cold weather in a cabin with the plump windowpane. He said he was going' to pass the cold weather in a cabin with the plump Widow Payne.

Softly I crept over to the stove, then out'a the cabin, knowin' what I had to do. Since Aunt Sarah surely weren't goin' to fetch the sheriff with me, I'd have to fetch him myself. I broke a heap'a branches off'a the pine trees next to Aunt Sarah's cabin and made pineknot torches like the ones the posses used at night when they was trackin' criminals. Then I set the torches 'twixt the logs in the railin'a the porch, tellin' myself I was doin' the right thing. Soon as I put a match to one'a them branches, I knowed the sheriff'd see the blaze and reckon a killer was loose in the hills. The sheriff'd know the flamin' signal jest like Dowser knowed his sign in the dirt.

But I couldn't stay and wait for the sheriff. I had to run away from the cabin. Before I knowed it, that one torch had lighted the others and all the waters from all the springs Dowser ever found couldn't have quenched that fire.

I done a heap'a talkin' to Frank on that machine about the buryin' ways but there was so many ways to tell him about. Some folks was buried proper in Weepin' Woman Hill and some was buried in the hollow in little boxes lined with lacy white cloth and some was buried under rocks and twigs deep down in a ravine and some was buried by rafters all black and sooty from fire. And some was buried under ponderous thoughts even though they done their chores and cared for their Pappy till he passed on.

I gave the postman the tape that I packed in a box with Frank's address on it. For a week I sat on the porch feelin' sure that Frank had turned the tape over to the law and waitin' for the sheriff to come for me, but nonetheless experiencin' a peculiar kind'a peace.

When I seen Frank crossin' the steppin' stones today, I was mighty surprised. He ate some more carrot puddin' and cracklin' bread before he took the tape out'a his pocket and said real sorrowful, "Thanks a lot, Miss Payne, but the recorder wasn't working right. There was nothing on the tape. I'll take this machine back and get it fixed. The kids and I'll visit in the spring and talk some more. You take the tape and keep it as a souvenir."

There's nothin' like the ties of kin, even distant kin, to lift a body's spirits up. I like that young fella even though I caught him in a whoppin' big lie. Before I mailed the tape I pushed the replay button and listened to my mind dowsin' out loud over fearful currents that seem to have settled down.

I walked off'a the porch to wave to Frank and I caught the first snowflake of the season in my hand. Real pretty it was, so lacy and white. For a long time I stood outside watchin' them snowflakes floatin' down and feelin' real thankful that they was tattin' a coverlet that'd reach down into the deepest ravine.

DOROTHY SALISBURY DAVIS

Old Friends

The two women had been friends since childhood, their mothers friends before them. Both were in their late twenties; neither had married. Amy intended not to, although she was beginning to lose some of the vehemence with which she declared that purpose. Virginia was still saying she was waiting for the right man to come along. She admitted herself to be an old-fashioned girl. One of the sadnesses in her life was that the men she liked most were already married. It made her furious when Amy would say, "Happily?"

"I suppose you think I should have an affair," Virginia said.

"Yes, as a matter of fact, it would be good for you."

"How do you know?"

"Well, let me put it this way," Amy would say, and the same conversation had occurred in some form or other a number of times, "it would be better than a bad marriage just for the sake of being married."

"According to you," Virginia would say, "there are no good marriages."

"Not many, and I don't know of a single one that came with a guarantee."

One might have thought that it was Amy who had grown up in the broken home. Her parents had only recently celebrated their thirty-fifth wedding anniversary. Whereas Virginia's mother had divorced her third husband, each of whom had left her better off financially than had his predecessor. She and Virginia were often taken for sisters. But so were Virginia and Amy. Or, to make Virginia's own distinction, she was always being taken for Amy's sister.

167

At one time they had worked for the same New York publishing house, Virginia as an assistant art director, Amy as an assistant to the senior editor. Amy's father, a retired executive of the firm, had arranged interviews for both girls after they finished college. The jobs, he insisted, they had got for themselves. Virginia stayed with hers. More than anything in the world, except possibly a husband who loved and respected her, she wanted her independence of her mother. Amy, to cap the interminable subject, once suggested that was why Virginia wanted a husband, to protect her from her mother.

"I am perfectly capable of protecting myself."

And that of course, Amy realized in time, was her friend's trouble. Nobody could do anything for her. She resented anyone's attempting it. Which made her yearning for a husband suspect: what Virginia really wanted, Amy decided, was a baby. This insight, as well as others just as profound if true, had slipped beyond Amy's conscious reckoning of her friend's character long before the weekend Amy reneged on the invitation to the country.

Sometimes months went by when they did not see each other. Amy, on inheriting an ancient cottage from an aunt, gave up her regular job for freelance writing, copy editing, and restoring the cottage. While not far from the city and not actually isolated, the cottage retained a rare privacy. It had settled deeper and deeper into the ground with the decades, and the mountain laurel that surrounded it was as snug as a shawl.

Knowing Virginia to be a Sunday painter, Amy thought of her whenever there was a change in nature. Such a change had come that week with the sudden November stripping of the leaves. The light took on a special quality and the long grass in the meadow quivered glossily golden in the sun and turned silver under the moon. She called Virginia on Thursday.

"Well, now, I would like to," Virginia said, mulling over the invitation aloud. "I half promised Allan—I don't know if I've told you about him, the architect?—I didn't actually commit myself. Thank you, Amy. I'd love to come."

Amy was on the point of saying she could bring Allan, the architect, and then it occurred to her that he might be an invention of Virginia's, part of that same old face-saving syndrome which, when they saw too much of one another, made their friendship dreary. She almost wished she had not called. However, they discussed the bus schedule and settled on a time for Virginia's arrival.

"If I miss that one, I'll take the next," Virginia said. There was always a little hitch to allow room for independence.

That very afternoon Amy received a call from Mike Trilling, one of the few men with whom she had ever been deeply in love. A newspaper correspondent, Mike had been sent overseas just when they had become very happy together. If he had asked it, she would have followed him, but he had not asked it, and she had been a long time getting over the separation. Except that she was not over it. She knew that the moment she heard his voice.

Her end of the conversation was filled with pauses.

Finally Mike said, "Are you still hung up on me?"

"What humility! Yes, damn you."

"You don't have to swear at me. I've got the same problem— once in love with Amy, here I am again. I'd come out for the weekend if you'd ask me."

"All right, you're invited."

"I'll rent a car and be there early tomorrow evening. We can have dinner at The Tavern. Is the food as good as it used to be?"

"I'll fix us something. It's not that good. You can bring the wine." She refrained from saying that he could take the bus, an hour's trip. There was no better way to put a man off than to try to save his money for him.

She postponed the decision on what to say to Virginia, and while she cleaned house she let her memory of the times she and Mike had been together run full flood. She washed her hair and dried it before the blaze in the fireplace. Mike loved to bury his face in her hair, to discover in it the faint fragrance of wood smoke; he loved to run his fingers through it on the pillow and to give it a not altogether gentle tug, pulling her face to his.

She could not tell Ginny that Mike was the reason she was asking her to postpone until the following weekend. It would be unkind. Anyone else might understand, but Ginny would understand even more than was intended: she would re-examine the whole of her life in terms of that rejection. Amy did not call her until morning.

"Ginny, I've had the most tremendous idea for a story. I was up half the night thinking about it, afraid to lose it, or that it wouldn't be any good in the morning. But it's a good one and I want to dash it off fresh. Will you come next week instead? I know you understand . . ." She made herself stop. She was saying too much.

"Of course," Virginia said, and her voice had that dead air of self-abnegation. "I envy you."

"Bless you for understanding," Amy said. "The same time next weekend. I'll be watching for you."

Once off the phone she gave herself up to the pleasure of anticipation. Almost a year had passed since she and Mike were last together. She had had a couple of brief encounters since, but no one had taken his place. She had worked. She had done a lot more work with Mike away than when he was around. They had not corresponded. He had called her on New Year's Eve. Collect, because he was at a friend's house and the British would not accept his credit-card charge. She had not asked him about the friend. She did not propose to ask any questions now.

At first it seemed like old times, their sitting before the fire with martinis, Mike on the floor at her feet, his head resting on his arm where it lay across her knees. His hair had begun to thin on the very top of his head. She put her finger to the spot, a cold finger, for she had just put down her glass.

Mike got up and sat in the chair opposite hers, brushing back his hair, something almost tender in the way he stroked the spot.

"I'm wicked, aren't I?" she said, carrying off as best she could what she knew to have been a mistake.

"Tell me about that," he said, purposely obtuse.

"Naughty, I mean."

"Oh, nuts. With the British, every other word is 'naughty.' Aren't I the naughty one?" He mimicked someone's accent. "It's such a faggoty word."

"I guess it is," Amy said.

He fidgeted a moment, as though trying to get comfortable in the chair, then got up and gave one of the logs a kick. "It's not easy—getting reacquainted when so much has happened in between."

"Oh?" In spite of herself.

He looked around at her. "I've been working bloody hard. Five months in Cyprus."

"I know."

"Does nobody in America read history?"

"I suspect the trouble is that nobody listens to those who read history."

"Did you follow my dispatches?"

"Every word, my darling."

Things went a little better. He looked at his glass. "I can't drink martinis like I used to. What kind of vermouth did you use?"

The phone rang and Amy, on her way to answer it, said, "Try putting in more gin."

It was Virginia, of all people. "I won't disturb you except for a minute."

"It's all right. I'm taking a break." She was afraid Mike might put on a record.

"I want to ask a favor of you, Amy. I got myself into a predicament. When Allan called a while ago, I decided I didn't want to talk to him, so I said I was on my way to spend the weekend with you. I don't think he'll call, but in case he does, would you tell him I've gone on a long walk or something like that?"

Amy drew a deep breath and tried to think of something to say that would not expose the extent of her exasperation. The most natural thing in the world would have been: Ginny, the reason I asked you not to come—

"I don't think he will call."

"Okay, Ginny. I'll tell him."

"Get his number and say I'll call him back."

"I'll tell him that," Amy said. It was all a fantasy, and in some way or other Virginia thought she was getting even. If there was an Allan and if these little exchanges did occur, she would then have to call Virginia back and tell her that Allan had telephoned her.

"Was that Virginia?" Mike said.

"Yes."

"Hasn't she hooked herself a man yet?"

"You damn smug—" Amy exploded, possibly because she was annoyed with both Virginia and him. But Virginia, being the more vulnerable and absent, got such loyal defense in the argument that ensued, she would have been stunned. Indeed, it might have changed her whole picture of herself.

Mike and Amy did reach a rapprochement. After all, it was his remembering Amy's complaints about her friend in the old days that had provoked his comment: she should blame herself, not him. After the second martini they were laughing and talking about old intimacies, and how they had used to put the third martini on ice for afterward. Such good memories and the kisses which, if they weren't the same, were better than most, sufficed to get them into the bedroom. There, alas, nothing went the same as it had used to.

"Damn it," Mike kept saying, "this never happens to me."

"It's all right," Amy said over and over again, although well aware he had used the present tense.

Later, watching him stoop to see himself in her dressing-table mirror while he knotted his tie, she said, "Bed isn't everything."

"That's right."

"But it's a lot," she said and threw off the blankets.

By the time she finished in the bathroom, he had gone back to the living room where he stood before the fire and stared into it. A fresh log was catching on, the flames like little tongues darting up the sides. He had not brought the martini pitcher from the kitchen.

"You can't go home again," she said.

"I guess not." He could at least have said that it was fun trying. But what he said was, "Amy, let's not spoil a beautiful memory."

"Oh, boy. I don't believe you said it. Not Mike Trilling."

"All right. 'You can't go home again' wasn't exactly original either. We aren't going to make it, Amy, so why don't I just take off before we start bickering again? No recriminations, no goodbyes, no tears."

Her throat tight as a corked bottle, she went up the stairs and got his coat and overnight bag.

On the porch they did not even shake hands—a turn and a quickly averted glance lest their eyes get caught, and a little wave before he opened the car door. When he was gone, she remembered the wine. It was as well she had forgotten it. A "thank you" for anything would have humiliated them both.

Returning to the house she felt as sober as the moon and as lonely. There was a whispery sound to the fire, and her aunt's Seth Thomas floor clock ticked with the slow heavy rhythm of a tired heart. Most things break: the phrase from somewhere she could not remember kept running through her mind. The old clock rasped and struck once. Hard through it was to believe, the hour was only half-past eight.

She called Virginia.

Her friend took her time picking up the phone. "I wasn't going to answer. I thought it might be Allan. Did he call me there?"

"Not so far, dear. Ginny, you could make the nine-thirty bus and come on out. The story isn't ready yet. I always start too soon. I'm botching it terribly."

"Thank you, but I don't think I will, Amy. I want to stay home by myself now where I can think things out comfortably. I'm a mess, but since I know it, I ought to be able to do something about it."

"You sound awfully down. Do come and see me."

"Actually, I'm up. Have a nice weekend, Amy."

Have a nice weekend: that was the *coup de grace*. Amy went to the kitchen and got out the martini jug. She closed the refrigerator door on an eight-dollar steak. The cat, her paws tucked out of sight where she sat on the table, opened her eyes and then closed them again at once.

Amy returned to the living room by way of the dining-room door. As she entered, she discovered a man also coming into the room, he by the door to the vestibule. She had not locked up after Mike's departure.

"Hello. I did knock," he said, "but not very loudly. I thought I'd surprise you."

"You have, and now that I'm surprised, get the hell out of here before I call my husband."

"Funny. Ginny didn't tell me about him. In fact, she said you didn't want one."

"You're Allan."

He had stopped. They both had, in their tracks, on seeing one another. They now moved tentatively forward. He was handsome in an odd way: his quick smile and his eyes did not seem to go together. The eyes, she would have sworn, took in everything in the room while not seeming to look directly at anything, even at her when they came face to face.

"Yes, I'm Allan. So Ginny's told you about me? I'm surprised, though come to think of it, I shouldn't be. She's told me a lot about you, too. Where is she?"

Damn Ginny. "She's gone for a walk." She regretted at once having said that. Now it was reasonable for him to expect to wait for her return. "Don't you think, Mr.—" She stopped and waited.

"Just Allan," he said, which she did not like either, the familiarity of it. No. The anonymity: it was more like that.

"Mr. Allan, don't you think if Ginny wanted to see you, she would have arranged it?"

"It takes two to make an arrangement, Amy." His eyes, not really on hers anyway, slipped away to the glass where Mike had left it. Her glass was on the side table near which she stood, the martini pitcher in her hand. He might well have arrived in time to have seen Mike leave.

He then said, "Should I confess something to you, Miss Amy— I guess that's what you'd like me to call you, but it certainly rings strange against the picture Ginny gave me of you—let me tell you the reason I crashed this party. I wanted to see the cottage, and I wasn't sure I'd ever get an invitation, leaving it to Ginny. It's pre-Revolutionary, isn't it?"

"Yes."

"Don't you need an architect?"

That disarmed her—he was a man with humor at least. "Will you have a drink?" She swirled the contents of the pitcher. "A martini?"

"Thank you."

"I'll get a glass."

A few steps took him to the table where Mike's glass sat. "If this was Ginny's glass, I don't mind using it."

No more lies. She hardly knew now which were hers and which were Ginny's. "It wasn't Ginny's glass," she said.

He brought it to her anyway. "Whoever it was, it won't poison me."

All the same, those eyes that just missed hers saw everything that passed through her mind. She wanted to escape them, however briefly, in the time it would take to get a glass from the other room. "That's ridiculous," she said. "Sit down, Allan. That chair is better for your long legs than this one."

His movements were such that she thought him about to take the far chair as she had suggested, but she had no more than stepped into the dining room than he was behind her.

"What a marvelous old room!"

Of all six rooms this was the plainest, with nothing to recommend it except the view of the garden and that was not available at night. One end of it had been chopped off in the nineteen-twenties to provide space for a bathroom. She took a glass from the cupboard.

"May I see the kitchen?" he asked, throwing her a quick, persuasive smile.

"Why not?" This time she stepped aside and let him go on by himself. The kitchen was straight head, not to be missed. He had an athlete's build as well as one's lightness of step, she observed as he passed her.

"Puss, puss, puss," he said, seeing the cat. She came wide-awake, stood up, and preened herself for him.

Amy kept trying to tell herself that it was she who was behaving oddly, letting her imagination run wild. She tried to think what he and Ginny would be like together. They were similar in a way she could not put her finger on. Then she had it: Ginny never seemed quite able to hit the nail on the head. God knows, he was direct enough, but his eyes slipped past what he was presumably looking at.

Well, he had made it to the kitchen and if there was something there he wanted—a knife or a hammer—there was no preventing his getting it. She turned into the vestibule, that entrance to it opposite the bathroom, with the purpose of making sure the shotgun was in its place alongside the porch door, more or less concealed by her old Burberry coat and the umbrella stand. She could not see it where she stood, but that did not mean it was not there. For just an instant she thought of making a dash to the front door.

"Amy?"

They very nearly collided, his coming in as she turned back.

"Is the kitchen fireplace a replica of the old one?"

"Probably."

"Afterwards I'll show you where I think the old one was." He caught her hand as though he were an old friend and led her back to the living room. When she tried to remove her hand he gave it a little squeeze before letting go.

She poured the drinks shakily. "I should have got more ice."

"Are you afraid of me?"

"Certainly not," she said.

"I'm harmless enough. You'd have to know that for a fact from Ginny's having anything to do with me."

She laughed, thinking how obviously so that was. If she knew Ginny. Sometimes she felt that she knew Ginny so well she could not possibly know her at all. Maybe there were two Ginnies. "Cheers."

The drink was strong enough, but it was going tepid.

"Would you allow me to get more ice and give these another stir?" he asked.

"I would allow it." She poked up the embers under the half-burned log. The sparks exploded and vanished. Ginny ought to have come even if she didn't believe the story about the story. It was funny how sure she had been that Allan was imaginary. Nor could she remember anything Ginny had ever told her about him. Had she told her anything? Or had Amy simply turned it off, doubting that there was a real live Allan?

He returned with the pitcher and the glasses, having taken them also to the kitchen. They now were white with frost. He poured the drinks, touched her glass with his, and said, "What else would you allow?"

Harmless? She said, trying to strike a pose of propriety without overdoing it: "I'd allow as how—I wouldn't allow much."

He shrugged. "No offense."

"None taken."

He started to shuffle across to the chair she had appointed his, then turned back. "What's much?" Having again amused her, he bent down and kissed her as she was reasonably sure he had never kissed Ginny. "Perfectly harmless," he said and trotted over to the chair while neatly balancing the glass so that he did not spill a drop. "Does she often take long walks at this time of night?"

"As a matter of fact she does."

"And if I'm not mistaken, we're at the full moon." He helped make the lie more credible. Knowingly? "Has Ginny talked about me?"

"Well now," Amy said, avoiding a direct answer, "I almost suggested that she bring you out for the weekend."

"How intuitive of me then to be here."

"I suppose Ginny has given you a complete dossier on me?"

"We do talk a lot," he said in a sly, wistful, almost hopeless way that again amused her. "Have you anything to suggest I do about it?"

She knew exactly what he meant. "A marriage proposal?"

"That's a bit drastic."

"It sounds archaic when you set it off and listen to it by itself— a marriage proposal."

"Or the title to a poem by Amy Lowell," he said. "You weren't by any chance named after her?"

"Good God, no."

"She did like a good cigar, didn't she?" he said, deadpan.

Amy sipped her drink and gave a fleeting thought to Mike, to the steak in the refrigerator, to the Haut Brion '61. And to the rumpled bed in the room back of the fireplace.

He put his glass on the table and got up with a sudden show of exuberance. "Shall I bring in more wood? I saw the pile of it outside."

"Not yet." Amy put the one log left in the basket onto the fire. While she swept in the bits of bark and ash, he came and stood beside her, bent, studying the fire, but stealing glimpses of her face. He touched his fingers lightly to a wisp of hair that had escaped one of the braids she wore in a circle round her head. "Your hair must be very long and beautiful."

"I've been told so."

"Ginny said it was."

"I wasn't thinking of Ginny."

"I wasn't either. Except in the way you hang onto somebody in the dark."

When they had both straightened up, he waited for her to face him, and then he lifted her chin, touching it only with the backs of his fingers as though to take hold of it might seem too bold. He kissed her. It was a long kiss which, nonetheless, didn't seem to be going anywhere until she herself thrust meaning into it. She had not intended to, but then the situation was not one open to precise calculations. He tasted of licorice as well as gin.

He drew back and looked at her. At that proximity his eyes did not seem to have the disconcerting vagary. He was, despite these little overtures, agonizingly shy: the realization came in a flash. Someone had prescribed—possibly a psychiatrist—certain boldnesses by which he might overcome the affliction. *Miss* Amy: that was closer to his true self.

He said, averting his eyes once more, "Ginny said we'd like one another . . . even though you don't like men."

"What?"

"She thinks you don't care much for men."

"What kind of woman does she think I am then? The kind who gets paid?"

Color rushed to his face. He backed off and turned, starting back to his chair in that shuffling way—a clown's way, really, the "don't look at me but at what I'm doing" routine which reinforced her belief in his shyness.

"I don't want another drink," she said, "but if you do, help yourself. I say what's on my mind, Allan. People who know me get used to it. By the sound of things, Ginny speaks hers too on occasion. I'd never got that picture of her."

"I shouldn't have blabbed that."

"No, you shouldn't." She started from the room, thinking: God save me from middle-aged adolescents.

"Where are you going?"

"To the bathroom for now. Then I'll decide where else."

She had not reached the door when he caught her from behind

and lifted her from her feet, holding her close against him, her arms pinned to her sides. He kissed the back of her neck and then with his teeth he removed, one by one, her plastic hairpins and let them drop to the floor. "Please don't be so fierce," he said, his mouth at her ear. She felt the dart of his tongue there, but so tentative, as though he were following a book of instructions.

"Put me down. Your belt buckle's hurting me."

Her feet on the floor, she faced him. "I don't have to be fierce at all," she said and loosened the braids, after which she shook out that abundance of rich brown hair.

He ran his tongue round his lips. "It's just too bad that Ginny's going to be walking in."

"She's not."

"She's not?" he repeated. Something changed in his face, which was certainly natural with that bit of news. "I don't believe you," he said, the smile coming and going.

She motioned to him with one finger as much as to say, wait, and going to the phone, she dialed Virginia's number. With each ring Amy felt less sure of herself, less sure of Ginny. Then, after the fourth ring, came the gentle slow-voiced, "Hello."

Amy held the phone out toward Allan. He simply stared, his head slightly to the side. It could not have been more than a second, but it did seem longer before Ginny repeated more clearly, "Hello?"

He was about to take the phone. Amy broke the connection, pressing her finger on the signal, then returning the phone to its cradle.

"I don't get it," he said.

"It was a change of plan. That's all."

"And not anything to do with me?"

"My dear man, I wasn't even sure you were real."

"Maybe I'm not," he said, and smiled tentatively. It seemed flirtatious.

Amy threw her head back. "There's one way to find out."

He gave a funny little shudder, as though a chill had run through him. Or better, something interestingly erotic. He wet a finger and held it up as to the wind. Unerringly he then pointed to the closed door of the bedroom back of the fireplace. He mentioned her to move on ahead of him. Had he looked in through, say, a part of the drapes at her and Mike? Or had Virginia told him that Amy slept downstairs? There did not seem to be much Ginny had not told him. With interpretations."Don't turn on the lights," he said.

Amy was not surprised. "We can always turn them off again.

"No." And then: "I'm able to see you in the dark."

A good trick. She said nothing. It was beginning to irritate her that Ginny had said she did not like men. Liking sex and liking men deserved a distinction, true. But she did not think it one Ginny was likely to make. And she had loved Mike. She had. Now it was over, ended. Nothing was beginning; nothing was about to be born. Except that you couldn't really tell. That was what was so marvelous about an encounter such as this: you couldn't really tell.

She bent down to remove her slippers. She felt his hand running lightly over her bare shoulder, sweeping the hair before it. A jolting pain struck at the base of her skull. Then came nothingness.

She awoke to the sound of voices and with a headache worse than any she had ever suffered. A woman's voice said that she was coming to. Like hell, she wanted to say; not if she could help it, not with all this pain. There was other pain besides that of her head, and with the awareness of it she began to realize what had happened. She tried to put her hand between her thighs. Someone gently pulled it away.

"Amy?"

She opened her eyes to the familiar ceiling beam with its ancient knot, the eye of the house. She turned her head far enough to see Virginia's round and worried face. "What are you doing here?"

A woman in a white uniform hovered alongside Ginny. She was filling a hypodermic needle from a medicine bottle. When Ginny glanced up at her, she moved away.

"On the phone," Ginny said, "I couldn't hear anything except the clock, but I'd know its tick anywhere. Remember when we were kids: 'take a *bath*, take a bath, take a *bath*, take a bath . . .' I decided I'd better catch the next bus out."

Amy gave her hand a weak squeeze. At the door of the room were two uniformed policemen, one of whom she thought she remembered having once talked out of giving her a speeding ticket. "How did *they* get in on the act?"

"I called the ambulance," Ginny said, and leaning close, she murmured, "You were"—she couldn't bring herself to say the exact word—"molested."

"I guess," Amy said.

One of the policemen said, "When you're strong enough we need the full story, miss. Did you recognize the intruder?"

The intruder. In a way he was, of course. She took a long time in answering. "Is there any way I can be sure he'll get psychiatric attention?"

The cops exchanged glances. "The first thing is to identify him so we can bring him in."

"And then I have to swear out a complaint against him?"

"If you don't, ma'am, some other woman may not get the chance to do it."

"To some extent it was my own fault," she said, not much above a whisper.

The cop made a noise of assent. Neither he nor his partner seemed surprised. "All the same, we better get him in and let the shrinks decide what happens to him. Okay?"

She thought of telling them of the point at which she had been knocked out and decided against it for the time being. "Okay," she said.

"Can you give us a description? Race, age, height, color of his eyes—"

"Ginny, I'm sorry. It was your friend Allan."

"Oh."

It was a little cry, scarcely more than a whimper.

"Would you give them his name and address? You won't have to do anything else."

"But, Amy, I can't. I mean, actually I've never seen Allan. He calls me and we just talk on the telephone."

HELEN NIELSON

Decision

Ruth had never been in a courtroom before. It was exciting—like something from a movie or the television. She paused just inside the doorway, the matron at her side, and as she did so the flashbulbs began to explode, and all the people in the room turned to stare at her. For just a moment she was startled and embarrassed. One hand automatically tugged at the front of her blue wool suit jacket—it had a way of riding up since she'd put on weight. Not that Ruth was plump. Her figure was good—too good for comfort, because Ruth, although she'd trained herself to conceal it, was excessively shy. But she was also feminine. She tugged at the jacket, and then she brushed a wisp of blond hair from her forehead—and all of this with such a well-practised concealment of emotion that the caption writers would be dusting off such phrases as "stony-faced tigress and "iceberg killer" to fit under those pictures in the afternoon editions. By this time the flashbulbs had stopped exploding, and a policeman was clearing the way.

Ruth walked forward to the table where Mr. Jennings was waiting for her. He pulled out her chair and smiled.

"Good morning, Miss Kramer. You're looking well this morning."

Ruth didn't answer. She sat down, and then Mr. Jennings sat down beside her and began to fuss with some papers in his brief case. Mr. Jennings was rather shy himself—and nervous. Ruth had heard it remarked that this was his first capital case, which accounted for the nervousness. Public Defender. She ran the words over in her mind. They had a good sound. This man was going to defend her from the public. No, that wasn't what the words really meant. Ruth knew. She'd learned a great many in her thirty-odd years, and she knew what just about all the words meant; but that's the way they sounded to her when she ran them over in her mind. She liked Mr. Jennings. He reminded her of Allan. Younger and more serious, but just as neat. That was the important thing. His white shirt was freshly laundered, his narrow tie was clipped in place, and his suit must have just come from the pressers. He was clean shaven and smelled of one of those lotions the ad writers call brisk and masculine.

But staring at Mr. Jennings would only make him more nervous. Ruth looked about the courtroom. The jury was in the box, their assorted faces wearing different degrees of strain. Ruth's bland face concealed an inner smile. The jury seemed even more nervous that Mr. Jennings. It might have been on trial instead of her. Then she turned and looked at the spectators. No trial since the Romans had fed live dinners to the lions had been complete without them. The public—society. That was a word that amused her even more than the faces of the jury—society. There it was in its assembled might, neither frightening nor particularly offended. Curious was a better word. Curious society awaiting its cue to acquit or condemn, because society never knew until it was told what to do. It was a like a huge mirror in which one saw not one reflection but that of a crowd.

If I smiled, Ruth thought, *they would smile back. If I waved my hand, they would wave their hands. They never do anything of themselves. They never act; they only react.*

That was society, and she was outside of it now because she'd broken the first rule. She'd made a decision. . . .

Everybody in the neighborhood could tell you how devoted Ruth Kramer was to her parents. Such a good girl. Such a hard worker. Such a good provider since poor old Mr. Kramer had had to stop working. There wasn't a mother on the block who didn't envy Mrs. Kramer's relationship with her daughter. Not many young people were so thoughtful. Not many cared so much. Everybody in the neighborhood could tell you everything they knew about Ruth Kramer—which was nothing.

Ruth couldn't remember when she'd started hating her father.

It might have been the time when she was five and caught him killing the puppies. They were newborn and hardly aware of life, and maybe it was the only thing to do, with times so hard and food so short; but it was horrible to watch him toss their bodies, still warm and wriggling, into the post holes he'd been digging for the back fence. It was even more horrible to hear him boast about it later.

"Six post holes, six puppies at the bottom. I saved myself all that work of digging graves."

"Otto, don't talk about it. Not in front of the child," Anna Kramer would say.

"Why not talk about it? She had to learn to save—work, money. Nobody can waste anything in life."

Otto Kramer had a simple philosophy. He never questioned life; he never argued with it. "A bed to sleep on, a table to eat on, a stove to cook on—what more do you need?" A very simple philosophy. Worry and fear belonged in a woman's world, and he had no sympathy for either. If Ruth had tears she could shed them in her mother's thin, tight arms. There was no other warmth in the world.

And there was no money to be wasted on the foolishness of pain.

"A woman is supposed to have babies. That's what she's made for. I ain't got money to throw away on hospital bills. It's all foolishness, anyway. It's all in a woman's mind."

Otto Kramer spoke, and that was law. Anna never argued with her husband. She just grew thin and pale and cried a great deal when he was away, and when her time came it wasn't all in her mind, after all. Hidden behind the pantry door, a child heard everything.

"You thick-skulled old-country men ought to be horse-whipped?" the doctor said. "You lost a son for your stinginess, and you damned near lost a wife! Leave her alone now until she gets her strength back—understand? Leave her alone or I'll take care of you myself!"

Crouched in the darkness behind the pantry door, Ruth didn't understand—except that in some way her mother was in danger from this man she was growing to hate, and needed protection.

She never forgot.

There were a great many things the neighbors didn't know about Ruth Kramer. They didn't know for instance, that when she was fourteen she slept with a knife hidden under her pillow. Nobody knew that. Not even her mother. But Ruth had watched and guarded for a long time, and by that time the quarreling and night noises beyond the paper-thin walls had taken on a strange and ominous significance. The knife was for her fear—a nameless fear that was doomed to silence.

Anna Kramer didn't like to talk about such things.

"Forget the silly things you hear, child. It's not for you to worry about."

But Ruth wasn't a child. She was fourteen. At fourteen it seems there should be an end to misery.

"Why don't you get a divorce?" she asked.

Divorce! A shocking word. Where had she gotten such an idea? Divorce was a sin! It seemed to Ruth that perpetual unhappiness was an even greater sin, but she didn't have a chance to argue the point. The tight, thin arms were about her again, closing out the world. She mustn't think of such things. She had her school work to think about, and that scholarship—

Ruth didn't win the scholarship. She suffered a breakdown and couldn't even finish the semester; but in a way, her sickness was a good thing. It gave her time to think things out. There had to be a reason for all this unhappiness, and there had to be a way out. If only they weren't so poor. If only there was a little extra money to fix up the house and have friends and live the way other people lived. Ruth thought it all out and then put the knife back in the knife drawer because it was foolishness, even if it were a sign of rebellion. She knew a better way.

There was no trouble about going back to school. School was an extravagance and a waste on a female. Work was good. Work kept young people out of trouble.

"I went to work when I was twelve years old," Otto Kramer said. "Fifteen hours a day and a straw pallet in the back of the shop. I had no time for racing around in old cars and playing jazz records all night like young people do nowadays. Hoodlums! Nothing but hoodlums!"

Ruth didn't argue. The old cars and the jazz records weren't to be a part of her life, anyway. There was no time. Work was for days and study was for evenings, because her father was wrong about education. He was wrong about a lot of things, but she didn't argue about any of them. Arguments and quarreling were a waste of time. She learned to withdraw from them—to tune out the voices behind the wall at night, just as she tuned up the music on her bedside radio. But she always listened with half an ear, and she never forgot to watch. And she never forgot her plan. Every problem had to have a solution, and she was going to find the solution for happiness. Otto Kramer's house remained a fortress from without; but within, it began to change. The floors were carpeted, the windows curtained, a plumber installed a new sink, and the iceman didn't have to stop by after the refrigerator was delivered. The plan began to work. Anna Kramer's face learned how to smile; but Otto's remained grim.

"Foolishness! Damn foolishness! Throw money around like that and you'll be sorry!"

And just to prove his point, he lost his job and never did get around to finding another one.

It might have been then that Ruth Kramer began to hate her father; but for the next few years she was too busy to think about it. Every problem had to have a solution. She did her positive thinking and took another course at night school. After that, she got a better job with longer hours. The problem was still there, but there wasn't so much time to think about it. What was happiness, anyway? How many people ever knew? When the quarreling was especially bad, and the tears too heavy—Ruth could never bear to hear her mother cry—she could set a balance again with flowers sent as a surprise, or some new piece for the shelf of china miniatures Anna Kramer so loved. And there was always the music to be tuned up louder so the neighbors wouldn't hear. From the outside everything was lovely. Nobody ever went into the house but the three people who lived inside, enduring one another while the years piled up behind them like a stack of unpaid bills. And everything in life had to be paid for sooner or later. Far back in her mind, crowded now with more knowledge that she could ever use, Ruth knew that.

The bills began coming due when she met Allan.

She'd never thought about men. They were in her world; but they were only names on the doors of offices, or voices answering the telephone. They sat behind desks that always held a photograph of the wife and children, and they sometimes paid compliments and gave raises.

"I wish we had more employees like you, Miss Kramer. I never have to worry about how you're going to do your work."

That kind of compliment—never anything about her hair-do, which was severe and neat, or her suits, which were tailored to conceal her thinness and build up her bustline. Men were hands on desktops, voices on the telephone, and signatures on a paycheck. They were the office wolf to be ignored, the out-of-town customer to be kidded, and the serious young man who missed his mother to be gently brushed aside. And a dour old man who now sat at home in his chair in the corner like a pile of dirty rags.

But Allan Roberts wasn't any of these things. Allan was that old bill coming due. If she'd known, she wouldn't have been so pleased when he called her into his office that first day.

"I like the way you work, Miss Kramer. You must have been with the company a long time."

A new engineer with top rating, and he'd noticed her out of the whole office staff. Ruth was flattered.

"Twelve years," she admitted, wishing for some reason that it didn't sound so long.

"Good. You know more about procedure than I do. You're just the assistant I need on this hotel job."

That's how it started—strictly business. But it was a big job— an important job. It meant long hours with late dinners in some hole-in-the-wall restaurant, with a juke box wailing and a lot of talk and laughter to ease the strain of a hard, tense job. It meant work on Sunday, with Allan's convertible honking at the curb, and Ruth hurrying out before he had time to come to the door. And eventually it meant talk at home.

"You're with this man an awful lot," Anna Kramer said.

"He's nice," Ruth admitted. "And smart. I'm learning a lot on this job."

"He looks nice. He dresses nice."

"He's got a responsible job. He has to dress nice."

"Your father used to dress nice. I'll never forget when I met him—silk shirt, derby hat, walking stick."

"My father?"

"Handsome, too. I remember thinking that I'd never seen such a handsome man—and such big ideas for the future."

They'd never talked like this before. Anna Kramer's eyes were far away; then they met Ruth's and changed the subject.

"I suppose you'll be working Sunday."

"I suppose I will," Ruth said.

"We'll miss church again."

"I keep telling you, you should make friends with the neighbors and go with them."

Anna sighed. Her eyes found the miniatures on the shelf.

"You know how your father feels about neighbors. I don't like to start a fuss and get you upset when we have such a nice home now."

Ruth worked Sunday. She worked many Sundays, and then, as much as she dreaded it, the job ended.

"But we're invited to the opening," Allan said. "When shall I pick you up?"

She hadn't counted on that. Working with Allan was fun. Dinner in those small cafés was fun. But a hotel opening wasn't like a concert, or a lecture, or a class at evening school.

"I suppose it's formal," she hedged.

"I hope so. You'll be a knockout in an evening gown."

He was kidding her, of course. Allan was a great kidder. Still she didn't like to refuse. It might even jeopardize her job. She took a lunch hour for shopping, because she'd never owned an evening dress. That was when she became the last person to be aware of what had been going on under those tailored suits all the years. Allan wasn't kidding.

Cinderella went to the ball. Poor Cinderella, who was always losing things. A dance floor wasn't much good to a collector of Bach, but Allan was gallant.

"I might as well be honest," he said. "It doesn't show because I have my shoes made to order, but I've got two left feet. Let's see how the terrace looks in the moonlight."

The terrace looked the way all terraces look in the moonlight. Ruth was trembling when she pulled away from him. They hadn't taught her anything like that in night school. But she was embarrassed, too. He must have known. He could go back to the office and tell stories in the washroom about how he'd frightened that strait-laced Miss Kramer who was so efficient in so many other things.

"You live with your parents, don't you?"

She'd expected that. She didn't have to answer. She already felt alone.

"I mean, you don't have any other ties to hold you here?"

She didn't expect that.

"To hold me?"

"There's a new contract coming up in Mexico City. A big one—six months, maybe a year. I'm getting the assignment, and I'd like to have you come along. I think we work well together."

She didn't expect that at all. Mexico City. A Latin beat from the dance floor came up behind them, a deep throbbing rhythm, and Ruth began to hear it for the first time. To hear it, and feel it, with a stirring and churning starting inside her as if something were being born.

And she could feel Allan's eyes smiling in the darkness.

"I think you'd like Mexico," he said. "I think the change will do you good. Anyway, you've got a couple of weeks to decide."

It was much after midnight when Cinderella came home from the ball. She stopped humming at the doorway and let herself in quietly, but she needn't have been so cautious. As soon as she switched on the lights, she saw her mother huddled in the wing chair.

"You didn't have to wait up—" she began, and then she saw her mother's face. "What is it? What's wrong?"

The face of a martyr taking up the cross.

"Nothing," Anna answered. "Nothing for you to worry about."

"Nothing? Then why aren't you in bed?"

Haunted eyes looked at her. A thin hand hugged at the throat of a worn robe, and the sleeve fell back to show an ugly bruise.

"Mother—!"

"Go to bed," Anna said. "You had a nice time, didn't you? Go to bed and don't worry about me."

"But you've been hurt!"

"It doesn't matter. It's happened before."

"*He* did it!"

An anger flared up as old as a knife tucked away under a pillow.

"Don't—don't talk so loud! He's asleep now."

"But you don't have to put up with this! You don't have to live with him!"

Anna's eyes swept the room. A beautiful room—perfect, like the miniatures on the shelf. The home she'd always wanted. Some plans did work.

"Maybe he's sick," Ruth said. "Maybe if he saw a doctor—"

"You know what your father thinks of doctors."

"But if he's violent—"

Anna wore a sad smile.

"I told you—it's nothing. It's happened before. You would have noticed if you weren't always so busy. He's an old man, that's all. An old man gets angry when—when he can't do what he used to do."

Anna fell silent. There was shame in her eyes for having almost spoken of the forbidden subject. She got up out of the chair and started toward the hall.

"You're not going back there?"

The sad smile came back.

"I told you—it's nothing. I shouldn't have said anything and ruined your good time. Go to bed now. It's all right. As long as I have you, everything is all right."

The arms closed about Ruth's shoulders in a good-night embrace. Nothing . . . nothing . . . Ruth turned out the lamp when she was gone and sat alone in the darkness. Nothing . . . She began to tremble.

Ruth didn't go to Mexico City. At the office her breakdown was written off to overwork on the hotel job. When she returned, Allan was gone. He never came back. For a time there was an empty place where he had been, a kind of misty pitfall with a mental sign in front of it: "Keep Away—Danger," and then the emptiness began to fill up with odds and ends of more work, more books, a course in clay modeling, and a season's ticket to the symphony. At home she played the music louder to drown out the endless quarreling, and learned not to mention separation, or a doctor, or doing anything at all.

On her thirtieth birthday, Ruth bought her first bottle of whisky. She kept it in a closet where her mother wouldn't find it. Good people, who didn't do sinful things—such as not facing problems—didn't drink. The bottle helped on the long nights when sleep wouldn't come. A little later she dropped the modeling class because she'd lost interest in it, and the homework was cluttering up her room, and she had to stop going to the concerts because they made her nervous. But she couldn't sit around the house watching the slow death come. She drove out nights, and in time found a hole-in-the-wall bar where a three-piece combo wandered deep into the wild nowhere, and a sad singer sobbed out the woes of the shadow people, who feel no pain and dream old dreams that never come true because they live in the land of no decisions.

There were objections, of course.

"I wish you wouldn't go out so much alone," Anna Kramer said, "especially at night."

Ruth laughed. She laughed a lot lately.

"Alone? How else could I go?"

The hurt look, and then—

"We used to take such nice rides on Sunday."

"I'll take you for a ride on Sunday."

"But every night—out. Honestly. I don't know what to make of you any more. You'd think I had enough trouble with your father!"

"Oh, God—!"

Then a door would slam, the music go loud, and she'd dig the bottle out of the closet.

The trouble at the office was a long time coming. It wasn't her fault. Everything cluttered, everything in a mess. The youngsters were coming in—fresh and eager and green. No use trying to teach them anything. They knew it all. It got so that Ruth hardly talked to anyone except the clown in the sales department who told ribald jokes and made her laugh without knowing why. The trouble was a long time coming, but it came suddenly when it arrived. With gloves, of course. Working too hard. Too much responsibility. Not a demotion, understand, but the hours will be shorter and, of course, the pay. Ruth understood. The strange thing was how little she cared.

She didn't go home after work. She drove around for a few hours, and then drifted back to that hole in the wall where the shadows moaned, and crouched, and waited. Now it seemed that they were waiting for her—that this was the destiny she'd been bound for all these years. This was what came of hiding behind pantry doors and trembling in the darkness with a knife under her pillow. She knew what was wrong. She couldn't bury it in the books or try to hide it in the bottom of an empty bottle any more. It crawled inside her like a worm of dread, and there was only one way to get rid of it. She ordered a double whisky to steel her nerve.

The shadow people moved about her with hungry faces. At first she'd come only to watch them; now she belonged. She had only to give the sign. They were waiting. One, in particular, a dark, dirty, unshaven man.

They went out together. They drove to a dark street—dead end. It seemed appropriate.

No preliminaries. This wasn't a high-school prom. He knew what she wanted. His mouth closed over hers, and his hands began tearing at her blouse. Ruth shuddered. The stirring that had started with Allan's kiss was churning up like an angry sea. A wall was crumbling. A high wall, a high tower—

But her hands were pushing him away.

He clawed at her, swearing softly. She pushed him back against the door.

"You crazy bitch!"

He came at her again, ugly and cruel. She saw his face dimly—unshaven, leering, smelling of liquor and filth. All of her strength went into her lunge. He fell backward against the door handle. The door opened, spilling him out in the street. She had the motor started by the time he'd scrambled to his feet. The headlights caught him for one wild moment as she backed away—

an angry and bewildered man, muttering curses and fumbling at his trousers.

She drove blindly, half sobbing. When it was far enough behind, she parked and sat alone in the darkness. The wall had started to crumble, and when a thing started it had to go on until it was done. She smashed the "Danger" sign in her mind and stared deep into the emptiness that was Allan's. Allan was gone. Allan would never come back. She'd never hear his laughter, or see the way his eyes crinkled, or feel that second kiss that had made all the difference. But the world wasn't over. There was other laughter and other eyes, and there *was* a difference! There *had* to be!

But before she could find it, there was one thing she must do. One thing for certain.

She drove home, noticing for the first time how the hedges had become shaggy and how the lawn had turned brown. There were so many things to do, and never enough time. She went into the house. Her father sat in his chair in the corner like a heap of dirty rags. Her mother looked up with anxious eyes. She hurried past them to her room. One thing she *must* do . . .

"Ruth! What are you doing? Where are you going?"

One suitcase was enough. The furniture, the lamps, the books didn't matter. Let the dead bury the dead. One suitcase and tomorrow was enough.

"Why are you packing? What's happened? What's wrong?"

No answers. No explanations. No trouble. Ruth closed the suitcase and started toward the door. They were there, both of them. The woman and the old man. Bewildered, frightened. She tried to get through the door without speaking, but they blocked her way.

"I'm leaving," she said.

"Leaving? For a trip? On business?"

"Forever," Ruth said.

"But why? What have I done?"

Tears were welling up in the woman's eyes. Ruth couldn't bear tears. She tried to push past. Her father was in the way.

"Who do you think you are?" he demanded. "You answer your mother!"

"There is no answer."

"You be careful now! You ain't so damn smart as you think. You ain't no better than us! You'll end up in the gutter like I always said!"

He shouldn't have said it—not ever, but especially not then. An ugly, dirty, unshaven old man. She looked at him and trembled, and then it started again—the shuddering, the churning inside.

"Let me go!" she gasped.

He tried to push her back into the room. He slapped her across the face, and the wall was crumbling again. She had the suitcase in her hand. She swung with all her might. She heard him go down, and then the ugly, evil face was gone. . . .

"Ruth—what have you done?"

He was on the floor—quiet and bleeding.

"Your own father! You've struck down your own father!"

Anna knelt beside him, cradling his bleeding head in her arms.

"Otto! Otto, are you alive? *Liebchen*—"

Ruth stared at them. The woman sobbing, her head bowed and her tight, thin arms, cradling him closer and closer to her breast. Her child. Her broken child caught up in the great-mother-lust, that subtle rape from which there is no escape save one . . .

And the wall was crumbling so that Ruth's breath came in great, silent sobs. When a thing started it had to be finished, one way or another. She moved slowly toward her mother.

The murmur of voices in the courtroom silenced, and everybody rose as the judge came to the bench. A handsome, dignified man graying at the temples. Stern and fatherly. He sat down, and everybody sat down. It was about to begin. Exciting. Just like in the movies.

And then a man came across the room and bent down to whisper in Mr. Jennings' ear, Mr. Jennings looked happy. He turned to Ruth.

"Good news!" he said. "Your father has regained consciousness. He's ready to testify that he struck you first—that you retaliated in self-defense."

Of course, Ruth thought. *Somebody has to look after him.*

"That gives you a good chance of getting off completely. We

should have little trouble proving that your mother's death was accidental. Everybody knows how devoted you were."

For just a moment Ruth felt the quick stab of panic; and then her poise returned, and she sat back quietly. The jury—only faces in a mirror. She'd never let them acquit her. Nobody was going to send her back to that house now that she'd made her decision.

ESTHER WAGNER

Contemporary Gothic

Michael Harker had had an old-fashioned education and upbringing, of which he was often made to feel ashamed. When his wife died and he moved with his small son David to another town, he was impelled in his loneliness to seek the sort of house and household he had always longed for—with a longing he was now unable to fight. So he bought a huge old house on a lot so large it was almost a park.

The house was one of the last of its kind in the town—indeed in the country, thought Harker—and his mind filled with a savoury blend of shame and pleasure whenever he walked through its long halls, glanced into its big rooms and up at its high ceilings, sensed its dark corner, roomy attic, and many-chambered basement.

Harker had never been poor, and was now almost rich. But his adult life had been lived in houses very different from this. His wife had liked breakfast nooks, dining areas, bedrooms on the same floor as the living room, half basements, patios. Largeness in a house was for her a matter of windows. Harker's houses had all looked out on the world. The inward-looking, closing-out houses of his boyhood had become identified in his mind with backwardness and unenlightenment.

He hired the most old-fashioned of household help, a plump, kindly woman named Mrs. Poole, who lived on the third floor. Harker, who in his married life had known only cleaning women, cateresses, and baby-sitters, felt guilty about this comfort, too. It was altogether too reminiscent of his mother's and grandmother's establishments. He felt he was backsliding, and backsliding with a voluptuous sense of sin.

196

When an opportunity for reparation presented itself, he was only too glad to take advantage of it. He hired a baby-sitter, who had never done anything in her life but baby sit. Harker felt familiar with her; she was like the help hired by his late wife in that she didn't do very much. But by paying her the small weekly sum which she asked for as "pocket-money," and allowing her to occupy a little basement room, formerly the gardener's apartment, he could tell himself that he was not only helping the girl get a college education but that he was doing an expected thing—hiring a baby-sitter.

Moreover, the girl did not violate the beloved spirit of his house. She seemed much at home amid the non-Philippine mahogany panelling and blue grasspaper of the dining room; she had *wanted* the spooky little basement room, rather than anything upstairs. In some secret way she responded to the old house, and Harker valued this.

The girl was so young that it was hard to imagine her ever, outside real childhood, looking any younger; but then, Harker realised slowly, it was hard to imagine her, outside real middle-age, looking any older either. She was extremely pale, with a kind of luminous pallor which Harker easily recognised as the prevailing fashion in make-up. She was lean and tall, also in the prevailing mode, and so spare that you thought "She's been sick!" until you remembered how today's models look.

But there was the stranger youthful glow of that pale skin, triumphing over livid make-up; the victorious deep red of her lips, the rich red-brown of her eyes, the sheen on her black straight hair, and the careless-power in her swift walk. Harker knew they were all beyond the gift of any cosmetic house or modelling school. She had, too, the glorious confident mindlessness which helped him feel she was the contemporary feature he needed in his household. She knew nothing about anything. She could only make peanut butter sandwiches and Instant chocolate milk for David; Mrs. Poole found this unsatisfactory, and insisted on her own menus for the boy.

Harker knew that this was quite standard, and that it was Mrs. Poole who really needed re-education. Yet he had to admit that the sitter made him obscurely uncomfortable. He disliked seeing her bend over David. The long body, the long neck, the long black hair . . . well, Harker knew he was being absurd, and he knew too, guiltily, that he was something his last wife had called "over-read." His mind was haunted by images derived from his book-loving youth and his rather obsessive taste for old books, a taste which he felt was a sign of arrested development. He knew that after college it was expected you would forget all that. But he couldn't. And the girl reminded him of the blood-stained mouths of Borgia legend, of the deadly graces and phosphorescent beauties emanating from the victims and initiates of great Count Dracula.

Harker had always thought these old romances very pleasant, and had even thought warmly of the Count when he bought the old house, and imagined as a visitor to those tall rooms the lord of the dark Castle. But he gradually found these associations unpleasant in connection with the baby-sitter. He avoided the girl; after all, it wasn't *her* fault. She did not get home from college till early evening, and he never saw her leave in the morning. She was easy to avoid.

But one evening she appeared in the front hallway, coming in from a little-used entrance that led to the pantries, just as he was preparing to leave for an evening of work at his office. Nervous as always in her presence, he asked if she had enjoyed her dinner. She stared at him.

"Dinner?" she said. "Oh. That. Well, I haven't had it yet. But I wanted to ask you a favour."

Harker welcomed this.

"I saw this little kiln in your workshop down there," she said in her sweet, small, stupid voice, so thin and silvery for one so tall and striking. "I *like* those things. I had one of my own, but I wrecked it experimenting. It got all burned out and stinky. But if you'd let me use that little one I know I wouldn't wreck it. I see nobody else uses it."

"David doesn't care for it," said Harker quickly. "Please have it."

She gave him her little blank-eyed smile—not really a smile since she never opened her lips for it; she just curved her mouth a bit.

"Thanks," she said, and started to move swiftly away.

"Wait!" said Harker, wanting to show intelligent interest. "Experiments? Are you in science?"

"What?" she asked, drawing her thin brows together. "Oh, science! You mean at college. No. I'm in Home Ec."

"Oh, yes," said Harker. Trapped in his limited academic experience, unable to make the smallest remark about Home Ec, he could only come up with "I guess that's what in my day the girls took in high school and called Domestic Science."

"I guess," she echoed in the sweet blank voice.

"Well, he said, "let Mrs. Poole know if you dream up any revolutionary new foodstuffs," and immediately feared she would take this for sarcasm about her lack of effort in the kitchen. But she smiled the almost-smile again, blinked in the hall light, and vanished soundlessly through her door.

She was beginning to bother him. He even thought about her at the office. Was it a sign of his general out-of-touchness and old-fashionedness that he felt so odd about this very unsingular girl? Or *was* there something fishy about her?

He had a good friend in the town, a social worker who had been a college friend of his wife's. Hilda Grose had done a lot of work among "difficult" young people. Harker called her up, and was soon comfortably settled in her little apartment, confiding in her while he swirled and rattled ice in his fat glass.

"Well, did you check?" said Miss Grose in her most commonsensical way, sounding exactly like his wife when she had been faced with a domestic problem: bored, but ready to come to grips. "References?"

"Of course I called the college. They said she was okay; never been a resident there, but she gets some money from a relative abroad—sort of Continental background. But she was born in this country, and makes the rest with these part-time jobs. Grades okay. Really no trouble of any sort."

"Well, Mike!" said Miss Grose. "Anyway, it's nice you stopped by." She grinned at him in friendly scorn. Then she felt sorry.

"Look," she said, "can't you be a little more down-to-earth about what bothers you with the girl? All you've told me is that there's no boy friend trouble, no klepto trouble, no noise trouble, no trouble with David you can put your finger on. She looks weird—what girl doesn't, if she goes in for the business, the clothes and posture and hair and make-up now? What exactl-'

"Well," he said, shamefaced but stubborn, "why does a girl like that *want* to live in our house? You saw it before I bought it and *you* thought I was crazy. Remember the basement, that little gardener's room? That's the room she wanted! And *she* came to me for the job, you know. What if she lets somebody through one of those basement doors? What if she goes out and stays all night and I don't know anything about it? What if she's *hiding* somebody down there?"

"Oh, Lord! You've been watching too many midnight television shows. But look: why don't you just get rid of her?"

"I can't do that!" Harker meant it.

"Okay, okay! So if anything happens—I mean really happens— call me. You wonder if there's something funny about the kid; brother, with the ones I see every day, you wouldn't have to do any wondering. Betcha one thing: your little Miss Weird-O isn't going to have any surprises for *this* old girl."

Harker lost a dog, and a neighbour lost a dog. David had some bad nightmares, about which he was very close-mouthed. Mrs. Poole complained just a bit about a smell coming up through the registers. Harker found a dead cat in the garbage can.

On an obscure impulse, wishing to "check" once more, he called up the college again. The Dean of Women allowed him to perceive that she was used to these vague, troublesome calls from fussy people who didn't quite know what they were calling about. He tried hard to expel the question of the sitter from his conscious mind. Then once he saw her gliding down the main staircase, looking incredibly vital and dead-pale. He spoke quite sharply to her.

"Miss Graves!" he said. She did indeed look gravely at him as she came down.

"Aren't you going anywhere? I, uh, I rather thought someone your age would be going—do you have friends at the college?" He felt, like an object inside his ears, the heavy weight of his own mean inquisitiveness.

"Why, sure," she told him calmly. "I'm going to a dance right now."

"The dress is very nice," said Harker lamely, and indeed it was a striking affair of black silk, with a broad band of red going diagonally across the front like some knightly order. Perhaps *nice* wasn't the word, but . . .

"Thank you, Mr. Harker," said the Graves girl demurely, and passed him.

Harker read late that night, determined to gather a few facts, make some concrete observations, rid his mind. He left enough doors open, including the door to the basement stairs, so that he could keep reasonable track. She came in fairly late, but not very; she did come in from the garden, though-through one of the basement doors to which he had not known she had a key.

Suddenly he heard a wild scream from the upper floor. David cried with his nightmares, but this scream was new. Yet, with a curious steady impulse. Harker went not upstairs but down. As he ran to the basement he heard Mrs. Poole pattering along the upper hall to David's room.

Miss Graves was not in her little bedroom. The door was open: he could see her chenille bedspread, her writing table with the kiln in the middle of it, a bunch of shiny glass jars; but she was in the little basement bathroom just down the passageway.

To Harker's stark amazement he found himself pounding on the bathroom door. He heard an ordinary splashing from within, of faucet water running in a basin, but there was no answer to his knock. He ground his teeth, swore, thrust open the unlocked door.

Miss Graves was bent over, brushing her teeth. She straightened and reached with a darting gesture for a towel, which she applied immediately to her face. Harker stared. She buried her face in the towel, wiped and blotted. When she raised her head to look at him, her red-brown eyes were more red than brown.

Had he made her cry? But he stared in gaping horror at the reddening towel with which she had wiped away the pink froth he had seen all over her mouth; at the stained toothbrush still in her other hand, at the thin streak and blotches of red on the washstand, escaped from the water's cleansing tide.

Miss Graves herself had to break the silence.

"What is it?" she asked, and turned away to pout up her toothbrush, wipe the basin top, and turn off the water. Harker was still speechless. When she turned back to him, her mouth dropped at its soft curling corners and her face was full of a strange, dark woe.

"Mr. Harker!" she said, her thin little voice rising. Harker gesticulated towards the towel.

"I *know*," she said mournfully, and her head hung. "It's terrible. It's always been so *terrible*, ever since I was a kid! Nobody can do anything about it, no matter what the ads say, Mr. Harker, I've just *got* pink toothbrush, sensitive gums. They bleed and bleed. I wish you—" Her voice trailed away.

Harker felt with a cruel, glad pang of self-castigation that he had done an enormous thing. He knew how these minor defects could damage a girl's idea of herself, break her confidence, haunt her with humiliation.

"These things go away," he muttered awkwardly. "I'm terribly sorry . . . shouldn't, wouldn't ever crash in like this, but I had to ask you about David. We're having trouble with him. I couldn't make you hear—" And he felt himself blushing, heard himself stammering.

"The nightmares?" she spoke again in her small crystal voice. "I heard him yell, down the register. I went in there once when he woke up and he nearly had a fit yelling. Mrs. Poole said I'd better not go in to him again. Didn't she tell you?"

"Well, I thought you—do you know about any stories he's heard, programmes he's seen—anything that could be behind this?"

She shook her head. Harker backed away, muttering his apologies. But as he turned, he tensed up again, for there in the basement passageway, bare feet on his linoleum, stood a girl he had never seen, wearing a flannel bathrobe. He shouted at her, "Who are *you*?" taken aback, outraged by her pale thick-skinned thick-featured face, her stolid expression. Miss Graves moved quickly to his side. The stranger was silent.

"Oh, that's Celia," said Miss Graves. "Celia Graves. My

cousin. She's at the college too. I thought you wouldn't mind, Mr. Harker. She was at the party with me. I know I should have asked, but it was so late, I didn't think you'd—" The other pale girl gave nothing but a numb half-smile.

"It's all right," said Harker confusedly. He brushed past and went up to David and Mrs. Poole.

But the next day he called up Miss Grose and made a date with her for dinner.

"Well, something *did* happen."

"You mean the kid's got pyorrhea?" said Hilda Grose. Harker enjoyed her smile; he'd not seen a real smile for some time.

"I only told you that because I thought the laugh on me was coming to you. I mean the other girl. This Celia. So I was right, there's been somebody else in and out. She looks queer, too, queerer than my Miss Graves, if you want to know."

"How could that *be?*"

"Okay! I called up the college. That damned dean. She tells me there's no other Graves at the college—just mine. Cynthia Graves. So mine was lying."

Miss Grose had to admit she was getting interested.

"All right, Mike," she said. "Funny family goings-on somewhere—it's usually that. Look: send your Cynthia over to me tomorrow afternoon on some errand. I can talk to these kids. I'll bet you another dinner I can tell you a lot about this Celia after I'm through."

When he got home that night he had no trouble finding Miss Graves. She was in the kitchen, boiling water. Harker asked what she was making.

"Instant," she said tranquilly.

"Did Mrs. Poole order it for you?" he asked in a fussy, hasty tone. Mrs. Poole never served it and had always seemed to him completely ignorant of the product. He had not missed it.

"What? Oh! No, I don't drink coffee. I make this other stuff, sort of soup, like, in that kiln you gave me. I just come up for the water."

He told her of the favour he wished to ask her. When she heard of the call on Miss Grose, a little wary look crossed her face.

"What time?"

"Late afternoon. I know you have some late classes. Just go when you can." She nodded. Apparently the wary look had come simply from the thought of having to alter her schedule. Harker, a man of schedules not lightly rearranged, felt this reassuring.

"What'd I tell you?" said Miss Grose over the dinner he had to buy her the next day. "It's usually family. That poor kid! Both of them come from broken homes. Cynthia feels more like a sister than a cousin to Celia. Looks out for her. Gets her invited to college parties; pretends she's a student, but she works somewhere downtown. Only relative they have is some terrible old uncle in some weird part of Europe. He sends Cynthia a little money every year, but ignores Celia. Cynthia helps Celia, and it's clear they're sort of mutually dependent. The lie was just a reflex. Ignore the whole thing, Mike! Those kids have had tough times. Let her have Celia there whenever she wants! What skin is it off you? Don't give her reason to lie and evade, then the lies and evasions stop. Rudiments! Come on, I'll buy you a drink at home and play you some new records. You'll still get home early.

"That kid loves your house, Mike. You've done a good thing for her. They can't ever come out with their gratitude, but *I'm* grateful to you, Mike, on the kid's account." He responded warmly to her kind smile.

But he didn't get home early, after all. Mrs. Poole called him at Miss Grose's to tell him that a terrible thing had happened and the house was full of police. A police officer spoke to him and told him a girl's body had turned up in his alley. The officer didn't want to ask the housekeeper to take a look; she was too old. Shock. A neighbour had found the body. The police ambulance was there; would he meet them at the morgue?

Hilda Grose went with him, for she honestly feared that he was going to have an attack of some sort. Remorse and terror drained the blood from Harker's ruddy face. Knowing him, she was sure he'd find some way to blame himself.

In the car he began to mutter.

"Poor kid, poor kid! You just don't *know*, Hilda! You don't know how I . . . Why, I used to *amuse* myself, pretending that

what I saw about her was that she was a vampire or werewolf or
something! Why, I used to sit there for hours handing myself a
laugh, thinking the Instant she brewed for herself was instant
blood, that her sort didn't need to suck any more because of
modern science . . . glass jars . . . cats and dogs, raw blood for the
Instant . . . Why, I used to think, well, she can't really be a
vampire—she goes to classes all day and everybody knows they
can't get around by day . . . The *dean* knows her, she's there all
day . . . So I'd hand myself a laugh: I'd think, well, she's the new
type vampire; she's not interested in David anyway, more
interested in just staying in the house, wouldn't risk her place . . .
after all, they have their housing problems; they've learned to
adapt . . . Then I'd laugh, I'd *laugh* . . . that poor kid, with her
broken-home background and her pink toothbrush . . . and me,
laughing!"

Miss Grose was at a loss. She couldn't even believe he had
laughed as he said he had; he was too emotional now. Somehow
she realized that she was, after all, surprised. She really hadn't
known that Michael was like this.

She stuck with him when they went in for the identification, for
she was now seriously worried about Harker's condition. She had
gathered that something pretty gruesome was involved. But when
the sheet was pulled down, neither she nor Harker even shrank
from the sight of torn throat and lacerated young shoulders; they
were too stunned by the face, unmarked, pale, drained in death.

"That's not her!" said Miss Grose.

"No," said Harker, who had only half his voice, and whose face
was drained too. "It's Celia."

The officer was considerate. He took in without effort the shift
in the case. He assured Harker an alarm would be sent out. He
didn't dare be too encouraging, he said, but after all, there was
not even any indication that the dead girl had been with her
cousin at the time of the happening. It was possible Cynthia was
perfectly safe somewhere.

"We've got to get back to the house," said Harker, dry-lipped.

"I left a patrolman there, Mr. Harker," said the officer.

"Hilda," said Harker hoarsely.

"Of course I'll come with you, Michael," she said.

She was unable to control her sudden fascination with Harker's unsuspectedly complex mental processes. Alone in his car with him, she started to probe.

"Now Mike! This sort of thing does happen. There's been some rise lately in our figures on juvenile delinquency in this supposedly wholesome town. This case will turn out to be one of those statistics. Though I must say I prefer, like you, the Teenage Vampire stuff."

Harker said nothing.

"Just to pass the time, tell me how you'd have fitted this development in with your private joke."

Harker shot her a look, dull-eyed, obscurely panicky.

"The girl Celia wouldn't be her cousin at all," he muttered, "just some poor, near-half-wit she picked up. Too dumb. But not too dumb to go to college, of course, enrol, sit there, take care of there being someone there who was thought of as Cynthia Graves. The dean's going to say I'm wrong and it *is* Cynthia Graves, and you and I and Mrs. Poole are going to have to say different. That girl kept mine from having to go out by day. Also she was a sort of, uh, reservoir . . ."

Miss Grose giggled helplessly.

"*What* an imagination, Mike! But if she used cats and dogs for her Instant, why did she need Celia?"

"You can't live on Instant alone," said Harker in a deep sad voice. Miss Grose felt really quite excited. There was certainly more to Michael's case than she'd ever suspected. His wife Helen had always told her he had been insecure as a child, living in those large old-fashioned households full of servants and shifting generation-patterns. And all that reading . . . well, everybody knew how that studious type of boy is likely to turn out. His instability had been settled for a while by marriage to Helen; but Helen's death had knocked out more props than he had realised, and now . . .

"Hilda," he said. "I'd better tell you something. After this, even if the girl comes back, I can't have her in the house."

"Of course," she soothed him, though she privately thought

that Michael would never get anywhere that way, always evading, always refusing to face up to things.

"I can help you, Mike. I'm a wheel, after all, at the Home, you know, the hostel for young people from broken homes. It's a good place, comfortable, lots of group activities, expert counselling."

"If she comes tonight, will you take her to this Home right away?"

"Of *course*, Mike."

The policeman met them at the door. No Miss Graves, nor any word. Mrs. Poole had taken David to bed, and was sleeping in the little boy's room.

"Hilda," said Harker, "would you do something for me? I'm going to sit up tonight. Don't argue, please! I want you to take David back with you. He's fond of you. I'd feel more comfortable if he were with you until we get this thing more nearly cleared up. Let me go up now and get him and drive you both back. I'll come for him in the morning before you have to leave."

Miss Grose was quite pleased to do this, for she liked David and got on well with him.

Harker went up to get his son from the bedroom. He found the boy's small nightlight on, as always since the nightmares. He could see the orderly features of the old housekeeper, relaxed in deep sleep, her breath coming evenly, her hair neatly confined in a fine grey net, a net which suddenly moved Harker, for it reminded him of others he had seen, made of real hair, in the days before synthetics. He determined not to wake Mrs. Poole, to let her have her slumber unbroken for once. He lifted the sleeping boy from his cot.

David barely woke at all and was installed at Miss Grose's with a minimum of fuss. Harker drove back slowly.

On the second floor of his house he heard a slight stirring, and moved towards the door of David's room, feeling that since Mrs. Poole had been wakened after all, she must be informed of David's absence. The room was dark, though. As he walked down the hall towards it, there suddenly appeared in the doorway the tall beautiful form of Miss Cynthia Graves.

Harker banished from his mind, with discipline, every morbid thought that was there.

"There you are," he said. "You've heard about your cousin. But I have some good news for you." He drew closer to her, looking past her at the door-panelling, the wallpaper, anything but at her face. "I've made a much better arrangement for you. Miss Grose whom you met this afternoon is going to get you into the young people's home where she does much of her work. This will be better for you, now that your cousin is gone."

"Celia's not gone."

"She's dead, Miss Graves."

"I know. But she'll be around. Death is a prelude."

Harker was moved by this most unexpected revelation of Miss Grave's calm faith. Still, his regressive self was stubborn.

"Miss Grose will be coming for you in the morning."

"The morning," said Miss Graves quietly. "I'll have to get ready. And I'll need some more."

"Mrs. Poole—" began Harker, without paying attention to this last remark. But he fell silent, looking past Miss Graves into the dark room, and seeing in the pale hall light a large dark pool on the floor.

He shifted his gaze, slowly bringing his eyes to rest at last on the face of the baby-sitter.

His whole being was invaded ruthlessly by a sudden deep sensuous delight in the girl's astonishing beauty. Her thin lids dropped over her eyes as she swayed in the doorway.

"You killed her," said part of him.

"I *had* to have more," the thin silvery voice assured him. "Please. I had to."

He put his hands on her shoulders.

"Mr. Harker! I'm sick. I didn't tell Miss Grose everything. After our home broke up, my mother—she was so sick, Mr. Harker." The light voice deepened and went on, rhythmically, in a slow and lyrical incantation. "Her mind was sick, her mind and mine, so sick, so very, very, very . . ."

Harker crushed her to him, just as they say in the old novels. He closed his eyes, so did not see the long-fanged gleaming smile, full and wide for the first time since he had known Miss Graves. But he knew, for he saw it in his mind's eye; knew it in his secret, educated heart; and in a great swoon of voluptuous awareness he surrendered, made ready in the last bone of his body and the last recess of his spirit for the piercing, ultimate kiss.

JOYCE HARRINGTON

Sweet Baby Jenny

I never had a mother, leastways not one that I can remember. I must have had one sometime, 'cause as far as I can tell I didn't hatch out from no egg. And even chicks get to snuggle up under the hen for a little space before she kicks them out of the nest. But I didn't have no hen to snuggle up to, or to peck me upside the head if I did something wrong.

Not that I would ever do anything wrong. Leastways not if I knowed it was wrong. There are lots of things that go on that are pure puzzlement to me, and I can't tell the right from the wrong of it. For instance, I recollect when Ace—that's my biggest big brother and the one who taken care of us all after Pop went away—I recollect when he used to work driving a beer truck round to all the stores in town and the root cellar used to be full of six-packs all the time. I said to him one day, "Ace, how come if you got the cellar full of beer, I can't have the cellar full of Coke-Cola? I don't like beer." Guess I was about nine or ten years old at the time and never could get my fill of Coke-Cola.

Well, Ace, he just laughed and said, "Sweet Baby Jenny"—that's what they all called me even after I was well growed up—"Sweet Baby Jenny, if I drove a Coke-Cola truck you could float away to heaven on an ocean of it. Now, just drink your beer and learn to like it."

I wasn't ever dumb, even though I didn't do so good in school, so it didn't take much figuring to catch onto the fact that Ace was delivering almost as much beer to the root cellar as he was to Big Jumbo's Superette down on Main Street. So it didn't seem fair when I got caught in the five-and-dime with a lipstick in my pocket for him to come barreling down and given me hellfire and damnation in front of that suet-faced manager. I just stood there looking at him with pig-stickers in my eyes until we got out to the truck and I said to him, "What's the difference between one teensy-weensy lipstick and a cellar full of beer?"

He says to me, grinning, "Is that a riddle?"

And I says, "No, I would surely like to know."

And he says, "The difference, Sweet Baby Jenny, is that you got caught."

Now I ask you.

It was different, though, when he got caught. Then he cussed and swore and kicked the porch till it like to fallen off the house all the while the boys from the beer company was hauling that beer up from the root cellar and stowing it back on the truck. When they drove away, I says to him, sweet as molasses, "Ace, honey, why you carrying on so?"

And he says, "Dammit, Jenny, they taken away my beer. I don't give a hoot about the job, it was a jackass job anyway, but I worked hard for that beer and they didn't ought to taken it away."

"But, Ace," I says, hanging onto his hand and swinging it like a jumping rope, "ain't it true you stolen that beer and you got caught and you had to give it back just like I did with that lipstick?"

Well, he flung me away from hill till I fetched up against the old washing machine that was resting in the yard waiting for somebody to fix it, and he yelled, "I ain't stolen anything and don't you ever say I did! That beer was what they call a fringe benefit, only they didn't know they was givin' it. They don't even pay me enough to keep you in pigtail ribbons and have beer money besides. I only taken what I deserve."

Well, he was right on one score. I didn't have anything you could rightfully call a hair ribbon, and I kept my braids tied up with the strings off of Deucy's old Bull Durham pouches.

Deucy, you maybe guessed, is my second biggest big brother and a shiftless lazy skunk even though some people think he's handsome and should be a movie star. Ace's name in the family Bible is Arthur, and Deucy is written down as Dennis. Then there's Earl, Wesley, and Pembrook. And then there's me, Jennet Maybelle. That's the last name on the birth page. Over on the death side the last name written in is Flora Janine Taggert. It's written in black spiky letters like the pen was stabbing at the page, and the date is just about a month or so after my name was written on the birth page. I know that's my mother, although no one ever told me. And no one ever told me how she died. As for Pop, there ain't no page in the Bible for people who just up and go away.

Deucy plays guitar and sings and thinks he's Conway Twitty. Says he's gonna go to Nashville and come back driving a leopard-skin Cadillac. I'd surely like to see that, though I don't guess I ever will. That Deucy's too lazy to get up off the porch swing to fetch himself a drink of water. It's always, "Sweet Baby Jenny, get me this and get me that." Only thing he's not too lazy for is to boost himself up to the supper table.

That don't keep the girls from flocking round, bringing him presents and smirking like the pig that et the baby's diaper. They all hope and pray that they're gonna be the one to go to Nashville with him and ride back in that Cadillac. And he don't trouble to relieve their minds on the subject. You ought to hear that porch swing creak in the dark of night. They are just so dumb.

Now, Earl and Wesley, they try. They ain't too good-looking, though they do have the Taggert black hair and the Taggert nose. I remember Pop saying he was part Cherokee and all his sons showed it. But while Ace and Deucy came out looking like Indian chiefs, Earl is crosseyed and Wesley broke his nose falling out of a buckeye tree and lost most of his hair to the scarlet fever. So they try. They are always going into business together.

Once they went into the egg business and we had the whole place full of chickens running around. They said they would sell their eggs cheaper than anyone around and make a fortune and we'd all go off to California and live in a big hotel with a swimming pool and waiters bringing hamburgers every time we snapped our fingers. Well, people bought the eggs all right, but what Earl and Wesley kind of forgot about was that 200 chickens eat up a lot of chicken feed and they never could figure out how to get ahead of the bill at the feed store. I could have told them how to do it was raise the price of the eggs and make them out to be something special so everyone would feel they had to have

Taggert's Country-Fresh eggs no matter what they cost. But Earl and Wesley just shoved me aside and said, "Sweet Baby Jenny, you are just a girl and don't understand bidness. Now go on out and feed them chickens and gather up them eggs and let's have some of your good old peach cobbler for supper. Being in bidness sure does make a man hungry."

Well, pretty soon the feed store cut off their credit and there wasn't nothing left to feed the chickens, so we had to eat as many of them as we could before they all starved to death and that was the end of the egg business. Earl and Wesley, being both tender-hearted and brought down by gloom, couldn't bring themselves to kill a single chicken. I like to wrung my arm off wringing those chicken necks. I used to like fried chicken, but I don't any more.

Pembrook, he's the smart one. He don't steal, sing, or go into business. He's off at the state college studying how to be a lawyer. He's the only one used to talk to me and I miss him. I was always planning to ask him what happened to our mother, how she died, and why Pop ran off like he did. But I just never got up the nerve.

Pembrook writes me letters a couple times a month, telling what it's like up there at the college. It sure sounds fine. He's always going on at me how I should go back to school and finish up and come to the college and learn how to *be* somebody. Well, I'd kind of like that, but who'd look after the boys? Reason why I didn't do so good in school was I never had no time for studying, what with looking after the boys like I was their mother instead of Sweet Baby Jenny like they call me. Only Pembrook never called me that.

Another thing I always meant to ask Pembrook and never did is how come I come out looking like a canary in a cuckoo-bird's nest. Pembrook looks more or less just like the other boys, though he keeps his black hair real clean and he wears big eyeglasses on top of his sharp Taggert nose. His eyes are dark brown like theirs, and he weathers up nice and tan in the summer sun. But in summer my freckles just get more so while the part in between the freckles gets red. And my hair, which is mud-yellow most of the time, gets brighter and brighter and kinks up in tight little curls unless I keep it braided up. And never mind my eyes. They're not a bit like the boys'. Greeney-blue or bluey-green depending on the weather. As for my nose, it couldn't be less Taggert if it was a pump handle. Small and turned up and ugly.

Could be I taken after my mother, though I don't know that for a fact 'cause I never set eyes on her nor saw any picture of her.

Pembrook says I'm pretty but that's just because he likes me. Pembrook says I look a lot like Miss Claudia Carpenter who is regarded as the prettiest girl in two counties, but I never saw her to make the comparison. She's the daughter of the town's one and only bank president. She's a year or so older than me, and she don't stick around much. Got sent away to school and always taking trips here and there. Can't be much fun, never being home in your own home place. Pembrook told me our mother used to help out at the Carpenter household, at parties and such or when their regular maid got sick. Maybe I could get such a job and put aside a little money, just in case I ever decide to do what Pembrook says.

One thing I do remember about Pop before he went away. He used to tell me stories. He used to sit himself down in his big maroon armchair and he would sit me down on his lap and he would say, "Now, listen. This here's a story about a bad little girl." The stories were always different but they were all about a girl named Bad Penny. She was ugly and mean and spiteful and nobody liked her. She was always making trouble and in the end she always got punished. Sometimes she got et up by the pigs and sometimes she got drowned in the creek. Once she got cut up in little bits by the disc harrow. And another time she fell into the granary and suffocated in the wheat. But she always came back, as mean and nasty as ever, and that's why she was called Bad Penny. After the story Pop would take me up to my room and put me to bed.

I liked the stories, even though they scared me some. I knew pigs didn't eat little girls, but I was always pretty careful around the pigpen. We don't keep pigs any more, but we had a few then and I used to carry the slops out to them.

Well, things got so bad after Ace robbed the gas station down at the crossroads and got recognized by Junior Mulligan who just happened to be having his pickup truck filled up with gas at the time and never did like Ace since the time they two went hunting together and Ace claimed it was *his* deer and knocked Junior into Dead Man's Gully and broken his leg. So off Junior went to the police and they come and drug Ace out of the Red Rooster Café where he was treating everyone to beer and hard-boiled eggs.

It was sad and lonesome around the place without Ace to stir things up, and quiet with Deucy's guitar in hock and him not able to sing a blessed note through mourning for it. Earl and Wesley tried selling insurance round about, but nobody we knew could buy any and the folks we didn't know wouldn't. So it was up to me.

I harked back to my idea of going as a maid like Pembrook had told me our mother had done. I didn't mind working in someone else's house, though Deucy said it was undignified and not befitting a Taggert. Far as I could see, Deucy thought any kind of work was undignified except maybe wearing out the porch swing. So one morning I washed my whole body including my hair, and cut my toenails so I could put shoes on, and got out one of our mother's dresses from the wardrobe in the attic, and made ready to go see Mrs. Carpenter. The dress fit me right well, though it was a little long and looked a bit peculiar with my high-top lace-up sneakers but that was all I had, so it would have to do.

I walked into town, fanning the skirt of the dress around me and blowing down the front of it from time to time so the sweat would not make stains on the green-and-white polkadots. I got to the Carpenter house before the sun got halfway up the sky, about the time Deucy would be rolling out of bed and yelling his head off for coffee. This was one morning he'd just have to find his own breakfast. I stood for a while with my hand on the iron gate looking up at the house. It was a big one, shining white like a wedding cake, and there must have been about two dozen windows on the front of it alone. It set back from the street on what looked like an acre of the greenest grass I ever saw sloping up to a row of prickly bushes that trimmed the porch.

I'd seen it before, times Ace used to take me riding in the beer truck and tell me how all he needed was to rob the bank and then we'd be living in this part of town alongside the rich folks. But I never really took a good close look, 'cause I thought he was joking. Now I looked until I got to shaking and wondering if I ought to march right up to the front door or sneak around to the back. I stood there so long I felt like my feet had taken root to the pavement, and if I could only get loose I'd run home and stay there forever.

But then I thought about how there was less than a half a pound of coffee left and just enough flour for one more batch of biscuits, and I pulled open that iron gate and set my face toward the big front door. It felt like an hour that I was walking up that path with my feet feeling like big old river rafts and my hair jumping out of the braids that I'd combed and plaited so neat. But I got up on the porch and put my finger on the doorbell and heard it ding-donging away inside. I waited. But the door stayed closed.

It was pretty door, painted white like the rest of the house, and I studied every panel of it and the big brass doorknob and the letter box beside it while I waited. I wondered if I should ring the bell again. Maybe no one was home. Maybe I'd come all this way for nothing. They probably wouldn't want me to be their maid even if they were home. The green-and-white dress was sagging down around my shinbones and my sneakers were covered with road dust. Maybe I'd just go home and wait until I got a better idea.

I turned away and started down the porch steps, and then I heard the door open behind me and a sharp voice like a bluejay's said, "Yes?"

I looked back and saw a tall skinny woman staring at me with a frown betwixt her eyes that made me shiver in spite of the heat. "Miz Carpenter?" I said.

"Yes, I'm Mrs. Carpenter," she said. "Who are you? What do you want? I'm very busy."

My throat got choked and I couldn't swallow, so when I said, "I come to be your maid," I thought maybe she couldn't hear me, 'cause I couldn't hear me myself.

"What?" she said. "Speak up. What's this about a maid?"

"I come to be it," I said. "If you'll have me."

"Well, sakes alive!" she said, showing all her yellow teeth. "If you aren't the answer to a prayer! Where did you spring from, and who told you to come here? Well, never mind all that. Come in the house and let's get started. You look strong. I just hope you're willing."

"Yes, ma'am," I said, and quick as a wink she drug me through the house and into the kitchen and right up to the sink where there was more dishes than I'd ever seen in my life and all of them dirty.

"Just start right in," she said. "The dishwasher's right there. I'll be back in a few minutes."

Now I'd seen dishwashing machines in the Sears Roebuck wish book, but I'd never been right up close to one. I knew what *it* was supposed to do. I just wasn't too sure what I was supposed to do. And I didn't trust anything very much except my own two hands. So I started getting those dishes as clean as I could before I put them in the machine, just in case we had a misunderstanding. They were the prettiest dishes I ever did see, even when they was all crusted with dried-up gravy.

Mrs. Carpenter came back in a few minutes carrying a pair of black shoes and a white dress. She plopped herself down on a kitchen chair and smiled at me. "What's your name, child?"

"Jennet Maybelle."

She didn't let me get the Taggert part in, but went right on talking.

"Well, I'll call you Jenny. That Marcelline quit on me last night right in the middle of a dinner party, and I was just about to start calling around when you walked in the door. I'll pay you five dollars a day plus meals and uniform, but you have to pay for anything you break, so be careful with those dishes. Each plate cost twenty dollars."

I put down the plate I was holding and tried to think what it could be made of. It didn't look to be solid gold. Our places at home were old and cracked and been around as long as I could remember. I didn't know what they cost. When one got broke we just threw it down in the creek bed behind the house along with all the other trash.

Mrs. Carpenter was still talking. "Now you can't be wearing those sneakers around the house, so I brought you an old pair of Claudia's shoes. Maybe they'll fit. And this uniform might be a little big for you, you're a skinny little thing, but we can cinch it in with a belt."

I didn't think much of her calling me skinny when she so closely resembled a beanpole herself. But I didn't say anything. The shoes looked nice with just a little bit of a high heel and shiny black, and the uniform dress was starched and clean.

She stopped talking for a minute and started looking me over real close. Then, "Haven't I seen you somewhere before? I could swear your face is familiar. Where do you come from?"

I pointed in the direction of home and said, "Out Clinch Valley Road." I was going to tell her how my mother had once worked as a maid for her, but she didn't give me a chance. She jumped up, left the shoes on the floor and the dress on the chair, and shook her head.

"I don't know anyone out that way. You can change your clothes in the maid's room back there." She waved her hand at a door on the other side of the kitchen. "And when you finish the dishes you'll find me upstairs. I'll show you how to do the bedrooms."

The day wore on. I didn't break any dishes and figured out on my own which button to push to start the machine. It sure gave me a start when it began churning and spattering behind its closed door, and I prayed it wouldn't go breaking any of those twenty-dollar plates and blaming it on me. Mrs. Carpenter showed me all over that house and told me what I was to do. At noon, she showed me what to make for lunch. We both ate the same thing, cold roast beef left over from the night before and some potato salad, but she ate hers in the dining room and I ate mine in the kitchen.

I drank two glasses of ice-cold milk and could have drunk some more, but I didn't want to seem greedy. In the afternoon she set me to washing windows. It wasn't hard work, I worked harder at home, and it was a treat to be looking out at the roses in the back and all that green grass in the front while I polished those windows till they looked like they weren't there at all.

Along about four o'clock she hauled me back to the kitchen and told me what Mr. Carpenter wanted for his dinner. "He's very partial to fried chicken, but nobody seems able to make it to his satisfaction. I know I can't. And he has the most outrageous sweet tooth. I don't eat dessert myself, but he won't leave the table without it."

Well. I set to work cooking up my specialities. I'd had lots of experience with chicken, and my peach cobbler was just about perfect, if I say so myself. Mrs. Carpenter left the kitchen to take a nap after telling me that Mr. Carpenter expected to sit down to his meal at 6:30 sharp.

At 6:30 sharp I brought in a platter of fried chicken and Mr. Carpenter whipped his napkin into his lap and dug in. He didn't even look at me, but I looked at him. He was a freckly sandy man with gold-rimmed glasses and a tight collar. He still had all his hair, but it was fading out to a kind of pinkish yellowish fuzz. His eyes were blue, or maybe green, it was hard to tell behind his glasses, and his nose turned up at the end like a hoe blade.

I'd fixed up a mess of greens to go with the chicken and he dug into those, too, dribbling the pot liquor down his chin and swabbing it away with his fine napkin. Mrs. Carpenter pecked at her food and watched to see how he was liking his.

When I brought in the peach cobbler he leaned back in his chair and sighed. "That's the best meal I've had in years, Marcelline."

"This isn't Marcelline," said Mrs. Carpenter. "Marcelline quit last night. This is Jenny."

He looked at me then. First through his glasses and then without his glasses. And then he polished his glasses on his napkin and put them back on and tried again. "Ah, ha!" he said. "Jenny. Well. Very nice." And he got up from the table and left the room without even tasting my peach cobbler.

Mrs. Carpenter was after him like a shot. "Paul! Paul!" she hollered. "What about your dessert?"

It didn't matter to me. Peach cobbler is best while it's hot, but it's just as good the next day. I carried it back out to the kitchen, finished cleaning up, and got back into my going-home clothes. I did hope that Mrs.Carpenter would pay me my five dollars so I would have something to show to Deucy and Earl and Wesley, so I hung around for a bit.

But it wasn't Mrs. Carpenter who came into the kitchen. It was him. He stood in the doorway, pulling at his ear and looking at me as if he wished me off the face of the earth. Then he sloped into the kitchen and came right up to me where I was standing with my back against the refrigerator and took my chin in his hand. He held my face up so I had to look at him unless I closed my eyes, which I did for half a minute, but I opened them again because I was beginning to get scared. Then he put his hand on my shoulder and took the collar of my dress between his fingers and felt of it softly. At last he spoke.

"You're a Taggert, aren't you, girl?"

"Yes, I am. I'm Jennet Maybelle Taggert." I spoke up proudly because I'd learned in the little bit of time I'd spent in school that lots of folks thought Taggerts was trash and the only way to deal with that was not to be ashamed.

Then he said something I didn't understand. "Am I never to be rid of Taggerts? Will Taggerts hound me to my grave?"

"You look pretty healthy to me," I said, adding "sir" so he wouldn't think I was being pert.

He didn't say anything to that, but took his wallet out of his pocket and opened it up. I thought he was going to pay me my five dollars, so I got ready to say thank you and good night, but he pulled out a photograph and handed it to me.

"Who do you think that is?" he asked me.

Well, I looked but I didn't know who it was. The photograph was in color and it showed a girl about my age with yellow curling hair and a big smile. She was wearing a real pretty dress, all blue and ruffly, like she was going to a party or a dance. I handed the picture back to him.

"She's real pretty, but I don't know who she is."

"She's my daughter, Claudia."

I didn't know what else to say, so I said again, "She's real pretty."

"No, she's not," he said. "She's a spoiled brat. She thinks she's the most beautiful female creature that ever trod the earth. But she's useless, vain, and unlovable. And it's all my fault."

I didn't know why he was telling me all this, but it was making me fidgety and anyway I had to get home to get supper for the boys. They'd be pretty upset that I was so late. "Well," I said, "I guess I'll be getting along."

"Don't go." He grabbed my arm and hauled me over to where there was a mirror hanging on the wall and made me stand in front of it. "Look there," he said. "Who do you see?"

"Well, that's just me." I tried to pull away from him, but he held on tight.

"That's a pretty young woman," he said. "That's what a young woman is supposed to be, decent and clean and modest. I wish you were my daughter, Jenny Taggert, instead of that hellion who won't stay home where she belongs and behaves so no man in his right mind would marry her. How would you like that? Would you like to live here and be my girl?"

Well, I felt my neck getting hot, 'cause Ace had told me that when a man starts paying compliments there's only one thing he's after, and I'd sure heard enough of Deucy speaking sugar words to his ladies on the porch swing.

"Excuse me, Mr. Carpenter," I said, "but I got to be gettin' home and would you please pay me my five dollars so I can carry home some supper to those boys?" I know that was bold, but he was making me nervous and it just came out that way.

He let go of me and pulled out his wallet again. "Is that what Clemmie's paying you? Five dollars? Well, it's not enough. Here and here and here."

The bills came leaping out of his wallet and he stuffed them into my hands. When I looked, I saw I had three ten-dollar bills. Not only that, he started hauling out the leftover chicken that I had put away and shoving it into a paper sack.

"Take the peach cobbler, too," he said, "and anything else you'd like. Take it all."

"Now I can't do that. What would Miz Carpenter say?"

"I'll tell her I ate it for a midnight snack." He laughed then, but it wasn't a happy-sounding laugh. It sounded like something was breaking inside him.

"Thank you, sir," I said, and skedaddled out the back door before he could think up some new craziness that would get me into trouble.

His voice came after me. "You'll come back tomorrow, won't you?"

"Sure thing," I called back. But I wasn't so sure I would.

All the way home I pondered on Mr. Carpenter and his strange ways. But I just plain couldn't figure it out. All I could think was that having so much money had addled his mind and I thanked God that we was poor and couldn't afford to be crazy.

I put it all out of my mind, though, when I reached the dirt road that led up to our place. The moon was just clearing the top of the big old lilac bush at the edge of the property, and its kindly light smoothened away some of the ugliness you could see in daylight. The house looked welcoming with lights shining from its windows, and there in the dooryard was Pembrook's dinky little car. I ran up the porch and busted into the house, shouting his name.

They was all gathered in the kitchen and I could see from their dark Taggert faces that I had interrupted an argument. But I didn't care. I set the Carpenter food down on the table and said, "Here's supper boys. Dig in." Deucy and Earl and Wesley did just that, not even bothering with places but snatching up that chicken in their fingers.

Then I sat down and took off my left sneaker and pulled out the money. "There and there and there," I said, as I counted the bills out on the table. Deucy's eyes bugged out, and Earl and Wesley shouted, "Whoopee!" as best they could with their mouths full of drumstick meat.

Pembrook looked miserable.

"Where'd you get all that, Jenny?" he asked.

"I went as a maid," I told him.

"Where did you go as a maid?"

"To Miz Carpenter."

"And she gave you all that?"

I was about to lie and say she did, but I was never very good at lying. It makes my nose run. "No. He did."

"You're not to go there any more," said Pembrook.

Well, I'd just about decided that for myself, but I wasn't about to have Pembrook, much as I dearly love him, telling me what not to do. "I will if I want to," I said. "And when did you get home, and how long you staying for?"

"Forever, if I have to, to keep you out of trouble."

"That's pretty nice trouble," piped up Deucy. "Thirty dollars for a day's work and all this food. You ought to have some, Pem."

"Shut up, you idiot!"

I had never seen Pembrook so angry. Taggert blood boils easy, but until this minute Pembrook had always managed to keep his temper under control. He turned back to me, his eyes glittering and mean, like a chicken hawk about to pounce.

"You are not to go back to the Carpenter house, not ever again. You are to put it right out of your mind. And tomorrow I am going to mail that money back. And that's the end of it."

I only said one thing. "Why?"

"Never mind why."

Well, that did it. I had worked hard for that money. Whether it was five dollars or thirty dollars, it was mine. The first money I had ever earned. And Pembrook had no right to take it away from me. I had done nothing wrong, as far as I could see, and it wasn't fair for him to punish me. I reared back in my chair, looked him square in the eye, and opened my mouth.

"Pembrook Taggert, in case you hadn't noticed, I am no longer Sweet Baby Jenny. I am a woman growed and able to make up my own mind about things. You can't stand there and give me orders and tell me to never mind why. I took it from Pop and I took it from Ace and I been taking it from these three, while you've been off at your college learning your way out of this mess. I ain't gonna take it no more."

The hard bitterness faded from his eyes and he took my two hands in his.

"You're right, Jenny," he said. "There are things you ought to know. Come out to the porch swing and I'll tell you."

"Don't make it a long story," Deucy called after us. "Ardith Porter's comin' over tonight and we got things to discuss."

But it was a long story that Pembrook told me. One that went back through the years to the time before I was born. All the boys knew it, but Pop had sworn them on the Bible never to tell me. It accounted for all the things I'd wondered about and never had the gumption to ask. If I had asked, they wouldn't have told me, although Pembrook said he was mighty tempted from time to time because it was my life and I had a right to know.

He told me that Pop wasn't my true father, that Mr. Carpenter was. He told me that about a month after I was born, our mother had told Pop the truth and packed her bag and said she was running off with Mr. Carpenter to have a better life than scratching around on a poor old dirt farm. He told me that Pop had choked the life out of her right there in the bedroom with me looking on with my blind baby eyes from the cradle beside the bed. And then Pop had gone to Mr. Carpenter and told him the whole thing and got him to hush it up because the scandal wouldn't have done anybody any good. They gave out that our mother had died of childbirth fever.

The tears were rolling down my face, but I managed to ask, "How could you keep on living here, after he did that?"

"Well," said Pembrook, "Ace was the oldest and he wasn't but twelve. We had nowhere else to go. And he was our father."

"What happened then?" I asked. "Why did Pop run off?"

"He didn't," said Pembrook. "He lies buried under Mr. Carpenter's rose garden."

He went on to tell me how the years went by and Pop took up drinking and the farm went even further downhill until it was just a wasteland. Then one day Pop got it into his head that Mr. Carpenter ought to be paying money to take care of his child, meaning me. He went up to the Carpenter house, full of liquor and hate, and demanded a thousand dollars. Pembrook and Ace tagged along behind and listened outside the window of a room that was full of books and a big desk and a hunting rifle on the wall over the fireplace.

"I seen that room," I told him. "Miz Carpenter calls it his study."

Pembrook nodded. "That's where Pop got it."

He said how he and Ace heard them arguing in the room, and Mr. Carpenter shouted that it was blackmail and he wouldn't stand for it, and then there was a lot of scuffling around, with Pop shouting that he would kill Mr. Carpenter for ruining his life. And finally there was a shot. Just the one shot, but it was enough. They peeked over the window sill and saw Pop lying on the rug bleeding his life out, and Mr. Carpenter standing there like a statue with the rifle in his hands.

They were about to run away home, but Mr. Carpenter saw

them and made them come into the house and help him carry
Pop out to the rose garden. The three of them dug up the roses
and put Pop in the ground and planted the roses back on top of
him. Then Mr. Carpenter told them to get on home and keep
their mouths shut or he'd have the marshal come and chuck us
all off the farm and into reform school.

And they did, until this minute.

"I guess," said Pembrook, "I guess that's why Ace is so wild,
but that's not the way to fix it up. That's why I'm studying to be
a lawyer. One of these days I'll know how to take care of Mr.
Carpenter legally and make it stick. So that's why I don't want
you going back there, Jenny. You're likely to spoil my plan, and it
isn't good for him to be reminded that you exist. I need to get
him off guard when I'm ready."

I wiped my eyes and blew my nose and said, "Thank you,
Pembrook, for telling me. Now I understand."

"And you won't go back."

"I'm going to bed."

And I did. But I didn't sleep. I lay there pondering over the
things that Pembrook had told me, trying to find the right and
the wrong of it. Our mother was maybe wrong for pleasuring
herself with Mr. Carpenter, but if she hadn't I wouldn't be here.
Pop was wrong for taking life away from our mother, but she
gave him cause in his eyes. Mr. Carpenter was wrong for
shooting Pop, but the Taggert blood was up and Pop probably
attacked him first. Hardest of all to think about was me being
Mr. Carpenter's daughter. If it was true and he knew it, how
could he have let me live all these hard years as Sweet Baby Jenny
Taggert while that other girl, that Claudia, had everything her
heart desired and then some?

Just before dawn I decided what to do. The boys, even
Pembrook, were all sound asleep. I got up quiet as a mouse and
dressed in our mother's green-and-white polkadot dress and my
high-top sneakers and snuck out to the barn. The barn used to be
a busy place, but it was still and empty that morning. No more
cows to bellow for me to come and milk them, no horses to gaze
sad-eyed after an apple or a carrot. Way in the back, behind the
piles of rotten harness, in a dark corner draped over with

cobwebs, I found what I was looking for.

It was a can of stuff that Pop used to put down to kill the rats that infested the barn and ate their way through the winter fodder. There wasn't much left in the can, and what there was looked dry and caked. Maybe it was so old it wouldn't even work any more. But I scooped some out with a teaspoon and put it into one of Deucy's Bull Durham pouches and set off down the road.

I kept up a good pace because I wanted to get there before Mr. Carpenter went off to the bank, and before the boys woke up and came after me in Pembrook's car. The morning was fresh and cool, and I didn't sweat one bit.

When I got to the Carpenter house, the milkman was just driving away. I went around to the back, picked up the two quarts of milk, and knocked at the back door. Mrs. Carpenter opened up. She looked sleepy-eyed but pleased to see me.

"Why, Jenny," she said, "you're here bright and early. Come in. Come in."

"Yes, ma'am," I said. "I came to make breakfast."

"Well, that's wonderful. Mr. Carpenter is shaving. He'll be down in a few minutes. He likes two four-minute eggs, I never can get them right, two slices of toast, and lots of strong black coffee. And now that you're here, I think I'll go back to bed and get a little more beauty sleep." She giggled like a silly girl, waved at me, and pranced out.

I put the milk away and started in making the coffee. There was an electric coffee pot, but my coffee is good because I make it the old-fashioned way. I boiled up some water and when it was bubbling away, I threw in the ground coffee, lots of it, to make it nice and strong. Then I turned the fire down to keep it hot while it brewed, and I cracked an egg so I could have an eggshell to throw in to make it clear. And I emptied out the stuff that was in the tobacco pouch right into the pot.

When I heard his footsteps on the stairs I put on another pot to boil up water for his eggs. He came into the kitchen smiling and smelling sweet.

"Well, Jenny," he said. "You came back. I'm glad, because you and I are going to get along just fine. You'll be happy there. I'll see to that."

I got out a cup and saucer.

"I been hearing things, Mr. Carpenter," I said. "Things I never dreamed of."

He frowned. "What things have you been hearing, Jenny?"

I poured coffee into the cup.

"I hear that you're my daddy."

He sank down into a kitchen chair. "Yes," he said, "that's true enough."

I put the cup and saucer on the counter to let it cool off a bit so it wouldn't be too hot for him to take a nice big swallow.

"I hear that you shot our Pop and buried him in your rose garden. They're mighty pretty roses you got out there."

He held his head in his two hands. "They swore never to tell you. Those boys swore."

"Pembrook told me because he's afraid I'll come to some harm in your house." I set the cup and saucer on the table in front of him.

"Oh, Jenny, sweet baby Jenny, I would never harm you. If anything, I'd like you to come and live here and be my daughter and let me give you all the things you should have had."

"Don't call me that. I'm not a baby any more."

"No, you're not. You're a fine lovely woman, just like your mother was. God, how I loved that woman! She was the only wonderful thing that ever happened in my whole life. I wanted to take her away with me. We were all set to go. We could have gone to some other town or to a big city where no one knew us. We'd have taken you along. And we'd have been happy. Instead, she died."

"Pop killed her. Because of you."

"You know that, too." He sighed. "Yes. He killed her and I killed him, and I've been living out my days in an agony of remorse. There's no one I can talk to. Clemmie doesn't know any of this. Sometimes I wish I were dead."

"Drink your coffee."

The water for his eggs was boiling. Gently I rolled the two eggs into the pot and stuck two slices of bread into the toaster. He left the table and came to where I was working.

"Jenny." He put his hands on my shoulders and turned me

around to face him. "What can I do to make it up to you? I'll do anything in my power, and believe me that's a lot. You name it. It's yours."

I thought a minute. Would it be right or wrong to take from this man? I was having my usual trouble figuring out the difference between the two. Would it be right or wrong to let him drink the coffee?

Then I said, "Could you put Pembrook through law school?"

"Consider it done."

"And Earl and Wesley, can you find jobs for them? They're good workers, only down on their luck."

"Tell them to come to the bank."

"And what about Deucy? Would you get him a new guitar and a ticket to Nashville? He sings real fine."

"Not only that. I know Johnny Cash personally. We'll work something out."

"Now this one's hard. Can you get Ace out of jail and set him on a straight path?"

"The warden is Clemmie's cousin. And I own a ranch in Wyoming. He can go there and work off his wildness. But what about you, Jenny. What can I do for you?"

I shrugged. "Oh, I guess I'll just live here for a while. I can help Mrs. Carpenter and sort of keep an eye on things."

He hugged me and planted a big kiss on my cheek. "That's my girl," he said. "That's what I was hoping you'd say. You'll never regret it. Mmm, that coffee smells good."

He was heading back to the table and his coffee cup. But I got there first and swiped it out from under his nose.

"That's coffee's cold," I said. "Come to think of it, the whole batch is bitter. I tasted it before you came down. I'll make some fresh."

I poured all the coffee down the drain and dished him up his eggs and toast. We drank the fresh coffee together, and he went off to his bank.

And that's the way it is now. Pembrook's way *is* better, and he's studying real hard. He'll graduate sooner now that he doesn't have to work his way through. Earl and Wesley really like being bank tellers, and Deucy has his leopard-skin Cadillac and all the girls he can handle, although he says he misses the porch swing. Ace sent a photograph of himself on a horse wearing a big old cowboy hat. He looks funny but he says he's doing fine.

And me? Every day while the roses are blooming I cut some and put them in the house. Mrs. Carpenter just loves them. I'm waiting. Someday us Taggerts are gonna dig up that rose garden.

RALEIGH BOND

Meet Athalia Good

I was almost finished with the Battle of Fort Henry when the messenger came in. He held a large manila envelope and looked at me tentatively until I stopped typing.

"Best?" he asked.

"No. Goode," I answered and jabbed my thumb toward the stairs. "Best is up a flight."

He stood there a moment, checking the address on the envelope and listening to the clacking of my machine. As he was going up I pushed a button under my desk to alert Athalia that something was headed her way. She must have been expecting it because no light went on over the intercom box. So I kept typing.

The "Best" referred to is Best Detective Agency, owned and operated exclusively by my wife, with no help, hindrance or interest from me. Athalia's been in her line quite a long time and listens politely to my suggestions, but she's under no obligation to follow them. Neither would I be under obligation to do more than listen if she stuck her nose into my business.

After all, what could we add to each other's work? My books on American history always do well in the mass market and the name Byron Goode is greeted with some respect even in academic circles, circles which I don't frequent.

Even as a kid I loved the more popular books on the subject and all during my years as a newspaper reporter I planned writing the definitive, yet entertaining study on a number of eras and wars. I finally did, much to my colleagues' amazement, calling my epic *The Call of Battle*, being the first really dramatic and in-depth recreation since Kenneth Roberts of Arnold's March to Quebec. I only mention this because I want you to know I was at

230

work on it long before I met Athalia.

She doesn't claim I'm responsible for her success either, since we came together while I was covering a murder case in New York for my paper and she was involved in the investigation on behalf of an insurance company. Before that she worked as an operator for various detective agencies and for a brief while was connected with the federal government as an investigator for a Senator. So we were both on the path of our careers even before we fell in love and got married.

I quit my job on the paper to devote myself full-time to writing after the sales of *The Call of Battle* justified such a move, and she handed in her resignation to the insurance company to start her own firm, calling it Best Detective Agency because, as she quipped, it sounds better than Goode.

We decided to hit the road for California and found a small house in Los Angeles on Melrose Place, set back from the street and covered with vines and surrounded by trees for privacy. We live in the rear—the two front rooms are reserved for our offices. Since I welcome any interruption from the typewriter I took over the ground-floor room, which is bigger, and stocked it with my ponderous collection of research books and files while she went upstairs with her paraphernalia.

I don't go up there very often, finding the décor less than what I imagine a private-eye's conclave should be. There's no wooden hat-rack, no cracked plaster or empty gin bottles. While it is unmistakably a business office, the little glass statuettes and potted plants, the pastel prints and slightly pink walls, do not spell Sam Spade or Philip Marlowe by any means. Thank God I got her to fill her magazine rack with more varied fare than *Cosmopolitan* and *Ms.*, even though it means having to read my historical journals quickly before they're snatched up and taken to the upstairs land of no return.

Anyway, being no detective I had no curiosity about what was in the envelope the messenger brought that day, except to note that the label bore the logo of the insurance company where Athalia used to work. It was probably a request for assistance which she gets from time to time from her old employers.

I knew I'd find out about it at supper because we always

discuss our work day over a good meal and a bottle of wine—a sort of professional courtesy. I know she's no more interested in my current book on Grant's Tennessee Campaign than I am in who swiped what from where; but we are interested in each other. So we listen.

"It's a bank embezzlement job," she told me, dishing out her excellent chicken limone while I opened a bottle of Auslese. She likes cooking which I suppose is an even trade for my directing her clients upstairs and letting them think I'm her receptionist.

"It's three hundred thousand dollars' worth, which is small potatoes to the insurance company, so they're not sparing any top operators on it. They asked me to look into it even though the guy who did it confessed and committed suicide. Maybe."

"Maybe?"

"Well, it can be read that way," she went on, sitting at her place and sipping the wine. "There was going to be an audit at the end of the week. The day after it was announced the guy is found dead and there's a shortage in his accounts."

"Why didn't he just hop a plane for parts unknown?"

"That's also a possibility."

I sighed and looked up at her, knowing this was supposed to goad me into asking more questions. I do it myself when I see her interest waning, spouting cryptic remarks like, "I'm beginning to wonder if Stonewall Jackson wasn't gay."

"His name is Ralph Swann," she continued, taking my look for the question. "He was assistant to the manager of the Merchant's Bank in Encino, and he was found dead in his garage the night before last. In the back seat of his car were two suitcases, and it was later discovered that he had booked space on a flight to Bombay, with a stop in Paris to change planes."

"I thought you said he committed suicide . . . maybe."

"He was sitting in the driver's seat with his foot on the gas pedal. His wife had been away visiting her family for the past week and was scheduled to return that night around eleven. She was surprised when her husband didn't meet her at the airport as he had promised. When she got home she found a note reading 'Sorry, darling. Try to forgive me,' and a garage full of carbon monoxide."

"It doesn't make sense. If he had his bags packed, why suicide?"

"Good point," she conceded, and I felt just like a detective. "The police theory is that Swann, fearing discovery because of the audit, decided to slip the country while his wife was out of town. He writes the note, goes out to the car, becomes overcome with remorse, and asphyxiates himself."

"What do they expect you to do," I asked, "prove otherwise?"

"The insurance company couldn't care less about how he died. What they want is the missing three hundred thousand. It wasn't in Swann's suitcases, and the police haven't been able to turn it up."

Since Athalia had accepted the case it meant I would not be working on the Battle of Fort Henry the next morning. As I've said, I have the writer's longing for any excuse not to write and one of Athalia's rare exhibitions of cowardice supplies it. She is absolutely terrified of taking the driver's test. Since she never needed it in New York I could claim I'm atoning for marrying her and taking her to the automotive civilization of California, but in truth I do it because we enjoy being together.

I waited in the car, warming up the engine, while she completed a last-minute call and then came out of the house. Watching her trim figure in the smart-looking pants suit, the crisp confident stride of her walk, and as she drew nearer, the lovely intelligent eyes behind the heavy horned-rimmed glasses, I was again reminded how lucky I was. Sliding into her seat she told me one problem had been cleared up.

"It wasn't suicide. I just got the autopsy results and the cause of death was a heart attack. Swann was probably dead two seconds after he put his foot on the pedal."

"Does his wife confirm he had a bad heart?"

It turned out she did. Mrs. Swann was a washed-out woman who looked older than her years. She lived in one of those small stucco houses that make up much of Burbank with an interior someone had worked hard at to make as drab as the exterior.

"I always made sure Ralph went to the doctor regularly," she assured us through a thin whiny voice. "He had three attacks within the past two years."

I thought I sensed a tone of resentment about this, but Athalia went about her interrogation by treating Mrs. Swann with what appeared to be sincere sympathy.

"Did you notice anything peculiar about him in the past five months? I understand that's when he was made assistant manager at the bank."

"That's true," answered Mrs. Swann. "It brought in more money but we didn't see each other as much any more. He worked far into the night at the bank, but when he was home on weekends he seemed more cheerful than usual and more helpful around the house."

"I don't want to upset you by going over the night you found him, but I understand the police have returned the suitcases he had in the car. Could I see them, please?"

Mrs. Swann led us to the bedroom where the two cases were lying on the bed. "I haven't had time to unpack them, so they're just as he left them. You can see what a messy person he was. Never folded anything right, never put things where they belonged. I always had to do everything for him."

I began to wonder why it had taken Ralph so long to fly the coop while Athalia went through the luggage. Both cases were well-worn and in the larger one she found a change of underwear, socks, and shirt, one suit practically wrapped in a ball, some shaving gear, a few handkerchiefs, and two pairs of shoes. The other one was a small carry-on case with another pair of shoes, more linen, cuff links, a set of keys, and a toothbrush.

"Those keys are for things around the house," Mrs. Swann told Athalia when she saw her examining them. "Cabinets, doors, a chest. The police tried them all out before they returned them."

We thanked Mrs. Swann and sympathized with her plight as she followed us to our car. She had by now accepted her husband's guilt and seemed to look upon it as another failing, like his messiness and cheerfulness, designed only to make her suffer.

"I've been thinking," I told Athalia as we drove out of Burbank. I paused to allow her a sarcastic rejoinder but she seemed definitely interested. "The plane trip. Isn't it a curious way to get to Bombay, via Paris? After all, it's much quicker just to head across the Pacific from California."

"Oh," she answered with a tinge of disappointment. "I don't think Swann cared where he was going, so long as he got far away and in the quickest possible time. The flight was booked around ten thirty that night, and the clerk who took the call remembered that the party asked for the first international flight out. It happened to be Paris. He was then asked for the next connection to the east which was Bombay, although it meant a three-hour stopover. It does prove one thing, however."

"What's that?"

"That the trip was a last-minute decision, not a premeditated plan. Which isn't odd because Swann learned of the audit only that day." She then looked out the window and said absent-mindedly, "I thought you were going to bring up something else."

We drove the rest of the way in silence.

Walter Hallward was the manager of the Merchant's Bank, but we had learned by phone that he had not come to work that day because his wife was ill; so we drove to his home in Los Feliz. It was one of those palatial affairs that smacked of old money, probably built around the time when Los Angeles was a summer resort for turn-of-the-century millionaires.

Hallward was a gray-haired man in his fifties with pouches under his eyes and over his belt. A butler brought us to his study which was richly paneled and lined with first editions and first-rate sculpture. He looked up from his desk with the expression of a harried beagle and indicated chairs, somewhat mystified by Athalia's presence. As an afterthought he half rose until she was comfortably seated and then plopped back in his chair, turning his attention to me.

"You'll have to forgive me if I seem brusque. I've just returned from a business trip this morning. On top of this situation at the bank I've also had to deal with my wife's illness."

He seemed to take it as personally as Mrs. Swann had taken Ralph's peccadillos.

"There's no doubt it was Swann who stole the money?" asked Athalia, and I noticed her back feathers ruffle a bit when Hallward directed his answer toward me.

"None. He was the only one who had access to that particular account and the faked notations are in his handwriting."

"How long had it been going on?" Athalia's voice rose slightly. Again to me. "As far as we can tell—"

"Mrs. Goode is asking the questions," I cut in gently, picking up a magazine from a nearby table. It wasn't *Cosmopolitan*.

I didn't see his reaction, but I could feel the room temperature drop about ten degrees. Finally his voice resumed, cold and emotionless, but slightly softer since it was now directed toward Athalia.

"About four months ago. I don't mind telling you what a disappointment it is. I trusted Ralph very much. He represented the bank when I had to go out of town for meetings and conferences. He came here for dinner. I looked upon him as my own son—"

He was interrupted as the door opened and a servant stood there tentatively.

"Mrs. Hallward is feeling better and asked to see you, sir."

"Tell her I'm busy," he snapped."I'll be there when I can. And make sure she stays in bed."

The servant looked somewhat shocked at this but withdrew. Whatever Hallward was busy at it certainly wasn't us because he rose and told us that if *we* had any further questions they could be answered by his secretary at the bank. We took our leave but noticed that Hallward returned to his desk, ignoring his wife's summons, and busying himself with a few papers.

"I'm probably missing the really important point again," I said after we got into the car, "but isn't that place a little too ritzy for a bank manager?"

"No. You've brought up something I agree is important. And yes, it *is* too ritzy. Being a bank manager pays quite well, but we're not exactly talking about Chase Manhattan."

Indeed we weren't, because the Merchant's Bank was a small one-story affair, shaped with all the architectural grandeur of a safety-deposit box.

Hallward's secretary, Karen Allenby, was a magnificently built blonde who towered over Athalia. Once she learned that Athalia was conducting the examination, she regarded me with the same mystification that Hallward had shown to my wife, and I got the feeling if I had asked a question she would have answered Athalia.

However, she would have got the same come-uppance from her. That's the way we operate.

As it was, Miss Allenby was more interested in unburdening some long pent-up resentments and responded more eagerly than I expected when Athalia turned her inquiry from the bank books to Hallward's private life.

"Mrs. Hallward is the daughter of Addison Quincy," she informed us and I remembered that Quincy, the last president and chairman of the board of the Quincy Orange Juice Company, had passed away about three years ago. "He left her everything, an estate that ran into millions. Mr. Hallward married her against her father's objections. He thought Mr. Hallward wasn't prosperous enough for his precious little girl, even though he had risen from teller to manager of this bank in ten years' time."

"It's odd that he still stays here. Why doesn't he enter the Quincy Company or use his wife's money to establish his own bank?"

Miss Allenby seemed to bridle at the thought. "Because he's much too fine a man to take advantage of his wife's wealth." I felt a little guilty about the five dollars I had borrowed from Athalia last weekend when I couldn't reach the bank and never paid back. "Besides," she added bitterly, "Mrs. Hallward doesn't fully control her estate. Her father knew her for what she was, a spoiled brat who never had to lift a finger for herself in her life. She used to gamble away half of her allowance and spend the rest on extravagant clothes and jewelry. He made it a stipulation in his will that she had to answer to a board of trustees for every penny, and she uses that as an excuse for begrudging her own husband any share of the estate—that is, for business purposes."

Her eyes almost filled with tears as she shook her head at the injustice of it all. "I've been with Mr. Hallward for many years. I still take care of many of his personal affairs, arrange his trips for the bank, even pick out some of his clothes. It's tragic to see a man like him kowtowing to someone like her."

I got the distinct impression that she would much prefer to be the one Hallward was kowtowing to. Athalia's interests seemed to run toward other lines.

"How did you feel about Mr. Swann?"

Miss Allenby's lips twisted in distaste. "I felt nothing about him. He was a little mouse. He was supposed to be an assistant manager but I never considered him as anything but an errand boy who just followed Mr. Hallward's orders. That is, when I, or anyone else for that matter, even considered him at all."

After examining the doctored books Athalia spent some time drifting around the bank, chatting with employees and reading a few memos from Hallward which Miss Allenby provided.

"I think I know what you're doing," I told her on the ride home.

"What?"

"Studying Hallward's handwriting. It seems to me he could use three hundred thousand dollars as much as Swann. Maybe to buy Miss Allenby some new clothes."

"So why did Swann pack his bags when the audit was announced?"

"The errand-boy type, remember? Following orders from Hallward. He would take the rap and Hallward would make it up to him later, after knocking off the missus and getting all that orange-juice money for himself. How's that for detecting?"

She didn't answer. In fact, she didn't say much all evening, even at supper. I tried to bring her out of it in my usual way, by being so boring about my own field that she'd start talking about hers in desperation.

"I'm moving on to the Battle of Fort Donelson now. That was much more interesting than Fort Henry. For instance, after the Confederate soldiers attacked Grant he noticed a lot of them had food in their knapsacks. He couldn't figure out why soldiers should carry food into battle and then realized it meant they weren't attacking him out of strength. They were trying to escape the fort and needed the rations once they got away. From then on he knew how weak the enemy was, pressed the siege, and won."

Even this bit of deductive reasoning failed to bring her out of her mood and she spent rest of the evening playing her electric organ, which someone had once given her as a fee.

The next morning I was relating Grant's victory to my typewriter when Hallward appeared at our front door. He seemed even more out of sorts than before and I wondered how Athalia had managed to get him to come over, but all the while I was feeling elation at my own victory. So I had been right after all.

He informed me he had an appointment with my "employer," and I told him I had been so busy making coffee for the office I hadn't had time to check my calendar. I made him wait ten minutes out of pure cussedness and then told him he could go upstairs. As he went I buzzed Athalia and then noticed that the intercom light came on. That meant she wanted me to listen in on their conversation, but it also meant that if I went on typing it would be heard in her office. I sat there patiently, listening to her door open and close.

"Mrs. Goode, I got your message. Do you really know where the three hundred thousand dollars is hidden?"

"That's right, Mr. Hallward. Please sit down." There was the sound of leather creaking and then Athalia went on, "First of all, there's no doubt that Mr. Swann took the money."

"I didn't know there *was* any doubt."

"Maybe not in *your* mind."

I settled back in my chair, wondering if that was why she wanted me to keep the intercom open.

"However, there is some doubt concerning Mr. Swann's supposed flight to escape capture."

"Supposed?"

"Yes. I felt there was something wrong about it the moment I examined the contents of his suitcases. Certain things did not seem right. I didn't realize they were all pointing to the fact that Mr. Swann was not planning to leave the country at all. Then it all began to fit in last night during a very perceptive illustration from history concerning what someone would take with him during an escape." So I had been of some use after all. "For instance, keys."

"Keys?"

"Mr. Hallward, if you were planning to quit your old life entirely and make for parts unknown forever, would you even think of packing your house keys?" She paused but there was no reply. "Or put in two suits and not include a single tie?"

"The man was in a panic. He didn't have time to think."

"He apparently had enough presence of mind to make plane

reservations, with a stopover in Paris after a long trans-Atlantic flight, and the prospect of many more hours in the air before he reached Bombay. I'm sure you've traveled to Europe, Mr. Hallward. Tell me, would you be inclined to pack your shaving gear in the luggage that you would check and not see again until you reached your final destination; or would you include it with the hand luggage you carry on board yourself? Didn't Swann consider how he would look when he hit Paris or Bombay after all those hours in the air and waiting in the airport? His wife said he was messy and yet he remembered to put his toothbrush within reach."

"Where does all this get us?"

"To the simple fact that Swann did not pack those bags and therefore never intended to escape. But someone wanted to make it look as if he did. "Who?"

"Are you saying that I—?"

"No. No man would pack another man's bags and forget his ties or lock up his shaving gear. No man would crumple another man's suit into a ball or put such a stock in having three extra pairs of shoes. Suits, even to the most careless man, are still the main article of wear and treated accordingly. And a variety of shoes is not as important to men as they are to women. Swann's bags were obviously packed by a woman, but by a woman who had never packed a man's suitcase before."

There was another sound of creaking leather indicating that Hallward was shifting in his chair. Then Athalia went on.

"Now, that eliminates Mrs. Swann. Even if she came home earlier than she admitted, found Swann dead from a heart attack, and devised the idea of making it look like an escape attempt, she deplored her husband's messiness and probably always packed when he went off on a trip, which was fairly often if the worn condition of the bags is any indication. She would have remembered his ties, put his shaving gear within easy reach, folded his suit, and given him extra socks rather than extra shoes.

"As for Miss Allenby, even though she's single most executive secretaries learn masculine needs in a hurry—luggagewise, that is. They're almost as knowing as wives, and she told us she takes care of your trips often, which I believe is more than your wife does."

There was another pause and I thought I heard heavy breathing.

"I've heard that your wife has been surrounded by wealth all her life which means she's had servants to do her every task. That sort of person wouldn't know that shaving gear is more important to a man during a long trip than cuff links. To her that would represent jewelry which must be kept near at hand along with a toothbrush. But ties? Would she consider ties while packing a bag? She who always had everything done for her."

"What would my wife have to do with someone like Swann?"

"It wasn't Swann, but the three hundred thousand dollars he could get for her. Oh, I know she has millions but every dollar she spent had to be accounted for, so she might as well have been poor, or as dependent as some wives are on their husbands for an allowance. That can tax anyone's self-respect, Mr. Hallward. Moreoever, she likes to gamble, indulge in extravagances, but is denied the use of her own money.

"Then along comes Swann whom you said you had to dinner at your home. He was a drab little man with a drab little wife, a man whom women like Miss Allenby treated with contempt. It must have thrilled him beyond words when Mrs. Hallward showed him attention. His own wife said he began to be more cheerful and even helped around the house, sure signs of guilt." I made a note not to fix the washer next time. "He was glad to supply her with money in return for the favors she gave him during those times he was supposed to be working late at the bank and you were away on trips."

"This is outrageous! How dare you—!"

"The night after he heard about the audit he called her, knowing you were again out of town. Fortunately, Mrs. Swann was also away, so he made your wife come to him, threatening to tell you everything unless she helped him make up the shortage. She had to agree and probably invited him to accompany her to your house where she could give him some jewelry to pawn. He wrote a note to his wife who was returning soon, apologizing for not meeting the plane. It was while he was writing it that he had his heart attack. I never wondered why there was no signature. Husbands don't usually sign notes to their wives. 'Sorry, darling.

Try to forgive me.' That's the kind of thing my husband leaves me when he takes the car unexpectedly while I'm out."

I save my literary talents for my books.

"When your wife realized he was dead she got the idea of the attempted escape, to ward off any investigation that would lead to her. She called the airport and picked any plane that would make it look like a desperate flight from the law. But when she packed his bags she made nearly every error a person with her background would make, including the keys. Somehow she carried him out to the car, put him behind the wheel, started the engine, and left, hoping we would come to the conclusion that we all did come to."

"You can't prove any of this."

"I think I can. There's one weak link in all this. You realized that when you returned home and found her in hysterics. A woman who had been pampered all her life hasn't got the strength to stand alone. She told you everything and begged for help. Naturally you had to make sure she didn't talk to anyone else, so you pretended she was ill and stayed home to keep an eye on her.

"Of course you did all this because you wanted to avoid scandal, the chance you'd be held responsible by the bank and laughed at as a deceived husband. But there was another reason. Everyone whom I talked to at the bank confirmed that you had always been servile to your wife because of your position. 'Kowtowing' was what Miss Allenby called it. But you certainly didn't sound servile when we visited you that morning. You didn't have to be. You had a hold on her now and forever, which meant her wealth and position now belonged to you alone. Like men of your type, Mr. Hallward, you only know two ways of acting—as a coward or a bully."

If this guy was as Athalia described, I couldn't understand why he was just sitting there. I didn't have long to wonder.

"So," Athalia went on, "you see I do have a line of inquiry to give the police. How long do you think Mrs. Hallward will stand up to their questioning? Suppose some of her bills are checked against the money from her estate? Suppose certain gambling establishments are questioned? That's why I called you here. To see if you wanted to settle this the easy way."

The sound of his chair falling back on the floor was heard and his voice grew strident with fury. "Damn you! Do you think I'm going to let you ruin things for me now? When I've finally got her where I want her? Why should I show her any mercy? She and that swine cheated me behind my back! But it wasn't his fault— she made him do it! You're all alike—every one of you!"

I heard his feet stamping on the floor and he gave a vicious growl. Then there was silence. Athalia's voice came quietly over the intercom.

"Byron?"

"Yes."

"Don't turn off the tape recorder yet. Perhaps Mr. Hallward would like to say a few more words into it."

"All right," I answered and looked to heaven. So that was why she wanted me to leave the intercom open. I knew she wasn't in any danger. We have another signal to indicate she needs help, which isn't very often. We also don't have a tape recorder.

"Would you mind dialing the police for me?" Athalia said. "It's hard to do it with one hand."

The wood-scraping noise was Athalia opening her desk drawer where she kept that rust-filled automatic which neither of us ever loaded, since we both detest firearms.

I told her I'd phone and flipped off the intercom, first typing the last three letters of a word I had left unfinished.

There wasn't much in the papers about it. Of course they had enough influence to keep from being arrested, especially after Mrs. Hallward's board of trustees promised to pay back the $300,000. Even Mr. Hallward, who could have been sent up as an accessory after the fact, got off scot-free, except for the divorce which followed soon after. But I understand he and the new Mrs. Hallward (née Allenby) are reasonably happy.

There was an item on the back pages of *The New York Times* which I read while I was in New York visiting my publisher. He and some others from the office took me out to dinner in some bar-restaurant and while we were sitting in a booth I glanced at the paper and read how the Merchant's Bank was now entirely solvent after Swann's embezzlement, thanks to prompt police work and the cooperation of the insurance company. No names were mentioned, which is fair since the company pays the bills; but it does seem hard on a fellow who would like to point to the article while sitting with some guys in a bar and say proudly, "My wife did it."

FLORENCE V. MAYBERRY

A Goodbye Sound

"**S**hut up, Joe," I said. "You bore me."

Joe looked as if he would cry. I can't stand a man who goes around all the time looking as if he could cry. Joe's that kind.

"Well—" He cleared his throat, a nasty, fluttering sound. It was too bad, I knew it was wrong, but Joe couldn't take a deep breath without irritating me. "Why can't you look at me like you do at everybody else? Like just smile nice at me sometimes. Like for instance you don't even know those guys standing over there, they're just waiting for a table and you never saw them before, just happened to look their way. And you give 'em a big smile like you were the hostess out here." A hesitation. "Or maybe you do know them."

"Whether I do or not is not your affair. Now listen, Joe, you've been after me to go out with you for months. So I'm out. With you. So why not cool it, lay off the witness-box stuff."

"Sure, okay, Lolly."

"Laura!"

"Okay, Laura."

What's a woman to do with a man like that? *Roll over and play dead, Joe, sit up and beg, Joe, fetch me my slippers, Joe.*

"Order anything you like, hon, the world's yours tonight."

"The prime ribs, please."

"Yeah, that's good, that's the ticket, best thing on the menu. Hon, you can have prime ribs every day, every night, if you'd only want it that way I just finished a quarter-million-dollar contract. Lol—Laura. Your old man—" He choked it off, trying to laugh. "I mean your old ex-husband is in the bigtime contracting now. Kept slogging along until I made it."

"Maybe I ought to go back in court and try for alimony this time. First time it would have been like a suing a four-year old kid for his nickels." *That's right, ruin his fun, be mean, you shrew.*

"I told you, if you'd only hang on a little while, maybe make me feel like I was something, I'd make it." He tried to laugh again, but it was like the laugh was hiding behind a door, afraid to come out. "I'm slow, hon. But right along with that, I'm too dumb to know how to give up."

That was for sure. He's telling me? Divorced two years and every week, regular as clockwork Joe telephoned. *Hon, let's try it again, willya, Lolly, willya just go out to dinner with me and talk a while? I get terrible lonesome, you gotta eat anyway Hon, do you need any money, I gotta few bucks ahead, construction's picking up. Hon, hon,* over and over. So once in a while I gave in, like throwing a dog a bone. Damn a man like that. Who needs his money? I make plenty doing beauty work.

"Prime ribs for the lady. Medium-rare, same as usual, hon? Baked potatoes, all the fixings. Same for me. Don't give the lady no coffee till later, she drinks it with dessert. That still right, hon?"

A crawly feeling shivered my back, crept into my jaw. My teeth started to chatter. Nerves, I mean, like before a fit.

The food came, beautiful stuff because we were at Eugene's where it's maybe the best in Reno, but I looked at it like it was poison. Joe did that to me, always. He didn't mean to, but he did. Slender I always was, but by the time Joe and I broke up I was nothing but skinny. Chemical reaction, maybe. Or maybe I'm just mean. But I think it's more than that. I'm a one-man woman.

I never should have married Joe. My fault, of course, because I knew I shouldn't and he didn't. That's why I stuck it out with him for three years and then let him hang around these past two years. No woman ought to marry a man when she loves someone else she can't have.

"Joe, are you still smacking your mouth after every swallow? You come to a swell place like this and still eat like you're in a truck-stop diner."

"Sorry, Lol—Laura. Hon, I keep telling you, I need a nice woman to shape me up, make something out of me. All I do any more is hang around with guys. Honest, Laura, you're the only one. I tried going out with other women but it's no use. Not after you."

See what I mean? What he should have done was reach that big paw of his across the table, smack me hard, and walk out. Never phone again. And I tell you, that would have been a big relief, no more anticipating that call every week, trying to think up new ways to say no.

"Eat up, hon, come on, tear into that meat. Or you'll get skinny again, like you were after—"

"I don't want to talk about it, Joe."

"You should of kept the baby, Laura, maybe that's what turned you bitter. I wouldn't of cared it wasn't mine, anything yours is mine far as I'm concerned. You should never have—"

"Damn you to hell!" Whispered, so the tables around couldn't hear. "You dumb stubborn ox, you still believe I'm a murderer! That I deliberately killed my darling baby, my poor lost baby! How many times do I need to tell you I *wanted* that baby?"

"Well, hon, I wouldn't of cared it wasn't mine. I told you that when you told me about it, right from the start. You were honest with me, and I said if it's yours, why, I'd love it no matter who it looked like."

Maybe now you won't keep thinking I'm the witch you started out thinking I was. Who wouldn't act like a witch, getting reminded every day that I loved someone I couldn't have? Besides hanging onto the conviction I had murdered my unborn baby. It was a miscarriage, not an abortion. Joe was determined not to believe that, perhaps in the hope that I had deliberately rid myself of my last attachment to Chris. Well, he was wrong. It was a miscarriage. My baby's silly mother cried too much.

"I like Chris myself, Laura, I wouldn't of cared. Because I understood why you went for the guy, you just a green kid and him knowing how to handle women. Only when you found out he was married you should of broke it off. But that's the trouble, women get took in by a good line, him throwing money around, regular guys don't have a chance."

"Joe, I have to go. I don't feel well."

"Aw, hon, we barely started eating—"

"You stay, Joe. Eat yours and mine, too. And don't call me again. Ever. Just leave me alone." I got up, skimmed past the tables and waiters, fast.

It felt good in the open air, a nice warm night, the moon big and bright. The white clean moonshine seemed to shower me off, wipe away what Joe stirred up, and I stopped wanting to cry. Nevada's moon, I think, must be the most beautiful on earth, so brilliant, so white. I felt like diving into its glow, swimming in it.

"You're moon mad," Chris used to tell me. Then he would say in his soft, gentle voice, slurred by a Danish accent, "So am I, little Laura, when I see you in the moonlight and hold you in my arms." How many millions of men have said those same dumb words to how many millions of dumb girls? So it wasn't the words, it was the way Chris said it.

A taxi moved up to me, ready for a passenger. I opened the door and got in. But I couldn't close the door because Joe was holding it, all 200 pounds of him. "Hon, why take a cab when I gotta car? I'll pay the guy his fare, he won't lose nothing. Listen, hon, you gotta eat something—Listen, fella, I'm not taking your fare, here's a couple bucks, come on, Lol—Laura."

Two couples going inside the restaurant stared at us. One of the women looked like a customer of the beauty salon where I worked. And it was so dumb, squabbling in front of Eugene's. So I got out and let Joe lead me to his big car. A good one but all dusty, with rope and a can of oil in the back, and papers, chewing-gum wrappers, and gravel on the floor in front.

"I know what you're thinking, Laura, didn't wash his car before he picked me up, Well, hon, I been out on the job, way off the paved roads, in soft dirt. So I got to carry extra oil and a rope in case. And I barely got back tonight, tore back like crazy, didn't want to disappoint you, hahaha!"

The poor guy. Oh, God, the poor guy.

"How about a little run up to Virginia City, hon? It's warm down here tonight, be cooler up there. Those old ghosts chill the place off, huh, hahaha!"

"Okay."

Might as well. I wasn't going to get rid of Joe any more than you can break a bulldog's hold on something he's locked his jaws on by smacking his rump. I switched on the car radio, the knobs gritty under my fingers, put it on loud so Joe would need to shout to be heard; a man can't shout forever.

Lovely music, a great "mood" program, bittersweet, haunting. It drowned out Joe and I spun out with it, far out. It was easy to forget it was Joe beside me, he was merely a broad-shouldered male figure. But pretty soon, dreaming with the music, he was more than that. He was Chris.

Chris beside me while we zoomed along, not toward Virginia City but toward Carson City and Lake Tahoe. Five years ago. A time when I barely knew Joe—he was only one of the men who worked for Chris. Once in a while we would bump into him and other employees of Chris in some night spot. And they would all cluster around Chris as if he were a magnet and they were iron filings. The same way I did.

I try and try to figure out why Chris was so attractive to everyone. But I never can put it in words. He simply was. Sitting beside him could put me on a cloud, soft and gentle, yet somehow firm and secure at the same time. His voice was so tender. Once I heard him speak when he was angry, not to me but to a stranger who tried to dance with me. Even then his voice was tender, a velvet-covered steel trap closing gently, but unstoppably, around the man.

In size he wasn't as big as Joe. But he exuded a mountain feeling, a mountain covered with grass and the sun streaming over it. A dopey woman in love? True. Absolutely true.

Joe shouted over the music and drove away Chris and my dream. "How about you and me trying it again, Laura, whaddaya say? You're acting like you're a million miles away. Put your mind on me a little bit, hon."

"Joe, turn around. I don't want to go up to Virginia City. Tomorrow's a big day at the beauty shop and we're shorthanded. Turn back to Reno at Steamboat Springs."

"Aw-w-w-w, hon! Just when I'm feeling good, you back beside me. Listen, take tomorrow off. I'll give you whatever it takes to make up your lost pay."

"I don't need your money, Joe."

"Please." His voice was uneven, shaky. "I need to be a little happy once in a while."

So I said, okay, okay, and we went up the steep climb from the valley, around the last bend, into Virginia City. Tourists ambled up and down the long main street, gawking at the store windows, going in and out of the fake oldtime saloons, laughing as if it was a ball, you know, gay like fun. And all the time it was nothing but an old dead town, faked up for dollars. It gave me the creeps. Like watching people laugh in a funeral parlor while they ogled a fancy old-fashioned coffin.

We got out of the car and drifted with the crowd, Joe hanging onto my arm. But even with the crowd, with the tinpanny piano music coming out of a bar and Joe trying to make talk, I couldn't stop being back with Chris. The thought of him simply wouldn't go away. It wiped out Virginia City, Joe, everything.

Chris, darling, are we going to be married? Someday, I mean.

Little girl, don't worry, let me take care of that. Don't you worry your pretty head about that. I have problems. I need to handle those problems first.

I'm sorry to bother you, Chris, it's just I love you so. I suppose a girl shouldn't keep telling a man how much she loves him but it's the way I feel. I'm no good at pretending.

He had patted my hand then, tenderly, almost as a father would pat his daughter, and said that was why he loved me, my eyes so deep and true, they couldn't lie, nor those sweet lips—

"Wanta go inside one of the joints, Lol—hon? Have us a little fun?"

"Damn!" I said. "I'd as soon dance on somebody's grave."

Joe's jaw dropped and his eyes turned moist. Poor guy, poor guy. Why couldn't he just fade away, leave me alone?

"It's Chris," he finally said. "I can tell. You're thinking about Chris again. When you gonna get him out of your system? After the way he done you dirt."

"He didn't! I was twenty-one. I can take my own blame."

"Hon, you were nothing but a dumb little kid, barely twenty-one. What's twenty-one mean, it ain't magic. And Chris close to forty, smart, wheeling and dealing with Nevada's big shots, knowing all the angles."

"Take me home!"

"Okay, hon, have it your way. But I still think it was a damn shame, leaving you so mixed up you can't love nobody but him."

"Shut up, Joe!" *Shut up, shut up, shut up, why tell me what I know too well?* I'm like my great-grandmother and she was Indian, full-blooded. Outside I'm blonde as a Scandinavian, but inside of me I'm Indian. And Indians don't change loyalties easily; when they get set on an idea, that's it. Forever. At least that's what I've heard. Anyway, that's how I am. For me, Chris is it, and always will be.

Joe did what I said, shut up, led me back to the car, and we headed for Reno. The moonlight turned the night into a twilight, only more shimmering, just as it was the night Chris and I drove to Tahoe. Our last night together. I remembered I had leaned close to the windshield, let the moonlight bathe my face, smiled at Chris. So he drove off on a side road and took my face in his hands. "My beautiful little girl," he said.

"Yes, Chris."

He kissed me, then drew my face back to the windshield, into the moonlight. "No wonder you love moonlight, little Laura, you're moonbeams made flesh. This is how I want to remember you. Always."

Something was wrong about the way Chris said that. A strange inflection, a goodbye sound. As though he had dropped a pebble into a well that I had expected to be full, but there was no splash. Lost. Gone. A goodbye sound.

I swallowed hard to keep back a question about that, because something told me I didn't want the answer. I've heard, too, that Indians are psychic. Anyway, I didn't ask. I smiled instead. If some crazy thing was going to happen, if I was going to lose Chris, I didn't want him to remember ugliness.

Chris drove back to the highway, and that night I think we dropped into every nightspot around the Lake. Joe showed up in one of the clubs and then kept following us from place to place, hanging onto us like a burr. Truth is, Chris seemed to encourage him. He would have had to, otherwise Joe wouldn't have stayed. Chris knew how to get rid of people he didn't want around.

Once I whispered, "Tell Joe to get lost." But Chris only patted my hand and said, "Who can blame the man? He's in love with you. Who wouldn't be in love with you?"

Without any thought it popped out. "Maybe you wouldn't, Chris." Was that my Indian great-grandmother coming out in me, knowing the way all primitive people know?

We kept dancing, Chris silent. Finally he said, "Little girl, you've picked up the feeling of what I have to tell you tonight. Not all, but part. I do love you. But tonight is goodbye for us. Our last time together. That's why I want to remember your face, everything about you. Darling, it has to be. The end, I mean."

"Why?" It was a weak, strangled sound.

"I've learned in business, no use explaining. When the end comes, face it, quick, sharp, no turning back. It's simply I have too many involvements, business, everything. It won't work out." He bent and kissed my forehead.

My head floated up among the colored, spangly lights, my body a numbed automaton on the dance floor below. Then my head fell back on my body, and all of me was numb, too numb to be surprised that a smile had frozen on my face. Who wants to remember a tear-streaked face?

"Dance with Joe, little sweetheart, he's been waiting for that all evening," Chris said, when we went back to our table.

Joe stood up and looked at Chris as if he was going to lick his hand. My smile was still frozen as Joe led me back to the dance floor. Over his shoulder I watched Chris call the waiter, speak to him. Then he looked toward me, smiled, nodded his head approvingly, turned and left. Just left. That's all.

The numbness suddenly went away and I started falling into a black pit. I clung hard to Joe while I was doing it, and he squeezed back. "Aw, honey, what's this? Huh? You go for me a little bit?"

I shook my head.

"I sure wish you would, baby. Just a little, you know, like at least be friendly."

"Chris has left me," I said. "So I'm dead. Mind playing hearse and taking me home?" My voice sounded flat and far off, like someone else talking.

Joe's head swung toward our table. "You mean he's gone?" I nodded. A wide happy grin spread over his face. "Gone," he said with satisfaction. "Well, now let's you and me have some fun for ourselves. We don't care if—"

"I care," I said. "Please take me home."

Joe led me back to our table. The waiter came over and said, "The gentleman with you said to bring you anything you want, it's his party, all paid for."

"Laura, honey, the night's young. And the first time, me with you, Chris doing this for us. It's like a dream, lemme dream a while."

"Take me home, Joe. Otherwise I'll call a cab."

Now, all these years later, I was telling him again, *Take me home, Joe.* Time hadn't changed anything.

We curved down the mountain from Virginia City, saw the valley spangled with lights, and Reno a shimmer of neon toward the north.

"Hon, didja hear what happened today? You musta, the way you're all sunk into yourself tonight."

"Hear what?"

"Chris got divorced today."

It couldn't be true. It was a crazy made-up daydream, an idiot fantasy that fairy tales come true.

"His wife finally got onto him. Took him for a bundle."

Good. Take every dime. That way I can prove it's Chris I want, not money.

"I'm really sorry, Lol—Laura. Honest. You may of always thought I only cared about what I wanted. Like, only wanting to hang onto you. But honest, all along I felt bad for you, the way you were hook, line, and sinker for Chris. He wasn't worth all that, not that he ain't a great guy. That is, with guys. But not worth all that grief. From you."

"Well, you don't have to be sorry for me any longer, Joe." All the sad five years of waiting for something I never expected to get wiped out! Because here it was, the pot of gold at the end of the rainbow. Laughter bubbled out of me—the first time I had laughed like that since Chris went away. "Not any more, Joe!"

"Gee, hon, that's great. Really great." I looked at Joe affectionately. He was kind, actually sweet, to be glad just because I was glad.

"You see, I was afraid you'd be all broke up. I mean, I figured you'd been holding onto the hope that someday you and Chris would finally make it. Then when he got his divorce today and right off married that kooky kid from New York. I mean, right today. I figured you'd take it hard."

The valley's lights went out. Blown out the way one blows out an oil lamp. When they came back on, they were blurred and my head was dizzy.

"But since you're taking it good like this, maybe I got a chance with you after all."

Keep talking, Joe, so I don't have to.

"Hon, I'll never stop loving you. You're so beautiful. I mean, looking at you sideways like now, you're like a beautiful statue or something. Honest, when I first saw you with Chris, it kinda made me sick, you so young and little and pretty."

To disinfect a wound, split it wide and rub salt in it. I may die from it, but the wound will be clean.

"Joe, is this true? Or are you making it up to try to make me forget Chris?"

He looked stunned. "Why would I make up a thing like that? Anyways, you could check, couldn't you? Oh, Lord, you're not taking it cool after all. But you'd have to find out sometime. Honest, I thought maybe you'd already heard."

"How did you find out?"

"Hell, I do business with Chris. See him all the time. So today late, when I first got in from the job, I went to his office about something. And Chris invited me to the party he's throwing tonight, even introduced me to the kid he just married, she was there, that's how I know she's kooky, giggling and crawling all over Chris."

"Where's the party?"

"I'm not going. Gee, hon, think I'd take you home and run off to that party?"

"I'm going to the party. Take me, Joe."

"Now listen, that's no good, you got a bad sound in your voice, you don't want—"

"Take me to the party, Joe."

"Hell!" Joe said.

The party was at the Mapes Hotel in a private suite, the door wide open, come-one-come-all, so we walked right in. Flowers were everywhere, in baskets, in vases, gift cards thrusting from them. The room smelled like a funeral. When my father died, the funeral parlor smelled exactly like this wedding party.

The guests, laughing, milling around, were only a moving color-dotted blur. And in the center of the blur was Chris, sharp and clear, with a small blur beside him that bounced and jiggled and swung on his arm. Chris looked just the same. Smiling, eyes blue as the sky after a good clean rain. Stocky, strong. And he saw me. As Joe and I came in, he was looking toward the door.

Chris dropped the bouncing blur off his arm and walked to us. He kept smiling. Smiles, I knew from five years before, don't really mean anything. "Hello, little girl," he said. "It's been a long time." Tender, loving voice. I had to bite my lips to keep them from trembling. "I hoped you would come to wish me happiness."

The small blur skipped over to us and caught hold of Chris. It shook its shaggy curls from its little heart-shaped face, came out of the blur, pursed its mouth into a pout, and asked, "Aren't you going to introduce wifey, hubby-doll-boy?"

Hubby-doll-boy introduced us. "Valerie, these are special friends, Laura and Joe Walker. You've already met Joe, remember? At the office. Joe used to work for me but now he's my competitor, a real great guy."

Joe stepped forward, grinning, pleased. "Congratulations, you two. Yeah. May you look as good on your fiftieth anniversary."

"Oooo, super, isn't that darling, Chrissy, just super darling!" Valerie cooed.

Chris took my hand. It shouldn't have sent an electric shock through me. But it did. "And little Laura is a very special lady I've known a long time. A lovely *lady*." Emphasis on *lady*.

Valerie's big brown eyes narrowed as she looked me over. "Oooo, lovely, just simply lovely-lovely. Chrissy angel, kiss me, I've not been kissed for five whole minutes, m-m-m-!" She stood on tiptoe, holding up her face, nuzzling the air. Chris bent and kissed her, red creeping over his face. "Mm-mm-mm, not that way, Daddy, big-big kiss!"

He kissed her again and she snuggled against him. Then he did it another time, on his own, a long hard kiss. He didn't have to do that. He could have waited until I couldn't see him.

I began to hear the voice. Not a real voice. Not mine or anybody's. Just a voice in my mind. It said, *I'm going to kill Chris, then I'll kill myself.* Flat, no anger, simply a fact.

I didn't argue with the voice. Why argue with what had to be? But I began to think, how? Should I use fingernails? The heel of my shoe? Hit him with a compact, stab him with a lipstick, choke him with a five-dollar bill? Those were my weapons.

Joe grabbed my arm and led me to the buffet spread. "Eat something, hon, you're kinda sick looking, you oughta eat something."

"Maybe some water."

"It ain't healthy not to eat."

No knives on the buffet table. Forks, but can a fork stab deep enough to kill? The cake cutter? Nothing but dull prongs.

My knees started to tremble and I went to a chair and sat down. A standup ashtray was beside the chair. Light metal, hollow inside. Put a bump on the head, nothing more. I tried to think what my Indian great-grandmother would have done. Latched onto some brave's bow and arrow, or a tomahawk. A shotgun, if one was around. But her great-granddaughter wouldn't know how to pull the trigger on a gun if one was in her lap.

Chris was watching me over the top of Valerie's shaggy little head. Still smiling, but not comfortable. Uneasy. I never saw Chris uneasy before. He turned his eyes away, too quickly. Guilty.

Joe touched my shoulder, leaned down and whispered, "Hon, don't keep starting at Chris that way, you're giving the guy creeps. After all, it's his wedding night, he ought to be let to be happy."

Why, I wanted to ask, just why? But that would have taken strength. I wanted to save all my strength to do what I had to do, before Chris left. Already he and Valerie were going around to their guests, bidding good night, Valerie giggling, snuggling. Chris moving quickly, in a hurry, people making cracks about that. Finally they headed in my direction.

"Go away, Joe," I said. "This is between Chris and me."

"Now, Lol—Laura—"

"Go away."

He shuffled off miserably. Then the bridal couple came to me, the last one in the room. I stood up, my weapon ready. Say it loud, scream it. *Chris, you never saw our son. I grieved about losing him as well as his father. He never drew breath, but do you suppose in some other world he wonders what happened to his father and what made his mother cry so much?*

"Good night, Laura. Please wish us well."

I opened my mouth. "How—" *How does our son feel about us?* I swallowed. "How—how nice to see you again, Chris."

It wasn't easy, but I smiled. Smiles don't mean anything but they're not ugly. It's better not to remember ugliness. "I wish you well."

They turned, walked away, out of the room, out of my life. Gone. Would that be the same as dead?

Joe shuffled back. "Come on, hon, let's go, you look all in. Hey, maybe you could eat a hamburger or something now. You know I worry about you, Lol—Laura."

"Joe, don't waste your time and feelings on me."

His face screwed up like an ugly baby's who isn't sure whether to cry or not. "I wish I could stop. But some things you can't help."

I knew about that. That I understood.

"Okay, Joe. Buy me a hamburger."

So Joe and I went downstairs to the coffee shop and had hamburgers. Like maybe a funeral feast?

SOURCES AND ACKNOWLEDGEMENTS

EQMM in the listings below refers, of course, to **Ellery Queen's Mystery Magazine**, to which this collection owes an obvious debt, and without which much excellent writing would not, I suspect, exist.

'What Have You Been Doing All Day?' 1973 by Kelly H. Blau, first published in **EQMM** No. 359, Oct. 1973. Reprinted by permission of the author.

'Bluebeard's Bathtub' 1962 by Margery Allingham Carter. Reprinted by permission of the Estate of Margery Allingham.

'A Quiet Day in the County Jail' 1958 by Craig Rice, collected in **Cream of the Crime** (Mystery Writers of America, Inc., 1962). reprinted by permission of Scott Meredith Literary Agency, Inc.

'Front Seat' 1978 by Ruth Rendell, first published in **EQMM** No. 421, Dec. 1978. Reprinted by permission of the Author.

'From Out of the Garden' 1966 by Charlotte Armstrong. Reprinted by permission of Brandt & Brandt Literary Agents, Inc.

'The Girl Who Loved Graveyards' 1983 by P. D. James, first published in **Winter's Crimes 15** (MacMillan, 1983). Reprinted by permission of the Author and Elaine Green.

'Dapper Johnny Brown' by Ruth McKenny first published in **The New Yorker**.

'If You See This Woman' 1966 by Dolores Hitchens, first published in **EQMM** No. 266, Jan. 1966. Reprinted by permission of the Estate of Dolores Hitchens.

'The Heroine' 1945 by Patricia Highsmith, first published in **Harper's Bazaar**. Reprinted by permission of the Author and Diogenes Verlag.

'Curses' 1982 by Carol Clemeau, first published in **EQMM** No. 474, Jan. 1983. Reprinted by permission of the Author.

'Danger — Women at Work' 1956 by Miriam Allen deFord, first published in **EQMM** No. 47, Dec. 1956. Reprinted by permission of the Authors Estate.

'Hidden Springs' 1980 by Barbera Callaghan, first published in **EQMM** No. 440, June 2, 1980. Reprinted by permission of the Author.

'Old Friends' 1975 by Dorothy Salisbury Davis, first published in **EQMM** No. 382, Sept. 1975. Reprinted by permission of McIntosh & Otis, Inc.

'Decision' 1957 by Helen Nielson, collected in **The Bloodhound Anthology**, ed. Scott & Sidney Meredith, 1958. Reprinted by permission of Ann Elmo Agency, Inc.

'Contemporary Gothic' 1961 by Esther Wagner, first published as 'Miss Weird-O' in **EQMM** No. 99, April 1961. Reprinted by permission of the Author.

'Sweet Baby Jenny' 1981 by Joyce Harrington, first published in **EQMM** No. 453, May 20, 1981. Reprinted by permission of the Author and Scott Meredith Literary Agency, Inc.

'Meet Athalia Good' 1981 by Raliegh Bond, first published in **EQMM** No. 462, Jan. 27, 1982. Reprinted by permission of the Author.

'A Goodbye Sound' 1974 by Florence V. Mayberry, first published in **EQMM** No. 366, May 1974. Reprinted by permission of the Author.

While every effort has been made to trace authors and copyright - holders this has not always proved possible. The editor and publishers would be glad to hear from any such parties so that omissions can be rectified and corrected in future editions of the book.